Hammerborn
Hammerforged Book One

ANDY WANG

For Kent, Grace, and John.

Nine realms forged from darkest night
Nine realms as one shining bright
Yggdrasil gave birth to life
Yet quickly rose war and strife

By Asgard's might wars did cease
Aesir forged a world of peace
Playful are the Jotnar's lives
Jotunheim does grow and thrive

Vanaheim brings balance nigh
"Peace to all," Vanir reply
Man, the fields they reap and sow
Midgard's bounty do all know

Svartalfheim yields much prized ore
Dokkalfar dig to earth's core
Ljosalfar among the trees
In Alfheim they grow tall, free

Fire in Muspelheim e'er burns
In Niflheim ice doth churn
And in Hel all come to rest
To Valhalla go the best

Nine realms forged from darkest night
Nine realms as one shining bright

PROLOGUE

Hooves thundered across the frozen tundra. The legs of the massive war horse were a blur of gray and white, a roiling cloud of churned ice and snow billowing in its wake. From horizon to horizon the land was a flat expanse of unbroken white, a sky of deep blue stretched high overhead. The amber sun hung low in the southern sky. At this place in the north and at this time near the summer solstice, it would not set for weeks. Despite it being the hour of midnight, the clear, bright disk of light bathed the distant southern horizon in a fiery blaze of orange and red. The lone, mounted figure noted all of this as he rode through these desolate wastes where nothing else stirred except the cold, biting wind. Horse and rider felt the barest chill as steam rose from the beast's flanks and its hot breath snorted out in a steady rhythm. Although encrusted with ice the rider's dark hair and beard stood in stark contrast to the white of the snow and the gray of the horse's coat. They had been running for days in pursuit of their elusive quarry.

"Just a bit farther, Sleipnir!" Odin called out to his mount, the timbre of his voice full of excitement and anticipation. "We're so close, I can smell the sulfur of the dragon's breath."

His left hand held onto the beast's mane and his thighs squeezed tight. Sleipnir was no ordinary horse to be bridled and saddled. They had a bond of mutual respect, a shared purpose in the defeat of this malignant blight, the dragon known as Nidhogg. With this sense of purpose and drive the majestic horse never stopped, never tired as they rode across the nine realms in their pursuit. They had chased Nidhogg from the towering peaks of Svartalfheim in the south, across the fertile Midgard plains to the Svelbjarg Mountains of the north, through Isabrot Pass and Jotunheim, and now across the frozen tundra of Niflheim. Despite losing sight of the dark silhouette in the sky, Odin knew that there was only one place here that could provide sanctuary for the dragon—Yggdrasil, the World Tree. It was well isolated, surrounded by the inhospitable and punishing icebound plains of Niflheim.

Slaying this monster would be his legacy. Nidhogg was an ancient and powerful dragon, the only creature to escape the Great Awakening, when the Aesir united the people to tame the land and rid the world of such terrible monsters. Those stories had been ingrained in Odin as he was groomed to inherit the throne. Beginning with his grandfather, Buri, and then Odin's father, Borr, they had culled the savage beasts and tamed the land, heralding an age of peace and prosperity. Yet even their combined might was not enough to destroy every monster. Garmr the hellhound, the lindworm broodmother Fafnir, and mighty Jormungandr the Midgard serpent—those beasts too powerful to kill had been trapped beneath the unbreakable roots of Yggdrasil, the World Tree. Now Nidhogg was the only one that remained free.

Odin tightened his grip on the enchanted spear, Gungnir. Crafted from Yggdrasil itself, the six-foot-long haft terminated in an iron blade two feet long; etched runes of power ran along its entire length, unbroken across wood and metal. The energy it exuded was at once reassuring and daunting. Odin carried the weight of generations in his hand. Forged in the crucible of Muspelheim by his grandfather, Buri, the weapon had then been carried into battle by Borr. During the Great Awakening all of the people had rallied behind Gungnir's power and banded together to beat back the savage darkness and make room for civilization. The indomitable weapon had slain the most terrible of those ancient beasts. Now, with Nidhogg so close, the spear thirsted once more.

"Soon enough you will drink Nidhogg's blood," Odin said to the spear. Thoughts of his father came unbidden. Borr, who had wielded Gungnir against so many infernal monsters, was slain by this elder dragon. After his death Gungnir had then passed to Odin. Gunnar, a newly minted valkyrie and the only survivor from his father's retinue, had brought the spear back. Although she would have gladly sacrificed her life in such a spectacular battle, Borr had entrusted her—ordered her—to bear the sacred duty to return

3

Gungnir to Asgard if he fell. And fall he did, a final sacrifice to halt the dragon's rampage. Yet even then a bloody and broken Nidhogg had barely escaped the savage battle that left Borr and a dozen valkyries dead.

Now, decades later, the dragon had reemerged at long last. And though Odin regretted leaving Gunnar behind, this task was his responsibility and would be his glory to avenge his father's death. Feeling the weight and power of the spear in his hand, Odin reminded himself to thank the valkyrie for it when he returned triumphant.

But even with such a devastating weapon, the creature's fiery breath was capable of turning him to ash before he could get near enough to use it. As Sleipnir carried them closer, he ran through all that he knew of Nidhogg. In addition to its fiery breath, the dragon was covered in iron-hard scales and spikes. Its powerful jaws were filled with teeth as long as swords, and each of its talons extended out like a spear.

Yet in spite of all of this, the pull of filial duty and triumphant glory was irresistible. The Aesir were no cowards, and Odin less so. Trusting in his skill and power to give him the victory this day, he urged Sleipnir forward, covering the final stretch with one last burst of speed.

The green canopy of the legendary tree broke the horizon, appearing to sprout up out of the ice. Even from this distance Yggdrasil was gigantic. From miles away it dominated Odin's field of vision. He had never before seen such a majestic spectacle. Finally, they arrived at the cliff's edge. "Shh, Sleipnir," Odin spoke in a calming tone to Sleipnir as he dismounted. The horse was panting hard, flecks of foam and spittle falling from the beast's mouth and freezing solid before hitting the ground. Despite his gentle patting, it remained agitated and eager, sensing the battle to come. Odin looked around wary of the noise. The dragon had thus far seemed unaware of his arrival and he preferred it that way. Against that terrible beast the element of surprise would be a key weapon.

"I'm sorry, but this fight is for me alone. Stay here and rest well; you've earned more than your share of oats and apples today," he said, loosening a feed bag and spilling its contents on the ground.

And so he left the majestic horse and approached Nidhogg's sanctuary on foot. He stripped off the travel furs that had kept him warm on the journey through the bitter cold of Niflheim. That left him with a simple leather cuirass as his only armor; the spelled plate and mail of war were not suitable for the hunt. As he readied himself, Odin's breath caught in his throat at the sight before him. It occurred to him that none had laid eyes upon the World Tree since his father created the realm of Niflheim centuries ago.

Yggdrasil stood in the center of a lush and verdant caldera a league in diameter. Seemingly excavated into the ground, the valley was surrounded by sheer cliffs of granite and ice over two hundred feet tall. The canopy of the tree itself rose another two hundred feet above the surrounding precipice, its broad, flat leaves of green contrasting with the barren, colorless tundra. Adjusting his grip on Gungnir's haft, Odin saw the same dark wood on the World Tree's trunk rising up from the valley floor. A modest spring near the massive knotted tree roots appeared to be the only source of fresh water in the valley. It belied the warmth and humidity of the air as hot sulfurous gases bubbled out.

A flourishing grass plain full of flowers in a rainbow of colors surrounded the tree. It was a paradise, a place full of life and beauty. At the center of the valley prowled the terrifying creature with spiked scales, black as volcanic obsidian, covering its hide. Huge, leathery wings sprouted from its back and flexed idly as it shifted and stalked its domain beneath the World Tree. Despite its imposing size, the dragon moved with a self-possessed majesty and grace, making the barest of whispers as it snaked through the tall grass.

With one last glance over the edge down the two-hundred-foot drop, Odin turned his back and walked away. He silently thanked his father for telling him of the hidden entrance into the caldera as he made his way down through the passage and out into the valley below.

As a skilled hunter, Odin was well practiced in stalking prey. The grass was tall, and a slight breeze blew through the valley; the gentle rustling of the foliage covered the sound of his approach. From the hidden opening he planned a circuitous approach to the dragon as the sun began to rise above the caldera's rim.

For the briefest of moments, the final rise obscured his view of Nidhogg as he steeled himself for the attack. Odin burst over in a sprint but slid to an abrupt halt when he realized the dragon had moved and was nowhere to be seen. His head swept side to side and he spun around, but still he saw nothing. His confusion vanished in an instant when flecks of bark cascaded down the trunk of Yggdrasil. Craning his head, he saw the dragon peer out from behind the trunk, up near the canopy. Liquid flames dripped from its jowls and smoke curled out of its nostrils.

The battle began in earnest as Nidhogg pounced, shaking the ground as the beast landed where Odin had been. He escaped being crushed by the narrowest of margins, his lightning reflexes and powerful muscles throwing him several yards away. He got to his feet just as the air exploded with Nidhogg's fiery salvo. Using the enchanted spear, Odin split the incoming gout of fire with a pointed thrust so that the tongues of flame broke around the spearhead like waves breaking around the prow of a ship. Char, ash, and glowing embers swirled in curling vortices through the air around him as he dashed into the inferno.

His charge startled the great dragon, catching it off guard. If it had been slower, Odin would have surely found his mark and run the beast through with Gungnir. But even for so large a creature, it was incredibly fast and agile. After suffering a deep cut across its flank from the Aesir's daring counterattack, Nidhogg took to the air and stayed out of Gungnir's reach. Odin patted at his armor where the flames had found purchase, extinguishing them. Watching as the dark silhouette wheeled in the air, he adjusted his grip on the enchanted weapon, poised to throw. As the beast flipped and dove at him, he brought Gungnir back down into a defensive stance as he reconsidered his strategy. He could not miss; once Gungnir left his hands, he would be utterly defenseless.

The dragon wheeled above, hammering at him again and again. Gungnir kept the brunt of the flames at bay, though the force of each blast pushed against the Aesir, his feet leaving deep furrows in the ground. Soon Odin was driven with his back up against the towering cliffs with nowhere to run. He watched the winged silhouette circle around for another pass, and desperately looked around for some option, some avenue of escape.

As the dragon swooped in low with another blast of fire, Odin turned and struck the cliff at his back with Gungnir, letting loose the energy imbued in it from the World Tree. The wall trembled and split, an avalanche of rock and ice came crashing down on their heads. But Odin was ready. The powerful weapon made short work of the crushing snow and rock, and in moments Odin extricated himself, standing ready to finish off his prey. He was tired though; channeling that power through his body had left him incredibly weakened, and he felt it. Without any energy left to give, Gungnir was just a spear, though still devastatingly sharp and unbreakable.

For a moment there was just a blanket of rock and ice in front of him. Then a powerful wing broke through the debris, beating rapidly as it swept away at the rock and snow. Beneath the rubble a glow bloomed, and Odin knew the dragon was readying a fiery blast. Acting on instinct, he thrust the spear at the exposed flank; but Nidhogg's thrashing wing blocked Gungnir from its true mark, and instead the weapon pinned the limb to the dragon's body and punctured its lung. An intense geyser of flame erupted out around the spear as the dragon roared in pain. The fire hit Odin with tremendous force as it engulfed the entire left side of his body and up across his face and sent him flying out of the caldera.

With that, the dragon burst free from the avalanche. The fiery jet abated into a kind of molten fire that cauterized the wound around Gungnir, sealing it in place. Nidhogg scanned the surroundings and spotted Odin on the cliffs above. It leapt into the air, but with its right wing pinned the beast crashed into the cliff face.

Odin had landed on the ridge above the valley. The fall knocked the wind out of him and fractured several ribs and other bones while the fire ate at his armor and clothes. The cold permafrost of the tundra did little to quench the dragon's flames. Wounded, in intense pain, and without Gungnir, Odin rolled on the ground several times until he extinguished most of the flames, and then he turned to rest on his back. He stripped off his still smoldering leather cuirass through shouts of agony. The entire upper left side of his body was badly burned, as was the left side of his face. His eye's vitreous humor had burst in the heat and the skin cauterized over the socket. If Freya or one of the other skilled Aesir healers had been here, they

7

would have been able to use their Mithlivald magic to heal him and save his eye. But that was idle fantasy. He gritted his teeth through the searing pain. He had come here on his own and would face the consequences on his own as well. Odin was not an expert in the healing arts, but he could summon its basic energies to quench the burns.

That final effort drained him; the view through his right eye darkened around the edges before he lost consciousness.

—

Odin's body lay still and smoldering, the smoke and steam the only movement in the vast, empty tundra. Even the cold arctic winds paused their near-incessant howling. Bit by bit a golden light, dim at first, glowed around the body. With one bright flare, Odin convulsed and bolted upright, gasping for air.

"What—" he panted as a towering gray stallion nuzzled him. As he moved to pat the horse's head, he noted the dull aches in his limbs and looked around him. He had no way of knowing how much time had passed since the sun still hung low in the same position along the southern horizon.

The air was heavy with the smell of charred flesh and burnt hair. The left side of his body was covered in blistered skin, though the last vestiges of the golden light danced over the wounds and extinguished the heat. Odin reached for his face. His fingers found nothing except scar tissue where his left eye should have been. As his hand fell away his remaining eye looked around, searching. What was left of his clothes and armor were strewn all around him, most of it reduced to ash.

He rose to his feet with great effort, leaning upon Sleipnir for support. Though the valley was hidden, the towering tree rising from its center was not. The Aesir and his horse approached the edge, and as he peered into the caldera a simple "huh" escaped his lips.

Even having lost Gungnir and his left eye and being physically scarred, he had, somehow, succeeded. Pulling himself onto Sleipnir, Odin headed home. *The nine realms would never see Nidhogg darken its skies again*, he thought, a smile of grim satisfaction playing across his lips.

8

CHAPTER 1: WODENSDAEG

Sounds of splashing and high-pitched squealing drifted across an idyllic little fjord. Not far from the rocky shore stood a modest homestead, nestled among a lush, alpine forest. Bright sunlight danced across the serene, azure water. A young girl with light blond hair, tightly braided, struggled with a very active fishing pole.

"Pabbi, come quick," cried the lively, six-year old. "I've caught one all by myself!"

"Hold it tight, Una, I'll be right there," Aric called out, himself in the process of hauling in a fishing net with a couple dozen of his own catches within. He continued to be amazed at the bounty the land and sea provided, grateful that his lanky, wiry frame could provide for his family. His own father had lost an arm to a prowling vargr by the time he was Aric's age, and they had still been able to survive and prosper. Securing the net to the shore with the economical and practiced movements of an experienced fisherman, he hurried over to help little Una bring in her catch.

From the corner of his eye he watched as Dagmaer stood upright and wiped the sweat from her brow. She was splitting firewood with their small, well-worn hatchet. Her flaxen hair was bound in loose braids to keep it out of the way and her taut muscles glistened from her exertions. Aric smiled at her as she caught him staring and winked.

"This summer has been a bountiful one," she said to no one in particular as she gathered up the split logs. With an armload of firewood, Dagmaer went to stoke the fire in preparation to smoke the fish that Aric and Una were bringing in.

"Dagmaer," called Aric a few moments after she'd gotten the smoker started, "look at what we've caught." Hauling the net full of

9

fish in his left hand, Aric carried Una in his right, slung over his shoulder; she, in turn, was carrying her own little fish. "It's a tiny minnow. She's so small that I was going to toss her back into the water, but it looks like she caught something so I think we shall keep her."

Una broke out into a giggling fit and promptly dropped her fish. Fortunately, Dagmaer was there to catch it before it hit the ground.

"Well, if this little one is half as good at catching fish as you are, then we might not starve when winter comes," said Dagmaer as she scooped Una from Aric's shoulder and tossed her up into the air.

Once Dagmaer set Una back down and she caught her breath, the little girl turned to Aric. "Pabbi?" Una asked. "Do you think my fish is big enough to offer to the gods?"

"I don't know," he said with feigned skepticism, "the gods can be awfully picky about the offerings that they accept." Holding up Una's fish, Aric squinted at it thoughtfully. He turned it over and hefted it from hand to hand, making deep, throaty grunts of contemplation. "Aha!" Aric exclaimed, "I thought so."

"What is it?" Una jumped up and down, trying to see. Aric stood taller and stretched his arm holding the fish toward the sun as if to get a better view. Undeterred, Una climbed up Aric as if he were a tree. Starting at his leg, she worked her way up his back and perched on his shoulder. Draped over his head she squinted hard at the fish, her head resting on Aric's. "I don't see anything."

After holding the fish as far from Una as possible, Aric quickly brought the fish right up to Una's face, so close that she went a little cross-eyed. "The gods will be very pleased with you. This is quite a rare and special fish. Do you see this deep blue stripe running down its body?" Aric asked, pointing to a barely visible coloration.

"Uh, yes?" replied Una with a tilt to her head and a perplexed look on her face.

"Well, take my word for it," said Aric, holding the fish back out at arm's length. "That stripe means that this is a rare blue ghost pike." In one fluid motion Aric repositioned Una so that she sat upon his shoulders, and he passed the fish to her. "Yes, the gods will be rather impressed with this fish. In fact," he said, pausing for dramatic effect, "you should make the offering yourself."

"Really?" Her eyes widened as she held the fish close to her chest.

"Yes, it's about time you attended your first Wodensdaeg Festival as a contributing member of Murtrborg," Dagmaer said as she brought Una down from Aric's shoulder and took her hand. "So let's get you cleaned up and we can all head to the village for the offering celebration this evening."

———

As Aric, Dagmaer, and Una walked the familiar road into town, they saw that Murtrborg's town square was a flurry of activity. On any other day this was a small, sleepy town of loosely connected homesteads. However, today was the first Wodensdaeg after the autumnal equinox. In honor of the Aesir and their lord, Odin, a festival was held to celebrate the year's good fortune and to offer up their share of bounty in supplication to their gods. The larger towns and cities held elaborate celebrations full of parades featuring exotic beasts, mummers, acrobats, and minstrels. Out here, on the fringes of the northwestern region of Midgard, the celebration was more modest, though no less enthusiastic.

"Have you ever met Odin? Where do the Aesir live? What does Wodensdaeg mean? What do they look like?" Una rattled off a barrage of questions while bouncing on her toes.

"No. In Asgard beyond the clouds of the Rainbow Bridge. It means Odin's day. They are the most beautiful beings in the nine realms." Aric answered every one of her questions as fast as she asked them but paused after this last one, looked to Dagmaer with a smile, and added, "Well, second most beautiful."

Dagmaer smiled and her cheeks flushed as she leaned over and gave Aric a quick kiss.

"Will Helga and Thor be there? Is everyone bringing food? How do I give Odin my fish if he's not here?"

The smile on Aric's lips never faded though his free hand ran through his hair as he struggled to keep up with her torrent of questions. He took a deep breath and exhaled a sigh of relief when Dagmaer began singing a familiar song and Una broke off from her interrogation to join in.

> Come friends and fam'ly
> Come bounty of the year
> Odin favors us
> And brings to us great cheer
>
> Celebrate as one
> Bright birds fly and fish splash
> Asgard smiles on all
> Wodensdaeg's come at last

Aric and Dagmaer pulled their small cart laden with offerings: a variety of fresh-caught and smoked fish, extra firewood, mushrooms and root vegetables they were able to cultivate in their small garden. Una sat upon the front edge of the cart, carefully cradling a small, cloth-wrapped package containing her "blue ghost pike." Despite not having anything resembling formal or fancy clothes, the small family was neatly groomed and had cleaned up well for the festivities.

"You shouldn't lie to her," whispered Dagmaer.

"I didn't; it *is* quite a special fish that she caught," Aric said with a goofy, exaggerated grin.

Dagmaer just sighed and rolled her eyes.

"Okay, so maybe it's not a 'special' fish," conceded Aric, "but it is the first one that she caught on her own. I was twice her age before I caught my first fish. That makes it special by any reckoning." He beamed a smile at her that was at once sly, silly, and smug.

"You didn't catch your first fish until you were twelve?" Dagmaer said, her eyes wide and her right hand at her lips, her left outstretched in an exaggerated pose. Aric smirked, recognizing it as a fair approximation of a melodramatic gesture they had seen in one of the Wodensdaeg plays the previous year. "It's a wonder we haven't starved to death years ago."

"Funny," Aric said dryly. Then his eyes widened and he gasped. "She's six already?" The smirk faded in a long exhale as Aric ran his hand through his hair. "It seems like just yesterday she was just learning to walk. Okay, okay, maybe I wasn't twice her age, but you know what I mean."

"Indeed I do." Dagmaer smiled back and gave Aric another quick and playful kiss on the cheek.

"Good Wodensdaeg to you," the village leader, Hege, said with a raised eyebrow at their antics. Standing at her side was another woman dressed in polished armor. They greeted all of the villagers as they approached the center of town. Hege was the community and spiritual leader of their little hamlet. "May the gods smile on us all this day."

Dagmaer nodded in deference while Aric gave a full bow of respect. Una followed her father's example. Hege was the gythja, village priestess and local representative for the Aesir. Though she was not yet in her fourth decade of life, the heavy responsibilities of leading even this small village showed in the graying hair at her temples. Like all of the villagers, she was lean and had a physique that spoke of hard labor and meager rations. Her clothes were as simple and austere as everyone else's save for the Svelbjarg ram shawl she wore around her shoulders.

"The gods show us much generosity in our harvests throughout the year, and so we gladly share our bounty with them," Hege said. She preached the same sermon year after year. Nevertheless, the festivities of the offerings made the ceremony enjoyable for everyone.

This festival was Hege's pride and joy. Their village was small, and this was a chance for them to come together as a community and show their appreciation for all that they had. As the families arrived, Gythja Hege greeted each and every one of them, directing them to the clearing in front of the great hall. At the center, a wooden dais was piled high with a variety of food and goods. Although they sent a portion of their harvests to Asgard every month, this annual festival required an additional tithe, one that all were glad to give in celebration. It was a difficult life, living month to month; there was never quite enough surplus for them to rest or seek wealth or leisure. Each family showed their reverence to Gythja Hege and her guest as they passed by and then proceeded to place their offerings upon the platform.

When it seemed the whole village was present, Gythja Hege

held her hands up for silence. "On this day we celebrate the wise and benevolent rule of Asgard," she said with a warm smile. "We welcome Odin's envoy, one of the venerated valkyrie."

She gestured beside her to the young woman, gleaming in ornate, ceremonial armor. Despite the warm weather of the season, the woman wore full plate armor over a gambeson of fine silk and a hauberk of glittering chainmail. Etched into the cuirass were an image of Yggdrasil and intricate knot patterns, with nine gems arranged around the tree. Draped over her shoulders was a cloak of fine fur made from the hide of a giant Svelbjarg mountain goat. Every aspect of her attire evoked a sense of awe in Aric, and he could see the same look in others as they bowed to the valkyrie.

But beyond the ornamentation, it also exuded an aura of violence and battle that made the woman intimidating. Her sword, sheathed at her waist, and the spear that she carried in her hand were more utilitarian and designed for efficiency in combat. To Aric's eyes they were no less impressive than the jeweled armor and looked to be expertly crafted from expensive materials. Runes etched into the blade and shaft of the spear glittered in the light hinting at hidden power. The pommel of her sword bore the crest of the valkyrie, two swans flanking a crossed sword and spear.

The woman was beautiful and youthful in appearance, even with her stoic expression. Aric saw cold intensity behind her eyes hinting at a long life spent in grueling combat, probably fighting terrible beasts and villainous brigands. Perhaps she had even fought in the Aesir-Vanir War. As an Aesir, she could have been centuries old. She stood at attention, aware of her surroundings yet with a haughty and detached attitude; the flick of her eyes was the only acknowledgment of the villagers as they passed by, carrying their offerings.

"Who's that?" asked a wide-eyed Una, pointing at the stranger. The village was tiny, and everyone knew each other, so the presence of outsiders was obvious. And in her armor, Gythja Hege's companion stood out even more.

"She is one of the Aesir," replied Dagmaer. "They come every year to attend our festival."

Aric looked at Una with a smile and livened up the answer. "Most likely she's a valkyrie from the regiment stationed in Bruborg. They're the most celebrated warriors in all of the nine realms," he said, brandishing an imaginary sword at her. "The gods send them as emissaries to all of the towns to witness the Wodensdaeg Festival celebrations and accept our offerings." He bent low and with a cupped hand whispered to Una, as if sharing a secret, "In fact, I've heard that in the larger cities, like Halvard, some of the gods themselves attend."

"Wow," Una breathed. "What are they like?"

"They are graceful, beautiful, and powerful," replied Aric. "They protect us and provide for us. They keep all citizens of the nine realms safe and secure. That is why we honor them every year with this festival, to pay homage to them."

"To hear your father tell it, they deliver us from the womb and suckle each of us at birth," Dagmaer joked with a roll of her eyes.

"Hush, Dagmaer," Aric whispered sharply, throwing a quick glance at the valkyrie. "We show our respect to the Aesir, at the very least on this day of all days."

"All that I'm saying is that we do a fair share of the work on our own," she said with a nonchalant shrug. "It's not the gods who bring in the fish or mend the nets when they break. We work hard for our bounty, don't we?" Dagmaer said as she tousled Una's hair, sending the little girl off giggling.

Running ahead, Una went straight to the valkyrie. "Thank you for my fish," Una said deferentially as she presented the wrapped package to her. "My father said that it's a very special fish. I caught it all by myself."

The Aesir's sharp eyes gave Una a quick assessment, though her expression and posture did not change. Aric could not tell if she was annoyed or entertained by Una's antics. With a slight arch of her eyebrow and without the slightest hint of emotion, she said, "I thank you, child. It is a fine fish. Please, place it upon the dais." She gestured toward the growing pile. "Odin thanks you for your offering."

Aric hurriedly approached. Bowing low at the waist and taking Una by the hand, he said, "Praise unto Odin, glory to the Aesir."

And to Una, he smiled. "You did well."

15

—

By early evening all of the families had arrived and the dais was piled high with all of the staples of the region. Grains, fruits, vegetables, fish, and game of all varieties adorned the dais. A small caravan with a merchant and humble troupe had arrived in time for the celebration. The children played together while the adults socialized, bartered, gossiped, and exchanged news. It had been some time since Aric had seen many of his neighbors. The air filled with laughter and chatter as old friends gathered together and met again with smiles.

As the sun began to set and the torches were lit, Gythja Hege took her place again in front of the great hall facing the dais. In the gathering darkness of the sky the moon and stars twinkled into sight and added to the festive atmosphere. The assembled villagers numbered just over a hundred people. The valkyrie, ever composed and stoic, stood to Hege's left and observed the ceremony.

"Friends," Hege began, her voice clear and loud despite her age. "Today, on the first Wodensdaeg after the autumnal equinox, we here at Murtrborg honor the Aesir, who protect and watch over us. The bounty before us shows that Odin loves and provides for even the least of us." At this, Una had the biggest smile possible on her face and Aric had to place a hand on her head to keep her still.

"Although the savage Jotnar were the first peoples birthed from Yggdrasil, the golden Vanir and the bright Aesir rose to bring order to the world. The Vanir and Aesir fought for the right to rule but soon learned to come together as one. After the Aesir-Vanir War, Odin led them all, united as the Aesir, and brought peace and prosperity to the nine realms," Hege said. "Instead of each realm competing with one another as separate nations, Odin joined us together as one large, interconnected community. It falls upon us humans in Midgard to cultivate and harvest all of the food that is distributed to the other realms." Aric stood a little taller, his chest puffed out with pride. He ignored Dagmaer's small smirk and shake of her head. "The graceful Ljosalfar of Alfheim produce lumber while in Svartalfheim the stout Dokkalfar mine ore, gems, and other minerals. In Muspelheim the Eldjotnar refine and work that metal and wood into weapons for the Aesir and tools for the rest of us. The quarries of Jotunheim produce stone for building…" She paused as

16

her expression turned dour. "...and the Jotnar laborers serve to remind us of the consequences of warring against Asgard.

"Our toil and hard work reaped what Odin gave, and now we return it so that he knows that we love and honor him in return." The valkyrie gave a distracted nod as Hege spoke. "We honor the Aesir with this offering and pray for their blessing in the coming year."

And with that the small troupe of performers, a traveling band of actors and minstrels, performed a modest show of some of the more spectacular Aesir fables. Most of the villagers never traveled beyond the confines of their quaint fjord, and these performances were their only window to the outside world. The first act opened with a comedic piece in which the cunning Jotnar Heimskr caused mischief for the Aesir. Because they were the first people to arise from the World Tree after all of the beasts, most stories about the Jotnar race often depicted them as fierce and terrifying monsters, villainous savages who lived in the wilds of the frozen north who feared and despised peace and civilization, more animal than man. Although none in Murtrborg had ever laid eyes on a Jotnar, everyone knew that they were covered in blue fur with wicked fangs and walked on all four limbs as often as they walked upright.

Aric smiled, grateful that the troupe began with this piece where a Jotnar was shown as a buffoon and oaf. A comedically small animal skull rested atop his head and branches protruding from his furred cloak. The actor's skin was painted blue to mimic the blue fur that covered all Jotnar. Though he had a fool's facade, he proved quite cunning and twisted the words of the Aesir to pit them against one another, causing a good deal of bickering amongst them. The villagers in unison laughed and booed at Heimskr's antics, and then burst into cheers when Thor entered the scene. He was played by the largest man Aric had ever seen, draped in faux finery with fiery red hair that trailed down his back. Using a flimsy wooden mallet as the legendary warhammer Mjolnir, the red-haired Thor proceeded to chase Heimskr around the crowd to the delight of the children; even Una shrieked in excitement. With a flourish he clobbered Heimskr over the head, and the audience cheered again.

This was followed by several other performances ranging from dramatic reenactments and poetry recitations to songs and small feats of juggling and acrobatics. They told the story of the Jotnar's evil influence, how it corrupted the rival race of gods, the Vanir, and precipitated the war. This time the Jotnar were portrayed as monstrous, blue-furred beasts with frightening heads and wicked horns crowning painted animal skulls. A regal and elegant woman took the stage in the role of Freya, Leader of the Vanir. Her skin was painted gold with hair black as night. Wrapped in finery she was dressed like the Aesir. But unlike them, she had vines and branches that bound her. They originated from a Jotnar at her back, whispering into her ear. With a wave of her hand the Jotnar attacked the Aesir, once again led by Thor. Despite the troupe only having eight members, the mummers staged a huge battle with the Jotnar actors often lunging at the crowd, eliciting gasps from the adults and squeals from the children. Aric could see that even though Una reacted in surprise with the other children, she had a smile on her lips and giggled at their capering. Final victory was gained when the red-haired Thor of the Aesir freed the golden-skinned Freya of the Vanir from the Jotnar influence and united them together as one race and banished the blue monsters to the frozen wastes of Niflheim, represented by a blue-and-white-painted canvas sheet.

The crowd stood and cheered. All of the actors and musicians stood forward and bowed in turn. The troupe then parted, and the crowd quieted as the venerated valkyrie, stoic still even now, took center stage.

She spoke with a clear, sharp voice. "On behalf of Odin, I accept your gifts and bestow upon you the protection and favor of Asgard. May you continue to find peace and prosperity as one town among many. The roots of Yggdrasil connect us all. Nine realms united are strong."

"Nine realms united are strong," the crowd repeated in unison.

At that, four attendants approached the dais, one for each corner. Bearing torches, they ignited the offerings in a smooth and practiced manner. The kindling and tinder bundled beneath the platform flared and soon the fire spread to engulf the piled offerings. The fragrant smell of burning food wafted heavy in the air, the pillar of smoke rising high into the dark night sky.

Gythja Hege intoned a clear note that seemed to originate from the bottom of her feet and rise through her entire body, and the village joined her in the traditional prayer song to the Aesir. They had all learned this paean from a young age. Dagmaer had taught it to Una and they sang it often. Aric could hear the sweetness of her voice add to the music of the village, and Dagmaer chuckled, looking at the big, goofy grin on his face.

> Summer is ending
> We have planted and played
> Winter still slumbers
> Look at all we have made
>
> Oh hark and be glad
> Bright birds fly and fish splash
> We reap the harvest
> Wodensdaeg's come at last
>
> Come friends and fam'ly
> Come bounty of the year
> Odin favors us
> And brings to us great cheer
>
> Celebrate as one
> Bright birds fly and fish splash
> Asgard smiles on all
> Wodensdaeg's come at last

The valkyrie looked on. The flickering light from the raging bonfire danced across her polished armor. Once the conflagration had engulfed the entire dais, the doors to the great hall opened and Hege proclaimed, "The gods have received their share; now it is our turn to celebrate!"

The entire village made their way into the great hall. Una stared, mouth agape at the tables laden with food and drink. As a fishing village, their primary staples were herring and shellfish, and

Aric pointed out to her the food that they had brought. He then identified and explained some of the less familiar cuisine on display. Many of the other families grew their own vegetables and hunted small game to supplement their diets. Goats not only provided milk for cheese, but their meat was an added treat for this celebration. The boiling cauldrons took in many of those things and provided warm, hearty stew for all. However, since this was the Wodensdaeg Festival, they had treats brought in from all over Midgard: sweet and gooey honeycombs from Mjodrmork, slabs of beef and wheels of hard cheeses from the vast herds of the central plains, and wheat and other grains from the faraway fields of Veizlakr became piping hot loaves of fresh bread. The bread was a particular delight and a hearty addition to the feast. They ate it with everything: dipping it in the stew, spreading honey over it as dessert, or just eating it plain, savoring the crunch of the crust and the warm, soft core. And through it all, casks of honeyed mead flowed freely into everyone's drinking horns and wooden cups as each villager gave a boisterous toast that ended with a shout of "Skol!"

In the corner, the minstrels began to sing the centuries-old tale of Odin's battle with Nidhogg. It was a story that all knew well:

> Ere the monsters had all been slayed
> Peace in the world was nearly won
> Dark'ning skies a shadow held on
> For Nidhogg had escaped Borr's blade
>
> None escaped death in dragon's fire
> Naught left for the funeral pyre
>
> Even Mighty Borr could not best
> Swift and strong the dragon did fight
> Sadly 'twas Borr Nidhogg did smite
> All of Asgard sent him to rest
>
> None escaped death in dragon's fire
> Naught left for the funeral pyre
>
> To avenge Borr, Odin fought on
> He tracked the dragon to its lair

'Neath Yggdrasil the battle flared
The epic fight left only one

Odin vanquished the dragon's fire
Nidhogg sent to the fun'ral pyre

The lord of all nine realms had fought with all of the strength and guile a god should have. And although it had cost him greatly, both the physical toll and the loss of Gungnir, he rose triumphant having slayed the monster and saved them all. It was yet another shining example of the might and benevolence of the Aesir.

While everyone had filed into the dining area, one person was conspicuous in her absence. Even among the crowd, her armor would shine like a beacon. Una tugged on Aric's hand and asked, "Where did the valkyrie go?"

———

"Where did the valkyrie go?" Aric whispered to himself. "Where had all of the Aesir gone?"

It had been three years since that last full day of the beautiful, unobscured, life-giving sun. Aric thought back on that Wodensdaeg Festival often over the years. That was the happiest day of his life. Everything had been so perfect then; his little family was complete, the harvest was in, the celebration had been joyous, and the start of winter was supposed to be months away.

Then, with no warning, snow flurries began falling as a cold wind blew in from the north. An unbroken blanket of storm clouds rolled in soon after, and winter had not left since. The Aesir disappeared from Midgard at that same time. No emissaries came from Asgard to collect their food production or distribute wares from the other realms. All of the reports from neighboring villages was the same—the gods had abandoned Midgard. Yet not all had abandoned this land.

In a small, forested fjord in Murtrborg, the dull thud of an axe echoed in the vast desolation. Even this dead, gnarled tree held

21

on to its patch of land. The ground had turned to permafrost over the course of this fimbulvinter, this cold, cruel, and unending winter. While the sun sometimes shone through the clouds and the snows abated, the climate remained harsh and inhospitable.

Even leaner and more wiry than before, Aric was a shadow of his former self. His hair was matted and unkempt, hanging down past his shoulders. A scraggly beard now spread across his face, and his eye sockets and cheeks were hollow and emaciated. The muscles in his arm twitched and strained with each stroke of the axe as Aric hacked at the husk of a long-dead tree. His arms tingled with every movement on the verge of becoming numb. Still he did not, would not, stop. Although its anemic trunk had scant enough wood for his purpose, it was the last tree for miles around that the blunt little hatchet could cut down. In the nearby homestead, two shrouded bodies awaited the completion of his task.

CHAPTER 2: HAMMERSTRIKE

The ringing of a single axe striking a shield was lost amongst the cacophony of the battlefield in the northern region of Asgard, near the city of Halvard. As the gateway to the north, it was poised atop the cliffs above the Calder Lake and dominated the landscape. Its once fertile fields were trampled underfoot as gods and monsters fought for control of this strategic city. Heavy storm clouds and a dense, cold mist rolled in from the north accompanying the invading force. As the Jotnar Army poured down from the Svelbjarg Mountains, the Aesir realized this was the best opportunity to hold them at bay. The two armies collided, the charging Jotnar crashing like a wave against the indomitable shield wall of the Aesir.

What had begun as a guerrilla insurgency in Jotunheim had now escalated into an all-out war. The garrison at Halvard had sent urgent word to Asgard requesting reinforcements, and they had arrived just in time, though they were vastly outnumbered. The dense mists enshrouding the Jotnar camp made precise estimates of the enemy number difficult to nail down.

Like the rest of the army, Brunhilda had been briefed on all of this during their hasty assembly and march. But even though these were critical details to the Aesir's battle strategy, they were the furthest things from her mind as she reveled in the thrill of combat. On her left arm she blocked a strike with a round, heavy shield made of oak with an iron boss in the center. She then returned four slashes and thrusts from the sword in her right hand, a three-foot blade of polished steel more than half her height. The golden pommel, with the swans flanking a crossed spear and sword, flashed against the blue spray of Jotnar blood. As she struck and turned away another attack, her bright red locks flowed around her shoulders, bound in loose braids. She wore no helmet and was armored in simple leather armor reinforced with metal plates. Their orders were to defend the line and hold the Jotnar Army at bay. Yet with each foe slain Brunhilda took a step forward, one after another.

"Fall back in line!" From a dozen yards to her right Thor's voice thundered over the clamor of the fight. When she did not react, he shouted louder, "Now, Brunhilda!"

It took a moment before she resumed her position at the front with the rest of the army. "Yes, sir!" The wicked grin faded from her face as her lips drew into a thin line. "Just let us loose, sir!" she called out as she dispatched a Jotnar with ease.

"We will hold the line until Halvard has been evacuated." Thor caught and threw down a Jotnar attempting to jump over the wall of Aesir troops. "We hold them until reinforcements arrive," he yelled as he brought his formidable warhammer down with a sickening crunch onto the fallen figure, "and then we will crush them!"

She deflected an attacking Jotnar with ease and dispatched her with three strokes, all while keeping Thor in the corner of her eye. She followed and respected Thor, not because he was the eldest son of Odin and next in the line of succession, but because he was a phenomenal fighter in his own right. His powerful physique was evident through his heavy plate armor and open helm from where his flowing red-blond hair and beard burst out. Even beyond his strength and skill was his weapon, unique and a sight to behold—the enchanted warhammer, Mjolnir. With a handle four feet in length and a massive head of iron, it was adorned with runes of power and ornate knot patterns. She knew the legends as well as anyone in the nine realms: Forged by Thor's great grandfather, Mjolnir had been used to tame the land, beating back monsters and flattening mountains to create the rich, fertile plains on which they now fought. Seeing it now, as he swung it with an effortless grace, she could almost feel that power. Resplendent in his armor of a gold-trimmed and polished steel cuirass over a mail hauberk, he commanded the army with a booming, powerful voice, shoring up the flanks and keeping the surging Jotnar forces from breaking through and threatening the Halvard civilians.

Looking down the Aesir frontline to her left and right, she saw a haphazard assembly of fighters from Asgard. In their haste to head off this threat, they had to cobble together a fighting force in very little time. Brunhilda did not think they were terrible. In fact, like all Aesir soldiers, they were well trained and disciplined. Yet she found that they lacked the passion, the enthusiasm of the valkyries, of her sisters-in-arms. With fewer than fifty individuals, the valkyries were comprised only by those shield maidens who passed a grueling selection process. Those who made it through possessed power and fighting prowess unrivaled in all of the nine realms. *It's too bad there were only two of us close by when this call came out*, she thought.

"Vali had better get here with those reinforcements quick," Gunnar grunted as three Jotnar fell back from her sword slash, "or he'll miss all of the fun."

While Thor led the Aesir Army, the valkyries were commanded by the fierce and battle-hardened Gunnar. As tall as Thor, Gunnar's physical presence was just as intimidating, and her close-cropped raven hair and golden complexion identified her as Vanir. However, her armor of a studded leather jerkin and simple steel bracers was more practical and less gilded than his. Like Brunhilda, Gunnar was armed with a sturdy shield and sword. The valkyrie sword was inscribed with runes along the blade's fuller and the hilt was capped with a golden pommel, etched with the valkyrie's crest.

Even as the Aesir defenders repulsed the waves of the Jotnar Army, the two valkyries seethed with the desire to jump into the fray and fight unleashed in the thick of battle. If Brunhilda had thought of the Jotnar as people, she might have felt sorry for them. Every time they pushed forward, they broke against a daunting wall of shields, bristling with swords held by the first line and backed up by subsequent lines armed with spears, thrust through the gaps of the forward shields. Most of the attacking Jotnar never made it close enough to touch the shields, much less injure any of the Aesir. Nevertheless, the Jotnar soldiers were many, and as the bodies piled up, they pushed them against the frontline. The ground crunched beneath Brunhilda's boots. As each Jotnar died, their cold, blue blood chilled the air and covered the ground with a thin layer of frost. Brunhilda gave the cold little thought as the Aesir weapons and armor dispelled the blood's effects. They were enchanted with wards of Reginvald magic, which protected the Aesir from those base powers.

Brunhilda sneered at her enemies. Her sword tore through them with ease, even though the animal hide and bone armor was reinforced with scavenged metal plating. Their helmets, made from armored animal skulls—auroch and giant Svelbjarg ram—proved more resilient and gave the Jotnar terrifying, horned visages. Combined with their fur-covered arms of various shades of blue and green, they looked like a monstrous army of undead animals. Along with their primitive armor, they wielded heavy, rough-forged weapons that they employed to brutal effect, bashing the Aesir at every opportunity. In some instances, by sheer physical force they were able to smash through the Aesir frontline. Yet every break in the line was filled by the second and third tiers as the fallen Aesir were hauled to the back of the company by their comrades.

"Stay in formation! Hold the line!" shouted Gunnar over the cacophony. "We have to give the people more time to get to safety!"

"Shore up the right flank, they're threatening to break through!" added Thor above the noise of battle. He and Gunnar and a few of the other battlefield commanders coordinated the distribution of the Aesir Army to maximize their effectiveness in protecting the retreating civilians.

During a brief respite Brunhilda looked out over the Jotnar horde. They were not just lashing out in anger. There was a calculated intelligence and planning to their movements. From an abbreviated briefing she knew that the Jotnar maintained supply chains and focused on taking strategic points, establishing footholds into the realms south of the Svelbjarg Mountains. Before the Jotnar forces arrived at Halvard, the city leadership had begun evacuating the civilians. But with reports that other attacks were underway elsewhere, the Aesir tactical position here was tenuous.

The lines of the Jotnar Army surged forward as a thunderous roar sounded. Suttungr, their leader, had arrived at the frontlines, his troops chanting his name. Brunhilda thought that she saw the very mists swirling and parting around him. He was clad as any other Jotnar, with no ornamentation to indicate his rank, yet his presence was undeniable, his aura of power and confidence energizing the Jotnar near him. At Suttungr's side strode a mountain of a Jotnar. He wore no helm and had instead half of a ram's skull adorning each shoulder. *This must be the one called Hrym*, Brunhilda thought, recalling initial reports from the field.

Brunhilda had not seen him until now, nor did she see where he and Suttungr had come from, but she could feel the Jotnar rallying around them. As they flowed to Suttungr, she saw a break, a direct path to him. In a flash she dropped her shield and leapt into the Jotnar horde, hacking at every foe she passed.

"Brunhilda! Get back in formation!" Gunnar shouted, trying to lunge after her.

Brunhilda ignored her. She was in a near trance, unaware of anything other than her target and the obstacles that stood in her path.

After downing one spear-wielding Jotnar, Brunhilda snatched up his weapon in her left hand. With deft footwork she evaded an attack from another Jotnar as she slashed him across the gut. Continuing in one fluid movement, she hurled the spear at Suttungr. Her throw was precise and found its mark, punching through a gap in his armor. But instead of crumpling into a heap, Suttungr grabbed the spear and pulled it out, and a burst of light flashed from his wound. He tossed the spear aside and turned his attention to her. Even though she could not see his face, she knew that he wore a smug look of disdain.

"Flimsy, garbage Jotnar weapon," Brunhilda spat under her breath. Undeterred, she pushed forward as she hefted the reassuring weight of her sword, feeling the tingle of Reginvald magic that flowed through it.

Although surrounded on all sides by Jotnar, Brunhilda had succeeded in carving a path to Suttungr. He lifted his sword and assumed a familiar fighting stance, inviting her challenge. At first she thought that he was mocking the Aesir style. But as they fought she started to recognize some of his movements. It was subtle at first. He had the lumbering, forceful movements of the Jotnar, but with the flick of his wrist in a riposte or the way he set his feet for a lunge she saw similarities to formal Aesir training. She logged it away in her memory for now and kept her mind focused on the present, pressing the offensive. After several parried strikes, she slipped through his guard and cut at his exposed flank. The glancing blow was pushed away by some kind of magical barrier with a burst of gold and blue sparks.

She could feel the Reginvald enchantments of her sword vibrating like a struck bell. Brunhilda had fought the Jotnar before, but her spelled sword had never reacted like this. The Jotnar's more powerful individuals sometimes wielded their own magic, Ethlivald. This was different though. With no time to process this feeling, she dodged and struck again, with more ferocity and her full weight behind the blow. This time the magic barrier erupted in proportion, the resulting burst almost knocking the sword from Brunhilda's hand. It was not just through her strength or sheer force of will that she kept her grip; her mouth was agape and her eyes opened wide at the swirling block of ice that now encased her hand and the hilt of the sword within.

She barely recovered her composure in time to deflect Suttungr's follow-up attack. That strike shattered her frozen sword and knocked her to the ground. As Suttungr prepared to deliver the killing blow, a rune-covered warhammer struck him full in the chest. Brunhilda looked up to see Thor standing above her, and Gunnar engaged with Hrym nearby. What shocked her more was that Suttungr was still standing after such a powerful impact, his protective barrier having held fast as frost sprouted on the hammer. The runes etched across the weapon flared, dissipating the ice before it could take hold.

Suttungr looked unfazed while the other Jotnar pressed in around them. Brunhilda saw the strain on his face as Thor poured his life's energies into Mjolnir, unleashing its power. Golden light illuminated the engravings as he swung and hit Suttungr again, breaking through the sword that he had brought up in defense. Bolts of lightning exploded out, and a concussive wave of sound and light knocked down Brunhilda along with everyone else in the immediate area.

As her vision cleared, Brunhilda could see that Suttungr was down as well. With a labored groan he shifted and attempted to rise on shaky feet. She stared in disbelief. It was not possible. This hammer had leveled mountains; he should have been obliterated or at least dead.

Even Thor had dropped down to one knee, Mjolnir on the ground, with arcs of electricity spidering all over his body. His face was contorted in a grimace as he struggled to move, his muscles seeming to have seized up. Hrym barreled by, knocking him down with a hurried slash of his cleaver as he rushed to Suttungr's side.

With Hrym supporting Suttungr and looking ready to finish off Thor, Brunhilda stepped up to protect her lord. "Withdraw now or die!" she shouted. Her braids had come loose in the battle and her hair billowed like flames dancing around her head. Wielding a jagged Jotnar sword in her left hand and the shattered valkyrie sword still frozen to her right, she was rage incarnate. She could see Gunnar had brought the Aesir Army to bear against the recovering the Jotnar line. In the face of all of this and with Suttungr injured, Hrym carried his leader off while calling for the army to fall back.

"We will meet again, valkyrie!" yelled Hrym over his shoulder.

"Count on it, giant," Brunhilda sneered back with as much venom in her voice that she could muster. Gunnar then grabbed her by the collar and hauled her back while others tended to Thor.

They had held Halvard, though the toll was heavy. And while this day brought a small victory, other divisions of the Jotnar Army continued to wreak havoc in the neighboring provinces. Still, a smile spread across her face as she relished the opportunity to face Hrym in battle again. For now, however, she allowed Gunnar to drag her off; barely able to feel her right hand.

CHAPTER 3: CONSEQUENCES

"That was damned reckless and stupid!" bellowed Odin. His right eye bored into Brunhilda as she stood opposite him. The burnt skin and hollow socket on the left side of his face was not what caused her to shift on her feet. It had been a long journey back since the battle of Halvard and they had stopped only long enough to change horses along the way. Vali had arrived soon after with a large contingent of the Aesir Army, at which time Gunnar had taken her, Thor, and a smaller group back to Asgard.

The injuries Thor had sustained from Hrym had seemed simple enough, but something about the encounter with Suttungr had prevented the Aesir healers in the field from treating him. And so they had brought Thor home to Asgard where he could be treated by their chief healer, Fostra Eira. Gunnar had also brought Brunhilda to answer to Odin for her actions.

He slammed a fist onto the arm of his chair. "What in the bowels of Hel is going on in the north?"

He was sitting at the far end of the war room on a dais raised above the others. The lord of the Aesir and the nine realms was centuries old now, though all the Aesir had the appearance of near ageless immortality. The streaks of white in his hair and full, braided beard only hinted at the vast panoply of events he had witnessed. Two ravens as black as midnight sat perched atop his throne and a fierce wolf sat at his side. Its hunter eyes focused on Brunhilda while another wolf stalked the shadows along the back edge of the room.

The war room of the Aesir was the epitome of grandeur in Asgard. Even Odin's throne room was not so ornate. Weapons and trophies adorned the walls, and skins and furs of legendary beasts from the past hung from the rafters. Brunhilda's eyes shifted from these decorations and fell upon the central table; made from a solid block of wood, it was eight feet in diameter with an intricate relief map of the nine realms carved into its surface. Detailed stone figures upon the map represented the Aesir Army spread across the known world while carved, unvarnished wooden markers indicated the known positions of the Jotnar Army.

Around the immense, circular map table sat the pantheon of the Aesir leadership. Though for centuries there had been twelve seated around the table, including Odin, today only nine of the seats were occupied. Baldur's death decades past had been tragic. As one of Odin's sons, his place was kept vacant, preserved in his honor. The place to Odin's left, Thor's rightful seat, was also currently empty. In another chair Frigg sat in silence, the embodiment of grace and composure even in the face of her husband's outburst. She counseled Odin and spoke for him when he was away, a less common occurrence since returning from his duel with Nidhogg. On Odin's right sat Freya. Odr had abandoned Asgard centuries ago, but his place was preserved by his wife, and she oversaw the strategic and tactical decisions of the realm. As the leader of the Vanir during the Aesir-Vanir War, she secured her position as a concession of the treaty ending the war. She was the epitome of beauty in Asgard, with long, flowing raven black hair and skin the color of pale gold. Her knowledge and mastery of Vanir magic, combined with her impressive physical skills on the battlefield, made her the ideal person to be the chief tactician of the unified Aesir.

Thor and Sif led the separate deployments of the military under Freya's watchful eye. Thor commanded the Aesir Army abroad, covering all of the nine realms while Sif oversaw Asgard's defenses and domestic forces.

Brunhilda understood why they were present. A look of mild annoyance tugged at the corners of her mouth as her eyes passed over the others. Freyr, Ydun, and Bragi were all Vanir. They, along with the Aesir lords, Tyr and Heimdall, were in charge of the various other duties from economics and infrastructure to governance and adjudication. They should not even be in the war room, let alone sit in judgment of her, Brunhilda thought with indignation.

"When the Jotnar began this uprising three years ago, you assured us that it would be a simple matter to put down this rebellion, Freya," Odin said.

"Their tactics thus far have been…" Freya paused as she considered her words. "…unconventional." Pointing out several locations on the map, she continued, "They began as small pockets of unrest disrupting supply lines and stealing resources. Our initial responses of going into Jotunheim and making examples of individual Jotnar had appeared to stop them. It wasn't until a month ago, when we lost contact with Isabrot, that we knew they had returned. It's as if they were testing our responses and capabilities before striking in force." She took a deep breath. "They're employing techniques and strategies they've never used before. Their leader, this Suttungr, is taking tactics straight from Aesir war books."

"Though the battle of Halvard ended in a functional stalemate, Suttungr's injuries leave the region in less immediate danger," Gunnar offered with some positivity.

Freya acknowledged this with a nod. "But with such a vast territory to cover and so many dispersed settlements that need protecting, the remaining Aesir Army cannot be pinned down to the defense of a single city. I'm sad to report that after centuries of peace, most of our towns have been lax in the building and maintenance of their defensive fortifications," she said, indicating Halvard and the other vulnerable locations on the map. "We have to aid the other villages in evacuating to a more defensible position. Until we can ensure the protection of all of our citizens, the army will not be able to fully commit to a counter offensive to quash this uprising."

"They, too, are spread out," Gunnar replied. "Should we not cut through their lines and attack Jotunheim directly?"

"It would do us no good," Freya replied. "Our scouts report that while they receive some supplies from Jotunheim, Suttungr leads from the field and they have intentionally left Jotunheim undefended. After all of these centuries, they still don't view those frozen lands as their home. Any attempt to seize their civilian populace would merely dilute our forces for weeks, all to capture a worthless prize. They have fully committed all of their assets into taking the fight to us. No, we have to destroy them here in Asgard."

"My apologies, sir," Gunnar offered as she stood at attention, and even without looking Brunhilda could tell that she had a sneer directed at her. "As valkyries, we train for battle. I fear that the excitement overcame Brunhilda's better judgment. Our failure at

Halvard is my responsibility."

Brunhilda also stood at attention beside Gunnar, facing Odin across the table. "I did what I was supposed to do, what I was trained to do," she spoke with a note of irritation and defiance. "I saw an opening and I took it. If I had succeeded, that would have been a quick end to this little uprising of theirs."

"You didn't succeed, did you?" interjected Odin. "Instead, you rushed headlong into a volatile situation and exposed your comrades to what could have been a crushing defeat. According to Gunnar's report, if Thor had not stepped in to shore up the line and hold off that mountainous Jotnar, you would have been cut off and surrounded. Then they would have pushed through and slaughtered the fleeing civilians as well as the Aesir Army. Ever since this damned uprising began, the other realms have become increasingly unsettled as well. Our army is spread thin, maintaining order throughout the nine realms. We cannot afford mistakes like this."

He paused to catch his breath. In a calmer voice, Odin continued, "We brought order to the world. As its architects and leaders, we have an obligation to conduct ourselves in all ways with dignity and a rational head."

Brunhilda bit her lip hard, nearly drawing blood. It took every bit of restraint for her not to laugh aloud at his words. Having demonstrated at an early age her gift for fighting, she had risen through the ranks of the army. Brunhilda's bravado and skill did much to impress her superiors. Never much of a team player, her many rash decisions were often overlooked and actually encouraged in light of her successes. She had brought much glory and renown to herself and Asgard when she single-handedly slaughtered a motley band of brigands who had been raiding Aesir supply convoys.

That said, there was that time she had struck Gunnar. They had gone into Svartalfheim to settle a dispute between the Dokkalfar and the Ljosalfar. Brunhilda had flown into a berserker rage, pummeling them even as the ran in fear. Gunnar tried to restrain her, and that was when Brunhilda hit her. Whether it was due to her battlefield frenzy or her fondness for drink, she could not say. Brunhilda was thrown into an iron cage they used for prisoners to cool off or sober up, whichever was necessary. No formal charges were brought to bear as to the Aesir these actions were far from unique. Even Gunnar had laughed it off after a week when she let her out.

A quaver of irritation crept into her voice. "We are, all of us, bred and trained for combat. You underestimate the capabilities of our army as much as my ability to fight. You should set us loose to obliterate the Jotnar instead of playing at nursemaid with the villagers while you—"

"While I commend your enthusiasm, Brunhilda," interrupted Freya, a look of warning in her eyes, "when we fight, we must fight with care and preparation. We have techniques to resist and break through Jotnar Ethlivald. And if you had taken the time to coordinate with your fellow soldiers—"

"I was prepared!" shouted Brunhilda, losing her temper at last. "I know better than anyone how to deal with Jotnar frost magic, but this was different. There was something else to it, something that I've never encountered before." Struggling with her words, she paced and gesticulated with her arms. "There was something familiar to it yet different at the same time… something like Reginvald intertwined with Ethlivald. That's what blocked me, that's what allowed the ice to take hold of my sword and, I suspect, even resist Mjolnir's power. If I hadn't charged in, he might have hurt more of our troops with this magic, caused more damage, and killed more of our people."

"That's… that's not possible," said Freya. Her voice faltered and was quiet. "Those energies are incompatible. It would be extremely difficult… no one should be able to do that."

"There was one who did learn to do that, wasn't there?" challenged Brunhilda.

"Loki," Odin whispered. The assembled Aesir grew silent and shifted in their seats as they looked to each other and then back to Odin. "No, that would be impossible. He perished years ago. He fell to the great dragon, Nidhogg. Not even I was a match for that monster's terrible power," said Odin. His hand reached up and stroked the scarred flesh where his left eye used to be. "Loki's survival would have been impossible."

"Not if he was truly able to protect himself with the combined strength of Aesir and Jotnar magic." Freya, looking ashamed, added, "This is my fault for teaching him. He brought me insight into their power, Ethlivald. How could I have known then that he would use our teachings against us, sow the seeds of revolution among the Jotnar nation… and kill Baldur?" With that, several of the Aesir either lowered their heads or turned to look at the other empty seat at the table.

"If he is alive and has succeeded in combining our magics, then we must find a way to defeat him before he can recover and march on Asgard," said Freya, steepling her fingers in contemplation. "With that power and the Jotnar Army behind him, he is nearly unstoppable."

The assembled Aesir burst into heated arguments and cries of concern. Some angry shouts were directed at Freya while others discussed attacking the Jotnar with all due haste, and still others spoke of withdrawing behind Bifrost altogether. Amid this sea of noise and chaos, Odin closed his eye and looked to be deep in thought. Brunhilda noticed this and held her tongue, waiting to hear what he would say.

"We need Gungnir." Odin's voice boomed above the din. The hall fell silent.

"How is a lost weapon supposed to break through a defense impervious to Mjolnir?" Brunhilda asked. Though the question came from a place of skepticism, her tone was tinged with intrigue and curiosity.

"My grandfather, Buri, imbued Mjolnir with his very life's essence when it was crafted. It may be that Suttungr's defense is designed to counteract Reginvald," replied Odin. "Boelthor, leader of the Jotnar during the Great Awakening, bound his own life to empower Gungnir. With Ethlivald at its core, it will penetrate Suttungr's shield." After a pause he added, "It must."

"The bards sing that Gungnir was destroyed when you slew Nidhogg, but we know the truth. Both survive, trapped at Yggdrasil, surrounded by the Niflheim wastelands," Freya said. She locked eyes with Brunhilda. "Someone will need to fetch it."

A wry smile emerged on Brunhilda's face.

"To retrieve Gungnir," continued Freya, "we will need a small group of warriors. We can't afford to send a large army on this endeavor. With the Jotnar Army rampaging through the borderlands, we will need the bulk of our forces in reserve to defend the outlying provinces. So whomever we choose for this undertaking must be disciplined, clever, and intelligent." She cast a sidelong glance at Gunnar. "This group must not only be able to slip past the Jotnar Army, they will need to devise some stratagem to subdue Nidhogg and retrieve the spear. If Odin was unable to defeat this beast head on, the group that we task with this mission must be able to find another way to deal with Nidhogg. This will be a perilous mission, and there are no guarantees that anyone will succeed much less survive. While Thor is the ideal person to lead this mission, Fostra Eira does not know when he will be well enough to travel and fight."

"I will go!" Brunhilda proclaimed, stepping forward and almost knocking over some pieces on the table.

"Ha!" scoffed Gunnar as she stepped up beside her. "You are the last person to whom we would entrust a mission as important as this."

"It is my right. As the one who confronted Suttungr and discovered his power, I am entitled to satisfaction. If we need Gungnir to defeat him, then it is my duty to retrieve it."

"You disobeyed orders and broke ranks," hissed Gunnar. "You are entitled to disciplinary actions, not critical missions."

"As always," Freya interrupted, "the valkyries are your responsibility, Gunnar."

"Thank you, my lady."

"However," continued Freya, "in this case, disciplinary actions and the mission at hand may be one in the same. I leave it to you to assemble your team, Gunnar; however, Brunhilda is certainly one of our most talented fighters, and she may prove more of an asset on this mission than in the defense of refugees and guarding the realm with the regular army."

Gunnar gave Odin a sharp look. He considered the options for a moment. His eye lingered on Brunhilda before turning back to Gunnar.

"The tactical and military decisions belong to Freya," stated Odin. "She is your commander and she has my confidence."

Gunnar remained silent as the other assembled Aesir acknowledged Odin's decision. Brunhilda had a self-satisfied smirk on her face, though it vanished when Gunnar turned her icy stare to her.

"As you say, my lord," Gunnar replied with a bow of the head.

"So how are we going to do this?" asked Brunhilda.

Freya stood. "Choose your team, Gunnar, and have them prepare their gear and be ready to leave at a moment's notice. We will depart as soon as we've devised a suitable plan. The road to Yggdrasil will be long and treacherous."

CHAPTER 4: FIMBULVINTER

Far to the southeast, beyond the horizon, a brief flash of lightning reflected high in the clouds. A short time later a low, powerful rumble of thunder could be felt, if not entirely heard, as it washed over the land. Along the quiet shoreline a solemn figure paused in his actions and raised his head and looked northeast. At last Aric had completed his meager boat. It amounted to little more than a floating platform of driftwood and planks stripped from his small home, barely able to keep its precious cargo above the waterline. Upon this barge there was a meager pile of kindling and a bed of dry lichen. There, with the utmost care and reverence, Aric laid two shrouded bodies. Kneeling on the shore by the boat, he closed his eyes and began to speak.

"I'm sorry that I could not be a better husband... a better father. I would gladly give up my own life if it meant that you both could live." Aric's voice cracked and faltered. "But the gods ignored our offerings of food. They abandoned the land and they abandoned us. So much food wasted. Food that could've... I only hope that they haven't also abandoned us in death. May this last act grant you peace in the afterlife." Aric coughed out something between a sob and a gag, unable to continue. He buried his face into his hands and his body convulsed. Long minutes passed until the bawling quieted and he regained his composure.

He pushed the makeshift boat out into the fjord with care, ensuring that it did not take on too much water. Retrieving his meager wooden bow he picked up one of his last two arrows. Aric sparked his flint to set its tip, covered in pine pitch, alight. Taking a deep breath, he drew the arrow back and released, sending it into the bed of kindling and lichen. The flame took hold and the figures were soon engulfed in the burning pyre. As he stared into the blaze, Aric lowered his head, fell to his knees, and cried, reminded of all he had given up to the fire.

CHAPTER 5: THE JOTNAR REGROUP

Meanwhile, in the Jotnar camp, Hrym kept a watchful eye as Suttungr lay in a semi-catatonic state. His body was bathed in a golden glow as well as a layer of sweat. Within the security and darkness of his personal tent, Suttungr allowed his magic to work undisguised. In the shifting illumination of the enchanted light, Hrym could make out the scars and burned skin that covered Suttungr's body from head to toe. Most of the burns were old and a permanent reminder of past trauma. The new injuries radiated out from a single point of impact, where he had been struck full force by Mjolnir's power. A dark bruise blossomed out from his chest where the impression of Mjolnir's head could be seen. Spidery, fractal lines of charred skin extended from there, crisscrossing the pre-existing burns. Hrym contemplated the severity of these wounds, wondering to himself how much worse off Suttungr would have been if not for his magic. Any other being in the nine realms would have been annihilated by such a terrible blow. Even now Hrym would have sworn that he could still smell the ozone and feel the crackling electricity in the air from that strike.

The aftermath of the battle had left the Jotnar forces scattered, with the less disciplined troops having fled in the face of Mjolnir's awesome display of power. But the conviction and commitment to the cause redoubled in those who had been closest to the battle between Suttungr and Thor. Immediately they had spread word of his miraculous survival. In fact, many of those who had deserted the battle found their way back to the main Jotnar encampment at Halvard, more than a few out of a morbid curiosity to see if Suttungr had, in fact, survived or if these were wild fabrications.

—

While Suttungr recovered under the healing powers of Mithlivald,

Hrym made certain to maintain a visible presence in the camp, walking among the assembled Jotnar and lifting their spirits. "We have done what no one thought possible. We have stood face to face against the mighty Aesir Army, and we did not break," he said. Hrym's voice carried through the assembled crowd in the Aesir common language so that all would understand him. "Even against the indomitable Thor our dauntless leader stood his ground and won glory for the Jotnar people!"

A low murmur swept through the army. Then a clear voice rang out, "If Suttungr did so well, where is he now?" This defiant question came from a young Jotnar in the crowd and gave credence to the doubts and questions of the skeptics. Arguments began to heat up between those who claimed to have witnessed it firsthand and the cynics.

Before things could escalate, Hrym raised his arms to call for silence. "And who are you to question the leadership of the one Jotnar who has done more for our people than any before?"

"I am called Skrymir," spoke the youth, "and I did not join this fight for glory. We've suffered for centuries under the oppressive Aesir. We should be fighting for all Jotnar, not for the personal glory of Suttungr. Look at all of the lives that were lost when we tried to seize Halvard. We should focus on retaking our ancestral lands of Jotunheim. That should be enough. Let us put our efforts into securing our homeland. Halvard was never ours; leave it to the Aesir. How many more Jotnar have to die?"

Before Hrym could reply, the flap to Suttungr's tent opened with a flourish and the charismatic Jotnar emerged, clad in his battle armor with a beaming smile on his face. The crowd calmed at his presence. "I am here," his voice boomed, loud and strong, giving no hint of his recent injuries. "Until now we've been slowly claiming worthless territory, simply pushing the Aesir out of Nyr Jotunheim, out of Niflheim. Yesterday we had our first true encounter with the proper Aesir Army, and we were not cowed. We held our ground and showed them that we are not to be trifled with.

"However, it wasn't a decisive victory. If we stop now, the Aesir will think us weak and they will retaliate against us in force. But

41

if we strike at their heart and win, we will have proven our strength. And we will ensure that they never lord over us ever again. We are bound together by our righteous cause, freedom for all from the tyranny of the Aesir. This isn't simply Jotunheim against Asgard. We are not just one realm of the nine, we fight for all people in the land of Ymir!"

The crowd erupted in cheers and drowned out Skrymir's attempted retort. Suttungr walked among his people, stopping often to see to the comfort and needs of a few individuals. He walked past Skrymir, looking to Jotnar on either side of him and ignoring his presence. But Hrym did not turn away and stared down upon the youth with so much ire and menace that those standing nearby moved away.

Suttungr energized the crowd and renewed confidence in everyone, quieting the doubt and dissent in all save for Skrymir. Soon enough the mood of the camp eased into merriment, with Jotnar regaling each other with tales of their feats during the previous day's battle.

"Jotnar," Suttungr called. "For centuries we have lived under the cruel yoke of the Aesir. After the Vanir betrayed us to them in the Great War, we have lived as slaves to both races. Our lush, verdant Jotunheim was taken from us and they exiled us to the barren wastes of Niflheim. We were bound to toil in servitude, rebuilding their shining city of Asgard while we dwelled in squalor. They have kept us divided and isolated from each other. Even our cousins in the south slave away smithing the weapons that they use to subjugate and slaughter us.

"Though our own weapons are crude compared to theirs, we have the power to stand on our own and face down the Aesir. They have underestimated us for too long. Now is our time. We will overthrow our oppressors and take our rightful place as the true leaders of the all the land!"

Suttungr made his way back to his tent in the midst of cheers and yells, Hrym just a step behind him. When Suttungr reached the open flap, he paused and faced his people again. "Take this week to rest and rejoice. Once we have celebrated our victory and filled our ranks with reinforcements from Niflheim, we will continue our march on Asgard."

With that he stepped inside and, once no longer visible to the other Jotnar, collapsed. Hrym was at his side before the Jotnar hit the ground. He carried Suttungr to the cot and removed his armor. As Suttungr fell back to his resting state, the familiar golden glow returned.

"Hrym," Suttungr called in the Jotnar language through clenched teeth. *"Let them celebrate, but carry on with the plan. We must ensure that our forces continue to press the advantage."* He paused with teeth clenched as the Mithlivald energies flared around Mjolnir's impact point. *"If we are to succeed we must keep the Aesir off balance, moving back, spread thin, and scrambling to anticipate which of the other towns in the region we will strike next,"* he continued. *"We cannot give them time to rally, lest they come with all of their might and destroy us. Even with my power I cannot hope to be victorious alone."*

"As you command," replied Hrym. He bowed his head and then left.

CHAPTER 6: REUNION

Brunhilda walked the familiar streets of Asgard. While she may have disobeyed orders on the field of battle, she was glad not to be confined to the brig, free to roam about her home city. The holding cells were most often used to incarcerate visitors from the other realms not used to the ways of the capital. After all, to serve and fight for the empire was the highest honor for which any Aesir could hope. No one in the history of the Aesir had ever deserted the army, punishment or not.

Nidhogg. The name still echoed in her ears. She smiled a broad, toothy grin knowing that she would have the honor of challenging the Aesir's greatest foe. Flexing her fingers and rolling her shoulders, she relished the chance to test her limits. While open warfare against Asgard was unheard of since the end of the Aesir-Vanir War, there were all manner of beasts and brigands that continued to roam the outlying territories. Since none of the other realms were permitted to field their own armies or forge metal weapons, responsibility to address these issues fell to the Aesir.

There were also the occasional scuffles among and between the other races that needed to be dealt with. Brunhilda often marveled at the tactics and fighting skills that the other races displayed. Though they lacked the weapon, armor, training, and discipline of the Aesir Army, they proved to be quite resourceful and driven when pushed. Still, none of these threats ever posed a significant menace to her or Asgard. Now, in a rapid succession of events, she had found three challenges worthy of her: Suttungr, Hrym, and Nidhogg. She let out a gleeful laugh, though no one gave her a second look.

As she walked down the shining boulevards, she wondered how there could be any doubt that the Aesir were the rightful rulers of the nine realms. The splendor of Asgard was unrivaled. Every building, from the smallest shops down the side streets to the grand taverns along the main thoroughfares, were architectural marvels. Many of the buildings towered in impressive spires reaching toward the sky. As impressive as they may have seemed, they paled in comparison to the central palace that served as the seat of Odin's power. The palace gleamed in day and night, its walls constructed of the finest marble. It and the capital city itself were more than simple objects of beauty; they were paragons of the power of the Aesir. During the Aesir-Vanir War they reinforced the walls and defensive structures of the city and the palace. And though they did not anticipate another attack on their venerated capital, they rebuilt it even stronger after the war had ended.

Even to her, someone who had grown up among its riches, the gleaming towers and pristine streets with their lively crowds still inspired awe. At this time of the evening, the taverns and food vendors were doing brisk business. Warm, inviting light from myriad hearths bathed the streets in a golden glow. Among the throngs of people here the violence and chaos of the battlefield seemed familiar yet also very distant. War and combat were integral parts of their way of life. All of the Aesir nobility earned their station and rank through their deeds and accomplishments on the field of battle or rite of passage. Whether it was done by hunting down monstrous beasts or nefarious bands of thieves, each and every one had proved their mettle.

The hearing before Odin earlier in the day still left a bitter taste in Brunhilda's mouth. Risk and sacrifice were intrinsic aspects of war. She had seen an opportunity to cut down the Jotnar leader and put a quick end to the conflict, so she had taken it. And the acclaim of slaying such an impressive opponent would have been an additional perk. Even if she had been cut off and surrounded and had fallen in battle, she would have been proud to die so gloriously. But to be harangued for taking that initiative had felt petty and simplistic. Odin of all people should understand the glory of the battlefield after all of his exploits in the Aesir-Vanir War and his own pursuit of Nidhogg centuries earlier.

She shook her head, the smile returning to her face. She was done thinking about Odin for now. It had been years since she was last in Asgard, and if the quest for Gungnir was as dangerous as they made it out to be, then she was determined to enjoy herself for now. "Skogul, Hilder!" shouted Brunhilda as she approached two of her fellow valkyries. "When did you arrive?"

"Just this morning," Skogul replied. "Ever since the reports of the troubles in the north first began, reserve units were called up for active duty."

"Obviously we jumped at the chance to come back to the capital in preparation for the eventual counter-offensive," Hilder added. "We hear their leader faced off against Thor and survived."

"That's just the kind of challenge we're looking for," Skogul said, punching and slashing at an imaginary opponent.

"Those Ljosalfar running around the trees too boring for you?" Brunhilda dodged and weaved Skogul's movements. She ducked a punch and gave her a rib-crunching bear hug.

Hilder joined the embrace and briefly lifted them both off of their feet. As they separated, Brunhilda looked them over. While all who joined the ranks of the valkyrie were skilled fighters, even among them these three were remarkable. Having trained together, Brunhilda, Skogul, and Hilder were not only friends but rivals as well. They competed with each other in all aspects of their lives, from the number of beasts and enemies slain to drinking contests and their romantic conquests.

All three women were in peak physical condition, as evidenced by their hardened, athletic physiques. Though none would be described as masculine, neither did they saunter about in courtly dresses. And in truth, there were few Aesir women who were not well versed in the arts of warfare and combat. In battle, men and women fought alongside each other. However, the most fierce and capable division in the army, the valkyries, was comprised solely of women.

"Ah, those thieving tree-jumpers never come out for a stand-up fight," Skogul said with a pout. "We either have to chase them down or set traps. It's so tedious."

"I'd prefer your assignments in the north any day," Hilder agreed. "Those Jotnar bastards don't hide or bandy about. They come out swinging."

Hilder had the light hazel skin and dark, long braids of a Vanir. She was also the largest of the three, both in height and sheer muscle mass. Despite the imposing figure that she struck, she was quite jovial and boisterous, with a blunt and straightforward sense of humor. To Brunhilda she quipped, "Although I heard that you got knocked on your ass by some Jotnar *hrodi.*"

"Don't be absurd, Hilder," Skogul said. Her pale blonde hair, evocative of sunlight on snow, flowed about her in a wild, untamed mass, an Aesir trait inherited from her father. In contrast, her golden complexion showed her Vanir lineage. Whereas Brunhilda and Hilder had more lean, muscular builds, Skogul maintained somewhat softer and more feminine features, though she was no less formidable in battle. "The Jotnar are undisciplined savages. No self-respecting valkyrie would be beaten by their ilk."

"Thank you," Brunhilda said, nodding her head to Skogul.

"She was probably drunk and tripped over her own feet," Skogul continued, and she and Hilder broke out in laughter. Unlike Hilder, Skogul liked to come at situations from different angles. Just as she did in combat, so too did her humor take a more clever, circuitous route in finding her mark. As a sharp-eyed scout she prided herself on teasing out these varied approaches and figuring out the best one. Although Hilder hit harder, Skogul fought smarter.

"Don't be silly," Hilder said. "Even drunk she found a way to escape from the brig on more than one occasion. And that time, when Freya was so mad that she trussed her up in the stockade after stealing—I mean, borrowing," she corrected just as Brunhilda was about to interrupt, "Freya's prized cloak of falcon feathers. Still, even then she had managed to free herself from that contraption."

Brunhilda chuckled with her friends and playfully punched both of them in the arm, before all three embraced once more in a group hug.

"I wasn't drunk at Halvard," Brunhilda replied, draping one arm across Hilder's shoulder and the other arm across Skogul's, "but tonight is another matter entirely."

———

The capital city was far removed from the fighting in the north.

However, news of the Jotnar uprising and Thor's injuries had reached even here. The taverns were abuzz with news, rumors, and speculation about what had occurred at Halvard. So when the three valkyries walked into the Sundered Anvil Tavern, there was a marked break in conversations as the crowd inside recognized Brunhilda.

"Gossip travels faster than the wind it seems," she commented when the noise resumed, and the three friends moved through the room.

Being valkyries meant that they were recognized as soon as they opened the door. Even if their faces were not known, the crest on the golden pommels of their swords spoke volumes. And their status carried with it certain advantages, as some of the regular infantry troops cleared out to make room for the trio as they approached.

"Pay them no heed, sister," replied Hilder as they took their seats at the now vacant table in a secluded corner of the main floor. The tavern owner had personally brought over three tankards of mead before they even sat down.

"So what in Hel's name happened out there?" asked Skogul.

"Something strange is definitely going on among the Jotnar," Brunhilda said flatly after taking a long draught of mead. As they gave a brief toast to fallen comrades, she recounted the events of Halvard. Not wanting even more rumors to spread, she kept her tone hushed when she spoke about the strange magic that Suttungr had used to protect himself. Her friends sat in silence while Brunhilda related her tale, though Skogul bit her lip and rocked back and forth.

Once Brunhilda got to the conclusion of the war council meeting, Skogul immediately said, "I'll volunteer!"

"We both will," Hilder added, giving Skogul a look to keep her voice down. "Skogul's one of our best scouts, and after all of the shit that I had to deal with in Svartalfheim, I sure as Hel should have the pick of my next assignment. I swear, if I ever see a deep mine again…"

"So what happened out there?" Brunhilda asked with genuine concern.

Hilder waved her off and drained her tankard. "It's nothing really. Let's just say that there are still plenty of nasty things living in the deep, dark holes of the world."

"We'll go to Gunnar and Freya first thing in the morning,"

said Skogul, bringing the conversation back to the matter at hand. "Imagine getting to see Yggdrasil, fighting Nidhogg, and wielding Gungnir." Her eyes gleamed. "No Aesir has set eyes on any of those since Baldur…" She trailed off and looked away. Loki's actions leading to Baldur's death made that the darkest day for the Aesir since the end of the Great War.

"For very good reason, Skogul," Hilder said, as she placed a comforting hand on Skogul's shoulder.

"So, could it really be Loki?" Skogul whispered.

Brunhilda took a long drink from her mug while her friend waited, rocking back and forth in her seat and biting her lower lip. "Seems like the most likely conclusion," Brunhilda finally answered. She smiled, enjoying Skogul's squirming. "He and his sister are the only Jotnar who were welcomed in Asgard after the war," she said with a shrug. "And even that didn't last long."

"According to Odin and all who were present," Hilder said, looking at Brunhilda as if to confirm, "Loki and Baldur were killed at Yggdrasil during that incident with the vargr Fenrir and his pack. Loki may have ambushed and stabbed Baldur in the back, but Nidhogg incinerated them both. I doubt that a Jotnar would be able to survive dragon fire."

Skogul leaned in, whispering in an even more hushed voice, "Well, I heard that Lord Odin was so enraged by the betrayal that he thought death was too good for Loki. And so he pulled the traitor from death's door away from the infernal hound, Garmr, on the threshold to Hel to face retribution. Odin then seized him by the neck and bound and imprisoned him beneath Yggdrasil, destined for all eternity to have a serpent above him dripping venom on his face and—"

"We've all heard that tale," Hilder said, rolling her eyes and cutting her off. "That's just a story spread among the Jotnar to keep their hopes up that he may one day return. He and his sister, Jarnsaxa, are their heroes."

Skogul had that look on her face that said she was not convinced, her mouth twisting a little. Hilder snapped, "By Odin's beard, Brunhilda was there!"

"Yeah, but she said she didn't see it, didn't you?" the excited, wide-eyed Skogul asked.

Brunhilda let out a little sigh, "We had just fought Fenrir's pack of vargr, and so we missed the actual incident." Skogul burst into a smile. "However," Brunhilda continued, ignoring Skogul's smile turning into a pout, "I did arrive in time to see two figures being consumed in Nidhogg's flame. There was nothing left for Odin to imprison let alone drip venom on for eternity."

"And where would he find a snake that would just sit still and do that?" Hilder added with a playful smirk and a jab at her ribs.

By now they were on their third round, their voices growing louder and merrier, but this had put a damper on them. A disappointed frown soured Skogul's face.

Hilder had a look of deep thought and concentration. "In any regard, this will be a treacherous mission. We'll need a large contingent of highly skilled soldiers to battle a dragon like Nidhogg. We have to be prepared."

"Tomorrow!" shouted Brunhilda, slamming her now empty tankard on the table. Some of the nearby patrons jumped in surprise.

Hilder cocked an eyebrow. "What?"

"We need to be prepared tomorrow," explained Brunhilda. She grabbed another tankard of mead from a serving girl walking by. "Tonight we drink!" she said, standing up. She tossed a pouch of coins to the girl and yelled, "A round of mead for everyone!"

The tavern patrons erupted in a hearty cheer as the revelry continued long into the night.

CHAPTER 7: JOTUNHEIM

"Whoa, calm down now," the Jotnar shepherdess said in an even, reassuring tone. She was short of stature, particularly in comparison to the livestock she tended which was fifty head strong, with a quarter of them juveniles. The mature, wooly aurochs dwarfed the shepherdess, towering half a yard above her head at the shoulder. Even the playful juveniles were three times her bodyweight, and their frolicking play could knock her down if she did not pay attention.

Another younger shepherdess was watching the young calves play, encouraging their exercise. Even covered with a light dusting of snow the aurochs' downy brown coats did not serve to camouflage them in the tundra, though they did add to their bulk and kept them nice and toasty, the shorter shepherdess thought as her fingers sank into the soft fur of a friendly bull. Not that they needed to hide, she observed as she ducked under four-foot long arching horns as one beast turned to nuzzle her.

Her face was covered all over in a pale blue fur that transitioned into an unruly mane of hair that cascaded down her back. About her shoulders she wore a mantle of thick animal furs. In addition to a simple satchel slung across her body she carried a sturdy, well-worn staff. Her garb was plain and the staff was no different, adorned with a rough iron ball capping one end. It gleamed as it caught the sunlight. She held it with a light, natural grip in her hand.

The spring sky was a bright and cheerful blue, with the sun shining pale and warm in the east as it began its long, daily trek. Wide open tundra spread out around them with the treeline of the boreal forest about a hundred yards to the south. The wind shifted and the herd calmed a bit.

Pulling her wooly mantle a little tighter against the breeze, the elder shepherdess looked upon her herd with admiration. Even this far north, in the near-arctic region of Jotunheim, these aurochs seemed comfortable covered in thick, shaggy coats and insulated with thick layers of fat. Oblivious to the chill of the early morning air, they returned to rooting around in the snow, searching out their favored snack, the tender flower buds of the purple mountain saxifrage. Still, as the wind shifted again, many of the three dozen adult aurochs paused their grazing and raised their heads, grunting and calling in quick, agitated notes while shuffling in place and stomping at the frozen ground.

"Something's spooking them, Hertha," the younger shepherdess said as she scanned the horizon, her attention pulled from the juveniles. A sudden gust of wind chilled her, causing the light teal fur of her face to bristle. She was taller than her sister and was also bundled up in hides, carrying a staff of her own. Even though it was a balanced staff without the awkward iron-capped end, she fumbled with it while trying to deal with a stamping, agitated bull.

"Really? Do you think so, Jorunn?" Hertha said with a roll of her eyes as she corralled a wayward calf. "Keep your eyes to the south, where the wind blows. They're smelling something there."

As the pair moved to stand between the herd and the treeline to the south, a blur of gray and white burst forth. Hertha looked up and saw a wolf almost as large as an auroch, barreling toward her. In the wan light of dawn it cast no shadow and looked for all the world like a wraith made of claws and teeth. Its coat was coarse and stiff, bristling around the neck in a mane of furry spikes. It moved across the open field with barely a whisper, the shushing of snow the only confirmation of its corporeal presence. Hertha swallowed hard, holding down the abject terror rising in her gut.

"Vargr!" Jorunn shouted, panic in her voice as she took two hesitant steps back.

Hertha said nothing. With slow and deliberate motions, she slid her feet out just wider than shoulder width and bent her knees, ready to spring. She held her staff at the ready, her eyes focused on the snarling beast. The aurochs, seeing the approaching vargr, huddled into a protective circle with bulls at the fore, their heads lowered, a wall of fur bristling with horns defending the calves in the middle.

The vargr jumped. Although it was swift and blinding awash in the churning snow, Hertha swung her staff with strength and precision and rapped the vargr soundly across the shoulders with the iron-capped end. The monstrous creature bounded back several yards avoiding the next swing, fur bristling, its hackles raised. A snarl at its muzzle curled back its lips, revealing a set of sharp, nasty teeth, saliva dripping as its heavy panting clouded the frosty air. A low, loud growl rumbled from deep within its chest, and the aurochs moved in unison back a step or two. Even Jorunn shifted her weight to her rear foot, matching Hertha's stance.

The vargr's breath froze in the air as its intelligent eyes darted from Hertha to the aurochs to Jorunn. It lunged forward with a snap of its jaws. Hertha anticipated it and swung, but her staff touched nothing but air. While she was off balance, it dodged around her, bounding straight for Jorunn.

Hertha watched her sister bring up her staff as the beast bowled her over. Jorunn was young and still weak, and she struggled to hold the vargr back, just avoiding the reach of its gnashing teeth. Her arms locked, holding the staff against its body, straining, on the verge of collapsing. The vargr pushed, its full weight upon her, jaws snapping inches away from her face and spittle flying at her. Just as it felt like her arms would give out, the vargr pulled its head back. Then it struck again, quick as a flash, jaws closing on the staff and snapping it in two.

In those brief seconds Hertha recovered her footing and threw her body against it, bowling it clear off her sister. It scrambled to its feet just as she unleashed a flurry of attacks upon it. Blow after blow struck the animal in the shoulders, in the flanks, not letting up or giving it a moment to recover. With one final brutal swing of the iron-capped end, she caught the beast full in the head and sent it sprawling.

The vargr tried to get to its feet, but its eyes were dazed, and it swayed and lost its footing. It shook its head, its legs faltering. As Hertha lunged forward, the vargr fell and stumbled before it bolted back to the treeline, tail between its legs.

Hertha offered her hand to Jorunn, who was still on her back in the snow. Jorunn looked at the proffered hand and then to her own. Hertha could see that the young shepherdess was in a state of shock, her hands clenched around the broken staff, one half in each hand. With a firm and gentle touch Hertha's fingers pried open Jorunn's death grip, and the pieces fell with a whisper into the snow. Hertha grasped her hand and pulled her up.

"You gave me quite a scare there," Hertha said as she looked over her younger sister with care. Her examination was rough and thorough, finding only some minor scrapes and bruises. Once she was certain that there were no significant injuries, Hertha embraced her. Jorunn stiffened at first, trembling all over. It took a few moments before her muscles relaxed, and she released her breath and began to breathe again. Jorunn buried her face in Hertha's shoulder and brought her arms up to return the hug.

"T-Thanks," she eked out along with a shuddering sob.

"Shh," Hertha said, and supported her sister with a small squeeze. "This was your first vargr attack. Don't worry, you'll get the hang of this. The next time one of those beasts attack, you'll be the one sending it on its way with its tail between its legs."

—

A lone Jotnar walked the long path to Gastropnir. The blazing orange of the setting sun illuminated the blanket of clouds above. Jorunn had hit a growth spurt over the last few years, filling out her figure and growing out her hair. Hertha would hardly recognize her the next time they met. Faint sounds of activity floated in the air and Jorunn urged on her auroch in the final stretch to the town.

Jorunn never tired of the kaupstefna, Gastropnir's market plaza. The whole village was there, trading and bartering for goods with the arching roof of arctic shrubs overhead. Foliage and flowers complemented the myriad wares on display, creating an oasis of color amid the monochrome world outside. While cooking fires did much to illuminate the space, columns of ice filtered and reflected the light from braziers distributed throughout. Savory aromas from the food stalls wafted throughout the covered space, protected from the harsh elements outside, while livestock brayed and carried on at the opposite end. The loose collection of vendors hawking their wares was accompanied by a modest crowd engaged in spirited haggling and gossip. Everyone worked during the day and gathered in the evenings to trade goods and stories.

For Jorunn it had been a long, tedious, boring day. Arriving at last, her shoulders slumped in relief, the well-worn staff, capped with a ball of iron weighed heavy in her hand. As the metal cap caught the fading light, she thought of Hertha and the grand adventures she was probably having in Suttungr's army. Fighting for the Jotnar homelands against the Aesir, in the lush forests of Vanaheim or the golden plains of Midgard, was a far cry from their days protecting the herd from vargr at home.

And yet as Suttungr rallied their people to reclaim their ancestral lands, Gastropnir was the only home Jorunn had ever known. It was a moderately sized village in Jotunheim, or at least she heard it was. Although she had never lived anywhere else, the stories she had heard spoke of cities a hundredfold larger. With Gastropnir's residents numbered just above a thousand individuals—at its peak it had just as many aurochs and twice as many Jotnar—she felt like she knew just about everyone.

A young auroch calf walked behind her, led by a length of rope tied loosely around its neck. It was lashed into a sturdy harness as it pulled a small cart laden with a sizeable mound of frozen manure patties. The cold kept the odor in check, but the smell was still quite pungent. No one gave it much notice though as everyone greeted the young Jotnar with a cordial smile and nod.

"Good evening, Jorunn," Knute said in their ancestral Jotunmal tongue. Jorunn acknowledged the ancient bone carver and nodded with deference. His once deep blue fur had paled to a mottled gray with some streaks of its original color. He was one of the many elder Jotnar who could not march with Suttungr and join the uprising. Many of his generation had already done their duty, having fought and died in the Aesir-Vanir War. Those who had survived this long were a hardy lot and well respected.

Jorunn always looked forward to his stories about the majesties of their old homeland, the epic battles of the war, and how things would improve when Suttungr overthrew the Aesir. After the devastation of the Great War, Odin had taken many steps to keep any realm from rebelling again. The measures were far reaching and ranged from controlling the flow and access of resources to keeping the other races isolated both from each other and from themselves in small, spread-out towns and villages. In addition, all those in the nine realms were required to know and only speak the language of Asgard. However, since Suttungr's uprising, the people of Jotunheim were reclaiming their old traditions, most notably by speaking the Jotnar language. Here in Gastropnir, so far removed from Asgard, they had been able to hold on to their heritage in secret, and now they rushed to embrace the old ways.

"Hi, Knute," Jorunn gave him a warm smile as she set up her stall. *"Any news from the warfront?"*

"I hear that Hertha has been really making a name for herself with Suttungr," he said. *"You should be proud of her."*

"I am," she said with a little too much enthusiasm. While she was proud of her sister, she also just missed her. Hertha had raised her since they lost their parents, so when she left, Jorunn had felt pride and honor, but also the acute pain of losing her only remaining family.

Hertha had been among the first to rally to Suttungr's side. Although throngs of people had jumped at the chance to join the fight, the thought of war gave pause to just as many. Suttungr was a charismatic speaker and had traveled to all of the Jotnar villages. In the end, all able-bodied Jotnar had joined up while the elderly and young were put to work on the domestic front. Suttungr's tactics relied on the army taking most of their supplies from defeated enemies, but soldiers and aurochs still came from Jotunheim.

As Jorunn unhitched her auroch, she ran her hands through its wooly coat. Soon, this juvenile would be mature enough to be added to the army. Most of the prime aurochs had already been taken to serve as pack animals to aid the army in moving and striking quickly, transporting supplies, and allowing them to evade Aesir counterattacks. When young Jotnar and aurochs came of age, they were conscripted into the military effort and sent to join Suttungr. Next year Jorunn would qualify along with a good number of her herd. And though she was eager to see Hertha again, she was wary at the prospect of fighting, killing, and dying in the war.

The evening wore on and Knute and Jorunn sold their wares. Because he was an elder of the town, many people stopped by to deliver reports and updates to him. Word of the battle of Halvard reached even here. And while most spoke in awe and reverence of Suttungr's stand against Thor, others saw this as an escalation by the Aesir and feared what this would mean for Jotunheim. With all of their soldiers far away to the south, those still in the homeland were vulnerable, and they feared the threat of retribution. While the danger to them felt real and near, Jorunn just worried about her sister.

CHAPTER 8: BIRGJAVALE

Two days after Brunhilda's hearing, Skogul stood with Hilder and Brunhilda in the troop marshalling field. An ominous wind blew in from the north, giving the pre-dawn air a bone-chilling quality. The eastern sky was just beginning to lighten through the ever-present clouds as the three valkyries prepared their mounts for the long journey ahead. Most warfare and combat, even for valkyries, was conducted on foot. When they did fight on horseback, they usually rode more formidable destriers. These mere rounceys were less intimidating, but their advantages of speed and endurance were far more important now. This minor detail communicated volumes to Skogul's keen scout eyes. The urgency of this mission would test their stamina. Even so, she kept a smile on her face.

"This will be the stuff of legends," Skogul said, hopping from one foot to the other with nervous energy. "Bards will sing of our exploits for generations!"

"Where's everyone else?" Hilder said curtly. Early mornings found her to be cantankerous, and Brunhilda sympathized. But when Skogul grabbed Hilder by the shoulders and hopped up and down, she caught Hilder cracking a grin and hopping too.

"Not sure," said a bleary-eyed Brunhilda with a dismissive shrug. "Gunnar told us to be here before sunrise, 'ready for a long and grueling journey.'" She imitated Gunnar's voice and wagged a stern finger at the others. "Maybe we're really early." Brunhilda looked around at the empty courtyard again. "Or really late."

"I'm just glad that they let both of us join this mission. Future generations will learn about us as minstrels sing rousing, epic ballads of our exploits at Wodensdaeg festivals throughout the nine realms. And our astounding feats will entertain audiences until the end of the world!" Skogul said, her arms held overhead in triumph.

"Wait, isn't this a punishment for Brunhilda?" Hilder asked

with sudden realization, shaking the last vestiges of sleep from her head.

"Yes," conceded Brunhilda with an exasperated sigh, "thanks for not rubbing that in every chance you get."

"So this mission will be an honor for us but punishment for you?" Skogul asked quizzically. "How does that work?"

"That's a good point, Skogul," Hilder added, arms crossed. "If anything, it's punishment for us to have to babysit you."

"The honor, sisters, is that you are allowed to witness my superior martial skills. Meanwhile, I'm punished by having to carry your weight."

"That's not what it felt like at the Sundered Anvil that first night," interjected Skogul. "I distinctly recall a fight breaking out, and Hilder and I had to jump in to cover your back." As she spoke she bounded up behind Brunhilda, standing back to back and miming fighting off attackers.

"I was just getting us some practice fighting a tavern full of drunken fools. That's what it's going to be like fighting against the Jotnar," said Brunhilda. She pushed Skogul off of her, a cocky smirk curling the corners of her lips.

The lighthearted banter continued as they finished their preparations. The wind faded and the air grew still in the empty courtyard. Guards walked high above along the walls of Asgard.

Skogul snapped to attention when she noticed Gunnar and Freya approaching. Brunhilda and Hilder followed suit. Gunnar was dressed for travel and led several horses. A chill ran down Skogul's back as caught sight of Freya. She was also dressed for travel. Although a skilled warrior in her own right, Freya had not been in the field since fighting against the Aesir in the war; her official role saw her directing strategy from Asgard. However, with Thor still in recovery, someone needed to take over leadership on the frontline. Freya's intellect and mastery of magic made her the most qualified to lead the Aesir against this new threat.

"Fall in, valkyries," said Gunnar, cutting through the jocularity as she approached. "This mission is a gamble, and for good or ill it's one that we must make. Freya will accompany us back to

Halvard and explain the plan along the way. Even with spare horses it will still take days to get back to the front. We will break in the evenings to water and rest the horses, though we will not sleep long."

"Where are the rest of the troops?" asked Skogul, her hand raised.

"It's only you," replied a somber Gunnar. "You three are the entire team. A full-frontal assault against Nidhogg didn't work before, and too large of a company would have difficulty sneaking past the Jotnar. With their army marching on us, you're all that we can spare."

"So," said Freya, placing her hand on Skogul's arm to lower it. She nodded toward Hilder and Brunhilda. "Thank you for volunteering."

With that they all mounted up, the three valkyries giving each other anxious glances. Ever fastidious, Skogul mentally reviewed the standard practices for these types of long-distance endurance runs. Each of them would lead a spare horse bearing their gear. They would swap horses at regular intervals to allow their mounts a brief respite as they made the trek to Halvard. That first day would be easy but taxing as they pushed the limits of the horses' endurance. They had to take advantage of the secure and well-paved roads now to make up for time lost when they traveled through rougher country.

As the scout, Skogul was the more forward-thinking of the trio. If she were in the enemy's position she would dispatch spies to watch the roads closer to Halvard. Their final approach would need to be circuitous, going through less traveled terrain to avoid prying eyes. Yet these concerns were trivial considering the magnitude of their mission, and she still did not know the details. The rumble of hooves and the howl of the wind made communication difficult, which was just as well; each woman was focused on the task at hand, and each understood that this would be the most dangerous and the most important undertaking of their lives.

By evening they had covered a considerable distance and stopped at a small tavern in the quaint town of Birgjavale. They all dismounted and stretched out their limbs with groans and sighs of relief, though Skogul knew that they were all eager to continue. Yet even with the spare horses to distribute the load, they still needed a break, the horses most of all. She drew her arm across her forehead and found her sleeve dirtier than it was before. Still, she beamed out a smile through a grime-covered face at each of her companions. With their armor packed away and the dust of the road caked on them, they looked much like the other travelers within.

"Remember," Freya whispered as they approached the stable hand, "we're simple travelers heading toward Veizlakr to inspect our grain shipments. Talkative civilians would be an unfortunate liability. Brunhilda." Freya stopped her before she dismounted. "The horses are your responsibility."

Skogul's keen senses were difficult to turn off as she noted their surroundings, looking for anything out of the ordinary, anything that might pose a threat. Compared to other commercial towns, Birgjavale was a quiet, provincial hamlet, yet its location, just off the main road out of Asgard, meant that it was no stranger to a wide variety of travelers. While the realms were well established as separate entities and travel by the other races was limited, there was much trade and commerce that flowed between the realms, all of it through Asgard. People from all of the other realms traveled and conducted business in this region. Larger cities would have crowded marketplaces and inns of various levels of refinement for all class of travelers. Birgjavale was something of a rest stop between the cities.

The tavern was only half full this particular evening. Most of the other travelers were content to take their ease in silence though there was plenty of chatter about the troubles brewing in the north. And while refugees had yet to make it to Birgjavale, they would be arriving soon enough. Skogul followed Freya to an empty table in a quiet corner of the tavern.

Though there was a consistent low din in the hall, Skogul's ears perked up as one group of rowdy patrons gossiped about the news of the day. There were four of them sitting around a table near the door, tankards of ale on the table or raised to their lips. Though there was a general boisterous nature to their tone—their faces were flushed and their mouths loose and wet—they spoke with anxiety about word from the frontier. She overheard them saying the Jotnar had attacked and begun retaking the annexed lands of Jotunheim.

"I heard that even the mighty Thor was struck down," the more rotund local with a full beard and a gin-blossomed nose said with a slur. "If he can't stand against those bloody Jotnar savages, then it might be time to get out of here. I always knew that the Aesir Army was more show than substance."

"Yeah, well, the way I heard it—from someone who was there, mind you—the Aesir Army was outnumbered a thousand to one," countered his slender human companion sitting opposite. "I'm surprised anyone could survive a fight like that. The whole Aesir Army will get crushed under the weight of an enemy that massive. It ain't a matter of 'if' but 'when' they'll break through. And woe unto those who stand in their way."

"Whatever happens, their grievance is with the Aesir. Leave us out of it is what I say," interjected the short, balding man sitting with them. His stout body and pale skin indicated that he was of Dokkalfar lineage. "That being said, there's nothing wrong with making a little money from the poor sods coming this way. It'll be a bonanza for us. I've stocked up on cheap food and blankets that aren't fit for animals but will fetch a good price from those sorry northerners."

Brunhilda had walked in during the course of their conversation. She glared at them, her hands balled into tight fists, and it looked as if she were ready to punch the bearded one in his face. Before Skogul could stand up, Freya was already there between Brunhilda and the group. "We are in the corner over there, sister," Freya said. Grasping her by the arm, Freya pulled Brunhilda away and to their table.

"Ignore them. We have more important matters to attend to," she said. As they dined on a simple meal of roasted venison, hard cheese, and warm bread, Freya leaned in and spoke in a low voice.

"You three are tasked with a heavy burden. As a team, you must succeed where even our illustrious Odin failed. As the senior officer, Hilder is in command while you're in the field." Brunhilda opened her mouth as if to protest, but Freya did not even glance in her direction. "Gunnar and I have devised a plan that will give you the best chance for success. From Odin's account, Gungnir was plunged into Nidhogg's flank and pinned one of its wings down so that it could no longer fly. Since it hasn't been terrorizing the nine realms, we can assume that still holds true. So at least that's one less difficulty."

Freya paused and took a deep breath. "It is still an exceptionally powerful and dangerous creature though. A direct assault will not work," she said stressing her last few words, eyes locked on Brunhilda. "Your objective is to retrieve Gungnir, first and foremost. We believe that the best tactic will be for one of you to distract the beast. The roots of Yggdrasil the World Tree are unbreakable, and if you can get it to chase you through there, then you may be able to tangle it up long enough for the others to pull the spear out. That will put two of you directly in the path of that dragon, so assess the situation carefully when you arrive before attempting this."

"Although to get to that point, you must first make your way past the Jotnar Army," continued Gunnar, "and then through the brutal and punishing realms of Jotunheim and Niflheim, just to get to Yggdrasil. Once you've done that and after you have outmaneuvered Nidhogg and retrieved Gungnir, you must then return to Asgard before the Jotnar Army arrives. Once we've rallied our forces, we can move against the Jotnar Army; and in a conventional war, we will dominate them. However, without Gungnir, defeating Suttungr himself will be impossible. This is a risky endeavor, but you three are our best hope."

"And how do we get past the Jotnar?" Skogul asked.

"I will enchant each of you with a glamour to disguise you as Jotnar soldiers," Freya said. "On myself the illusion is complete; however, on others the spell is not as thorough. From a distance your disguises will hold up, but if anyone gets too close, they will see the telltale glimmer of Reginvald magic. Since I will not be there to maintain these glamours, you must be able to concentrate and hold the image in your mind. As Aesir, we all have within us some connection to the energies of the World Tree. Some of us"—Freya flashed a brief burst of light from her hand that changed it to mimic Jotnar fur, skin color, and texture—"simply have more control of that power. If you lose your concentration, the illusions will disappear and you will be revealed." Another flash, and her hand returned to its normal appearance. "So be cautious, all of you." Though she did not call anyone out by name, Skogul thought she may have meant the last comment to be for Brunhilda.

"Once we reach Halvard, I will cast my spell. Then you will

have to slip in with the Jotnar and penetrate their lines. They do not have mounted troops, so you will have to move on foot and go swiftly. You will not be able to carry much with you, so be prepared to scavenge for food and water once you've made it beyond the enemy lines. I will stay with Gunnar to take command of the northern division of the army while Thor recovers. The three of you must find a way to succeed."

Skogul still held onto her excitement for this mission, only now it was tempered by the magnitude of the obstacles and its importance in the fight at hand. Her leg twitched with nervous energy. After finishing their meal, they stood up and headed toward the door. They would rest briefly with their mounts and continue along their way before the moon reached its zenith. Skogul noticed Brunhilda dawdling at the rear of the group, so she waited by the door after the others exited. She watched as Brunhilda passed the table of locals and stumbled bumping into the serving girl, knocking three tankards of ale onto them.

"My apologies," she said insincerely. To the girl she gave a wink and tossed her a gold coin that more than covered the cost of the drinks.

"Now see here—" the large, bearded one said and began to rise until the balding Dokkalfar placed his hand on his friend's arm. The Dokkalfar motioned with his eyes toward the sword hanging from Brunhilda's belt. Even though she was dressed in simple clothes and covered in a thick layer of dust from the road, the dim light of the tavern reflected off of the golden pommel, emblazoned with the sigil of the valkyrie of Asgard.

"Of course, not a problem," the bearded one muttered into his empty mug as he returned to his seat. His clothes were still dripping when Skogul followed Brunhilda out the door.

CHAPTER 9: RETURN TO HALVARD

Freya balked at the sight of the Jotnar Army camped out in the northern fields surrounding Halvard. Even with the reports from Thor and Gunnar their numbers were staggering. Pillars of smoke far to the east attested to more Jotnar causing havoc elsewhere. The Aesir forces had secured the city, their fortifications extending to the east to prevent a full siege and to keep the road to the south open.

Though the ground was covered in frost and shrouded with a mist centered on the Jotnar camp, Freya could see that many bodies littered the battlefield. Thankfully, no fallen Aesir remained. The Aesir would have conducted funeral rites for the dead, burned them in pyres and sent them off on the waters of Calder Lake. Like savages, animals, the Jotnar were content to leave their dead to rot. She had witnessed some formality in the Jotnar burying their fallen in ceremonies in the past while they were allied during the Aesir-Vanir War. Freya never could understand their desire to trap their spirits, entombed beneath the dirt. This grisly scene reminded her of those dark days of the war. With a shake of her head she focused on the task at hand.

The sun was setting in the west, dropping behind the cliffs above Calder Lake. Though Jotnar shrugged off the cold with ease, Freya could see many fires burning throughout their encampment; after all, they needed to stave off the dark and keep watch. She saw there were few hard fortifications, but the sheer number of tents and troops was daunting.

"The Jotnar Army will likely have guards and scouts looking for any travelers entering Halvard," Gunnar said as they reached the final rise before they would be visible. There was a broad, open plain that stretched out between them and the city, with no cover at all.

"How are we going to get in without being spotted?"

"Not to worry," Freya said as she forced herself to sit upright. "I can conjure enough magic to mask our approach." A pale glow shimmered across her hand followed by a burst of dense, rolling mists. With a sly grin she said, "Stay close and all they will glimpse in this twilight will be a bank of fog coming in from Calder Lake."

—

It was a great testament to the on-duty sentries that they reacted at once and without losing composure when five women appeared out of the heavy mists, covered in the mud and dust of the road. Freya did not enjoy having spears pointed at her face, but she was proud of their poise.

"Kari, Olf, stand down!" Gunnar ordered.

Recognizing the voice of the valkyrie commander, they snapped to attention. Junior soldiers and stablehands hurried to attend to the women and their steeds. Moments later the five were in the central command tent of the Aesir Army to be briefed on the current tactical situation.

In the absence of both Gunnar and Thor, the young and capable commander Vali had been overseeing deployment of the army in the region. When Freya and the valkyries entered, he and three other senior officers were gathered around a large wooden table with maps of the area and small carved figures scattered on them. Freya appraised the map, noting the distribution of troops and resources. Intricately carved alabaster pieces represented the various units of the Aesir: foot soldiers, archers, defensive, and supply. The Jotnar figures were rough wooden tiles with markings indicating unit type and size. It was difficult to categorize Jotnar units as they were all outfitted in a motley assortment of weapons and armor.

"Your presence honors us, Lady Freya," said Vali as he and the others rose to attention. "Commander Gunnar, it is a relief to see that you've returned as well." Though he sounded sincere, he did raise an eyebrow directed at Brunhilda.

"Greetings, Vali," replied Gunnar.

"We've no time for pleasantries or formalities," cut in Freya. "Give us a summary of the current situation. We have a mission of grave importance to undertake and no time to waste."

She visualized everything playing out on the map in front of her as he spoke. Vali explained the quick strike tactics that the Jotnar were using to keep the Aesir off balance. In the week following the first battle for Halvard, when Thor and Suttungr clashed, he reported that the Jotnar Army appeared to close ranks and simply settle in their encampment while the Aesir fortified the defenses of the city. Scouts reported Suttungr walking among the troops the following day, and then the Jotnar camp erupted in celebration that lasted for a week. It was an oddly Aesir-like ritual, mused Freya, to revel after a great battle; what could be greater than standing against the power of Mjolnir itself? It appeared Suttungr had developed quite a fondness for the trappings of life in Asgard; just one more piece of evidence that he might be Loki.

From the layout it was clear that the bulk of the Jotnar forces had massed around Halvard as something of a staging point. In addition, they had flanking forces threatening many of the nearby cities. The Aesir Army was spread thin, defending those cities and protecting the refugees as they fled south. Vali said that he led regular sorties against the Jotnar encampment, ensuring that Halvard was not completely besieged and cut off from reinforcements from Asgard.

Freya was tempted to order a full-frontal attack knowing that their troops were eager to bring the fight to the Jotnar. But she could not lose sight of the big picture: Their numbers were insufficient to mount an effective strike and defend Halvard and the nearby settlements. Also, with Suttungr back on his feet, she was wary of a direct confrontation without Thor and Mjolnir present. Fresh Aesir troops had arrived the previous week. Though they were able to integrate the reinforcements sent from Asgard with practiced efficiency, they were under a perpetual deluge of reports of Jotnar troops marching on other cities. Every move Suttungr made kept the Aesir on the defensive. And every day it seemed more Jotnar arrived to bolster their ranks.

"The situation is more dire than we suspected," Freya said with a frown. "If Suttungr has recovered this quickly, then he is much stronger than we suspected. And their army is growing larger and more daunting by the day." She stared intently at the map, her brow furrowed. "Halvard will soon be indefensible." Turning to Vali she asked, "Is the rest of the northern territory evacuated?"

"We have covered the evacuations of all of the major cities in the area that we could. However, we were unable to respond to every attack that the Jotnar Army has made," responded Vali, his gaze cast down at the map with several city names crossed out. "Scouts report that we lost six of the smaller towns. All of the inhabitants were slaughtered."

"Very well, we'll have to cut our losses." Freya's expression was stony and her voice even. The valkyries remained stoic as well, standing at attention, unmoved. "This is a full-scale war and we cannot save everyone. We must abandon the north and draw their army into attacking our more fortified territories. Once we've regrouped with our reserve forces, we will counterattack and put down this uprising once and for all."

"But what of Suttungr, m'lady?" asked Vali. "Will Lord Thor face him again on the field of battle? If he can withstand Mjolnir's power, how can he be defeated?"

"We have a plan," said Gunnar.

Freya held up a hand commanding silence in the room. After a few more moments she spoke. "We'll have to alter the plan to include our withdrawal from Halvard." Her eyes met Gunnar's. "The Jotnar host is too close and will attack our rear position as we fall back." She moved one Aesir piece toward the Jotnar camp as she scooped the others in Halvard to the south. "Gunnar and I will lead an assault on them just before dawn. We'll need all of the horses and your best riders, Vali. I doubt that we'll do substantial damage to their army, but we'll be able to throw them into chaos and disorder long enough to give the retreat a head start."

"It'll take days to organize and mobilize our supplies without the spare horses," Vali said. Freya gave him a withering stare. "We do have barrels of lamp oil and a cache of sapper charges. We'll gather all we can carry tonight and scuttle the rest."

"Even better," said Gunnar with a wicked grin. "I'll rig them up to trip lines. With luck, Suttungr will want to be the first one in."

Freya gave a nod of assent and turned to the three valkyries. "Your mission does not change," Freya said to them. "However, you will accompany the assault and infiltrate the Jotnar Army during the chaos of the battle. We're still counting on you three. Do not fail me."

She looked at everyone present, holding their gaze for a second to confirm that they all understood their part. With a wave of her hand everyone hurried out of the tent to prepare and carry out the plan.

—

The skies were still dark as exodus began. They had worked through the night in relative darkness to mask their activities, gathering their supplies and readying their soldiers for departure. Supplies that they could not carry with them were rigged with explosive charges, oil, and kindling. They would leave no resources here for the Jotnar Army to pillage. With the bulk of the troops escorting the supplies and the wounded set to depart to the south, the mounted forces gathered at Halvard's northern border. All up and down the line the soldiers readied their weapons and performed final checks on their equipment. The horses were agitated, sensing the tension in the air. Nearly all of the horses in Halvard were there. Messengers on swift mounts were sent to inform their other divisions in the north of the withdrawal.

Freya had briefed the rest of the officers during the night. She knew that most were not pleased with the order to fall back, but they were Aesir and would follow her orders. Drawing the Jotnar Army closer to Asgard would allow the Aesir to consolidate their forces and envelop their enemies.

While the mounted soldiers waited, Freya met with the three valkyries in private. They had taken the furs, weapons, and armor of fallen Jotnar troops and equipped themselves accordingly.

"Why don't we just use those mists to cover the retreat and sneak in with the Jotnar?" Skogul asked, wrinkling her nose as she tightened the straps of her pungent leather cuirass.

"That magic is Ethlivald," Freya replied. "The Jotnar themselves are accustomed to its effects and can see through it rather easily when nearby."

Skogul pouted as she inspected the Svelbjarg ram's skull that she would have to put on her head. With a sniff and squint she plucked a bit of flesh from a crevice and flicked it aside.

Freya approached them each in turn, whispered her spell, and then kissed them on the forehead. After each kiss the valkyrie shimmered and, in a wave that propagated out from that point, transformed. Fur covered their bodies: Skogul in a pale blue, a bit of her golden skin accentuating the color, while Hilder took on a dark teal coat, her black hair lightened as it shifted hue. When Freya came to Brunhilda, she paused.

"I saw what you did at the tavern back in Birgjavale," Freya whispered. "You need to keep your emotions and pride in check, or it will be the ruin of us all. We're counting on you."

"Yes, m'lady." Brunhilda bowed her head with downcast eyes.

"My blessing be upon you," Freya said as her lips touched Brunhilda's forehead. "May you all find success and your way back home." She looked at all three of them. With a shake of her head she knew that Brunhilda's blue fur with an auburn tinge might arouse suspicion, but it would have to do. "Victory or death."

"Victory or death," they repeated in unison.

With that they assembled with the rest of the soldiers, ready to charge forth from their Halvard defenses. Freya rode to the front of the army. She struck an intimidating visage atop her fiery destrier, having exchanged her utilitarian rouncey for this beast of war. Brunhilda, Skogul, and Hilder followed her closely.

The soldiers had assembled without speech or ceremony. Freya could be quite eloquent when called upon. Yet time and again she proved to be a woman of action, not words. Only two dozen mounted troops were present. They were rare and valuable enough that horses were not often used in battle, but these were extraordinary circumstances. Riding up and down the line Freya evaluated each pair, rider and horse. Each soldier met her steely gaze in turn. They had all volunteered for this despite knowing the daunting odds they faced.

Without a word, Freya drew her sword and led the charge. She could hear the chime of ringing steel as they drew their weapons and the thunderous chorus of hooves. A smile curled at her lips as she reveled in the rush of adrenaline. A dense mist rose up and around her, leaving a trail behind obscuring the disguised valkyries. If they focused the Jotnar would be able to see them, but Freya counted on their attention to be drawn to the galloping horde.

The Aesir Army announced their presence in a deafening roar. Freya's eyes went to the unmistakable figure moving to meet them. Gunnar's description had seemed ridiculous before, and yet now Freya found her words were woefully inadequate. A hulking, shifting mass of muscles covered in dark blue fur was first on the line. Even without the fearsome animal skull pauldrons and hide coverings, Hrym was an arresting sight. Harried and disheveled, he had not bothered to put on his armor as he rushed to organize the defense.

Chaos and confusion ran rampant in the Jotnar camp as they were caught unaware. Many Jotnar even broke ranks and fled in panic at the sight of the gleaming, armor-clad Aesir on horseback. Hrym had just organized the Jotnar into lines when Freya and the mounted Aesir first hit them. The sickening crunch of steel on flesh rang out in the brisk morning air. From the moment of the initial contact, Freya set the tone of the battle. She knew that this could not be a traditional fight with armies lined up and pulsing, slow-moving fronts. With these odds they would be crushed by the Jotnar horde in moments. Instead, the lightning attacks and swift retreats left the Jotnar with no targets to counter. Some Jotnar, not knowing what to do, ran after the horses, creating a chaotic and undisciplined line. In the resulting confusion Brunhilda, Skogul, and Hilder slipped off their mounts and broke away from Freya and the Aesir and mixed in with the Jotnar troops.

As the Aesir continued to hack away at the Jotnar, Freya felt a shift in the opposing lines. The rest of the enemy camp had finally roused to the sounds of battle. The fighting intensified as the defenders surged with reinforcements. Though they were outnumbered, the Aesir pulled back before being outflanked or surrounded and then returned to strike farther down the line where it was weak.

Hrym's powerful attacks—cutting down any horse and rider with a single stroke—gave Freya pause as she kept her attacks as far from the giant mass of blue fur as possible. Yet even with his demonstration of raw power, Hrym was not her primary concern. She, Vali, and Gunnar continually scanned the area for any sign of Suttungr. Vali had reported sightings of the Jotnar leader over the duration of the siege of Halvard, yet they had not seen him this morning and that worried Freya. Hrym was an exceptional fighter and competent battle commander but combined with Suttungr's magic the Jotnar would put an end to this raid before the Aesir could fully evacuate Halvard.

CHAPTER 10: INTO THE BREACH

The Jotnar camp was a roiling sea of bodies. The Aesir forces had turned the tables on the Jotnar, keeping them off balance and on the defensive after losing three soldiers to one of Hrym's lethal blows. A large number of the Jotnar soldiers were abandoning their posts and fleeing from the attack. Hrym called out to another Jotnar to shore up the left flank. The animal skull helmet and bulky armor did little to make up for Hertha's short stature. And yet she commanded the troops nearest her with great efficacy. Amid the chaos three Jotnar slipped in from the Aesir side into the mass of Jotnar rallying to defend the camp.

After dismounting with the others Brunhilda gave a little smile as she saw the three riderless horses run back to the south, their infiltration having been covered by the chaos and the fog. She, Skogul, and Hilder made their way to the rear of the Jotnar line before peeling off and joining the panicking masses fleeing from the fight. Brunhilda bit down on her lower lip as she tried to keep her hand from her sword. So many Jotnar wheeled around her, their guard down in a state of panic. It would be such an easy thing, she thought as her hand drifted once more toward the hilt of her sword. As her fingers closed around the familiar leather wrapping, Freya's words echoed in her ears. With more than a little hesitation, she released her grip and doubled her pace.

The trio moved with purpose, putting more distance between them and their fellow Aesir. They communicated with each other using quick hand gestures. It was jarring at first for Brunhilda to see blue fur covering her hands but she maintained her composure. They moved with a loose group heading north toward the rear of the camp. It was unlikely that the nearby Jotnar paid them any heed, but they needed to take as many precautions as possible to see their mission through.

Without warning, Hrym barreled into the crowd. It seemed impossible for such a large person to move with such speed and stealth. Just a moment ago he was at the front, rallying the defenders.

He yelled something in Jotunmal with deafening rage. Then in the common tongue, he shouted, "Get back to the front! We do not run from the Aesir!"

Brunhilda saw that not all were turned back by the sheer threat and power of his voice. Those who did not stop of their own accord he physically restrained and threw back toward the front. He was grabbing everyone he could, and Brunhilda realized that he was headed straight for her.

Remembering their last encounter, she craved the rematch with every warrior instinct in her body. Again her hand went to her sword, though both Skogul and Hilder flashed her sharp glances and emphatic hand signals. And once more Freya's words flashed in her mind as Brunhilda stayed her hand. She would not fight him here and now, but neither could she let him bar her from their mission. Eyeing another Jotnar running near her, she stepped into his path and kicked out his right foot midstride. That sent the unfortunate Jotnar stumbling, and he slammed right into Hrym while Brunhilda slipped away.

The Jotnar bounced off Hrym's barrel-chested body and fell to the ground, his helmet tumbling away. Brunhilda smiled as Hrym stopped to pick up the Jotnar, and she turned back and fell back in step with Skogul and Hilder.

"Good job avoiding him," whispered Skogul, breaking the silence. At this point they were beyond earshot of any other Jotnar. "I'm very proud of you. It looked like you were going to fight him right then and there."

"I was sorely tempted," Brunhilda replied. "We'd faced off during the first battle at Halvard and I promised him that I'd cut him down the next time I saw him."

"Hush! We're not safe yet," hissed Hilder, flicking her eyes behind them.

—

Suttungr had emerged from his tent at last. Raising a large horn, he blew a piercing note that gave everyone in the valley pause. From where he had fallen on the ground, Skrymir looked back to the source of the sound. The Aesir cavalry also reacted to the horn and pulled back from the fighting to regroup.

"Formations!" shouted Suttungr into the eerie silence where the din of battle had so recently filled the air. The disarrayed and scrambling Jotnar Army fell into line with uncanny speed and discipline.

"You can't fight for the Jotnar people from down there, Skrymir," Hrym said, and lifted him up off of the ground with one hand.

Skrymir brushed himself off and opened his mouth, ready with a verbal jab in response, when he caught a glimpse of the one who had sent him headlong into Hrym. A brief glint of gold had drawn his eye to the sword at her hip. The wrought iron of the Jotnar weapons was a far cry from the glittering metal that he saw. Even among the Aesir a weapon ornamented with gold was uncommon. He had seen swords like that before.

Forgetting the retort on the tip of his tongue, Skrymir looked at the attack and then back to the fleeing Jotnar with the golden sword. A queer feeling at the back of his mind arose. This attack did not make sense. Though the Aesir cavalry were causing a fair amount of chaos, they were doing little actual damage to their camp. Then it dawned on him: The attack was just a ruse.

"Hrym!" shouted Skrymir, pulling away from his grasp. "Something is very wrong here." Pointing at the Jotnar who had run into him, he said, "We have to stop her."

Since the rest of the deserters had responded to Suttungr's call, the three Jotnar became conspicuous as they continued to flee. Hrym eyed the trio for a long second before he called to several nearby Jotnar to follow. Launching into a dead sprint, he led the pursuit after the three deserters. By then the strangers had made it to the rear of the Jotnar encampment a hundred yards away. Skrymir ran as fast as he could but was unable to keep pace with the long strides of the huge Jotnar. Only a small contingent of soldiers were on duty to guard all of their supplies and pack animals at the rear where they were stored. All of the other Jotnar soldiers were rallying to Suttungr.

With a quick glance back, Skrymir could swear that Freya was looking right at them. And when it appeared that Suttungr would join in the pursuit of the deserters, Freya let out a fierce battle cry that reverberated across the valley and charged the line again. That drew Suttungr's attention and he gathered his forces to bear against the attack.

"Stop those three!" shouted Hrym to the six Jotnar guarding the auroch pen. Although they looked like the rest of them, by now it was clear that were not what they appeared to be. The guards at the auroch pen drew their weapons.

—

Following Hilder's lead, Brunhilda and Skogul drew their swords as they ran. The bright blades danced in the light filtering through the clouds overhead. Any doubt that they were not Jotnar were erased by the grace, skill, and speed of their swordplay. In a matter of seconds the valkyries dispatched their foes and continued on their way without missing a step. To call it a fight would give too much credit to the six Jotnar guards, Brunhilda thought, her face impassive, almost bored. She hazarded a look back and saw Hrym closing on them fast.

With a decision made, Brunhilda's face hardened and her brow furrowed. She skidded to an abrupt stop and wheeled around to face Hrym and the pursuing Jotnar.

"What are you doing?" Skogul shouted as she too slid to a halt.

"The mission is the only thing that matters. I'll hold them off and then catch up with you. You two go on and complete the mission," Brunhilda said, her voice solemn with a tinge of excitement.

Skogul's mouth dropped. "But... "

"No debate." Brunhilda's lip curled into a slight grin. "He's mine!"

Skogul surveyed their surroundings, her head flicking left and right. As her eyes fixed on something nearby she grabbed Brunhilda by the armor and said, "Pull your head out of your ass. We've got a mission and I've got an idea."

Running to the far side of the auroch pen, Skogul let out a fearsome roar and cut down the auroch closest to her startling the rest of the herd. Hilder and Brunhilda picked up on the idea and joined in. They shouted and swung their swords around and gave chase, whipping up the frightened beasts into a stampede headed straight for the pursuing Jotnar. Seeing the Jotnar break off in the face of dozens of charging aurochs, the three valkyries sheathed their weapons and continued on their way. Brunhilda's pace quickened as she thought ahead to their goals: Yggdrasil, Nidhogg, and Gungnir.

"I suppose that was a good idea," mumbled Brunhilda. "You were right."

"What was that, Brunhilda?" teased Skogul. "I think these glamours are affecting my ears as well as my eyes."

"All right," Hilder said, "those aurochs won't keep the Jotnar off of our backs for long. Let's put as much distance as possible between them and us."

"I just wanted to make sure that my hearing was okay."

"Come closer and I'll check for—"

Skogul shoved her away, and a spear meant for her heart instead pierced her shoulder. Brunhilda fell to the ground and her glamour shattered, revealing her true form. Bright red hair bloomed about her as the animal skull helmet flew from her head. Above her, Skogul drew her sword and whirled around.

Dazed, Brunhilda looked back at the auroch stampede breaking around one Jotnar. The giant figure was unmistakable, and as their eyes locked she knew that Hrym had recognized her too. She stared at him as her friends pulled her up. They checked her over and cut off the spear shaft, leaving the tip embedded and immobilized. Together, Skogul and Hilder supported Brunhilda between them and raced for the tree line. As they pulled her away, Brunhilda could just make out the aurochs still running amok and the Jotnar trying to contain the chaos.

—

"Fall back!" ordered Freya as she led the surviving members of her squad back to Halvard. She looked back to survey the damage and breathed a sigh of relief. They had slain close to three dozen Jotnar while only losing four. Including the valkyries' three horses, it was a significant loss. Still, it could have been much worse.

Even while they had charged the Jotnar frontlines and been in the thick of the fight, Freya kept an eye on the valkyries and almost left her post when Brunhilda was brought down by the spear. Only when all three valkyries continued on their way did a wave of relief wash over her.

"Was that enough time?" Vali asked as he rode up beside her.

"Did they make it through?" Gunnar asked behind him. "I saw Brunhilda—"

"They are through, though not unscathed," Freya said. "There is nothing more we can do now."

Gunnar looked back, her lips drawn into a thin, tight line, and gave a slight shake of her head. "Yggdrasil bless them."

"As for us, by the time the Jotnar recover from this attack, corral their aurochs, and organize a counter offensive, the withdrawal from Halvard will have a significant lead. We must now regroup with the main body of the Aesir Army and keep the Jotnar forces contained until we have Gungnir." She paused and echoed Gunnar as her eyes drifted past to the horizon. "Yggdrasil bless them."

CHAPTER 11: PURSUIT

Hrym eyed Suttungr standing among the smoldering ruins of Halvard. He did not often see his leader in such a state, with shoulders slumped and head bowed. The Aesir retreated as suddenly as they had attacked, but they did not return to Halvard; they had instead continued farther south, abandoning the city altogether. Now they knew why. There was nothing left of the Jotnar advance team sent in to the city. Not long after they entered, a series of powerful explosions rocked Halvard and ignited the buildings turning a once bustling and vibrant commercial hub into a blazing inferno. Some Jotnar were able to conjure Ethlivald ice, though none had any formal training. Even with the dense mist and chilling presence of so many Jotnar, it had taken hours for the flames to die off. Charred husks were all that remained of the once proud city.

"This was a costly battle, sire," Hertha said, approaching Hrym and Suttungr, a charred Aesir banner in one hand and one of the scout's helmets in the other. *"For both sides."*

With a nod of respect Hrym took the items from the diminutive Jotnar. Under his tutelage she had flourished as a fighter while learning tactics and strategy from Suttungr. Hertha had proven herself time and again on the field of battle to earn her position, second only to Hrym, despite her young age.

"We've liberated Jotunheim from the Aesir, and now we've taken one of their key cities." Suttungr's voice was strong though Hrym thought he heard a tinge of emotion. *"Soon we will crush the Aesir and then all of their venerated cities will be nothing but ash."*

"Without Mjolnir to hide behind, they flee before us," Hrym said with a self-satisfied grin. *"We will march victorious across Bifrost, and Odin will kneel before you while Asgard burns."*

"If you hadn't noticed, we also suffered heavy losses," said Skrymir as he approached them. *"And we didn't take Halvard, they abandoned it. This is no victory."*

"Skrymir," acknowledged Suttungr. *"What business have you here?"*

"The Aesir are up to something," he said, trying to force his way past Hrym. Suttungr gestured, and Hrym reluctantly allowed Skrymir to approach. *"They may have better training and weapons, but we have the advantage of numbers. Since the Great War they've spread themselves thin policing the nine realms. And with the decoy armies we've sent out, they don't have the manpower to protect every city. We dictate the terms of this war."*

Suttungr paused and considered for a moment. *"Their next move will be to retreat, lure us into a trap where they can neutralize our advantage, and wipe us out in one fell swoop."*

"Why do you think that?" Hrym asked, his brow askew in thought.

"Because it's what I would do," he replied. *"As luck would have it I've planned a surprise for their retreat from Halvard. I do hope that they will appreciate my parting gift."*

"There's more to it than that. The three who snuck through, the ones who got away during the auroch stampede, they were not mere soldiers. At least one carried a valkyrie sword," said Skrymir standing toe-to-toe with Suttungr. *"They're up to something."*

Hrym grabbed his shoulder and pulled him back, unnerved by the intensity of Skrymir's eyes.

"They pose little threat," Suttungr said with a dismissive wave of his hand, not even bothering to look at Skrymir. *"Even if they strike at Jotunheim, there is no tactical advantage."*

"All the more reason to suspect something." Skrymir shrugged out of Hrym's grasp. *"The Aesir would not dispatch three valkyries lightly."*

Suttungr turned his gaze to Skrymir and regarded him for a long moment. *"Very well."*

From behind Skrymir Hrym gave a wicked smirk. After years under Suttungr's tutelage, Hrym felt as if he knew what his leader was thinking. If the Aesir were indeed up to something, they would find out and stop them. In addition, this was the perfect opportunity to be rid of Skrymir.

"Hrym, take a small squad in pursuit. And take Skrymir with you. Perhaps he may prove his value in this endeavor."

80

"Me?!" Hrym reacted with a start and shook his head. *"You cannot send me away on this fool's errand as we prepare to march on Asgard!"*

Cold silence followed. Suttungr's expression did not change but a fire raged behind his eyes.

"Send me instead, sir," Hertha said, quick to volunteer.

"You will complete this task quickly," Suttungr said to Hrym, his eyes never wavering. *"Catch up to us at Asgard."*

"But—"

"You have your orders." Suttungr turned and walked away. *"Do not fail me. Hertha will be my second in your absence."*

Hertha bowed her head in acknowledgement and followed. Hrym just glared in silence, his fists clenched and shaking with rage.

———

"This had better be worth my time," Hrym said to Skrymir as they gathered gear and supplies from the armory. Skrymir grabbed two quivers full of arrows as he put his unstrung bow into a leather sleeve that he slung over his back. Hrym never went anywhere without his cleaver needing little else. Yet something caught his eye as they walked past the new additions to their armory: the sapper charges that Suttungr had taught the Jotnar to make. Not unlike those the Aesir had used to destroy Halvard. *"Suttungr will wage glorious war on the Aesir while I'll be stuck with you chasing down some rogue valkyries."*

"I don't care about your time. My goal is to look out for the best interests of our people," retorted Skrymir as he stuffed a satchel full of hardtack and a solid block of auroch cheese. *"Who knows what kind of trouble three Aesir might cause in Nyr Jotunheim? With all of our soldiers here our youth and our elderly have no protection, so let's just finish this quickly. Then you can return to your precious leader and his 'glorious war.'"*

"We are fighting for the Jotnar people. We're taking back our rightful place in the world," Hrym said grabbing Skrymir by the arm. *"Why can you not see that? Why do you constantly question Suttungr, he who has united us and led us to victory after victory?"*

"Because I don't trust him." Skrymir yanked his arm free. *"His thirst for war will not end until the world is little more than a charred and lifeless*

husk."

"*The Aesir gave us no other choice,*" Hrym retorted, rising to his full height. Though he towered over him, Skrymir gave no indication of backing down. "*Life in Niflheim isn't fit for vermin, and yet we've been forced to live there for generations. They treated us no better than animals. I'll be damned if they deserve any more.*"

He turned and pointed at three Jotnar standing nearby. "*You three. Grab your gear and keep it light. We're leaving now.*"

They looked at each other with uncertainty before they nodded and fell in behind Hrym. "Um, where are we going, sir?" a spear-wielding Jotnar asked in the common tongue.

Hrym's eyes glowered. "We go to hunt Aesir."

CHAPTER 12: THE HUNT

The alpine woods were sparse enough for the valkyries to move mostly unhindered, yet thick enough to break line of sight and allow them to obfuscate their tracks. Just as before, they kept their verbal communications to a minimum and moved with speed and stealth. Even with her sharp eyesight Skogul was impressed at how well the Jotnar armor was made for this. Made of animal skins and natural materials and with minimal metal and ornamentation, they were light and moved well while also blending in with the brown and white of the snow-covered trees. Hilder supported Brunhilda as they moved while Skogul alternated between scouting ahead and going back to mask the most obvious signs of their passage. After another hour of this, they stopped to tend to Brunhilda's wounds.

Looking closer, Hilder breathed a sigh of relief. Skogul had pushed Brunhilda far enough out of the way to avoid a life threatening blow. Brunhilda did not squirm or cry out, only gritted her teeth as Hilder pulled the spear out. They removed her armor and found a deep tear in her flesh. Skogul let out a sigh of relief to find that no bone was broken and no arteries were hit. Hilder cut strips of fabric from her tunic and used the material to stanch the flow of blood. It was far from a benign injury, however, as the spearhead was jagged and somewhat rusted, leaving a wicked gash that was likely infected. Although Hilder was Vanir, she was not a Mithlivald healer and so relied on conventional treatment. She cleaned and bound the wound as well as she could. "How are you feeling?" Hilder asked.

"I feel better than you look," groaned Brunhilda with a smirk.

Half sighing and half laughing, Hilder looked over at Skogul who also still wore a blue furred face. Nodding to each other, they closed their eyes and released the Jotnar images that they had been holding onto. The illusions shattered in a brief flash of golden light.

"Wait, no, it was better before," Brunhilda said, though her laugh quickly turned into a groan.

"Just shut up and drink some water," Hilder said and pushed a waterskin to her lips. "You've lost a lot of blood and we don't have the luxury of giving you time to recuperate. We have to keep moving."

"You think they're coming after us?" asked Brunhilda.

"Well, they might've thought us simple deserters at first, but they were clearly suspicious when they decided to try to kill you with a spear," Hilder said. "Once your glamour broke, I'm pretty certain they noticed your bright red hair."

"They might not think we're that important," Skogul said, pointing out a column of dark, billowing smoke rising from the south, visible through a gap in the trees. "I heard the explosions from our traps. They must be trying to take Halvard still."

"Whether or not they're coming after us, we still have a mission," Hilder said, her lips drawn into a thin line. "The longer we delay, the more Aesir will fall to Suttungr and the Jotnar." Locking eyes with Brunhilda, she said, "If you can't keep up, we will have to leave you here."

"First of all, this is my mission, so you're not leaving me anywhere." Brunhilda rose to her feet and secured her arm into a makeshift sling. "Second, even wounded I can outpace both of you."

"Okay, okay, no need to get so defensive. I just had to be sure," replied Hilder. "Skogul, scout ahead. I'll bring up the rear and cover our tracks. Now let's get moving."

—

In the waning light of dusk a lone hunter crouched in the snow and examined it for tracks. Clad in animal hides from head to toe the figure melted into the surrounding boreal forest. With tenacity and stealth the hunter had stalked his prey for the better part of a day. "Finally," he breathed out with a sigh of relief, "she's slowing down. It shouldn't be much longer now."

Quietly stalking and observing every miniscule sign, the hunter approached his quarry. He spotted her drinking from an ice-cold stream. Nocking an arrow to his string, he drew the bow to its full length, exhaled, and released. The arrow flew through the air with a slight hiss before striking the target in the neck, killing her in an instant.

As he emerged from cover, the hunter removed his hood, revealing a haggard human face with a scruffy blond beard. Aric walked over and picked up his prey by the ears. The female snowshoe hare was nearly as thin as he was. He went to work, pulling out a sharp flint stone to field dress the animal. Though a hatchet hung from his belt, its blade was now far too worn and dull for such precise work. Even in the dim light of dusk, Aric's practiced hands flew through their tasks with alacrity, and in moments he was on his way home with food and another pelt to add to his piecemeal clothing.

The small house, though it was never grand, was now little more than a shed for Aric to cower under in shelter from the elements. It had been a few days since his last successful hunt, but as hungry as he was he knew he had to ration out the hare to last as long as possible. The availability of game was scarce and there existed the very real possibility that this would be his last source of food if he stayed.

After sending off his daughter and wife, there was no longer anything tying Aric to this place. But it was difficult for him to imagine leaving what had been home to their small family. As painful as it was to be here alone, leaving felt even more unbearable.

For the moment he focused on the task at hand, pushing down any other thoughts. Aric had gathered enough wood for a modest fire. He carved off one of the hind legs and set it to cook on a spit. While that was going he cut the remaining meat into small strips and prepared them for smoking.

Aric ate the leg in silence. The meat was meager so he took his time and savored every last morsel. He even cracked the bones and sucked out the miniscule yet rich marrow. As he ate, he sat there staring at the small fire. Pulling out one of the larger strips that he had cut, he closed his eyes and lowered his head. "Odin, you have taken everything that I hold dear. I damn and curse you for taking my family from me. You have forsaken us, and so I forsake you in turn. But my family deserve better. The last thing that I ask of you—the last thing that I will ever ask of you—please accept this final offering for Dagmaer and for Una. May they find shelter in your care in the hallowed fields of the afterlife."

And with that Aric dropped the meat into the fire. For a long time he watched the fire consume it, not noticing how much his mouth salivated. Only when the drool fell onto his hand in his lap did he blink and wipe his mouth. Shaking his head, Aric gathered the remaining strips of meat and put them into his small smoker. He laid his head down and stared into the fire, a single tear leaving a trail down his grime-covered face as his mind drifted to a similar offering a long time ago.

—

One day, sometime the previous year—for who could keep track with no seasons—a light flurry of snow fell from a sky of unbroken gray. A feeble column of smoke rose from a small fire near the ramshackle house. After two years of the fimbulvinter, even this robust boreal forest had begun to show signs of distress. Many of the trees stood dead or dying and some had toppled, knocking down their neighbors. In the distance, other similar pillars of smoke could be seen. A lightly bearded and thin Aric stood beside the modest pyre with a small stack of smoked fish at his right side. Dagmaer and Una sat to his left, bundled in threadbare blankets and some stitched animal hides. All three shivered uncontrollably in the cold, gray morning.

"We should save more of the fish," whispered Dagmaer. Her face and body had wasted away and become gaunt and skeletal. Una, huddled tight to her mother beneath the coverings, was in still worse condition.

Aric lowered his head to look at the meager pile of fish. "We must demonstrate our piety to the gods with this offering. If we hold back they will know and not heed our prayers." Looking up toward the other columns of smoke in the distance, he added, "Our neighbors are sacrificing as well. This will surely return us to the favor of the gods. When this winter ends, the fish will return and our garden will bloom. Then we can restock our stores."

"Can't you see that the Aesir have turned their backs to us? If we do not fend for ourselves, we may not survive long enough to see the end of this unnatural cold," Dagmaer said with a hardened look in her eye. "It has always been up to us: our time, our skill, our labor."

"We mustn't anger the gods," said Aric as he placed the entire pile of fish upon the fire. "It has been a difficult two years since that first summer's snow. The small offerings that we made back then were insufficient to catch the attention of the gods. This time, together with our neighbors, this offering will surely bring the gods' attention and aid back to us. They will know, must know, of our suffering and sacrifice. We have to believe," he said tousling Una's hair, "for there is nowhere else to turn."

Aric sank to his knees next to Dagmaer and Una. Huddled together under their blankets, they held each other close. The fire flared up as the oils from the fish ignited. For a short while the smoke darkened and across the sky he could see the other columns of smoke do likewise. As if in answer, the snowfall lightened and, by the end of the day, abated, though the clouds remained. The snows had stopped before, but the timing of this particular break seemed auspicious, and the warmth from the fire filled him with the tiniest spark of hope.

CHAPTER 13: ISABROT PASS

Two sharp whistles sounded out in the muffled quiet of twilight. Geir, the spear-wielding Jotnar, and three figures converged in a small clearing in the woods. He walked closely behind Hrym along with the others chosen to join the hunt: Borghild, a broad-shouldered, experienced, and respected female warrior; and a quiet and wiry huntress named Ylva. They gathered around Skrymir, who was crouched with his face low as he scrutinized the snow.

Following the hastily masked trail leaving the battle at Halvard, Ylva and Skrymir had tracked the valkyries with ease. But after a few miles, the tracks disappeared. Geir feared the mission would be over before he had a chance to demonstrate his strength and usefulness to Hrym. He breathed a sigh of relief when Skrymir found a clue and they continued their pursuit. Now they had lost the trail again.

Hrym barked a question at Skrymir in Jotunmal.

With little urgency Skrymir gave a long-winded reply while stroking the fur along his jawline. His other hand slid over the contours of the snow near him.

"What are they saying?" Geir whispered to Ylva in the common tongue.

"You really should learn Jotunmal," Ylva said looking down her nose at him. "It's our heritage."

"Not all of us grew up in the hinterlands," Geir snapped back. "In Isabrot we lived under constant scrutiny. Anyone caught speaking Jotunmal was publicly whipped."

"Calm down, both of you," Borghild interrupted. "We're all on the same side." To Geir, she offered an abridged translation. "Skrymir picked up their trail and says that we'll catch up to them in a couple of days."

"I don't know how he can see anything," whispered Ylva

with a frown, as she squinted, "especially in this light."

"Indeed," agreed Borghild, "we searched for hours in the full light of day and couldn't find any tracks."

"Do you think he actually sees anything?" asked Geir, leaning in closer while looking at Skrymir out of the corner of his eye. "I mean, he could just be making all of this up to show up Hrym."

"They're good and they're being very cautious," said Skrymir in common Aesir, loud enough for them all to hear. "But they're also in a hurry with an injured member."

Pulling down a nearby branch, Skrymir drew a short knife from his belt. Hrym's eyes widened in recognition. The blade shimmered blue with Ethlivald magic. Touching the blade to the branch gave a brief spark of gold light as it reacted.

"Residual Reginvald energy; they came this way a day or so ago. Their tracks indicate that they're staying out of sight of the roads and moving north, toward Jotunheim." He made eye contact with Geir before continuing. "If that's their intended destination, they'll need to go through Isabrot Pass. We can cut them off before they get there."

"You have an enchanted blade?" Hrym asked, his eyes lingering on the weapon.

"It was my sister's," replied Skrymir with downcast eyes. "It's all that I have to remember her by. The Aesir killed her…" There was a quaver of emotion in his voice as he spoke. "…and when I find those responsible, I will strike them down with this blade."

Hrym gave a grunt and nod of approval. "How can you be sure that they're heading for Isabrot Pass?"

Skrymir took a few long breaths before speaking again. "Isabrot is the most direct route to Jotunheim," he replied, the timbre of his voice smooth and even once more. "There are other ways through, certainly, but Isabrot is closest. It would take an extra week to follow the Calder River west to the coast and go around the Svelbjarg Range. Isabrot Pass is guarded, but valkyries would be skilled enough to slip by under the cover of night. They might even choose to just fight their way through."

Hrym grunted with a nod. "You might not be completely

useless. I'll make sure that Suttungr hears of your contributions."

"I don't care what Suttungr thinks of me," Skrymir said with derision. "I'm looking out for the best interests of the Jotnar people. This isn't about me, you, or that megalomaniac."

Geir hoped that Hrym would crush Skrymir and be done with it. But the two Jotnar eyed each other with silent malice. Hrym stood, breaking the tension, and began moving toward the main road.

"We'll run ahead and set up an ambush at the pass," said Hrym, pointing to Geir and Borghild without looking back. "You and Ylva continue to track them from behind in case they deviate or change course. If all goes well, we'll surround them at the pass and kill them."

"We should question them first," argued Skrymir. "If they went to all of this trouble to get past our army, it must be of significant importance. Whatever they're doing, wherever they're going could benefit us."

"Suttungr gave us explicit orders," snapped Hrym, turning and jabbing his finger into Skrymir's chest, punctuating his next words. "We will hunt them. We will kill them. And then we will return to Suttungr in time to sack Asgard."

With that, Hrym started running with Geir and Borghild hurrying to catch up, leaving Skrymir with Ylva.

—

"Should we wake her?" asked Skogul, nodding toward the mound of piled furs that was Brunhilda. While the wound had not been severe, she had lost a good deal of blood. toward the end of the day she had struggled to keep pace but never complained. When they had stopped to make camp, Brunhilda had collapsed to her knees, though she did volunteer to take the first watch—right before she passed out. Skogul had taken the first shift instead.

"No, let her rest," Hilder said and rose from her light slumber. "I'll take the next watch."

"I found some thyme for dressing her wound and some nuts and berries to eat," said Skogul, holding up her items. "Game is pretty scarce out here. Not that we'd light a fire and cook anything."

"Good work," Hilder said, looking over at Brunhilda. "She'll need all of that if she's going to keep up tomorrow. We'll change her

90

bandages in the morning."

Skogul shrugged and stuffed her mouth full of berries. "By the way, we're being followed," she said as she chewed.

"What?" Hilder whisper-shouted. "How close are they? How are they even tracking us?"

"Well, they could just be messengers from the army carrying information back to Jotunheim," suggested Skogul after she swallowed. "But they don't seem to be moving with the urgency of messengers or following the roads or paths as a convoy would. I can't be sure that they've caught our trail yet, though they're looking for something and almost certainly that something is us. I would say that we've probably got about half a day's lead on them if they keep to their current pace." Looking at Brunhilda she continued, "We should be able to reach Isabrot Pass tomorrow evening. It will be a moonless night so we should have no problem sneaking past any guards there; with the bulk of their army at Halvard, there can't be much more than a skeleton crew guarding the pass."

"Very well," said Hilder with a furrowed brow.

Skogul could guess what was going through her mind. Setting a trap for the Jotnar would delay their mission but would prevent them from being surrounded at Isabrot Pass. If they threw caution to the wind and rushed forward at full speed, they might increase their speed but be far easier to track. They could break off to the west and circumvent Isabrot altogether, adding more than a week to their travel time. Before Hilder opened her mouth Skogul knew what she would say.

"Get some rest. We'll leave before the sun rises and we'll move fast. No more wasting time covering our tracks. Once we're through the pass we can lose them and any other pursuers. If we get caught on this side of the Svelbjarg Range our mission will be over before it's even begun." Shaking her head in disappointment she said, "This has not been a good start."

———

Letting out a slight groan, Brunhilda squinted her bleary eyes at the lightening sky. "What hour is it?" she asked with a start as she bolted upright. She winced at the pain in her shoulder when she tried to use her arm to support herself.

"Slow down," Hilder said in a low, calming tone. "It's just before dawn."

"Why didn't you wake me for my turn at the watch?" she asked as Hilder eased her back down to a reclined position. Brunhilda fought against her a little though went down without incident.

"We decided that it'd be better for you to be fully rested for today," replied Skogul, who was mashing some kind of poultice in the inside of her skull helmet with a rock. A fragrant herb scent wafted in the air.

"You'll have to move fast. We'll be off as soon as Skogul's redressed your bandages."

While Skogul applied the poultice and changed Brunhilda's bandages, Hilder told her that they were being followed and filled her in on the plan. Brunhilda nodded in silence. Hilder could see that she was frustrated, though she still wore an expression of intense focus. Even the sting of the poultice, which should have been bracing in the frigid, pre-dawn air, did not distract her. As a hardened warrior, Brunhilda, and in fact all three of them, had been through far worse.

Moments later their campsite was packed up and the trio was dressed and ready to go. Brunhilda stretched her shoulder, testing her limited range of movement. Hilder watched her through the eye holes of the Svelbjarg ram skull with a look of concern that did not disappear even after Brunhilda gave her a reassuring nod and pulled on her helmet.

"Smells better than before," Skogul said as she donned her own helmet. And with that they set off just as the light of dawn filtered in through the clouds.

CHAPTER 14: ESCALATION

The ringing of steel on steel punctuated the cold morning air. A blur of weapons clashed in the middle of the troop exercise field in the shadow of the royal palace of Asgard. A small crowd of off-duty troops gathered to watch as the preeminent warriors of the realm sparred. Lady Sif, commander of the royal guard at Asgard, panted with labored breath as she broke off from her clash with Thor. Most soldiers wore basic padding and used wooden or dulled weapons for such practice bouts. Sif wore her casual garments: a simple outfit consisting of a light tunic, pants, and knee-high leather boots. The brisk air did not bother Thor, who wore a similar ensemble. Although they eschewed any armor, their garments were tailored to fit and of the finest quality, and they both fought with sharp weapons that were not enchanted.

"It seems as if you're recovering well, my lord," said Sif as she parried a strike, "considering you had to be transported here on a stretcher mere weeks ago."

"Fostra Eira is quite skilled," Thor replied as he avoided a lunge from Sif and countered with a spinning strike.

"Though it seems they still have some work yet to do," quipped Sif. She had anticipated Thor's maneuver, and though he may have been fast enough to get inside her guard at full health, he was still weak, his swing slow and telegraphed. She avoided the strike and swept out Thor's feet from underneath him. He fell with a heavy impact and found Sif's sword pointed at his throat as he lay on his back.

Some soldiers watching in the background cheered while others grumbled in disappointment as they settled their wagers and laid down new bets.

"Physical wounds are simple enough to recover from," said Thor as Sif helped him to his feet. "Whatever magic Suttungr used to protect himself appears to have lingering consequences."

"Odin and Freya believe that this is a result of that Jotnar somehow combining Reginvald with Jotnar Ethlivald. We were never meant to fight amongst ourselves, so when the energies of Mjolnir collided with Suttungr's armor, the clashing Reginvald energies resulted in some kind of explosion," explained Sif. "At least that was Freya's theory. Baldur and Freya were the scholars when it came to magic. With her off commanding the northern army and Baldur..." Sif trailed off when Thor flinched at the name. "Regardless, once we have both Gungnir and Mjolnir, we will overcome Suttungr's magic."

"You know as well as I that that mission bears little chance of success. We have to be prepared to face Suttungr in combat. I must recover faster," Thor said, taking a fighting stance and beginning the next round of sparring.

Even with the strenuous exertion of their practice, they continued their discussion. In between strikes and parries Thor said, "We need to have a plan to crush the Jotnar Army. Without them Suttungr cannot win, even with his protective magics."

"Our division from Muspelheim should arrive within a week or two," said Sif as she dodged and countered Thor's attack, knocking him off balance. "With those combined forces"—block, thrust, slash—"we should be able to hold strategic points to at least"—a kick to the gut—"keep their armies and supply lines in check."

Having spent the last few weeks bedridden, Sif knew that Thor would be much more alert and engaged out here than in the war room for their daily briefing. It was better for her own sanity as well. She could not stand Thor when he was moody and restless.

"Still," she continued, "I fear that reducing our presence in the other realms will make us appear weak."

"Losing to the Jotnar will make us look weak," retorted Thor while also unleashing a series of counterstrikes. "We must defeat them decisively"—his dodge was slow as a cut in his tunic opened just above his navel—"on the battlefield with tactics as well as with magic." He eyed Sif while fingering the tear, and she gave him a smug look before she charged. "If we cannot put down these challengers"—he deflected her thrust and knocked her off balance—

"we will lose our authority among the other peoples."

He took a deep, calming breath as Sif regained her footing. The fight was about to get serious now. This was his favorite tunic that she had just cut. Thor lunged forward and thrust at her head before dropping his weight and swiping low. Sif twirled, narrowly avoiding the stroke only to find a booted foot sweeping across her path. That move sent her sprawling, though she turned it into a roll and came up to her feet. Thor was already behind her and just as he was about to swat her with the flat of the blade, the watch's horn sounded the approach of a messenger. He paused mid-strike as they and all of the spectators turned their attention to the west gate. Riding hard and fast, the mount foaming at the mouth close to exhaustion, the messenger dropped from his horse before it, too, collapsed. His legs were weak and shaky as he stumbled and crumpled to the ground at the feet of Sif and Thor. They acted immediately to tend to the bleeding, pale man.

"Trap," he moaned through ragged breaths as they bent down to him. "It was... a trap."

"Get a healer over here!" shouted Thor. "Now!"

———

"He's dead," Sif reported to the remaining pantheon of the Aesir gathered at the war council chambers. "After the retreat at Halvard, the northern division was headed back to Birgjavale to regroup with the rest of the troops. Before he died, the messenger, Einar, said that a trap had been set along the road. Jotnar sappers had found a way to lay explosives and set them off as the army approached. He said that he saw Captain Vali killed in the first series of explosions. Freya was consumed by the secondary explosions, along with many of our soldiers. Gunnar now leads the surviving troops and the refugees at Birgjavale." Sif delivered the news with a dispassionate voice; inside, she felt numb. "Einar was sent ahead to us with the news, though he had also suffered grave injuries."

"Freya's dead?" Odin's voice was thunderous. His words echoed amid the stunned silence from the assembled Aesir. "Hel's taint! How did Suttungr outmaneuver Freya?" Odin bellowed. "These vermin have been nothing but trouble. We were too lenient with them after the war; we will not make that mistake again." He stood so quickly that he knocked his chair back. Slamming his fist on the map table he ordered, "Recall all of our troops from the other realms. We will wipe the Jotnar nation from the nine realms."

No one spoke as Sif hurried to right the pieces. She distributed them on the map to indicate the advancing Jotnar Army and the retreating Aesir. Everyone bowed their heads in respect as Freya's marker was removed from the board.

"How did they get past our forces at Halvard to set those traps?" asked Odin as he regained his composure. Two attendants had righted his throne just as he sat back down. "We were holding Halvard precisely to keep the Jotnar Army to the north of our army. And where in the nine realms did they get their hands on sapper charges?"

"We're not sure, sire," replied Sif. "We need to send out reinforcements to Birgjavale. If our position is not defensible, we will have to fall back to Bifrost and fortify here at the shield wall, the Skjaldborg. I am ready to leave in force now."

"No," interjected Thor. "I am commander of our army and I will lead them. Sif, you are captain of the royal guard. Your duty is to protect Asgard."

"You can't, you're still recovering from your injuries," argued Sif. "If you face off against Suttungr before you've fully recuperated, he will kill you."

"One day I will die gloriously in battle." Thor stood and placed Mjolnir on the table with all of the weight and responsibility that it represented. The map pieces rattled at even that slight impact. "But I will not die by his hand. If Suttungr is indeed Loki, he has much to answer for, and he will answer to me!"

Sif shifted her gaze from Thor to Odin, her eyes pleading.

"Thor will lead the army," Odin decreed. The fierce look on his face brooked no argument. "We have underestimated the Jotnar thus far to our detriment. Let us see how they stand to the full might of Asgard."

He looked at Sif. "Make your preparations; you will march together at the end of next week with all of the reserve troops in Asgard. The soldiers from the south will assemble with Gunnar in

Birgjavale as they arrive."

"Next week, my lord?" said Sif with a note of impatience.

"We will take the next nine days to celebrate Freya's life and her sacrifice. She was one of our greatest generals and our most powerful magic scholar," said Odin with a solemn reverence. "She deserves nothing less."

———

For a week, revelries reverberated through the streets of Asgard. The troops stationed within the city had been commanded directly by Freya and celebrated her life with the most fervor. All of the citizens of Asgard respected her wisdom and power and honored her passing with such grandeur unseen since Baldur's wake years before. For this occasion the non-Aesir merchants and artisans who lived and worked on the western side of the Bifrost Bridge were allowed into Asgard, unrestricted. The majestic bridge was a marvel of engineering, held a hundred feet above the churning ocean below. The enchanted waters from Asgard poured over the edge, the mists catching the light, a rainbow visible nearly every hour of the day.

Now the people gathered at the docks of Asgard. A full armada sat on the calm water of Bifrost Bay, each ship crafted and ornamented to represent all nine realms. Their square sails were emblazoned with the valkyrie crest. The swans, spear, and sword of the crest were stitched into the sails with gold thread to honor Freya's Vanir lineage. Painted shields bearing the insignia of each of the twelve Aesir lords adorned the gunwales. Intricately carved dragon heads stood at each prow, their fierce eyes of precious gems blazed in the light of the setting sun. Without a body to honor, every ship carried a treasured possession of each lord as an offering to honor Freya's memory. On the lead ship Odin had laid his signet ring.

The throngs of people grew silent as Odin and the Aesir lords made their way to the dais at the front of the docks. Tens of thousands were in attendance. While the Aesir and Vanir made up a significant majority of the audience, other races were there as well— Dokkalfar, Ljosalfar, and even humans. No Jotnar were in attendance. None had been allowed in Asgard since Fenrir attacked years ago. None since Loki had betrayed and murdered Baldur.

One by one, the lords gave tributes to Freya. She was Vanir by birth, though after the Aesir-Vanir War their two peoples had merged as one, as the Aesir. And so she was honored in true Asgard tradition. Yet even within this coalition, there existed a hierarchy. The true Aesir spoke first—Heimdall, Tyr, Sif, Frigg. They each related epic tales of heroic feats. From thrilling hunts of fierce vargr and rampaging boars to battlefield victories during the Aesir-Vanir War. Even as adversaries they had great respect for her strategic acumen. While their stories told of her triumphs from the defense of Veizlakr and Utgard to the siege of Asgard, the Aesir were always portrayed as gallant heroes, dying in glorious battle to a worthy foe. The assembled masses roared in celebration when Thor stepped forward to speak.

"People of Asgard," he began, his voice quieting the crowd. "The Lady Freya was not only a great leader, she was unmatched on the field of battle. Her valor, strength, and wisdom brought our peoples together, and we are stronger because of it. She pursued knowledge and expanded the power of Mithlivald and Reginvald alongside my brother. And if he were still with us..." Thor choked down his emotions as the memories of Baldur's death burst forth. "Baldur would have some pretty words for this moment. He would honor Freya with some display of magic or a rousing ode while holding a drinking horn full of mead in one hand. Words were his domain, not mine."

He tightened his fist, comforted by the feel of the runes engraved into Mjolnir's shaft as he searched for the right words. The crowd fell silent in sympathy. Baldur always found a way to get the people around him to smile and laugh no matter what else was happening. Thor cast his gaze out toward the boats in the bay, remembering his brother's funeral. Even then everyone had found joy in recounting his many tales of mischief and merriment. A distant, sad smile appeared on his face.

The crowd began to shift in the long, uncomfortable silence. Frigg stepped forward and placed her hand upon Thor's shoulder. He straightened up and stood taller as his eyes focused once more on the crowd standing before him now, in the present. Thor shifted Mjolnir in his hand and felt the crackle of its pulsing energies. His eyes traced the knot patterns and the runes along the length of the weapon. "I will honor Freya through action, through victory!" Raising the warhammer overhead he unleashed a small burst of energy, a small display of its power. Electricity cascaded throughout the audience leaving a tingle on everyone's skin. The crowd thundered louder than before.

Thor stepped back and the Vanir spoke next. Ydun and Bragi attested to her knowledge and power with magic, of her connection to the energies of Yggdrasil and the nine realms. Though they were not as gifted in Mithlivald, they punctuated their eulogies with minor displays, conjuring patterns from flares of golden light.

Then Freyr stepped forward to speak, and everyone fell into a reverent silence. "Freya was not just the leader of the Vanir people to me. She was first and foremost my sister." He spoke in a clear, strong voice. There was a slight quaver to his voice, though none would fault him for it. "I loved her dearly and always admired her fortitude, her vitality. She struck like lightning in combat and her intellect was peerless. Her only weakness was her love and compassion for others." Again his voice shook with emotion though he forced himself to look out to the crowd.

"The Jotnar knew that they could not defeat her on the field of battle so they resorted to insidious trickery and killed her in a cowardly ambush," he shouted, his tone shifting from sorrow to rage as his hands clenched in white-knuckled fists before him. "This was all done while she was hindered, protecting refugees. The Jotnar feared her, and rightfully so. Now they will fear our furious vengeance!"

He was visibly shaking and full of emotion. Whatever more he might have said was lost as he stepped back, embraced by Ydun and Bragi. Thor and Sif joined as well, for Freya was their sister-in-arms.

"The glory and splendor of Asgard today is due in large part to Freya," Odin said as he took center stage. "I have been fortunate to have fought against her and then beside her. It was through her wisdom and strength that the Vanir and Aesir people joined together as one. This union has brought peace and prosperity to all of the nine realms." He paused as the masses cheered in agreement. When the noise died down he continued in a more solemn tone, "But now everything that we have built together is threatened. The Jotnar, out of spite and jealousy, have taken up arms and risen against us. They have taken the life of Freya, she whose impassioned advocacy spared them from extinction at the conclusion of the Great War."

The crowd shifted. What were once cheers now turned into chants for death to all Jotnar. After a week of celebration, many were besotted and bristled with drunken rage; and though many a fight had ensued before, here at this gathering Odin cultivated a more controlled, focused anger. He raised his hands to silence the people before continuing.

"Suttungr and the Jotnar Army continue to avoid our main army and strike at weak and vulnerable cities like Halvard. We have saved all we could and brought you all here within the safety of the capital. And it is here that the fury of the Jotnar storm will break like waves upon the rocks. They will topple before us and Suttungr's head will adorn a pike atop the shield wall, the Bifrost Skjaldborg!" The ovation deafened, yet above it Odin shouted, "For Freya!"

All of the people soon picked up the chant. The rhythmic cheer pulsed and grew as Odin turned and walked to the largest ship, the crowd parting before him. The hull was painted gold and its sail a field of black, the valkyrie crest shimmered with magic in the fading light. It was as if it was Freya in the form of a boat. Odin drew his sword and raised it high. The blade was emblazoned with runes that shone with their own light drawing every eye to it. In a shining arc, he severed the guyline that held the boat to the dock. On that cue the other boats were also released, set on their final journey, carrying Freya's spirit to the afterlife.

The crowd cheered as they watched the ships float with the current toward the thundering falls of Bifrost. Standing by, archers took their positions. Igniting their pitch-covered arrowheads, they drew and released, and each flaming barb traced a fiery arc until it struck its target, setting the flotilla ablaze. And as the ships crested and went over the falls, they were framed by rainbows in the mist creating an ethereal image, almost as if Freya was passing into the afterlife at that precise moment.

—

Gunnar looked away before the ships dropped out of sight. She was standing by herself, having returned to Asgard two days ago to treat her wounds and attend Freya's memorial. Her hands gripped the railing hard, knuckles strained and white. She had remained strong through the ceremony, but now her head was lowered and her jaw was clenched shut.

"It's not your fault," said Sif behind her.

"I don't need your pity," said Gunnar as she discreetly wiped her eyes. "We all did our jobs, but something sinister is afoot with the Jotnar. They are outmaneuvering us at every turn. I've never seen them this focused, this driven."

"Odin and Thor will lead us to victory. And we can't lose faith in Hilder, Skogul, and Brunhilda." Sif stood at her shoulder and looked out at the boats. "You said it yourself. They made it through the Jotnar lines."

"But not without difficulty. The Jotnar saw them and are likely hunting them down as we speak. If they capture or kill them, then Gungnir will be lost to us." Dropping her voice lower, Gunnar said, "Or worse, they may gain possession of the spear and be even more powerful. Not even Thor wielding Mjolnir would be able to stop them."

"Then it's up to us to put a stop to them before any of that can happen," Sif said, placing her hand upon Gunnar's shoulder. "Suttungr is just one person. We will grind his army into the dirt and contain him. We will remove the Jotnar threat even if we can't kill their leader.

"We can't lose heart now. It's up to us to avenge Freya's death and restore peace to the nine realms. This time we will wipe out this Jotnar scourge once and for all," she said as placed her hand atop Gunnar's, "like we should have done at the end of the Aesir-Vanir War."

CHAPTER 15: HUNTER AND HUNTED

The clouds in the western sky burned a fiery red as the sun dropped toward the horizon. Three shadows flitted through the trees and came within view of Isabrot Pass. A layer of virgin snow covered the ground surrounding the pass, yet there had been only the barest dusting of snowfall over the last few days. Jagged, rocky spires of the Svelbjarg Range rose up in an imposing and impenetrable wall of granite and ice. The only opening was the visible gap in the mountain's spine, and a gate with constructed and recently reinforced defenses barred the way.

Skogul had reviewed all of the documentation of Isabrot Pass in preparation for this mission. She ran through all that she knew of it, searching for anything out of place that might give her insight to what the Jotnar might have changed since capturing it.

Before the Aesir-Vanir War, the Svelbjarg Range stood as the border between Niflheim and Jotunheim. After being defeated in the war, the Jotnar were forced from their lush, rich home of Jotunheim and relocated to the cold and desolate Niflheim. Now Jotunheim was part of the Aesir and Vanir's new expanded realm of Asgard, and Isabrot Pass became the gateway to contain the Jotnar in their new home. Between the Great Awakening and the ending of the Aesir-Vanir War, the defenses at the pass were oriented against incursion from the north—not south, which was their current approach. Any defenses the valkyries might encounter would have been erected within the past few months, though Skogul doubted anything the Jotnar had cobbled together in such a short amount of time could pose a significant obstacle to them.

The churn of dirt and snow along the sides of the paved path were indicative of the undisciplined columns of the Jotnar Army. Even with a road wide enough for ten people abreast the tracks of marching Jotnar had crowded and spilled off of the smooth paving stones as they had moved down through the pass. Other, newer footprints circled the area in what were most likely patrol routes made by the few Jotnar guards standing watch now. Then she spotted it. They had hidden it well and a lesser scout would have missed it, but she could see signs of recent tracks heading north to Isabrot. Their pursuers had beaten them here. Skogul signaled a warning to the others.

"What's the problem?" Hilder whispered as she silently moved up next to Skogul.

"Aside from the gaps in their patrol and the lax disposition of the guards, they also tried to cover up the recent arrival of three Jotnar from the south," she replied, her voice so quiet that Hilder had to lean in closer.

"Our pursuers?" Brunhilda had joined them.

Skogul nodded. "It's a trap."

"It's about damn time." Brunhilda cracked her knuckles and flexed her neck.

"Well, they went to all of that trouble," Hilder said. "Let's not leave them waiting."

Brunhilda nodded. "Agreed." She and Hilder drew their swords carefully, the whisper of the blades clearing the scabbards barely audible. Yet in the tense silence it sounded to Skogul as if they were trumpeting their presence with a war horn.

Nocking an arrow, Skogul moved into a better position, took careful aim, and released. A hundred yards away, the arrow hit one of the guards in the head, and he was dead before his body crumpled to the ground. As the other guard spun around, Skogul sank another arrow through her throat, and she fell just as quietly.

Skogul nocked another arrow as she looked to the other sentry group. Just as she was about to exhale and release, her ear twitched at the faint hiss of an arrow already in flight. She ducked, narrowly avoiding the Jotnar arrow intended for her head, and instead it struck the downhill side of the tree that she had been hiding behind. The shot had come from behind them.

"Now!" a voice shouted as two more arrows zipped toward Skogul. She dodged one, contorting her body into a low crouch in the snow, avoiding being skewered by mere inches. The other was cut out of the air mid-flight by Brunhilda's sword. Hrym burst forth from the snow, flanked by Geir and Borghild along with a dozen additional troops. The remaining sentries also snapped to attention, lighting great braziers that illuminated the surrounding area. Having sprung the trap, the valkyries regrouped, now aware of all of their opponents. As they have done time and time before in war, they eyed their current tactical situation and calculated their odds of success.

All of this transpired in a fraction of a second before Skogul cried out, "Run!"

More arrows flew past them as the valkyries leapt off in a dead sprint to the west, away from the pass and toward the glare of the setting sun. At its current position, even through the clouds, the light was blinding to them, but at least it would blind the Jotnar as well.

And the Jotnar were coming in earnest.

CHAPTER 16: TO VALHALLA

Skogul, Hilder, and Brunhilda led Hrym and the Jotnar deeper into the alpine forests away from Isabrot Pass. The trees grew denser here, negating the ranged attack of the Jotnar archers. As valkyries, they had trained for precisely this type of mission. The dense vegetation also neutralized the Jotnar numbers advantage and would force them to fight and maneuver around the trees.

After running just over a mile Hilder pulled up to a stop and turned to face their pursuers. Skogul nodded as she lined up on her right. Putting away her bow she drew her sword at the same time as Brunhilda did on Hilder's left. Brunhilda slipped her right arm out of its sling though kept the sword in her left hand. There was no verbal communication between the three women. They calmed their breathing and prepared for the coming enemies. Battle cries from the Jotnar echoed through the trees. The crunching of snow underfoot and the breaking and snapping of branches heralded their approach. Off to the west the low roar of the raging Calder River filled the calm of the air before the fight.

Half a dozen Jotnar arrived together. Two of them still carried their bows in leather holsters attached to quivers at their hips. Skrymir slowed as he came near and drew his sword. Brunhilda recognized him from the battle at Halvard when they had broken through the Jotnar lines. Hilder's face was impassive as she flowed into the fight and met him head on.

Meanwhile, Brunhilda cut down another Jotnar as soon as she cleared the nearby trees. The Jotnar died without ever swinging her sword. Before Brunhilda could join Hilder's fight a spear jab cut across her path and forced her back. With deft skill and caution Geir launched an offensive barrage. The density of the trees did not impede his thrusts as Brunhilda found herself held at bay. While she lunged and parried with her sword, from the corner of her eye Brunhilda caught a glimpse of Skogul engaged with more Jotnar on the right flank.

—

Skogul guided her sword in flowing arcs while her graceful steps kept her untouched amid the wild, undisciplined Jotnar attacks. Borghild and two other Jotnar surrounded her, trying to trap her between them. Slicing and thrusting, the Aesir blade danced through their defenses. Skogul's eyes were half-open as she suppressed a yawn. With practiced, deliberate movements she ducked and slashed, side-stepped and disarmed one before drawing her sword across his throat, spilling the bright blue blood. With another series of parries, counters, and nimble steps, Skogul twirled between the other two, leading Borghild's blade through her fellow Jotnar's lung. Borghild was still in shock when Skogul drove her sword through a gap in her armor, piercing her heart.

Through her feet Skogul could feel the ground rumble and her eyes flared wide open looking for the coming threat. The other fighting paused as a small tree fell to the charging auroch skull covering the shoulder of a furry blue mass of muscles. Hrym arrived in time to see Borghild's death throes. Broken branches stuck in and jutting out of his animal hide armor told of all of the other trees that his huge frame had had to force his way through. Now in a fighting stance he squared off against Skogul. His feet danced around the trees with remarkable speed as he attacked.

Ducking under his first swing Skogul frowned as he chopped through the dead spruce instead of getting his blade stuck as she had guessed. Indeed she had to roll away from the falling tree instead of launching a counterattack. His overhead swings came faster and Skogul had to push herself to dodge the slashes. The dense forest that should have hindered someone so large instead prevented her from getting close enough to strike.

—

Hilder did not like the sound of all of the trees falling and branches breaking, but she knew that Skogul could handle herself and she had problems of her own. Before she could dispatch her opponent, Ylva joined Skrymir and set to firing arrows from behind him. Together the two were proving to be worthy adversaries, coordinating their actions of ranged and melee attacks to keep her contained.

They worked together attempting to corral her away from the others. Hilder recognized their strategy: to divide and conquer, get the valkyries isolated and overwhelmed. So instead she charged headlong at Skrymir. She barreled forward, even taking an arrow to her left shoulder, forcing Skrymir to leap out of the way. With a flash of her blade she cut through Ylva's bow, causing her to fall back, and whirled around just as Skrymir recovered and attempted his own strike at the distracted valkyrie. When she blocked his frost knife with her sword, the runes flared and a bright flash of blue erupted from the impact. Ylva leapt in at that moment, brandishing her curved bone knife. Hilder disengaged from Skrymir to avoid the lethal attack and took only a superficial cut to her right arm. As the two Jotnar faced off against her, Hilder smiled.

—

Brunhilda cursed her shoulder wound as a spray of golden blood came from a deep cut to her left leg. She had neglected her off-hand training as of late and was now paying for it. Gritting her teeth, she pushed through the pain and lunged at Geir as he recovered his stance. Her blade caught his arm as he scrambled away from her. He whipped the spearhead side to side, cutting off Brunhilda's advance. She ducked behind a tree to dodge his long reach. A bestial roar grabbed her attention and she took a brief moment to survey the fight from behind cover.

—

Skogul had scored a hit across Hrym's left flank, enraging him. Even with an abridged backswing his powerful, rage-fueled blow cut clean through the tree that she had ducked behind. Its trunk splintered and

107

came crashing down, barely slowing the Jotnar's cleaver as it hit her. Her sword blocked it and fared better than the tree against the devastating blow. Still, she had been thrown to the ground, dazed, her weapon knocked from her hand.

—

Everyone paused, frozen by the awesome display of might. Hilder was the first to act and took advantage of her opponents' distraction and made a quick feint at Skrymir. This drew in Ylva as she reacted to Hilder. As planned, Hilder was ready for her and landed a well-placed kick to her face followed by a powerful slash across her gut, eviscerating the Jotnar. Ignoring Skrymir, Hilder ran to aid Skogul. But he was already in her path as if he had anticipated that move.

Hilder's sword clashed with his frost knife, and the cold sparks ignited and filled the air. She was desperate to get to Skogul. With their faces close and eyes locked, she noticed Skrymir's eyes flick to her left for a split second. Hilder knew that he was trying to distract her. The other Jotnar was dead and there had been no one else nearby. Then she saw it: a silhouette moved in her peripheral vision. She disengaged from Skrymir to defend against this new threat. Yet as she turned she saw there was no one to fight. She turned back, but it was too late. The frost knife slid with lethal precision into a gap in her armor and found its way between her ribs, piercing her heart.

—

At that exact moment, Hrym had his cleaver poised over the downed Skogul, ready to strike the killing blow. Before he could bring down his sword, a fierce, primal scream cut through the air as a spear struck him. Hrym dropped his sword as he staggered back, the spear lodged in his left shoulder.

Brunhilda was running straight for him, sword in hand, following the spear that she had thrown. Behind her Hrym could see that Geir was down. It was his spear that had hit him. Of the dozen Jotnar that Hrym had recruited from Isabrot Pass, all were now dead including Borghild, Ylva, and possibly Geir. And for all of that, they had only killed one valkyrie. With the spear stuck in his shoulder and his sword gone, Brunhilda looked to finish this fight. Skuld had scrambled to retrieve her sword and was rising to her feet, her breath shallow and quick. Unarmed and facing two valkyries, he fell back a few steps. His mind raced while his eyes searched for a weapon, any weapon. As he turned, the strap of his satchel tugged against the spear in his shoulder. Eyes wide, he reached into the bag and pulled out an object the size of his fist and a flint stone. With a flick of the wrist sparks spewed forth and ignited the sapper charge.

"Skrymir, duck!" he shouted as he threw it at Brunhilda.

—

Brunhilda heard the Jotnar's yell. Even though she did not understand him and Skogul was between them, she saw the thrown object. In that half second she slid to a halt and her mind raced to process everything. Skogul's gait was irregular and later Brunhilda would recollect that she was still weak and off balance from Hrym's blow. Yet in this instant Skogul's sword lashed out at the small object. At mid-stride it was an awkward hit, knocking it down at her feet instead of batting it away.

Just as Brunhilda's eyes caught Skogul's, the charge exploded in a blinding flash of light and deafening sound. The concussive blast knocked her back, the silhouette of Skogul burned into her retinas.

Ears ringing and eyes blinded, Brunhilda fell over several times while trying to scramble to her feet, eventually finding a nearby tree to brace against. Frantically she rubbed her eyes with one hand, her sword held tightly in the other. As her vision returned she saw the place where the trees had been knocked down by the explosion. Ghost images flickered with every blink. In the clearing she thought that she could see Skogul's body, and beyond that were Hrym and the Jotnar who killed Hilder. They and the spear wielder she had fought were also recovering. The bodies of a dozen or so Jotnar were also scattered around, mist rising from their spilled blood.

Brunhilda steeled herself to charge in. But before she could take a step, she found her legs were unsteady and shaky and her ears were still ringing. No, not ringing—rumbling. Looking up toward the

Svelbjarg peak, she saw a massive sheet of ice had dislodged and broken loose. The explosion had triggered an avalanche.

The slab of ice, snow, and rock picked up speed as it careened down the slope. She saw a flash of blue light when the leading edge of snow and ice reached the Jotnar, though she did not give it much thought as the wall of rubble was fast approaching her. With a quick glance back toward Hilder and Skogul, Brunhilda hesitated for a fraction of a second before she sheathed her sword and ran. She ran harder and faster than she ever had before. The pain in her left leg was lost in the burst of adrenaline that coursed through her veins. Southwest and downhill she sprinted to the cliff's edge above the Calder River with half of the mountain crashing in a thunderous wave behind her. The roaring of the river ahead provided little reassurance. Brunhilda reached the cliff just as the wave of snow, ice, and debris caught up to her. As she leapt out into the void bracing to hit the icy waters below, she was struck by some debris and her vision of the sky went from a light steel gray to black.

—

"What in Hel's name was that?" shouted Skrymir, reverting to Jotunmal as he burst forth from beneath the snow. The last thing he remembered was the flash of an explosion before a wall of rock and ice plowed into them. He shook his head and tested his hearing by covering and uncovering his ears with his hands. His ram skull helmet was cracked and his body had taken a beating, though he had avoided any major injuries. Once again he thanked his strong bond with Ethlivald for shielding him; this wasn't the first time it had saved him. The ringing from a recent avalanche lingered in the air.

"It was just a small sapper charge," Hrym shouted back. *"It was the only thing I had with me."* He tried clearing his ears with his little finger while working his jaw open and closed. The broken shaft of a spear protruded from Hrym's left shoulder. His movements were stiff and he grit his teeth with each movement, but they were both alive. *"No need to thank me."*

"You could have killed all of us!" raged Skrymir as he leapt, grabbing Hrym by the collar.

"Well, I didn't, did I?" replied a surprised Hrym. He broke out of Skrymir's grasp and seized his arm, pinning him down to the

snow. *"Do not do that again."*

"If we kill them all, then we won't find out what they're after," Skrymir said, his words muffled as his face was still pressed into the snow. He turned his head to one side and spat out the slush. *"Think about it. Suttungr is hammering the Aesir on the battlefield. Whatever those three are doing is important enough to be away from the rest of the troops. Maybe it's something that could turn the war in their favor. We have to find out!"*

"Complain all you want, but if I hadn't done it then those valkyries would have killed us. We may not be able to interrogate them if they're all dead, but we certainly can't interrogate them if we're all dead either," he said as he released Skrymir. *"We had them outnumbered and had the element of surprise, and still they almost killed all of us!"*

"Yeah," grumbled Skrymir in agreement rubbing his arm, *"they were quite formidable."*

A patch of snow shifted as Geir broke through and gasped for air. Hrym walked over and pulled him out.

"Direct combat won't work," Skrymir said. He brushed off snow and stretched as he stood up. *"We'll need a different approach when we find that last one… if she survived."*

CHAPTER 17: INTRODUCTIONS

A light drift of delicate snowflakes found their way into the gutted little shack near the Murtrborg fjord. Curled into a ball under a tattered blanket of animal hides, Aric stared blankly out into the cold and empty world beyond his flimsy walls. The smell within his meager hovel had become quite pungent though he had become inured to it. These days he had almost no motivation to get up, let alone bathe.

After putting it off for as long as he could, the pressure on his bladder at last got the better of him and Aric rose from his stupor and trudged out to his usual spot at the edge of the woods. After he relieved himself his stomach rumbled with fury, and he realized how hungry and thirsty he was. Game was scarce this deep into the fimbulvinter, and even the fish had long since abandoned the frozen waters of the fjord. Any animal in the neighboring woods big enough to provide sustenance had migrated south or been eaten long ago.

Coming back inside, Aric looked around at what was left of his hovel. His bed consisted of a threadbare blanket and a small patchwork of animal hides laid on the cold, hard floor. The tiny room felt cavernous now that he was alone. Aric stared with intensity at the empty bed, as if maybe, if he looked long enough, he might still see them there. Alas the only things he saw, the only things he had left, were a dull little hatchet and his bow with one lonely arrow.

His feet propelled him forward of their own accord outside. The dappled light cut ethereal shapes on the ground as he walked. The shadows and light passed by in a blur of dun and pale white, and his eyes were dull and expression blank. Before long, he found himself up on the cliffs overlooking the fjord where he had set Una and Dagmaer adrift on their final journey days before. He stepped right up to the edge. Aric closed his eyes and took a deep breath. Small rocks and clumps of dirt cascaded down the cliff face as his weight shifted, his body teetering against a light, buffeting wind. In this moment he was oblivious to the rest of the world; it was almost peaceful.

In his mind's eye, he could still see the small funeral boat floating out to sea. He watched as it drifted beyond the fjord, its flames blended in with the fiery setting sun. Something flashed across his closed lids. Slowly opening his eyes he came out of his reverie when he noticed there was indeed something floating from the river out into the fjord.

A piece of metal glinted in the light near a large fragment of a tree trunk on the water. Though there was a moderate amount of other debris floating along with it, this particular piece grabbed his attention. He could not be certain, but it appeared as if there might be a person clinging to it. It was then that he realized how close he was to the cliff edge, and Aric stumbled back onto firmer ground, his heart in his throat. He made his way to a lower, safer ledge, keeping his eye on the detritus; in fact, he could not pull his eyes from it. He hesitated for a long moment—then dove in.

—

Brunhilda woke with a start in a cold, dark room. Though she was battered and bruised, her instincts kicked in and she was up on her feet in an instant, her eyes scanning the surroundings. She had been on the floor with a frayed, shabby blanket and some animal hides covering her. In a corner of the room a figure was huddled next to her Jotnar armor, with her clothes hanging on a line near a small pile of glowing embers. The figure had been studying her sword in the dim light but startled at Brunhilda's sudden movements.

"Take it easy," the gaunt figure said as he stood, his free hand outstretched in a placating gesture. Before he could say anything else Brunhilda sprang upon him, snatching her sword from him with one hand and pinning him against the wall with her left arm in one motion.

"Who are you," she hissed at him, "and where am I?" As she raised her right arm to point the sword at his throat, a sharp pain flashed through her shoulder. A lesser warrior would have dropped the sword, but she just gritted her teeth and held fast. She could also tell that her left leg was severely battered and bore her weight with difficulty. With raw menace she asked, "Where are the others?"

Gasping for breath, the man was only able to make weak, gagging sounds. Though his lips moved, he was unable to reply. He grabbed at her arm in desperation.

Brunhilda registered the thinness of the man and the fearful look on his face, and she lowered him to the ground. "You were alone when I found you," he said between coughs and gasps for air. Her arm, still pressed against his throat, had let up only slightly and her sword remained pointed at his face. "My name is Aric, and I live here. I found you half drowned with a bad shoulder, and it looked as if your body was beaten with giant clubs."

"It was a Jotnar," said Brunhilda in a low voice as if they might be overheard. "Everything's a bit hazy and confused right now," she continued as images flashed in her mind—running through the trees, the blazing setting sun, arrows flying by her head, swords flashing and flesh rending.

"One Jotnar did all of that?" the man, Aric, asked in shock.

"He had friends," she replied, "and so did I. We fought and, though we were outnumbered, we were winning." She shook her head as if dislodging stuck memories. "Then something flashed... an explosion?" She closed her eyes and pressed her sword hand to her head. They stood in silence for a moment. Brunhilda's muscles tensed and twitched as the images grew more chaotic and violent.

"Well," said Aric, "I made a simple poultice and applied it to your wounds, but I'm no healer." As he spoke, Brunhilda noticed that he was averting his eyes, trying not to stare at her.

She supposed it must be because her body was bare at the moment. As a warrior, Brunhilda had spent much time in Aesir encampments, in the wilderness, and outposts, among many other men and women, and had no qualms about being unclothed in front of others. Perhaps it would be a vulnerable position if she were facing an enemy, but she could see that he was emaciated and malnourished and posed no immediate threat to her. So for his sake she released him, drew up the blanket, and wrapped it about herself with her left hand, never letting go of the sword the whole time. Her left leg almost gave out when she put her weight on it. She cursed under her breath at her weakness. "Now, tell me where I am and how long I've been unconscious," she said in a stern yet less menacing tone.

"Uh… well," Aric said, still wary of the half-dressed woman brandishing a sword. "This used to be Murtrborg, a small fishing village in the northwestern territory of Midgard. Although these days it's just me. This cursed winter killed or drove out everyone else since the Aesir have abandoned us. Despite all of our faith and devotion and centuries of tithes and sacrifices to them, they've let the land fall to ruin." His shoulders slumped and he shook his head, "I'm sorry, I shouldn't burden you with my problems. I just thought you should know the lay of the land. You won't find much aid in this corner of Midgard." He retrieved a bit of smoked hare and offered a piece to Brunhilda. She accepted it, her sword still in hand, though she let it hang heavily by her side.

"I found you yesterday morning," he continued while gnawing on his own piece of meat. "You were floating out into the fjord. I think the hides that you were wearing got snagged on the wood."

"I suppose I owe you my thanks for these," she said, indicating the dressings on her injuries.

"I did what I could, but as I said, I'm no healer. You'll need to find someone else to properly tend to your injuries." Eyeing the gleaming sword in her hand and then the Jotnar gear hanging in the corner, Aric asked, curiosity in his voice, "You were dressed like a Jotnar but you said that you were beaten by one?"

Brunhilda gave a curt nod and stood fully upright, all of her weight on her right leg. She faced the gaunt, half-starved man, cowering under her towering gaze. "My name is Brunhilda, first shield valkyrie of the Halvard garrison. I am Aesir."

CHAPTER 18: THE BEST LAID PLANS

Cheers rose from the triumphant army. Suttungr picked up a battle standard of the Aesir Army and snapped the pole over his knee before tossing it and the banner into a nearby bonfire. The town of Veizlakr smoldered in ruins while the vast wheat fields all around them remained untouched. Illuminated by bonfires and the light of the burning village, the amber fields of barley glowed.

"Jotnar," Suttungr said and raised his hands to call his troops to order. "Today we have won another decisive victory against the Aesir. We've taken Halvard, Birgjavale, and now with the fall of Veizlakr we have cut off their food supply and claimed it for ourselves." He raised a sack of grain above his head before tossing it to the ground, the golden oats spilling out at his feet. "So tonight, we feast!"

Hertha directed the division leaders to oversee the distribution of food and scavenged weapons and armor. The towering bonfires added to the festive mood while a copious feast was prepared. Two dozen soldiers worked to dig several large pits among the fields. With so many at work, the task was completed before the sky was completely dark. The dead Jotnar were then brought and placed within the pits. After they were buried, Suttungr rose to address the army.

"Friends, brothers, sisters, today we were victorious. Yet even in that victory many of our brethren fell. Though they fell in battle, they were not defeated. They return to Ymir's embrace, back into the ground from whence we all arose. Tonight we celebrate their lives, because their sacrifice today is not their end, it is our future." Suttungr raised his fist and opened his palm to the sky, revealing a handful of oats. With a sweeping gesture he cast the seeds across the turned soil of the mass grave in front of him. "To the future!"

"The future!" echoed the Jotnar at all of the other burial mounds as they repeated his gesture.

—

In the dim light of Suttungr's tent, the alternating faint glow of blue and gold danced against the heavy canvas. He stood shirtless as he hunched over his craft table, his fingers tracing fine lines of Reginvald and Ethlivald energy onto long strips of metal. One hand held the strut in place as his finger engraved filigree onto the surface. Each time a line of Ethlivald crossed a line of Reginvald, sparks flared and he had to push his finger through as if it was a physical barrier. His teeth clenched tight and sweat dripped from his brow as he poured his will into wielding these powerful magics. The rivulets of sweat ran down along the contours of the scar tissue covering his entire body.

The sounds of cavorting and celebration from outside suddenly poured in. Suttungr pulled his hand back with a sharp grunt of pain from a small burst as his concentration broke. He spun around, glaring at the open flap of his tent.

"*Sir,*" said the messenger kneeling at the threshold, one hand holding the hide door open with her other on the ground supporting her. Their eyes met briefly before hers snapped to the ground, short of breath. Suttungr's eyes flared and his brows knit as he regarded her. "*News from Isabrot Pass. I have a message from Hrym,*" she panted. She kept her head bowed and eyes low as she spoke.

"*What news have you brought?*" he asked.

Suttungr approached her with confidence, calm returned to his fur-covered face. Light from the bonfires outside fully illuminated him in the tent opening. He saw a hint of confusion in her eyes when she rose to address him. Pristine blue fur covered his body and his winning smile caught the light. All evidence of burns or scars were now gone.

"*Suttungr, sir,*" she stammered. "*Hrym reports that they caught the valkyries attempting to cross Isabrot Pass. They killed two of them and were able to prevent their passing. They took heavy casualties and are taking reinforcements from the patrol stationed there to hunt down the remaining valkyrie. He requests that you deploy additional troops there to replace them, sir.*"

"Thank you for the report," Suttungr said with an easy smile. *"Isabrot will have to manage on their own. We cannot spare to lose any from the frontlines."* He looked out through the tent flap at all those who have followed him this far. *"This is our chance to change everything. If we lose at Asgard, Isabrot will not matter. Nyr Jotunheim will not matter. If we lose, they will wipe us out for this. There is no going back."*

"Yes, sir," the messenger said. She rose and quickly left letting the tent flap close behind her.

Suttungr stared at the space where the messenger had stood. What could the Aesir be chasing out there? He shook his head. Victory was close now. Whatever Odin was up to must not succeed. "Don't let me down, Hrym," he whispered.

Turning back, he returned his full concentration and power into his task. The telltale glow of magic shimmered and faded from his skin, revealing the scarred visage once more.

—

Odin crumpled the paper in his hand. His fingers closed tight, fist trembling with the intensity of his crushing grip. The king of the Aesir and ruler of the nine realms sat in the war room looking over the map of the world. Today the chamber was nearly empty. Only Frigg stood in attendance to Odin, along with his animal menagerie: the ravens Huginn and Muninn, and his wolves Geri and Freki. An exhausted messenger also knelt at his side breathing hard.

"We've lost Veizlakr," Odin said, his voice betraying no emotion. He stood abruptly, pushing his chair back setting his ravens aflutter. As he relaxed his grip, the paper fell from his hand. He waved off the messenger.

Frigg picked up the parchment and smoothed it out before tipping over the Aesir figure at Veizlakr and moving several other pieces on the map. The divisions led by Thor, Sif, and Gunnar continued to strike at the Jotnar armies. Yet for every victory they achieved, it seemed that they also suffered a strategically significant loss. Too few alabaster pieces were on the board to counter every Jotnar token.

"This will be problematic," Frigg said with a frown.

"Asgard has plenty of food."

"In the short term," she countered, "but what of the other

realms? If we neglect them for too long, they will starve. Our distributed resource system cannot sustain this kind of attack." Pointing to several food production regions, she said, "The Jotnar have captured key resources taking whatever they can and razing the rest. Between that and what we've had to slash and burn in retreat, we will run into massive food shortages when we finally defeat them."

"They know precisely where to strike to destabilize our supplies," Odin said, pointing at the regions hit the hardest. "By attacking our infrastructure and ability to distribute resources to the other realms, the other races will be incited to riot when they run out of food. Asgard is secure, but the other realms will either become distractions for us or allies to the Jotnar." Looking up from the table, he met Frigg's eyes. "Do they hate us so much that they would see the world set to ruin?"

Odin placed both hands on the table and bowed his head. His shoulders sagged and he exhaled a long, slow breath. He would never allow any of the other Aesir see him in such a state of weakness and exhaustion. Frigg was his wife and partner. She provided strength and wisdom; more than once he wondered if she could actually see the future, so accurate were some of her predictions. Freki came and pushed his snout under Odin's hand.

Frigg looked at the wolf. "The Jotnar have always opposed us. We had to practically drag them through the Great Awakening. They're jealous that the Aesir took up the mantle of leadership to protect the world from the monsters of old. We saw that come to a head during the Aesir-Vanir War. They blamed us for their problems then and now. Every war has its losers, and as such they begrudge the victors."

"It's even more than that, I think," Odin said, a frown returning to his face while he searched for the right words. "If we had simply beaten them on the field of battle, I think they could respect that. Instead we cut a deal with the Vanir, and so they not only lost, they were betrayed."

"That may explain some of it. These acts do feel more extreme, almost vindictive," she said.

"It is undoubtedly personal," Odin replied. "Loki blames me for the death of his sister. I may as well have killed her with my own hands as far as he is concerned. As if him killing Baldur hadn't been revenge enough."

"Then you truly believe that Suttungr is Loki in disguise?" Frigg asked with a raised eyebrow.

Nodding absently, he said, "He was the only Jotnar I've seen capable of even attempting Reginvald."

"Then why the charade? You would think he would be a rallying figure for the Jotnar nation."

"Perhaps he did not want to give away his secret. It is only because of Brunhilda that we even suspect his identity. Or perhaps he is merely a student or disciple of Loki." Drawing his hunting knife from his belt, Odin slammed it into the map at Veizlakr. "We shall ask him when he is bowed down before me in defeat."

CHAPTER 19: THE PACT

A raven's caw echoed out into the vast stillness of the fjord. A thin wisp of smoke curled out from the small shack near the treeline. Inside, Aric and the valkyrie were yelling at each other.

"You have to go," Brunhilda said as she paced around the hovel with a pronounced limp. "The Jotnar are tracking me, and they'll find this place. If you're here, at best they'll kill you and move on, and at worst they'll torture you until you tell them which way I went"—she raised a hand to forestall Aric's argument—"and then they'll kill you."

"If you're going, then just leave," yelled Aric. He never expected to be so confrontational and assertive with one of the Aesir. But when she had told him they needed to leave Murtrborg, his reaction had been instant and emotional. It also helped that she was fully clothed now. "This is my home," he said. "I can take care of myself."

She scoffed. "You can't fight them off with one arrow and a dull, little hatchet."

"That's not what—" Aric shifted toward his tools defensively. "I wouldn't fight them. I've lived my whole life here. There are plenty of nooks and caves to hide out and find shelter."

"They would find you," she said, emphasizing each word. "They tracked three highly trained valkyries through dense forests and snow drifts. Finding a single human would be simple."

"I saved your life," Aric mumbled.

"Yes, you did," she said, softening her voice. "And that's why I won't just kill you myself."

Aric pulled back with a start.

"I'm not going to kill you," she said, trying to sound

comforting and nonthreatening. Aric could tell that she did not use that tone often. "I'm trying to save you."

"I can't leave." Aric's eyes darted to Una and Dagmaer's empty bed rolls. "This is my home, this is where... I just—" His tears and emotions welled up and he turned and dashed out into the cold, dark night.

Aric ran a short distance away outside, stopping suddenly at the shore. There was a rare break in the clouds to the west. He caught sight of the broad expanse of the stars in the sky. As his eyes drifted down, he saw the still water of the fjord reflecting the night sky, creating a stunning, dizzying effect. The vast panorama of the heavens blended across the horizon and he thought about how small he truly was. Clouds of his breath rose up into the silence of the freezing air.

Snow crunched behind him in an awkward rhythm. It came to a halt a few feet away before the world was silent once again. As he stared at the sky, a single tear slid down his cheek as the trail it left froze. He stood like that for a long moment, letting the cold wash over his face and watching as the stars shone down on him.

"Do you have a family, Brunhilda, first shield valkyrie of the Aesir?" Aric asked without turning his head.

Her voice came after a brief pause. "All of the Aesir are my family, especially my sisters in arms, the valkyries... But if you mean, 'Do I have a husband or children?' then the answer is no."

"Then how can you possibly understand what I've lost?" Aric said softly. "What this place means to me?"

"Giving up and dying here will not undo their deaths nor will it honor their lives. This village, this house is nothing more than a tomb now. If the living do not survive and fight for the dead then the world would have ended long ago."

The silence stretched out as they stood there in the cold. He saw a bright orange dot near the horizon and imagined it was Una and Dagmaer's funeral boat, carrying them to the afterlife. As the time passed, Aric almost forgot that Brunhilda was there.

"Very well," she said quietly. "I won't make you come with me, but I still have a mission and I will see it through to the end." From the corner of his eye, he saw her turn her back to him. "Thank you for your hospitality, Aric. I'll leave tracks directed away from here. I hope that will be sufficient to keep you safe, though to be sure you should stay hidden for the next few days. Perhaps find a place far away to shelter in for a while. At first light I will be gone, and you may return to your… life." With a frown Aric thought that he detected a note of pity and something else in her voice.

Once again Aric stood alone in the frigid darkness. He closed his eyes and bowed his head, exhaling a long, cloudy breath. The crunch of snow echoed in the solemn night air, sounding the irregular rhythm of Brunhilda's steps. Turning his head, he could see Brunhilda cradling her right arm as she limped away, silhouetted against the luminous snow.

Brunhilda held her head high despite her own losses, despite her injuries. Her words echoed in Aric's ears and bored into his heart. He imagined saying something like that to Dagmaer after Una had died. Would she have fought harder to survive? Would she still be alive with him now?

———

Just before dawn broke over the fjord, Brunhilda woke and prepared for her departure. Aric's sleeping spot was empty and there was a small strip of cured meat laid on a cloth. She figured that he had already left and wanted to avoid facing her. Checking her bandages once more, she strapped on her sword, slipped her right arm into the sling, and went out the door.

Aric was outside waiting for her. "I'm not afraid of them," he said pointedly. "But maybe it is time that I moved on from here."

She looked at him with a warm smile and placed a gentle hand on his shoulder.

He gave her a rough branch stripped into a simple walking stick. He had a makeshift sled that must have taken a several hours to lash together, she guessed. "Where are we headed?" he asked as he slipped into a rope harness.

"North," replied Brunhilda. "I have to get to Yggdrasil, beyond Jotunheim, at the very heart of Niflheim."

"Yggdrasil?" Aric cried with a start. His mouth opened and closed and he took halting steps first in one direction then another.

"We're going to see the World Tree? We're going to just walk there? Through Niflheim? Through Jotunheim? How long—? Aren't the Jotnar trying to kill you?" His hands twisted as he spoke.

She held up her hand and immediately he quieted. She waited for him to breathe and calm down before speaking. "There will be no help for us along the way. We'll need to hunt and forage for food as we go. This will be a difficult journey, though a little less so with your aid," she said with a wan smile.

She caught his eye and saw that he understood; he knew how grateful she was, even if she did not say the words others would have found so easily. He shook his head then set his shoulders to the harness and began to walk north. Brunhilda kept a good pace despite her injuries. The limp would not—could not—stop her now.

CHAPTER 20: ELUSIVE PREY

Dawn broke to the rumbling of hundreds of feet trampling the ground. Cresting the low hills of the southern horizon the Aesir Army emerged. They had moved north at an incredible pace, and only through a sustained march were they able to reach Birgjavale so soon after the Jotnar had taken it.

Thor stood at the head of the Aesir Army, ready with anticipation. Being a commercial hub in the heart of Aesir territory, Birgjavale had never been fortified with many defensive structures. They would have been impediments to the flow of goods to and from the other realms. As such, the Aesir had not been prepared to defend it, and Thor was counting on the Jotnar to be ill prepared to hold it.

The enemy troops were numerous though not quite so many as he had anticipated. In fact, he was disappointed by this entire scenario. The Aesir were only outnumbered three to one as opposed to the ten-to-one ratio the scouts had reported.

"No sign of Suttungr or Hrym," Gunnar said as she stepped to Thor's side. "They don't stand a chance."

"They may have a trick or two waiting for us," Thor said with a slight note of disappointment in his voice. "This entire rebellion caught us by surprise. Overconfidence can be just as lethal as any weapon the enemy possesses."

He hefted the massive Mjolnir above his head as he turned to address his soldiers. "The Jotnar Army will break before us today; ready yourselves for the fight ahead." Returning his gaze to the north, he broke into a run and shouted, "For Freya!"

His army roared and joined him in the charge. The thunder of their booted and armored feet shook the ground beneath them. The

Jotnar Army responded with their own roar, and they rushed headlong to meet them on the field of battle.

———

It was a brief skirmish with no casualties among the Aesir Army. To all present, it was clear that these Jotnar were sacrificed. There had been just enough to give the appearance of a much larger force. And as the blood-red sunlight bled through the thin veil of clouds on the horizon, Thor walked among the fallen, searching. The blue Jotnar blood had a warm hue even as cold tendrils of mist rose from the ground.

"Garmr's taint!" shouted Thor as he slammed the head of an insignificant Jotnar commander into the ground. "Suttungr should have been here at this battle. He must have led the attack on Birgjavale. It's impossible that this wasn't their main army."

He let loose a long string of profanity and curses the entire walk to his personal tent. Royal guards stood on either side of the entrance to his personal quarters and held back the heavy canvas flaps for him to enter. His attendants brought him water and linens to cleanse him of the grit and grime of battle. Thor quenched his thirst with a tankard of mead as his armor was removed and wiped clean, ready for the next battle.

Refreshed, he returned to the command tent and updated the pieces on the map that represent the Aesir and Jotnar forces. Birgjavale once again had an alabaster figure atop it. Messengers from throughout the northern regions lined up to relay their latest information. They all stood patiently at attention and awaited their turn without complaint, even though many must have ridden all night and day to reach him. With each message Thor slid the wooden Jotnar tokens, one to the east over Veizlakr and another to the south toward Svartalfheim.

"According to the prisoners, the Jotnar Army has split into several distinct groups and were tasked with attacking the less defended cities and towns," Gunnar reported. "They say that Suttungr was heading south and to the west, though they wouldn't say if he was going to Alfheim or Svartalfheim. It would seem that they're not after our strongholds at all, just terrorizing our vulnerable territories and sowing seeds of chaos while creating panic in our populace."

"Divide and conquer." Thor frowned and stroked his beard.

"Or they're trying to tire us out. Getting us to chase ghost armies while they make overtures to the other realms," Gunnar said.

"Loki was always fond of creating illusions with his magic. If he's taught that trick to other Jotnar, then many of these troop movements could be worse than mere diversions; they could be complete fabrications," Thor said. He crushed one of the wooden pieces in his hand.

"We should follow Freya's strategy. Pull back and let them come to us."

"Freya was always better with devising strategies," he grumbled as he dismissed the last messenger and stared at the updated map. He took a deep drink from his horn of mead while evaluating the recent updates. "And look where that got her." He pointed to an piece just off to one side, gilded with gold filigree. Although her piece was no longer on the map he had kept it near. "Yet after father's speech we cannot simply return to Asgard and cower behind the Skjaldborg."

"We have won every battle that you've led, my lord," replied Gunnar.

He looked over at her. She still bore the scars and wounds sustained from the ambush that had cost them Vali and Freya. Debris from the explosions had cut her deeply. The Aesir healers could have mended her scars, but she had insisted on leaving as soon as she could hold a sword and march. Those scars reminded Thor of her toughness, devotion, and desire to return to the fight. At the same time, they whispered to him of their strategic failures.

"But I can't be at every battle," he said, slamming his fist onto the table and rattling the markers. Three of the Aesir pieces toppled over and all of the pieces shifted from their carefully placed spots. His eyes lingered on the figure that represented Suttungr on its side pointing to Asgard. The silence stretched out while Thor stared at it, his fist still clenched tight.

He gave a long, slow exhale as he stood upright and picked up the piece. "Freya was right. Out here we are spread too thin. It's time to pull back."

"What of the remote villages, sir? We need to evacuate them to the safety of Asgard."

"Yes, right," he said, taking a deep, calming breath. "Take a division with you and organize the evacuation of the east. Grab as many as you can but leave any who cannot keep up. We'll garrison a division here for three weeks to assist the refugees on their way. I'll take another division out to head off the Jotnar trying to reach Alfheim or Svartalfheim. The rest of the army is to return to Asgard and prepare for the Jotnar." He turned to Gunnar, who was nodding along. "Send word to Sif. Hurry. It will take all of us to bring this situation under control."

CHAPTER 21: PERSPECTIVES

"How's your leg?" asked a weary Aric. "Maybe we should slow down our pace. It hasn't even been a week since I pulled you from the water." After a moment of silence from Brunhilda, Aric continued, "That limp doesn't look like it's getting any better."

"I've had worse," Brunhilda said through gritted teeth. Though Aric was pulling most of their gear and supplies on the sled, she was still weighed down with her Jotnar armor and valkyrie sword. She was already frustrated at their sluggish pace.

"I really think that you should remove your armor and pack it up on the sled," recommended Aric. Brunhilda gave him a withering stare. "Or whatever you think is best, oh mighty first shield valkyrie of the Aesir," he said as he pulled the sled past her.

Beneath the snow her foot hit a rock, throwing off her gait. A sharp pain flashed through her leg. She suppressed a yelp, but the vision of Skogul being consumed in the explosion came to her mind, unbidden. Hilder's death had been quieter though no less traumatic to witness. This pain in her leg reminded Brunhilda that she was still alive; that she had survived when her comrades—her friends—had not. Tears welled up in her eyes and her emotions threatened to overwhelm her. Instead of breaking under the strain, she gritted her teeth, pushed her feelings down, and redoubled her focus on the journey ahead.

While she had been keeping pace with Aric since their departure before sunrise, she realized that he had been walking slower for her sake. Now, as he moved farther ahead, she struggled to keep up. With each footfall she felt the weight of the armor drag her deeper into the snow. Her exertions pulled at the dressings binding her wounds, and she could see drops of blood falling into the snow at her feet.

—

Brunhilda's eyes blinked open and, through a gossamer patch of clouds, she saw a handful of the brighter stars twinkling overhead. The layer of furs underneath her were warm and comforting. There was no moon tonight to compete with the magnificent celestial display visible through the branches of the surrounding trees. The stars twinkled in the dark sky, and the bright band of stars was just creeping into view. Just as Brunhilda was considering how long it had been since she last noticed them, she bolted upright with a start, pain flashing through her shoulder and leg.

Reaching for her sword she realized that it was not at her side and she was no longer armored. "What happened?" she groaned in a raspy voice as she looked around and found Aric propped up against a tree. They were tucked against a rocky outcropping, surrounded by trees. She was atop the furs piled on the sled and had fresh dressings on her wounds.

"You passed out," Aric said. "You lost a lot of blood, so I found a secluded place where I could drag you. We can stay here for a few days so that you can recover—"

"We don't have a few days," Brunhilda interrupted. "The Jotnar Army is marching toward Asgard. A crazed, giant Jotnar is chasing us."

"Fine," said Aric. He tossed her a bit of salted meat. "If we aren't going to stop, then you have to travel lighter. It'll be slow going if you collapse every day."

Taking a bite, she replied, "Point taken. When we've finished this mission and defeated the Jotnar, Odin will reward you handsomely for your help."

"Odin can take his reward and throw it to Hel for all I care," Aric snapped. "If I ever see him or any of the 'gods,' I'll curse them to their faces and spit in their eyes." His fists were tight and knuckles white, his body shaking. When his eyes met hers he unclenched and remembered to breathe, as he suddenly remembered that she was Aesir. Taking a deep breath, he regained some of his composure and looked away.

"It's always supposed to be such an honor and privilege to

serve the Aesir. Every month we paid our tithes, and every year we sacrificed our excess bounty to you. Yet when we needed you—really needed you—you abandoned me… us." Another deep breath. "After I help you, I'm done with everyone—the Aesir, the Jotnar… I just want to be left alone."

"But—"

"I don't want to talk about it!" His voice cracked. He turned his back to her and covered himself in the animal skins.

Brunhilda sat in silence and stared at the lump. For the first time she considered how the other races looked upon the Aesir. They were glorious and an awesome sight to behold in battle, and when they were resting they lived in the gleaming city of Asgard. She thought back to her most recent battle. A desperate group of bandits had hijacked a supply convoy, and the humans had proved too wily for the general army, so she had been brought in.

It had taken a concerted effort to hunt them down. They had an uncanny ability to sniff out traps and caravans set up as bait. Finally, employing some scouting techniques that Skogul had taught her, she homed in on them and found them distributing sacks of grain and crates of vegetables to a small, unmarked village whose great hall was a mud hut covered in straw, twenty feet across. At the time she had not given much thought to the specifics of what they were doing or why. All she knew was that they had stolen from the Aesir and their sentence was death.

Like cornered animals they had fought with desperation and with tenacity. Their only weapons were farm implements, modified to be more lethal. But against her and her hunting party of six Aesir, they posed little real threat. She carried out the immediate execution of the bandits and forced the villagers to return to Veizlakr to face the judgement of the local gythja. No one lived outside of Aesir law.

What was so important about their miserable little village that they fought so hard for? Having spent her days in the service of the nine realms amid the wealth of Asgard, she did not understand why anyone would fight so hard to live apart. The other Aesir that she knew and spent time with lived lives of idle comfort. How did the other races spend their days, she began to wonder.

—

The latest messenger from the front had just departed, having delivered news to Knute and a letter to Jorunn. With Hertha's rank in Suttungr's army she had been able to dispatch a letter to Jorunn. Jorunn sighed as she read about the vast, golden barley fields of Veizlakr. It was difficult for her to picture it in her mind having only known the dull, desolate tundra of Gastropnir, but she imagined something bright, warm, and inviting. Jorunn wrinkled her nose as an especially pungent odor broke her from her daydream. Even though she spent her days herding the aurochs and her evenings selling their milk, wool, and dung, the smell still got to her from time to time.

"Hey Knute," Jorunn called over after a snort and gag. The elder Jotnar grunted acknowledgement, not pausing or looking up. His concentration was on carving designs into the handle of a bone dagger. *"What was Jotunheim like? I mean old Jotunheim, not this place."*

He paused mid-stroke in his carving and looked up at her. *"How old do you think I am?"* he asked with no small amount of annoyance in his tone, his brow furrowed.

Jorunn dithered and mumbled as she tried to come up with an inoffensive reply. *"Hertha said you used to tell stories about life in Jotunheim before the war."*

"I'm just giving you a hard time," he said with a little chuckle. *"Yeah, I used to talk about it, but then Suttungr came along and started this new war. Ever since then it's been difficult to think about the old days. The last war saw us losing our homeland. I fear to think of what will become of us if we lose this one."*

"Sorry, I didn't mean to upset you," she said, bowing her head and looking at her feet.

"Bah, I'm an old Jotnar," he said, waving the apology off. *"Everything upsets me."*

That drew a small laugh from Jorunn. Knute set aside his tools and picked up the dagger. Eyeing the fine carvings, he gave a gentle blow to clear out the shavings. She turned to him fully in anticipation.

—

Back before the war, every inch of Jotunheim was covered in verdant forests and lush plains. We were Yggdrasil's first children, after all. The nine realms didn't exist as distinct, separate entities until after the Great Awakening, but that was before my time. Then, as now, we lived in harmony with the world around us. Even our fur grew in mostly as various shades of green. I wasn't always this dull, lifeless blue. In my youth the hair on my head and the fur down my back was a deep olive with pale stripes. It was quite striking, if I may say so. We blended in with our homes, grown from the trees and plants all around us.

I lived in the capital city of Utgard. It was a towering forest city. The trees were so large that four families could live in one with room to spare. And the fruits of those trees were the sweetest delicacies, blossoming year-round. We even had entire groves of trees that served as hanging gardens, producing a variety of crops. Things were so plentiful that we had an excess of time to get into mischief.

It was so unlike here, where we must work so hard and scrounge for every resource. We didn't domesticate the aurochs until we were exiled to Niflheim. Here it has become a necessity. The alpine trees bear no sweet or nourishing bounty, having to stand against the harsh, blowing winds of the north. It was difficult enough to get them to grow at all, let alone into the forests we have now. Trying to shape them into homes in these conditions is impossible. That's why we live in these low, boring hovels. Still, we thrive and find the beauty here. But that's who we are—like Yggdrasil, we're always connected to the world around us.

Still, things weren't perfect back then. We're not the kind of people who like being confined to rules and borders. We had more than a few "misunderstandings" with the other races and the Aesir were the least accommodating. Suffice it to say, we clashed with them one too many times. You know about "Aesir-Vanir War," as they like to call it. But there were many "lesser" incidences as well.

One that you might not have heard of involved a Jotnar named Thiazi and the Vanir Ydun. Thiazi was a splendid and gifted cultivator of fruits. But though his own fruits were impressive, the Vanir Ydun had the most marvelous golden apples. Thiazi spent much time with her, claiming that he sought to cultivate a grove of those trees in Jotunheim. I suspected that he was interested in more than her apples, and I wasn't the only one. Among her many suitors was one of the lesser Aesir lords, Honir. The Aesir can somehow turn coupling into such a tedious process, with ideas of monogamy and marriage. Honir took offense to Thiazi and slayed him when he found them together, claiming that Thiazi had abducted her.

Odin gave him a slight punishment, despite Ydun contradicting Honir's accusations. In the end Thiazi found no justice in Odin's court, as we would often find. Honir also lost as Ydun eventually chose Bragi as her husband, though that provided little solace for Thiazi's family.

—

He paused and cleared his throat when some prospective customers came to barter for goods. Jorunn attended to some patrons as well, getting some tubers and herbs in exchange for a few bundles of auroch dung. Yet even in this flurry of commerce she noticed the forced smile that Knute wore. His sad eyes and a note in his voice spoke of something in that story that weighed heavily on him. Still, he chatted up his patrons, as was his way.

Knute ended up with a workable bolt of homespun made from Svelbjarg sheep wool. He had gotten it for a knife and a set of bone needles. She did not think sewing was one of his skills, though she did know him to spend a considerable amount of time with the old seamstress. Perhaps she would whip something up for him in exchange for some carved and polished bone jewelry.

"You know the rest," he said when they were idle once again. With his eyes shut he pinched the bridge of his nose before continuing. *"Thrym, the war, our alliance with and eventual betrayal by the Vanir..."* Jorunn waited for him to continue, to tell her more about Jotunheim, about their people's history. He had gone off on a tangent with the story of Thiazi, but his reaction left her curious. She shuffled closer in an attempt to let him know she was ready to hear more. But with a wave of his hand he seemed to indicate that he was done talking.

She did not move back and just waited. When it became clear that he was not going to continue, she blurted, *"Was Thiazi—"*

"He was my brother," Knute cut her off.

They sat in silence for a long time. Jorunn thought of her own sister, now engaged in the war against the Aesir. Knute stared at his carving, his gaze distant and cold.

"Do you think things will ever be like they were before?" She asked with hope and longing, but with the look on his face she did not

expect a positive response.

Knute raised his head and looked at her for a long while, as if he were trying to divine the future within the depths of her eyes. His mouth opened and closed wordlessly once, then again. After a long moment he just bowed his head and returned to the bone knife, holding the blade and polishing the patterns in the handle.

CHAPTER 22: CHANCE ENCOUNTER

Another gray dawn cast its weak light through the skeletal branches onto the new-fallen snow. Brunhilda was already awake and gnawed on a strip of cured rabbit. Aric had brought an ample supply of salt to preserve what little meat they could find out in these northern wilds. It was just as well that she was injured; it seemed doubtful they would have squeezed more game from this sepulchral land. Brunhilda was used to surviving on much less during her training to become a valkyrie, yet a week of chewing on foraged roots and salted meat still annoyed her. Fond memories of her last good meal in Birgjavale resurfaced even as the brackish flavors assaulted her tongue. She allowed herself a brief moment to mourn Hilder and Skogul before reaffirming her commitment to their mission. Their deaths would not be in vain.

The first few days had passed without much incident. They were able to supplement these meager meals with some of the food that Aric had accumulated while living on his own. Brunhilda was steadily recovering, growing stronger day by day. Trudging through the snow was hard, tedious work and yet every evening after making camp she made sure to exercise her sword arm, running through drills to rehabilitate her injured body.

She had attempted to teach Aric some basic skills with the sword, but he had refused every offer. Instead he chose to spend the evenings using his hatchet to whittle additional arrows from whatever suitable wood they could find. He showed no interest in learning any other martial skill. By the end of the first night they discovered that they had almost nothing to talk about. Neither wished to speak about their losses, and any conversation about Asgard inevitably led to Aric vehemently denouncing the Aesir.

Brunhilda could only imagine what he had gone through, was going through. He had lived his entire life in that small human town near the sheltered little fjord, and by now he had traveled farther away from his home than he had ever been in his entire life. In the waning light of the evening she could often see the conflicting emotions play across his face. Her own thoughts of Skogul and Hilder still left her raw. The further they ran, the easier it became to forget and move on.

Five days of this routine—sleeping, eating, and walking in silence—put both Aric and Brunhilda in foul tempers. When Brunhilda felt strong enough, she helped Aric pull the sled laden with their supplies. Making their way through the powdery, virgin snow stunted the feeling of progress with each glade and copse looking alike. Several times Brunhilda could have sworn they already passed by this tree or that rock. She even stopped covering their tracks to make sure. Out here it was no longer a matter of avoiding other travelers on the roads; there simply were no roads to Yggdrasil.

However, on the sixth day Brunhilda pulled Aric to a stop and crouched down into the snow. His face wary and confused, he opened his mouth just as faint sounds of fighting trickled through the air, coming just beyond the next rise.

Brunhilda drew her sword, the rasp of the blade as it passed the scabbard a mere whisper. Its weight felt comfortable and reassuring in her hand. Even after shedding all of her armor for travel, her sword was the one thing that she insisted on carrying at all times.

"Leave the sled and stay out of sight," she whispered. "Bring your bow. If they get past me, you'll have to defend yourself." With quick and nimble fingers she strapped on the few armor pieces that covered her injuries, leaving the rest behind.

"Are you well enough to move or even fight?" hissed Aric. He fumbled with his bow as he strung it. She glared at him as he rifled through his quiver. With more care he pulled out shaft after shaft until he found the only one that had an actually lethal arrowhead. The others were simple sticks with no fletching, no nock, and no point. Her focus turned back to the source of the sounds, and she shushed him when he tried to get her attention.

Waving her hand dismissively, she crouched low and made her way to the rise. Walking had become easier, and her sword exercises had improved. Still, Brunhilda was not certain that she had recovered enough to take on Hrym and his squad of Jotnar again so soon and by herself. Those thoughts vanished as she crested the top of the rise.

In a small clearing a short distance away, a young human woman was fighting off two Jotnar. She had dark, wild hair and was dressed in simple traveling clothes. A satchel and heavy cloak sat at the edge of the clearing apparently discarded in haste. The woman's sword was of a simple, utilitarian design but appeared to be well crafted as she swung it in quick, graceful arcs, turning and parrying powerful strikes from the attacking Jotnar. Although she was having difficulty breaking through their guard she kept them from surrounding and overpowering her. Brunhilda had not expected to see anyone in this area let alone be impressed with the combat skills of a young human woman.

The Jotnar held swords and wore the crude, piecemeal armor of the Jotnar Army. Their animal skull helms loomed over the woman as they circled her, but her fierce expression showed no sign of fear. Brunhilda looked at them with a calculating eye, sizing them up. While they were no equal in skill to Hrym or the others she had fought near Isabrot Pass, they swung with precision and power. Still, the human was at a disadvantage against the two of them, though she moved with an acute awareness and at least was keeping the Jotnar a safe distance away.

"What's going on?" whispered Aric. He had moved up behind her, just below the rise. With his only arrow nocked in the bow and his dull hatchet tucked into his belt, he looked ill prepared for any kind of conflict. "Is it the Jotnar who are hunting you?"

"I don't think so," said Brunhilda. "This seems to be something else entirely."

Aric crept up to get a closer look. He covered his mouth just in time to stifle a gasp. "What in Hel's name are those creatures? Are those Jotnar?" His eyes widened in bright fear.

"Of course they're Jotnar. What else would they be?" hissed Brunhilda.

"I don't know, I've never seen one before," Aric stammered. "They look terrifying."

"They're just wearing animal skulls," she said with a shrug. "Unfortunately I don't have time to give a lecture on the intricacies of the Jotnar people and culture at the moment." Of course she would never admit that she knew exceedingly little about their people and culture.

"Cover me," she said without looking back to Aric, and ran toward the fight.

Aric looked from his one functional arrow to the two Jotnar and mumbled, "With what?"

Uttering a deep, guttural battle cry, Brunhilda leapt into the fray. The two Jotnar were startled by the sound and spun toward the sound. In their moment of distraction, the young woman took advantage and cut down the closest Jotnar from behind.

Powered by the rush of adrenaline, Brunhilda no longer felt her injuries as she swung her sword. She weaved through his defenses but could not cut through even the weak Jotnar armor. As she thrusted and blocked and parried, the pain and fatigue built up, and when the Jotnar struck with a shout, her injured arm buckled under the impact against her block and she dropped to one knee. The Jotnar stood above her, weapon raised—and then an arrow struck him on the helmet, stunning him. It was the opening that Brunhilda needed to thrust her sword upward through his head from under his chin. The Jotnar crumpled to the side in a heap.

"Thanks for the help," the young woman said as she sheathed her sword and offered her hand to help Brunhilda up.

"You were doing quite well for yourself considering there were two of them," replied Brunhilda, accepting the proffered hand. "Where did you learn to fight like that?" she asked with a hint of suspicion in her voice. "I've never seen a human with such skill."

In response the young woman drew a hunting knife and threw it past Brunhilda's head. It struck a tree trunk some distance away, and Aric jumped out from behind it.

"Whoa!" he said, startled. "I'm with her!" He dropped his bow and raised his empty hands. Brunhilda nodded in confirmation when the woman gave her a questioning look.

"My name's Aric, and this is Brunhilda," he said while straining to pull the knife from the tree.

"My apologies, Aric," the woman replied, returning to a

neutral, more relaxed stance. "I thought you were another Jotnar skulking around up there. You may call me Skuld." She gave a little bow. "Deserters from the Jotnar Army roam this area. They're more of a nuisance than anything, but since they cannot return to Jotunheim they prowl in and around these woods, acting as brigands and thieves."

"Well, that explains why they were here," Brunhilda said, looking at the two corpses. "What brings a lone human to this desolate part of Midgard?"

Skuld bowed her head, her hair falling across her face. "I was part of a caravan of survivors from Birgjavale—"

"Birgjavale has fallen?" interrupted Brunhilda. "How are the Jotnar mobilizing so rapidly?" She looked skyward in frustrated exasperation. "What happened to the Aesir Army? They were supposed to regroup there after Halvard weeks ago."

"There was a battered army that came through with some refugees from Halvard," answered Skuld. "But they had suffered many losses and left only a small contingent at Birgjavale before the wounded continued on to Asgard. The division stationed there were overwhelmed by the Jotnar. They seemed to focus their attack on the Aesir."

"You ran?" Brunhilda jabbed a finger at her.

"We aren't soldiers," Skuld countered, "and most of our group didn't even have weapons. What were we supposed to do against an army that was beating the Aesir?"

"So there are other survivors?" Aric cut in.

"Yes," Skuld said through clenched teeth. "I was part of a minstrel group and we were able to escape with some others. Somehow the Jotnar had cut off the roads to the east toward Asgard. They were pushing through with such haste that it seemed the safest place to go was north. In my travels I had heard stories of a small human settlement hidden near the border between Midgard and Jotunheim. If they'd managed to stay safe this long, then I thought it might be a good place to wait out this war or uprising or whatever it is that's going on."

Brunhilda had grabbed Skuld by the shoulders. "How long ago was this? Who was in command at Birgjavale? Were there any communications or orders from Asgard? How large was the Jotnar Army that attacked? Were they led by a Jotnar named Suttungr?"

Aric put an arm around Brunhilda and got her to release her hold of Skuld. The valkyrie shrugged off his arm and turned her gaze south in roughly the direction of Birgjavale.

"It's been about a week. Regrettably I don't know anything about your other questions," Skuld replied, breaking free from Brunhilda's grasp. "The attack came with little warning, and after that it was utter chaos. We ran and didn't look back. That evening we saw the fires from the town. They lit up the horizon," she trailed off, her eyes darkening at the thought.

They stood in silence. Then Aric gave a little cough, and Skuld blinked in surprise as she looked at the two of them again.

"Right," she said, shaking her head slightly. "We'd been on the road for quite a while, trying to avoid Jotnar. We finally reached the foothills of the Svelbjarg Mountains when we were ambushed by four Jotnar, including these two. We tried to fight them off, but we didn't have many weapons, and only a couple of us had any experience doing... this. Choreographed fighting is a far cry from the real thing." She paused and took a deep breath. "We killed two of them, but I lost everyone... so I ran, and these two chased me down. Thank the gods that you found me when you did. If you two hadn't shown up, I'm not sure I would have had the strength to fight them both much longer." She held up her trembling hands, though whether it was from fatigue or fear, Brunhilda did not know. "I think that all of this is finally catching up with me. All of the wanton death and destruction... it's nothing like the plays that we put on."

"I understand," Brunhilda said somberly, her gaze meeting Aric's eyes. "We've all lost people in this madness."

"Well, we've got our supplies just over that rise," Aric said abruptly, pointing in the direction from which he had come. "We should get out of here and find a place to hide out for the rest of the day in case more Jotnar come looking for these two."

As he turned toward the sled, Brunhilda collapsed into him. He was able to catch her and ease her to the ground; pulling away from her, he noticed golden blood on his hands.

"What's wrong?" asked Skuld.

"I think her wounds opened back up during the fight,"

replied Aric. Brunhilda could hear and feel him as he carefully checked her shoulder. Yet all of her sensations were dulled, as if she were far away. "She was wounded a few days ago. I'm not a healer and did what I could, but it didn't look good. We should've rested longer before setting out, but she was insistent that we leave as soon as she was mobile."

Aric felt her forehead. She was burning up with fever. "This isn't good. I think her wounds are infected. She was floating in the Calder River for a while before I found her. And who knows how filthy the Jotnar weapons are."

"I have some medicines with me," Skuld offered as she approached Aric. He stood to give her room to work. She pulled a small pouch from the satchel she had retrieved from the edge of the clearing. Brunhilda felt a warm, tingling sensation where Skuld's deft hands applied the medicines. As Skuld pulled away and stood up, Brunhilda's eyes fluttered shut.

"She should be stable enough for now," Brunhilda distantly heard Skuld say. "As you said before, we should get out of here before any other Jotnar come looking for their comrades. Start pulling, I'll clean up here and cover our tracks. I can do more for her once we've reached a safer location."

CHAPTER 23: DETOUR

As night fell, the three companions huddled under the shelter of a rocky crag. They had gathered everything of use from the fallen Jotnar and hidden the bodies before they left. Even with the possibility of hostiles nearby, they could not move too quickly. Aric pulled the unconscious Brunhilda on the sled while Skuld brought up the rear and covered their tracks. Skuld's medicine worked so well that by the time they made camp for the night, Brunhilda had regained consciousness.

"By Odin's beard this is getting absurd!" Brunhilda was a poor patient, although Aric was getting used to it by now. "I'm not yelling at you. I just—thank you for your help," she said to him as she stood up. Skuld hurried over to give her some support. "Thank you both."

"You should get more rest," Skuld said to her. "Those aren't minor injuries."

"Lying still has never suited me," Brunhilda said, drawing her sword. "I need to work through this."

"Well," Skuld said with some hesitance. "If you insist on doing something, I would be honored to practice with you."

The two women sparred in the waning light of dusk. Aric found himself staring before averting his eyes and busying himself with other tasks. Brunhilda was unsteady on her feet but she had insisted that she needed to be prepared to fight through her injuries. Once they had started, Skuld had a wide grin on her face as they fought. For the most part Aric ignored their idle banter, though he caught snippets here and there. Having traveled across the realms with her troupe, Skuld not only kept up with Brunhilda physically but handled the conversation just as well.

"I can't believe that I get to learn to fight from an actual valkyrie," Skuld panted to Aric after they had finished their practice. "This is such an amazing opportunity! How can you pass up a chance like this?"

Aric paused and looked up from his work. They had found some arrows on the Jotnar but they were too large for his bow, so he cut them down and scavenged the broken ones for parts. All told, he would have an additional eleven complete arrows to add to his meager arsenal.

"You know, you don't look like any valkyrie that I've ever seen," Aric said in reply.

"And exactly how many valkyries have you seen?" Brunhilda said, her brows arched and a smirk on her lips as she wiped the sweat from her forehead.

"I see—I saw one every year in Murtrborg," he said with a darkened expression. "There was always at least one in attendance at our Wodensdaeg festival."

"What's a Murtrborg?"

"It's the village where I'm from." When she gave no sign of recognition he added, "Where I pulled you from the fjord and saved your life."

"There is no chance in all of the nine realms that a valkyrie, an actual valkyrie, attended a festival in some tiny, remote human village on the farthest edge of nowhere," she scoffed with such disdain and certainty that Aric stopped fiddling with his arrows. "Less than fifty valkyries serve in the entire Aesir Army. We are the best of the best and have more important matters to attend to."

"But she had armor and a sword with the valkyrie's crest, a sword crossed with a spear flanked by two swans."

"Like this?" she drew her sword and thrust the pommel out to Aric's face for closer inspection.

"Y-Yes," he said with only a little conviction. "I mean, I think so. Gythja Hege said—"

"I think I can clear this up," Skuld said sheepishly. Her interruption was so graceful and forceful that they both fell silent. "As you know," she continued, "I traveled with a minstrel troupe—"

Aric's brows knitted as he listened.

"—and the smaller towns and villages would hire us to perform plays and sing songs during those festivals." An apologetic smile curled at her lips and she held up her hands in a placating gesture.

"Oh no," Aric whispered. He already had his face buried in his hands.

"But to add to the legitimacy and... well, *authenticity*," Skuld said, cringing at the word, "of the festivities, we also pose as Aesir... as valkyries."

"Is there nothing true about the gods?" he yelled into his hands. "I didn't think that it was possible for me to lose any more faith in the Aesir." Even muffled by his palms his voice audibly cracked, and he gulped for air, his throat convulsing.

Skuld softened and placed a hand on his shoulder. "It's not—" She paused, searching for the right words. "We weren't trying to trick you. The Aesir really do so much for us, for the nine realms, but they can't be everywhere. They can't do everything. Sometimes the gods need a little help, and so we help them."

Aric shrugged off her hand and stumbled away in a daze.

"Let him calm down," Brunhilda said, taking hold of Skuld's arm as she moved to follow. "This is good. He needs to know that the Aesir have limitations, that we're not omnipotent. He'll come back."

———

"So you're really headed into Jotunheim, huh?" Skuld asked after Brunhilda had related her story. Though she had proven to be very helpful, Brunhilda still suspected that there was something not quite right about her. On the other hand, they had begun to bond over their love of fighting and all things Aesir. Still, Brunhilda kept the destination and purpose of her mission secret.

Aric had returned well into the evening. By then the moon had come out and illuminated the clouds, giving the forest an ethereal patina. He remained sullen and distant, and sat apart from them, making a show of continuing work on the arrows.

"That's going to be a pretty rough trek," Skuld said to Brunhilda. "You won't likely find much help from the Jotnar with your peoples at war." After a moment of thought, she said, "It's a little out of the way, but you should definitely come with me to that hidden human settlement. They might have some supplies for you to stock up on."

"If that place isn't just another made up story," Aric said aloud, with a scowl.

"It does seem unlikely that there's a secret village unknown to Asgard. The nine realms work because all of the villages and realms do their part to contribute to the greater—" Brunhilda could feel Aric's icy glare without even turning around.

"Oh, it's real," Skuld said with a knowing nod before adding softly, "I just don't know exactly where it is."

Brunhilda shot her a questioning look.

"It's not as if they have road signs or make maps to hidden villages," she said with a shrug.

"So we're just supposed to wander around the Svelbjarg Mountains until we happen upon a hidden village?" Aric had stopped working on his arrows and just stared at her.

"Not exactly." Skuld said with a whisper and cupping her hand at her mouth. "In my travels throughout Midgard I've heard many a tale of a hidden human settlement. Nestled in the Svelbjarg mountains a roost of great falcons marks their secret valley, and runes carved into the living trees point the way to the entrance for those wily enough to decipher them."

"Well, that sounds like a load of auroch dung," Aric said. "Are we supposed to check every tree for runes?"

"If we see a flight of great falcons circling nearby," she added with a wink and a smile.

Aric rolled his eyes and returned to his arrows.

Brunhilda frowned. "We can't go back to Isabrot Pass, so our only other path north is to follow the mountains to the sea anyway. We'll keep an eye out for trees with runes and falcons circling overhead as we go." To Skuld she added, "Besides, it'd be a shame for us to have saved you only for you to die or be captured before making it to your destination."

"And I thank you for that," Skuld said with a low, formal bow. "For your aid I insist on paying for any and all supplies that you may require. I may have not made it out of Birgjavale with much, but whatever coin I have is yours."

146

"I assure you that the Aesir are grateful for your generosity, and when my mission is completed, you will be well compensated," Brunhilda replied.

"If you're both finished now, I suggest we get a good night's rest," snapped Aric. He turned away and mumbled something under his breath about falcons. Aloud he added, "I'll take the first watch."

"I think he's still upset about the Wodensdaeg valkyrie thing," Skuld whispered to Brunhilda.

"He just needs more time," Brunhilda replied under her breath. "After all that he lost, he doesn't like it when I talk about the Aesir. Let's just get some rest."

—

The clouds continued to filter the light into a uniform and gauzy illumination. Aric looked about and guessed that it was near midday. He focused on pulling the sled and taking each step, one at a time, to keep his mind from wandering—a task that would be infinitely easier if Skuld were not blabbering in a near unbroken stream of thoughts and observations. For someone who had seen as much death as she had, her attitude was oddly chipper.

"Though I've only been to Asgard a handful of times, each time I'm amazed by its beauty," Skuld said while helping him pull the sled that Brunhilda rested on. It had taken a lot of arguing, but Aric and Skuld were able to convince her that it'd be best if she were rested in case they needed to fight. "I mean, they created the nine realms, and you can see the splendor of their craftsmanship in every mountain and forest and fjord. Seeing their city is simply breathtaking. It really leaves a person speechless."

"I'd like to see that," said Aric in a low voice.

"After the Aesir put down this little war, I'm sure Brunhilda will take us both to see the hidden gems of the city," she continued in a cheerful tone. "I remember the Wodensdaeg celebrations in Birgjavale. They were always so magnificent. Odin himself once presided over the festival, and I swear that flowers floated down from the sky." She looked up as if she expected flowers to shower on

147

them at that very moment. After a pause when nothing happened, she turned to Aric with a smile on her face and asked, "What were your festivals like, Aric?"

"Was it really Odin or just some mummer dressed as him?" Remembering the last celebration was painful, and he wanted to avoid talking about it.

Skuld paused as she considered his quip. "I know that you think they've let you down, but just try to remember how much the Aesir have done for the world. The land used to be overrun by terrible monsters and lawlessness. Even after the first war with the Jotnar nation, the Aesir showed mercy in accepting their surrender and giving them land to live in. What's happening now... it's not their fault, they are trying to protect us—"

"Please, stop talking," Aric said, cutting her off. "I've lost more than you could possibly begin to understand. I'll help, but I don't have to like it, and nothing that you say is going to change how I feel. If I saw Odin, Thor, Baldur, Freya, or any of them, I'd spit in their face. Yes, the Aesir provided the land, provided all we needed, but we still tithed our share to them, didn't we? And when we could have used that extra, when they abandoned us, what did we have then?" His voice was strained and cracked. "No, I'm done talking about this. Go help Brunhilda, I'm sure she's eager to get up and stretch. I'll pull the sled by myself."

A look of disappointment clouded her face, but Skuld handed over the other strap and fell back to walk beside the sled with Brunhilda.

"Don't take it personally," Brunhilda said as they trudged along covering their tracks as they went. "He's not blaming you personally. He's still coping with his loss."

Aric ignored them focusing his thoughts to their surroundings. It had become difficult to tell if it would snow or not just from looking at the sky. The clouds were always present, threatening to storm. If they were lucky, a fresh dusting of snow would come and help to further conceal their tracks. As it was, their current efforts would make their tracks hard to spot, though it would not be so difficult for a skilled tracker.

—

148

"If he could just see the majesty of Asgard, I'm sure he'd gain a new perspective on all of this. They aren't perfect, but they've done amazing things," Skuld said to Brunhilda. "He's helping you out. At least that's a start."

"Reluctantly. Maybe if he saved the lives of Odin and the others, then he'd feel obligated to all of us," joked Brunhilda.

"I can hear you," Aric called back in annoyance.

"Yes, but you are Aesir. Shouldn't you be able to better explain the ways of the world to him?" asked Skuld, lowering her voice to a whisper.

"He's not ready yet," Brunhilda mused aloud. "Humans think of death in different terms from the way we do. I think being an Aesir gives me a skewed perspective. You would probably have better luck explaining things from a human's point of view. We all live in the same world, but I'm just beginning to understand that our experiences are completely different."

"You're not saying that the Aesir are to blame, are you?" Skuld asked, her lips drawn tight, brow furrowed, and voice severe.

"No," Brunhilda said quickly. "No, it's just that things are not as simple as I used to think. It doesn't matter now." She waved her hand as if to dispel the thought. "I just know that things aren't perfect. It will take all of us working together to ensure that something like this doesn't happen again."

—

"She was here not long ago," Skrymir said as he examined the abandoned little shack in Murtrborg. They had traveled for days following the Calder River looking for signs of the valkyrie along either bank. The debris from the avalanche could be found even this far out.

"Are you sure she wasn't just washed out to sea?" asked a skeptical Hrym. *"It doesn't seem likely that she survived the avalanche much less the rapids leading out here."*

"Ever the skeptic, Hrym." Skrymir unsheathed his frost knife and touched the floor of the hovel eliciting a dim spark. *"There are traces of Reginvald here. It's very faint though. She's got a couple of days' lead*

and help from whoever lived here, but she's injured. They're heading north and they'll probably stay off the roads. We'll catch them."

"*Very well,*" Hrym conceded, and whistled to gather the others. Along with Geir, four other Jotnar had been recruited for the task of hunting down this valkyrie. Hrym had taken everyone left from Isabrot. "You heard him," he said with a glint in his eyes. "We're on the hunt!"

CHAPTER 24: MAKING FRIENDS

By the fourth day after meeting Skuld, Aric was in an exceedingly foul mood and rebuked all attempts at conversation. He went off on his own to search for the hidden village whenever they stopped. Twice they had spotted birds in the sky that could have been falcons. Both times they had searched and found nothing.

From what they could tell, they were nearing the end of the Svelbjarg Range, so if this village indeed existed, it had to be nearby. Once again they saw a bird soaring overhead, but it was difficult to tell if it was, in fact, a falcon, much less a great one. Brunhilda agreed to stay with the sled and keep watch while Aric and Skuld went in search of a tree with runes carved into it. They agreed to return by sundown, whether they found anything or not. Aric went to search on his own, grateful to have some respite from Skuld's incessant chatter.

Without the distractions of the others, his mind began to wander, recalling some of the fun times he'd had with Dagmaer and Una. When not doing chores they would often play hide and seek in the woods near their house. Just as he thought this, from the corner of his eye he caught a glimpse of a girl running, hiding among the trees. "Una," he breathed. A breeze blew through the branches, and the light and shadow danced across the snow and created movement among the shadows. Shaking his head, he refocused on his task, looking for runes carved onto a tree somewhere.

Minutes later, something darted just behind him, and this time he spun around to follow it. It must be a small animal, thought Aric. They had not had a successful hunt in a couple of days, and their cured meat stores were running low. Not wanting to startle whatever it was, he crouched low and ducked behind some short,

151

dense brush. With great care, Aric pulled his bow from the sling on his back and strung it. He slid an arrow from his quiver and nocked it.

As he sighted along the arrow shaft, his target came into focus. The world went quiet and his breath escaped from his lungs. His lips formed his daughter's name, but no sound came out. Somewhere in the back of his mind, he knew it was impossible. His eyes watered and vision blurred as he struggled not to blink, until finally the stinging wind forced him to rub the tears away. With a shake of the head and clear eyes, he could now see the figure was not Una. It was a young girl. The hair and silhouette were familiar, but it was not her. For that one brief moment, he felt the loss all over again. Falling to one knee, he almost dropped his bow as his breath returned. His brow was covered in sweat despite the chill and his chest tightened as he gasped for air.

Her back straightened at once. She stood upright and looked in his direction. The girl's eyes rested upon him for a moment before she made to leave.

"Wait," he called, but his entreaty was too late as she bounded off. After a second's hesitation, he gave chase.

The girl appeared to be quite adept at moving through the snow without leaving a trace. So obscure were her tracks that Aric still was not certain that he had seen a real person and not a spirit or illusion of his mind. After getting turned around a few times, he found that he was lost, had even lost his own tracks among the low brambles.

"Who are you?" The voice was quiet, just above a whisper. The still, crisp air carried it so that Aric thought that the sound came from the snow itself.

"I'm Aric," he whispered in turn, still not sure that he was not hallucinating. "My friends and I have traveled a long way. We're looking for a place to rest and get some supplies."

There was a short pause. "Your friends look dangerous." Aric turned in place, slow and methodical, looking for the source of the voice in the deep shadows of the woods.

"They're friendly enough once you get to know them," he offered. "We're trying to get away from the fighting in the south." While not entirely a lie, it was not quite the whole truth. But the whole truth was a long story, and the details of Brunhilda's mission were confusing even to Aric.

"You should go," the voice said.

"Wait, please," he said, imploring. "My friend, the one with the red hair, she's hurt. I'm worried that she won't last long if we don't find a place to rest." His words hung in the cold air, unanswered. "Please, we've lost so many people... We're not here to cause problems. We just need a little help."

Moments passed by without any response. As Aric started to move back toward where he hoped the sled was, a small figure emerged from the tree well of a nearby spruce. She was slight and young, but otherwise healthy. He had never seen her before, yet Aric thought that she looked as Una might have, if she had lived to be sixteen. The young girl glided through the snow, leaving almost no trace. Aric could now see that she wore broad-soled boots that kept her from sinking into the snow and that her heavy, oversized animal hide cloak dragged behind and smoothed over her footsteps and the bounce of her gait broke up the drag marks.

"I'm Lif," she said in a strong, quiet voice as she looked Aric square in the eye. If she had been hiding out of fear, it did not show now. At her belt she carried a black, glassy hunting knife made from knapped obsidian. She had a couple of dead hares tied to her belt as well.

"Thank you for helping," Aric stammered. He turned his head left then right, "Uh, can you take us back to my friends?"

Lif said nothing as she turned and headed off in the opposite direction Aric had been going. Even though he was taller, he had to hurry to keep pace with her.

A short while later they found the sled where Brunhilda was practicing with her sword. Despite her obvious pain, her movements were powerful and graceful. She looked flush and was sweating profusely despite the chilled air of early evening.

"Looks like you've found a friend," she said in greeting, her sword pointed at Lif. Lif gave Aric a look of concern but did not back down or recoil.

"Put that away," Aric said hurriedly, placing his hand on Brunhilda's sword arm. "This is Brunhilda," he said to Lif. "She's not feeling well. And this is Lif." He gestured toward the young girl to Brunhilda. "She's agreed to lead us to her village."

"I'm pleased to meet you, Lif," Brunhilda said with a slight inclination of her head as she sheathed her sword. Lif just stared at her until Brunhilda turned back to Aric.

"Is Skuld back?"

"Not yet, but the sun is near setting, so she should be back soon."

"Can you find the way in the dark?" he asked Lif. She gave a single nod in reply. "Well then, when Skuld returns we'll all go together."

Brunhilda panted with labored breaths as she walked back. Aric dropped his bow and quiver as he hurried to offer her some support which she ignored. Picking up the quiver, Lif examined the arrows made from the scavenged Jotnar materials. She ran her thumb along the edge of the metal arrowhead.

"She doesn't talk much, does she," Brunhilda whispered aside to Aric. She sat with a heavy thud upon the sled.

"It wouldn't appear so," he whispered back, "but she does want to help. She could have left me lost out there, but she came out of hiding to guide me back here."

"Just as well. Skuld speaks enough for two," Brunhilda chuckled.

CHAPTER 25: COMRADES IN ARMS

"What do we actually know about him?" Geir whispered to Hrym as they trekked north.

"Not much, Geir," Hrym replied. "Not much at all."

"I don't trust him," Geir said with menace. "There is something peculiar about him and he openly questions both you and Suttungr."

"We'll keep a close eye on him. If he steps out of line again, I'll gut him myself," Hrym said, a wicked smirk curling the edges of his mouth. Though Hrym spoke softly, the deep bass of his voice carried in the still air. "But he's got a talent for this so we'll use him for as long is necessary." At this Geir smirked as well. They had found the sled ruts and footprints leading away from the fjord easily enough. At first Hrym had suspected a ruse, for the trail was not well hidden. Skrymir's theory was that the valkyrie was too injured and rushed to hide the tracks.

The foothills of the Svelbjarg Mountains were far milder than the harsh weather of Jotunheim. So even with a light dusting of new snow, these conditions were trivial to the Jotnar and so they made rapid progress at first. But after the first few days the tracks simply disappeared. The ruts in the snow ran straight into a patch of brush and did not emerge from the other side. They had spent the remainder of the afternoon searching until Skrymir had picked up the trail again. Four days in and this had become routine. Even the most minute details did not escape his sharp eyes.

"How did you become so skilled at this?" Hrym asked after the third time the Jotnar had picked up the valkyrie's tracks.

Skrymir grunted. *"I grew up in Nordbroddr. We had to learn these things to survive. Spotting vargr tracks before they found mine kept me alive. All children there were taught that early on."*

"Impressive," Hrym replied with a thoughtful nod. *"You must have been pretty tough to survive up there. Of course, the cruelty of nature pales in comparison to the cruelty of the Aesir. I lived in Isabrot, near the pass. We saw all of the Jotnar taken to work as slaves in Asgard. We saw them come back broken, if they came back at all."* Hrym looked down at his hands, he saw the bloody face of a female Jotnar, cradled in his arms; the small arms of a child. The screams as he tried to wake his mother echoed in his ears even now. Standing straight he dusted some snow from his shoulders and his voice was strong again. *"I was fortunate enough to have been working on the fortifications of Isabrot Pass when Suttungr came. He freed me from the Aesir whips. I owe him my loyalty… and my life."*

"You misunderstand. Life in Nordbroddr wasn't about me," Skrymir said. *"Our survival, our prosperity, came from the shared strength of our community. The Aesir prize individual achievement and try to break us by keeping us in these small, scattered towns. But we worked together to survive in Nordbroddr, to turn Niflheim into a home, and now to defeat the Aesir. We look out for each other and we honor our people, our culture. The Aesir banned it, but in our homes we spoke Jotunmal, we kept our heritage alive…"*

He trailed off as a look of confusion darkened his face, and he stopped abruptly. The tracks had vanished again near a small clearing.

Skrymir searched as usual and even drew his frost knife and poked about, its blade giving off a distinctive blue glow. The others stood idly by, waiting.

"I think he's run out of luck," Geir stated with a self-satisfied smirk.

"If he's run out of luck, then so have we," Hrym reproached Geir with a scowl. "Spread out and look for any sign of them!"

Skrymir rushed about, back and forth, following the frost knife like some sort of divining rod. *"This isn't right,"* he mumbled, his eyes darted back and forth as if he were expecting an ambush any second.

"What's the problem?" Hrym asked, his voice lowered to a whisper. He drew his sword. *"They've hidden their tracks before."*

"It's not that, it's this," Skrymir said, running the dagger along the surface of the snow. In his light grip the blade bounced and skipped without penetrating into the drift.

"I don't see any signs of Aesir magic," Hrym said in confusion. He

was looking to see the same gold sparks Skrymir had shown them before. *"It's just blue."*

"That's because it's Ethlivald," Skrymir replied, sheathing the blade. *"Not enough to react violently with my knife, but it was used here."*

Hrym raised his brows in mild bewilderment. *"Well,"* he said after a moment's consideration, *"we are fairly close to the Svelbjarg Mountains. There are bound to be some Jotnar out here. Deserters or others who had escaped the Aesir resettlement of Jotunheim."*

"This is no coincidence," Skrymir said with conviction. *"Ethlivald was used to blanket the ground in frost and cover all tracks."*

"Any Jotnar aiding the enemy deserves a slow and painful death," Hrym said, gesturing with his sword.

"We do not kill our own," Skrymir said with fire in his eyes and power in his voice. Standing to his full height, he remained physically dwarfed by Hrym's massive frame. Yet just as before, he exuded something beyond mere physical stature.

Hrym was undaunted. *"Death to Aesir collaborators,"* he said in a rumbling growl through clenched teeth. The threat in his voice was as plain as the dark blue fur on his face.

"Over here!" Geir shouted in the distance. Hrym and Skrymir glared at each other for a second longer before they went to Geir, who was waving and pointing at a notch in a tree made by a blade of some kind. A little farther away, one of the other scouts shouted and waved having uncovered two dead Jotnar buried in a snow drift.

"Perhaps they used the Jotnar blood to freeze the area and cover their tracks," Skrymir speculated aloud. "It's clear that these two were killed elsewhere." He gave the area a cursory evaluation. "Probably the clearing there, and then their bodies were hidden here."

"Maybe," Hrym conceded. He felt that Skrymir had almost stepped out of line. And his defense of possible Aesir collaborators gnawed at Hrym.

"There are only two ways to get north of the Svelbjarg Mountains," said Skrymir. "Isabrot Pass or the sea."

"Isabrot is back to the east," Hrym said with a smug expression. "And since they haven't gotten past us, it appears that we'll be heading west."

CHAPTER 26: HODDMIMIS HOLT

The entrance to the valley was hidden by a series of ridges and blind turns in a remote region of the Svelbjarg Range. Lif led the way, followed by Brunhilda, then Aric pulling the sled, and finally Skuld bringing up the rear and masking the evidence of their passing. The way was so well hidden that Brunhilda would have been sure they were lost if not for Lif walking with confidence in front of them. And even she might have been an apparition, for she walked so light atop the snow that she left no footprints. Brunhilda questioned if her fever had, in fact, broken, or if this was all part of some delirium brought on by infection.

As they emerged from the pass she was sure that she was back in Aric's hut hallucinating under a mound of warm furs. What they saw was a geological marvel—a lush caldera tucked away in the middle of the mountains. Enclosed by the steep ridges of the surrounding Svelbjarg Mountain Range, it stood in stark contrast to the dead lands they had just left. The moon remained hidden behind the clouds, yet its light bathed the area with a dim, cool illumination. Mists from the myriad hot springs gave the cluster of rustic, wooden buildings of the small village an otherworldly, dreamlike appearance. The wave of pungent, sulfurous air broke that illusion and grounded this all firmly in reality.

"Incredible," said Skuld, abruptly ending her most recent ramblings about the majesty of the nine realms. Only in the ensuing silence did Brunhilda realize that she had not noticed Skuld's prattling.

"Lif, is that you?" A watchman approached, carrying a lantern in one hand and in the other a staff with a sling blade attached to the end. Brunhilda kept her eyes on him although did not so much as move her hand to her sword hilt. He wielded the weapon like a halberd, though to her it looked more like a farming tool.

"Hi Elof," Lif said.

Elof gave Brunhilda and the others a questioning look and asked Lif, "You going to take them to meet with Gothi Frode in the morning?"

Lif nodded once, tossed the watchman one of her hares, and continued past. Brunhilda, Aric, and Skuld just followed her lead and pulled the sled with their supplies on it down into the lush valley. The watchman shrugged and walked back to the warm, glowing brazier that served as his outpost. He leaned his sling blade against a nearby tree with a crude iron bell and watched the quartet make their way to the valley below.

Lif led them to a small storage hut where they were to stay for the night. Sacks of grain and other supplies were piled in orderly stacks inside. They promptly took some straw packed into a corner and spread it out on the ground. Brunhilda collapsed onto the makeshift nest and passed into immediate unconsciousness. She barely heard Skuld ask Lif for some basic herbs and medicines.

Shortly after midnight, Brunhilda's fever broke and she finally eased into a peaceful slumber.

—

In the caldera the sky was bright long before the light spilled over the eastern ridge. The same clouds that covered the sky elsewhere covered the valley here as well. However, there was a difference in the quality of the light that helped this valley to feel brighter and more hopeful than the morose gray of the world beyond the surrounding ridges. The day enhanced the vibrant green of the lush vegetation to a spectacular degree. But the bucolic serenity was marred by the pungent tang in the air.

Lif arrived just after dawn to gather the group. Aric and Brunhilda were fully rested while Skuld retained her cheerful disposition despite not having slept as much as the others. As they walked in line behind Lif, they marveled at the incredible sights around them. Here it seemed as if the catastrophic winter of the last three years had never occurred. Skuld was full of questions that she felt no compunction in holding back. Lif maintained her taciturn demeanor and saw fit to ignore all of them.

The village was small, with no more than two dozen homes and additional structures. All of the dwellings were simple and solidly built. There did not appear to be any large dwelling or other building that would signify the home of a leader. They passed by the great hall, now empty. It seemed as if they had missed breakfast. Brunhilda thought they might be taken to the other large structure to have an audience with the town leader, but instead the building turned out to be a barn of sorts for some of their domesticated animals. They walked beyond the buildings to where most of the villagers appeared to be; the fields were abuzz with people tending crops or herding animals. They stopped short when they neared an elderly farmer checking the soil near some anemic barley plants.

"So these are our visitors, Lif?" he said as he stood up. Though considerably older than Aric, he had the bearing and power in his frame of a much younger man. He was simply attired and wore the dust and dirt of the field with a quiet nobility.

Lif nodded.

"Welcome to Hoddmimis Holt," he said grasping each of their hands in turn. "I'm Frode, the gothi of our little village."

"Gothi Frode," Brunhilda began in earnest, "I am Brunhilda, first shield valkyrie. I'm on a mission for the Aesir. We require supplies and provisions."

"I can offer coin to cover the costs," Skuld offered quickly.

Frode held up a hand. "Please," he responded, "we welcome you as guests, but we have limited resources. And your coin is of little use here."

"Aren't you're a gothi? Surely duty to the Aesir is enough to warrant your aid," Brunhilda said, a note of irritation creeping into her voice.

"'Gothi' is simply a title that we use here. We've had no connection with the Aesir or the other realms for generations. But you misunderstand me," Frode continued in a stern yet still friendly tone. "We cannot simply sell you supplies; what need have we of money out here? Neither can we give you any excess since we have none. I know we may appear to be prosperous, but we have to work the land hard just to survive. Despite the fertility of this valley, we have little to spare. Perhaps with your added labor, we may reap enough to accommodate your needs. We are nearing the harvest, and if your aid helps us to gather extra then you are welcome to it."

"We don't have the time to work the land," Brunhilda said with visible frustration. "There is a war raging out there right now and the longer we waste here, the more our people are dying."

"And how long do you think you'd survive out there in your condition?" Moving faster than he looked capable of, he gave her a light tap to her injured shoulder and another punch to her solar plexus. Despite her fever having broken, Brunhilda was still quite weak and slow in reacting to the attack. The two blows dropped her to the ground gasping for breath. Lif's expression did not betray concern or surprise at this.

"She'll be fine," Frode said, holding his hands up to Aric and Skuld who already had her sword halfway out of its scabbard. "It was just a demonstration of her current weaknesses."

"It was a sucker punch," coughed Brunhilda as she picked herself up from the ground, fists clenched. Aric and Skuld helped her to her feet while also restraining her from lunging at him.

"While you take some time to convalesce, your friends can help out with our labors." He placed a hand on Lif's shoulder and said, "Lif will explain the work that you two will be doing."

162

CHAPTER 27: HALCYON DAYS

It was almost like a normal life again. At least it was for Aric. Brunhilda noted how well he took to the work and fell into the routine of this domestic life. He relished in the simple straw bed that they had provided, and even she had to admit that it was comfortable. It had been far too long since they had slept in a proper bed. Every morning they rose at dawn and ate a simple, hearty breakfast with the other villagers before beginning a long day of tough labor: tending to crops and to animals, mending fences, carrying water, cleaning out animal pens, and all of the mundane chores of farm life. They began with the harvesting of a large field of barley. That first day's labor was difficult for Brunhilda. Not only were her stamina and mobility limited, she was also dismayed to find these stalks small, providing a paltry yield. At this rate it would take them another full harvest cycle to scrounge up extra food from these plants.

Skuld, however, tended the crops with great success. Although she reaped the same fields, she somehow finished the day with three times as much grain as anyone else. Despite the ease to which she took to this lifestyle, she was restless and spoke often of the outside world, especially when she spent time with Brunhilda. They whiled away the evenings together practicing swordplay as Brunhilda's strength and flexibility gradually improved. The village healer also tended to Brunhilda's injuries with various herbs and poultices. Their main treatment, however, was to have her soak in the boiling sulfur hot springs, which Brunhilda learned to enjoy after a hard day's labor.

—

At dawn of their fifth morning, Brunhilda accompanied Lif on her daily expedition to check traps and hunt for game. Large animals were nonexistent in the area and the smaller animals were scarce, but any success meant a welcome variety to the villagers' diet. Successful or not, Brunhilda relished the opportunity to stretch her muscles and test her limits; the medicines and hot springs having significantly improved her physical condition.

"Do you always go alone?" she asked Lif. A shiver ran down her spine once they left the comfort and warmth of Hoddmimis Holt and the cold air hit her face. Brunhilda was dressed in simple garb—a tunic and trousers with boots and wrapped up in her Jotnar-made auroch fur cloak, her sword on her hip. It was not effective for hunting but she never went anywhere without it. Lif was similarly outfitted but with a plain knife and bow, and an oversized cloak that dragged on the snow as she walked. She showed no reaction to the cold and simply nodded. "Thank you for letting me come along," Brunhilda continued. "Farming and sitting around in hot springs all day is driving me mad." What she did not say aloud was that all of that time spent alone brought her thoughts to Skogul and Hilder. As Aesir they were taught to celebrate glorious death on the field of battle. Now, however, away from all of adrenaline and excitement of combat, she realized just how much she missed her comrades... her friends.

As they walked, Brunhilda kept her mind to tracking and hunting, and experimentally rolled her shoulders and stretched her aching limbs. Her left leg was stiff, and she had to be careful to avoid pulling at her stitches. She also felt soreness in her right shoulder when she raised her arm above her head. Even without her armor, she did not have full range of movement yet, and it annoyed her.

They walked along in silence, checking the various snares that Lif had set. A few were sprung and needed to be repaired or reset, the animal tracks long since grown cold. All were empty.

Brunhilda put her finger to her lips and motioned to Lif. The girl nodded in response, her keen eyes having spotted the same thing. Near one of the tripped snares was a set of fresh snowshoe hare tracks. They followed, winding their way through the low scrub brush.

Eventually they came upon a dense bush laden heavy with

snow to where the tracks disappeared. Communicating through hand gestures, Lif nocked her arrow and drew in anticipation as Brunhilda approached, ready to flush their quarry. In a puff of snow, the hare suddenly bolted from the bush, running straight at her. It darted past, slipping between her legs, just as Lif loosed her arrow, almost hitting Brunhilda. Lif swiftly drew again and fired another arrow. This time she hit the scurrying creature through the neck, killing it instantly.

"Thanks for not shooting me," Brunhilda said as she gave Lif back the first arrow.

"Sorry," she mumbled, avoiding eye contact. She fidgeted with the bow in her left hand while she took the arrow with her right.

"Not used to hunting with others, are you?"

Lif shrugged in response.

"Not to worry," Brunhilda said, and tousled her hair with a sincere smile. "This wasn't the first and certainly won't be the last time someone shoots an arrow at me."

Together they retrieved the hare and removed the arrow. Brunhilda looped a leather thong around the animal's legs and hung it on her belt at her right hip. On the other side she wore her valkyrie sword, the pommel reflecting in the muted light. Brunhilda caught Lif gazing at it.

"You know," Brunhilda said, placing her hand on the pommel, "I was probably about your age when I first began training with the Aesir Army. I can teach you some things if you'd like. You're welcome to join myself and Skuld before supper when we practice."

Lif's eyes went from the sword to meet Brunhilda's eyes and she nodded once.

———

The evenings saw the three outsiders slowly building a rapport with the locals. Lif now spent the majority of her time with Brunhilda, hunting and checking traps, taking her to their healers and to the therapeutic mineral baths, and training with her and Skuld in the evenings. Brunhilda would talk about hunting, fighting, and life in

Asgard while Lif listened with rapt attention.

Brunhilda noticed Skuld had developed a mutual respect with Frode as she learned of the egalitarian structure of their village. They all shared in the duties and responsibilities of governance. It was interesting to see that for these people, the less they had, the more they shared. Though they kept many of the customs and rules of the nine realms, they had created their own life apart from that world, eschewing their benefits but also many of their problems. She engaged many of the residents in lively, civil debates about the strengths and weaknesses of their ideologies. Though neither were swayed by the other's arguments, Brunhilda could tell they gained a healthy respect for one another.

But Aric kept mostly to himself. His diligent work ethic brought respect from those he labored beside. While they dined together and conversed genially, he always seemed distant, his mind elsewhere. During their days in the fields Skuld often tried to strike up a conversation with him, but each attempt had been met with curt, one-word answers, if he replied at all.

—

The days settled into a comfortable and familiar rhythm. A week after their arrival the barley harvest was coming to an end and much more had been reaped than expected, leaving everyone in a pleasant mood. As they walked back amidst pockets of cheerful conversations, Skuld began to hum. The tune had an inkling of familiarity to all who could hear her. Gradually the melody grew in intensity and she began to sing, her voice clear and pure.

At first the words seemed strange to Aric, like an unfamiliar language. As the song continued though, he began to recognize the melody and the lyrics. Looking around he could see that same wave of comprehension wash over everyone else. It was as if she were singing to each and every one of them.

> Summer is ending
> We have planted and played
> Winter still slumbers
> Look at all we have made

Oh hark and be glad
Bright birds fly and fish splash
We reap the harvest
Wodensdaeg's come at last

Come friends and fam'ly
Come bounty of the year
Odin favors us
And brings to us great cheer

Celebrate as one
Bright birds fly and fish splash
Asgard smiles on all
Wodensdaeg's come at last

For Aric, images of clear water, silver beaches, and a balmy sun came unbidden to his mind. The warmth of hearth and home was almost tangible, though not from any external source. The heat seemed to spread from within himself. And though he did not see them, he felt as if he could feel the presence of Una and Dagmaer lingering just beyond his sight.

As the final words faded away on the lilting breeze they all blinked and came to as if waking from a dream. They applauded and a lightness of heart permeated the crowd, and friendly conversations began in earnest as everyone complimented Skuld on the beauty of her voice—almost everyone. Aric's gaze was turned to the ground, his breathing ragged and tears streaming down his face. He hurried on ahead of the crowd with a quickened pace.

—

Things were different as everyone gathered for the dinner that evening. Everyone was in the great hall as usual, pooling all of the resources they had gathered during the day: crops from the fields; eggs, meat, and milk from the chickens and goats; clothes and textiles; even firewood to stoke the hearth and cooking fires. But after everyone had eaten, Skuld rose and began to sing. These songs were traditional folk music of the southern regions of Midgard. And though not so penetrating or haunting as her first song, they enraptured the people of Hoddmimis Holt. After a long day of toil, they found new life and energy after her performances. Their hunched shoulders relaxed and their faces brightened as they engaged in conversation with each other instead of trudging home immediately.

Every evening after that they came together for supper in this new way. And although Skuld sang each time, she also invited others to participate and sing their own songs.

"Thank you for your hospitality," Skuld said, approaching Frode after her performance on the ninth day since their arrival. He was standing near the doorway of the great hall enjoying the camaraderie of the gathering. "We endured a great deal of pain and suffering along our journey and are truly grateful for this sanctuary."

"We should be thanking you," said Frode a warm and sincere smile on his lips. "This harvest has been our biggest ever, and your singing has brought cheer and happiness to our community. I don't think I've seen Lif smile since her parents died. But she smiles with a genuine lightness when you sing."

"This is quite a wonderful place that you have here," Skuld said as she gestured to the valley beyond the door. "I came here seeking simple shelter; instead I think I've found something more."

"You are more than welcome to stay and join us," Frode said, placing a hand upon her shoulder. "We would be honored to have you."

Skuld smiled and nodded in appreciation but said nothing as she walked out of the doorway into the pleasant evening air.

—

She followed a trail of footprints to one of the smaller, less frequented hot springs and found Aric sitting there, silently staring at his hands. Steam rolled off of the surface of the water, shrouding him in mist. The stars and moon were visible in the caldera tonight, its sky occasionally free from the persistent cloud cover that blanketed the rest of Midgard.

"Why didn't you stay for the rest of the songs?" Skuld asked.

"Do I sing so poorly that you can't stand to listen?"

She waited as he sat in silence, unmoving. But as she turned to go, Aric finally spoke.

"You sing beautifully," he said in a barely audible whisper, not looking at her.

"I'm just trying to bring a little joy and lightness here," she said.

"After all that we've been through and with all that these people have done for us, it's a touching and generous gift that you give."

"So why do you leave? Why don't you stay for the songs? I see you leave each night, in a hurry to go before you've barely finished eating. Is it so bad to feel happy, if only for a short while?"

Aric's mouth opened and closed several times. It almost looked like he was trying to remember the mechanics of how to speak. He closed his eyes and took a deep breath. "This should have been their life," he whispered. Turning to Skuld he held her gaze for a long moment. "Why would the Aesir take them and allow *me* to live?"

It felt like an eternity before she spoke. "You shouldn't be asking why," she said as she put a hand on his shoulder. "That won't change the past or make the future any brighter. Rather, you should keep them in your thoughts and consider how your actions will honor them. If they had survived and you had died, would you wish for them to live on in such grief and despair?"

He stared at her silently before she turned and walked back toward the village, softly humming a familiar melody.

CHAPTER 28: BACK INTO THE FIGHT

"Finally!" Gunnar shouted. Herding and guarding refugees had been tedious and frustrating for her. This final group was well on its way when the scouts signaled the approaching Jotnar Army. She had been itching for a stand-up fight, not against mere foot soldiers. Now her wish was granted as she spotted Suttungr through the chaos of the battlefield. He had been elusive since Halvard, though they suspected his presence at every Jotnar victory that left no Aesir survivors.

After ensuring the civilian leaders would keep the people moving south, Gunnar rallied her battalion into an offensive formation. The modest village of Hofborg had no fortifications and they were outnumbered, so her only available strategy was to bring the fight to Suttungr. And if she happened to kill him in the process, so much the better, she thought with a smile.

The fighting was intense and chaotic. One hundred Aesir were all that stood between the refugees and a thousand marauding Jotnar. Gunnar, flanked by her valkyries, cleaved a path through the horde. She knew that their best plan was to strike at Suttungr and force the Jotnar to his defense. Yet this course of action would put them smack in the middle, surrounded on all sides. None under her command hesitated as blood from both sides flowed freely in gouts of blue and gold.

Aesir soldiers were ingrained with the idea of glorious death in battle and were prepared to lay down their lives. And so they fought without regard for their own safety and cut a swath of death through the Jotnar host. For every Aesir who died, they killed five Jotnar. Despite those numbers, by the time Gunnar reached Suttungr there were only a dozen of her troops left.

Facing them, he raised his hand and the Jotnar soldiers encircled the Aesir but did not attack. Gunnar could only speculate why, but she would not turn down the opportunity to fight him in single combat. After Halvard's loss and Freya's death, she had been looking to bring the full wrath of the Aesir down on his head.

Pointing at Gunnar, he spoke one word: "Come."

Holding out her left arm, she waved off her soldiers. She knew that this was a trap, that he would have his magical shield in place, but in this moment she did not care. Dropping her own shield, she wrapped both hands around the hilt and ran straight at him. Gunnar was not as skilled as Thor or even Brunhilda in single combat, but what she did have was a tactical mind and centuries of experience. Having witnessed part of the fight at Halvard, she knew that a head-on attack would be folly. She feinted high and deftly moved to his legs before his blade could connect with a block. It was a simple yet effective move and should have gotten her inside of his guard, allowing her to cut into a gap in his leg armor. Instead, he countered it with ease. She pressed forward and pushed him back, though he seemed to be in control.

After a few of these dueling attacks and ripostes, Gunnar came in with a direct lunge, expecting Suttungr to block or sidestep. To her surprise he dropped his guard and moved into the line of her strike. Before she could disengage, her sword collided with his armor. The strange burst of blue and gold energy exploded as it had before in Halvard, and her sword was knocked free from her hand. When it hit the ground, the frozen blade shattered.

Gunnar's right hand was covered in a swirled block of solid ice. Before she could react, Suttungr swung his sword and cut her head clean off, her lifeless eyes saved from witnessing the ensuing massacre. The other Jotnar pounced upon the remaining Aesir, and in a matter of minutes the battle was over.

CHAPTER 29: DISCOVERED

"We're leaving before moonrise tonight," Brunhilda said abruptly, pulling Aric aside as he was returning from the fields. "Even if we haven't 'earned' our keep yet, I'm fit enough to travel, and we've wasted too much time here."

She had awoken with a start that morning, covered in sweat and short of breath despite her fever having broken days ago. Nightmarish visions of Gunnar's death and the burning wreckage of an Aesir village lingered long after waking. Aric looked as if he might argue, but then he said, "Yeah, it's time to go." He pulled away and continued walking to the great hall for supper. There was a sad, stiff aspect to his stride.

Brunhilda could sense that he wanted to say more. As she fell in beside him she said, "Listen, you've done everything that I've asked of you. Getting us this far was no small feat, considering the state you found me in." She paused and exhaled in something akin to a sigh. "This is my mission; you should stay here. This place has been good for me, and even though you try to hide it, I know that it's been good for you too."

Aric paused mid-stride. Brunhilda had seen a marked shift in his demeanor in the last few days. At first he had thrown himself into the daily tasks as if he were working to forget. But then something had changed and he had softened. And with all of the misery and suffering in the outside world this little village would be the perfect place for him to begin anew. She gave him a warm smile and pat on the shoulder as she started to walk ahead.

"What are you talking about?" Aric said, breaking the silence and catching Brunhilda by surprise. "You wouldn't make it a day out there without me. You're my responsibility now."

"Thank you," she said. There was a hint of relief or perhaps happiness in her voice, though she could not say which it was for certain. A slight smile turned up the corners of her mouth as they walked on together.

—

"Quiet night, Inge?" Elof asked as he walked up to the guard post, his sling blade resting on his shoulder.

"Yeah," came the reply from the stocky older woman who was currently stoking the brazier. "Dull as usual. Nothing ever happens here." She paused then looked back down into the valley to the great hall. "Well, except for your three visitors."

"Speaking of them, you missed some delightful songs tonight," Elof said. The serenity of the music still showed in his face. "That Skuld has a beautiful voice and she seems to know many songs and stories that I've never heard before. Next time you catch her, ask her to sing the one about Thor dressing up as Freya and—"

An arrowhead burst forth from Inge's throat, spraying blood into Elof's face. Her body dropped to her knees, limp and devoid of life, and then he saw dark figures behind her emerging from the gap. As he lunged forward to catch Inge's listing form, another arrow flew out and struck him in the right shoulder, spinning him around. Gasping, he scrambled toward the iron bell hanging in the tree. He drew back the sling blade to strike the bell with his left arm, but just as he did another arrow pierced him through the neck, and Elof crumpled into a heap on the ground, and his weapon fell from his lifeless hand.

Seven Jotnar stepped into the light of the brazier. Skrymir removed the arrows from his victims, wiped them clean, and placed them back into his quiver. Hrym stood over Elof's body and looked at the iron bell that he had been trying to reach. Down below in the caldera, warm, inviting light came from the buildings clustered below, making for a cozy, pastoral scene. Pulling the sword from his scabbard, Hrym struck the bell with his pommel, shattering the silence.

"Why'd you do that?" Skrymir asked with unmasked exasperation. His efforts to take out the guards silently had now gone to waste. He ripped the bell down and slammed it into the ground. It

173

made little difference though; the clear peal of the bell had rung out in the still night air and echoed down into the valley.

"*These are just humans,*" Hrym said, waving at the two guards dead on the ground. "*And not even soldiers. Without the two other valkyries, she doesn't stand a chance.*"

Geir stood to Hrym's right and glared at Skrymir with menace. Skrymir rolled his eyes. He knew Geir could not follow the entire discussion with his limited Jotunmal, but no matter what Skrymir said, he knew that Geir would side with Hrym.

"*We wasted so much time checking the west coast with nothing to show for it. If you hadn't stumbled across those snares and traced them here, we'd still be running around the Svelbjarg foothills like vargrs chasing their own tails,*" Hrym spoke through clenched teeth. "*I want them to suffer. I want them to fight. I want them to know that death is coming for them.*" A cruel smile curled at his lips. "*Besides, it's more fun when they're scared.*"

CHAPTER 30: SURRENDER

Aric had been securing supplies to his little sled behind the storage shed when he heard the bell first sound. "What's going on?" He emerged just in time to ask Frode as he raced by.

"Sounds like it's coming from the caldera's southern entrance," Brunhilda said as she hurried toward them, strapping on her sword and armor.

"It's the alarm," Frode said. "You should stay indoors. The last time it sounded was five years ago, when a vargr had strayed into our valley. The pattern of the ringing is supposed to let us know what's coming." Trepidation crept into his voice. "This time it just sounded once." And with that, he ran off to meet with the other villagers on watch reserve.

Brunhilda motioned for Aric to come as she followed Frode. He hastily retrieved his bow and quiver, now full of fletched arrows, from the sled. Nearby, Skuld trotted up to them with a sword in hand.

When they reached Frode and the other villagers, they could see Lif running toward them from the direction of the disturbance.

"Inge and Elof are dead," Lif called to them. "At least seven Jotnar came through the pass. They're right behind me."

"Get everyone indoors. We'll take care of the Jotnar," Brunhilda said, taking charge.

"Hold on now, this is our village," Frode said. "We've protected ourselves for generations and—"

A handful of arrows arced in and cut him off. Frode and two other villagers fell. Skuld cut one arrow out of the air while Brunhilda pushed Aric out of the way and avoided another one. The other assembled villagers scattered, screaming in panic. Aric scrambled to his feet and pulled the wounded Frode to safety, sheltered behind a large pile of logs stacked close by.

Five Jotnar burst out of the darkness, with the unmistakable frame of Hrym at the front. In the dim light they could just see menacing silhouettes adorned with the skulls and hides of beasts, their primal howls filling the air.

From farther back Skrymir shouted something in Jotunmal to Hrym while pointing at Brunhilda. Hrym did not look back or even acknowledge him; his eyes were already locked on her. Neither flinched or looked away as they drew closer. She had been waiting for this rematch since their first encounter at Halvard. This was her chance to avenge Skogul and Hilder. Brunhilda shifted the sword in her hand, its familiar weight reassuring.

Jotnar arrows were met with a return volley from behind her. That and a slight groan from Frode let her know that Aric had leapt to action and that the gothi was not dead. Having grabbed his bow and quiver, he loosed his own arrows, hitting several of the attackers. Brunhilda could see that Aric's arrows were crafted for hunting, not warfare, and had minimal impact against the armored Jotnar.

Within the first handful of minutes a dozen villagers lay dead or wounded. Brunhilda charged the final few yards at Hrym, flanked by another Jotnar. He easily blocked her thrust but his counter almost hit the other Jotnar. It was a calculated yet dangerous strategy. Brunhilda counted on their wild, undisciplined fighting style to work to her advantage. These Jotnar were not practiced at fighting together and she was determined to exploit that. With both focused on her, she had them stumbling and nearly hitting each other.

Brunhilda had another reason to keep the fighting close. Every time she tried to get some distance from them to rest the Jotnar archers fired at her. However, like a good tactician she had a plan. Lunging forward she made an exaggerated feint at Hrym and baited the other Jotnar to overcommitting to a strike. As Hrym attempted to block, Brunhilda turned on her heel, parried the thrust from the other Jotnar, and swung her blade up, separating the surprised Jotnar's head from her shoulders.

———

Meanwhile Skuld danced between Geir and the remaining two Jotnar.

Across the square Skuld's fluid movements played her opponents off of each other. She redirected the attacks of one opponent into the other. Geir was proving more difficult as he kept his distance with strategic thrusts, utilizing his spear's length advantage. In a risky gambit one of the Jotnar dashed past to flank Skuld, finding an opening in her defense. Before she could strike, Aric fired an arrow in desperation. It hit its mark and struck the Jotnar under her raised arm, causing her to drop her sword. Skuld wheeled around and landed a killing blow then gave a little wave and a wink to Aric.

From his blind Aric continued to pelt the enemy with arrows. He spotted one of the Jotnar archers break but he held his position and kept firing arrows at every opportunity. While unable to pierce the Jotnar armor, he was able to distract them at key moments, allowing some of the villagers to get away from the fighting.

"Cover us," Geir shouted over his shoulder. He and his partner broke from Skuld and ran at Aric while the Jotnar archer kept Skuld pinned down.

Aric released arrow after arrow at the two approaching enemies. Several of his barbs stuck though showed no signs of slowing them down. As they neared Aric tried to block a spear thrust that knocked his bow from his hands. He looked around frantically as he scrambled back, dodging his attackers.

Brunhilda had seen the Jotnar running for Aric and disengaged from Hrym with a well-placed kick. In a rapid succession of events, Brunhilda cut down one Jotnar and clashed with Geir. At the same time Skuld leapt forth to take on the archer, dodging and deflecting arrows as she charged.

———

Hrym brushed off the kick. He had been off balance, taking no injury other than getting knocked to the ground. As he readied to pursue Brunhilda a single arrow struck the half-skull pauldron on his right shoulder. Though it had done no damage at all, it got his attention. The shot had come from Lif who had, until then, managed to stay hidden. With a cruel smile Hrym charged at her, and in nine massive strides he closed the gap separating them.

Everything seemed to happen all at once: Skuld was mid-swing, the Jotnar archer bringing his bow up to block; Brunhilda had Geir's spear in her hand while she pulled her sword free from the other Jotnar's eviscerated gut; Aric blindly reached for his bow while unable to pull his eyes away from Lif, the Jotnar's sword already coming down.

A bright blue flare and loud crash of steel on steel rang out. Skrymir had stepped between Hrym and Lif, blocking the strike with his frost knife. The impact reverberated through the streets and left a dusting of frost over everything in the immediate area. Before anyone comprehended what had happened, Skrymir punched Hrym in the face and knocked him back.

"Leave her alone!" he said through gritted teeth.

"Have you gone mad?" shouted Hrym.

"We're not savages," Skrymir replied, leveling his blade at Hrym's exposed face. "We do not slaughter children." He spared a quick glance around. Skuld was pulling her sword from the archer, Geir was unarmed, and all of the other Jotnar lay dead. Brunhilda and the others saw what had happened and turned their attention to them. The other humans had regrouped and, though armed with mere farming implements, there were over a dozen of them. "It's over. We lost."

Hrym looked around him and saw that Skrymir spoke the truth. With a scowl, Hrym spat at him and took a step back turning to go. Then, faster than Skrymir thought possible, he continued the rotation and lashed out with his sword. Skrymir rolled with the strike as the blade cut into his right side and a spray of blue blood immediately steamed as it hit the warm air. His armor protected him against the worst of it, but Hrym's powerful stroke left a nasty wound. With that parting shot he retreated for the breach out of the caldera.

"If they don't kill you," Hrym shouted over his shoulder, "know that I will hunt you down and kill you myself!" He and Geir ran off together.

As Brunhilda, Skuld, and Aric came closer, Skrymir dropped to his knees while clutching his side, laid down his weapons, and said, "I surrender."

CHAPTER 31: THE ENEMY OF MY ENEMY

"I should be allowed to kill him!" raged Brunhilda as she paced back and forth in the village's great hall. "He's butchered many Aesir and humans and was probably the one who shot Frode!"

"He also saved Lif," Aric said, his voice meek while also filled with conviction. "That has to count for something."

"And he surrendered to us," Skuld added somewhat reluctantly. "To kill an enemy in battle is brave and honorable." Aric thought it sounded like she was quoting from some Aesir code of conduct. "Killing a defenseless foe is an act of cowardice; even this Jotnar would not tolerate it. Are you less honorable than he, Brunhilda?"

Brunhilda stared down Skuld, her jaw clenched and her fists shaking at her sides. Though he was no match for Brunhilda, Aric took a step forward as if to intervene. Without another word, Brunhilda turned on her heel, kicked open the door, and stormed out of the room.

"Well, speaking as one of the ones who were shot," said a bandaged Frode, sitting on a chair in the corner with his arm in a sling, "you both have valid points. While we've had to deal with the occasional dispute, we've never had to mete out justice on this level. And yet we cannot simply let him go. He might tell the Jotnar that we're here. It's bad enough that those other two got away."

"Perhaps those two are just waiting nearby. They might follow us if we leave soon," Aric speculated, his tone hopeful before he shook his head ruefully. He couldn't believe he was advocating being hunted down by Jotnar as a good outcome.

"They seemed intent on hunting down Brunhilda," Skuld said. "They wouldn't have strayed very far. You should be safe from them, so can't you just keep this one locked up here somewhere for the time being?"

"You've been here for a while now," Frode said. He pinched the bridge of his nose, his eyes squeezed shut. "Have you seen anything here that could serve as a prison? We're not equipped to hold anyone captive. And though I disagree with Brunhilda, there are many here who lost friends and family last night who want to see him put down." Looking Aric square in the eye, he said, "You're going to have to take him with you."

Aric, who was sitting, now stood up with his hands placating. "Now hold on a moment," he said. "It's hard enough keeping Brunhilda from killing him here; there's no way that she'd let him travel with us."

"She might, but then she'd give him a weapon and kill him in an 'honorable' duel the first chance she got," Skuld added with a shrug.

"Excuse me." The Jotnar gave a slight cough as he spoke up. "In lieu of killing me, perhaps I might offer a suggestion."

"Ah yes," Skuld said, and she walked over to him and grabbed him by the collar. In the light of day, with their prisoner securely bound and without the animal skull helmet, Aric found this Jotnar to be less frightening and, with the downy fur covering his face, almost friendly looking. "Tell us why you're chasing Brunhilda."

"Who? That angry Aesir?" He wore a feigned expression of naivete. "You should ask her."

Skuld raised her fist, ready to strike him.

"No, honestly!" he said as he flinched. "All we know is that the Aesir went to a lot of trouble to get her and two other valkyries past our defenses. We're just trying to find out why."

"That wasn't so hard now, was it?" Skuld quipped, letting him go. He fell to the ground with a thud.

"How do you know that he's telling you the truth?" Frode whispered to her.

She drew her sword in a flash, its point leveled at the Jotnar's throat before Aric could blink. "You wouldn't lie to me, would you?" The ringing of the drawn blade filled the air.

"O-Of course not, miss," he stammered with a nervous gulp.

"So," Skuld said as she sheathed her sword, "what shall we do with you?"

"Well—"

"We're not letting you go."

"Right. If I may continue?" Aric gave him a nod when Skuld did not respond. "It seems as if you're determined to travel north, into Jotunheim."

Aric looked to the door from which Brunhilda had departed and then back to the Jotnar.

He was looking at Aric now. "I can guide you through all of the hazards and pitfalls. It's very dangerous up in the north."

"She's a valkyrie," Skuld said. She turned to face him. "They're the fiercest, strongest warriors in the nine realms. She's survived tougher challenges; she doesn't need your help."

"The perils of Jotunheim aren't just vargr packs and other Jotnar, like Hrym and Geir," he offered, an earnest note in his voice. "They are the intangible dangers of exposure to the brutal cold, the lack of food, hidden crevasses. If you wish to stay off of the main roads, you'll need me to guide you. And I can go into the Jotnar cities and procure supplies without raising suspicions."

She gave him a skeptical look. "What's in it for you?"

"You mean other than your angry friend not killing me?" he said dryly. "Well, you'll have to agree not to kill any Jotnar while we're traveling through Jotunheim." He locked eyes with Aric again. "None."

Aric furrowed his brow. Although he had not killed anyone himself, he had had a hand in the deaths of several Jotnar. It would be easy enough for him to abide by that agreement. After he lost Una and Dagmaer, the mere thought of taking another's life filled him with grief and dread. Brunhilda, however, would be harder to convince.

"I want this war to end quickly just as you do. I'm not loyal to Suttungr. I think he's going too far in taking this war to Asgard. I fight to restore independence for us and to reclaim Jotunheim. Is it so much to ask that my people don't have to live as second-class citizens or slaves to the Aesir? So let me help you, and we'll all get what we want."

Aric still hesitated. The Jotnar's eyes searched his as he added,

"Nearly all of the soldiers are marching with Suttungr in the south, leaving the villagers defenseless. They are good people who aren't looking for violence."

"She wouldn't kill unarmed—"

"They will defend themselves if provoked," he cut in. "They may not have proper weapons, but we have long ago learned to use our meager tools to defend against vargr and their like. Your friend is quite a skilled warrior and would probably end up killing any and every Jotnar she runs across."

"And with your help, we'll get honest guidance?" Aric asked, and Skrymir nodded. "And in return we'll promise not to kill any Jotnar." Their prisoner raised an eyebrow and gave him a look before Aric added, "Including you." Aric exchanged looks with Skuld, who gave a curt nod in agreement.

"Tell her that I'll go with you to help keep him in line," Skuld offered.

"You can't," Aric argued. "You've already gone through too much, and you've reached your destination. This isn't your fight."

"No less than it is yours," Skuld replied. "After all we've gone through together, I'm just as invested in this as you." With a wry smile, she added, "Also, I've seen you fight. You'll need me if you get into trouble again."

"If you keep your end of the bargain, I'll keep mine," the Jotnar said as he locked his gaze on both Skuld and Aric. "My only concern is for the welfare of my people."

Aric stood silent for a few seconds and considered him and Skuld in turn. At this moment, his old life and family felt worlds away. He could scarcely comprehend the distance he had traveled from his past, both physically and emotionally. And yet he could understand this perspective, looking out for one's people.

He bent down to untie the ropes around the Jotnar's hands and legs. "My name is Aric," he said. "This is Skuld. We accept your deal."

"You may call me Skrymir," he answered, rubbing his wrists as circulation returned to his extremities. "And what of your friend, the angry one? Will she agree to these terms?"

"Brunhilda? Leave her to me," Aric said with a mixture of fatigue and hope. "It'll take some convincing, but I think I'll be able to talk her into it."

———

Aric found Brunhilda in the same spot that he had gone to when Skuld had confronted him. It looked quite different in the morning light though it was no less tranquil and beautiful. They stood for a while in silence before Aric related the deal that he had made on their behalf. She vehemently protested, but Aric put forth compelling arguments, and he knew he had won when he saw her hardened expression soften.

"I don't trust him," Brunhilda said with spite. "And I will kill him the moment when he betrays us—'when,' not 'if.'" She was right in Aric's face and jabbed her finger at his chest for emphasis. Then she turned around and walked back to the hall.

"Don't worry. If that happens, I won't stand in your way," he said as he fell into step behind her.

CHAPTER 32: STRATEGIC WITHDRAWAL

Thor's breath was labored and heavy as he knocked back three Jotnar soldiers in a single swing of the massive hammer, Mjolnir. This particular battle had neither lasted long nor been more difficult than any other. It was, however, the latest in a long, unbroken string of skirmishes over the past three weeks. After so many battles this particular fight was an indistinct blur, unremarkable from any of the others.

This Jotnar had to be the commander of this division, Thor thought with a weary sigh. He brought his hammer down, splitting the crude animal skull helmet and crushing the head within, scattering the remaining Jotnar soldiers in defeat. It was another insignificant and hollow victory without his eagerly anticipated rematch with Suttungr. Looking around at the scarred and ruined plains, he was not certain that he could call this a strategic victory. Fields once host to a vast, unending bounty were now scorched lands littered with the bodies of the fallen. Jotnar blood spilled over the lands and turned the ground to barren soil.

The Aesir troops raised a cheer as the last of the Jotnar soldiers fled back to the northeast. As the Aesir looked for survivors and tended to their wounded, Thor made his way back to camp. After most battles he would take time to celebrate with all who fought with him but the drudgery was getting to him. They had moved southwest and defeated every Jotnar battalion they encountered, with several of those turning out to be illusory legions. With no sign of Suttungr, Thor was concerned that the reports of envoys to Svartalfheim and Alfheim were ruses and their efforts were being wasted.

To his surprise, he saw Sif waiting for him as he approached the command tent. "What news, Sif?" he asked.

"It's Birgjavale," she said, standing at attention with her ordinarily neat hair a disheveled mess and grime on her cheeks.

"After we split off to engage these forces, Suttungr must have doubled back and attacked. They slaughtered the garrison we left there and burned the city to the ground."

"Those sneaky *hrodi* Jotnar outflanked us," cursed Thor. "Birgjavale's fall leaves the path to Asgard open and vulnerable. We have to get back!"

"It gets worse, sir," Sif continued. "We've lost contact with Gunnar's division. The last communication we received from them was from Hofborg."

Thor's eyes widened and his jaw dropped. "Our resources."

Sif nodded in agreement. "They're cutting us off. We need to prepare Asgard for a siege."

"How are they beating us?!" Thor shouted in a rage and smashed a nearby table.

—

Long columns of troops and refugees marched along the road to Asgard. Unlike the main road that ran through Birgjavale, this road was narrower, winding, and not well paved, but it was the more direct path along the border with Svartalfheim. Tall plumes of smoke rose in the distance from whence they came.

"This is the correct tactical decision," Sif said, seeing Thor's darkened brow. "The Jotnar were spreading us too thin trying to get to the other realms. At least now we know that their goal is not to reclaim Jotunheim or unify the other races. They intend to bring the fight to the very gates of the capital. Pulling back toward Asgard not only allows us to protect as many of our citizens as possible, it will also force Suttungr to face you in direct combat and not through these proxy battles."

Thor grunted in acknowledgement. He was in no mood to discuss the series of losses the Aesir Army had suffered in Midgard at the hands of the Jotnar. The battle of Halvard was the last time the Jotnar had engaged in traditional large-scale warfare. After Freya's death, the Jotnar Army had split into smaller autonomous fighting forces, terrorizing multiple cities and settlements in the region simultaneously. By the time the Aesir armies had mobilized, they were either too late or outmaneuvered. So despite his many triumphs in battle, Thor was returning to Asgard in defeat.

Sif rode beside Thor, the frustration on her face just as evident. "The messengers have reported that the reserve forces have arrived from Muspelheim. Reinforcement of the fortifications at Bifrost have begun in earnest. They should be complete by the time we arrive."

Thor grunted in acknowledgement. His eyes looked forward, but his mind remained stubbornly in the past, on his failure to kill Suttungr at Halvard.

CHAPTER 33: ONWARD THROUGH NIFLHEIM

"I knew the Svelbjarg Mountains weren't as impenetrable as we thought," Skrymir opined as they walked single file through a narrow crevasse. The sheer walls towered high above them on either side so that it was like looking up from the bottom of a well.

Skrymir observed this path had not been far from Hoddmimis Holt and was hidden just as well. It was not on any map and was certainly not well traveled. Lif had led the four of them to it before returning home, the goodbyes kept brief.

"So where are we headed?" Skrymir asked when they emerged from the pass into Jotunheim. Two days after setting out from Hoddmimis Holt and the tense silence was getting to him. "It'd be much easier to guide you if I knew our destination."

"I know where I'm going," Brunhilda snapped, looking around at the vast boreal forest around them. "You just let us know if we're heading into trouble."

Considering the last time that he had clearly seen her she was running away from an avalanche, Brunhilda now seemed spry and remarkably hale. Her pace was brisk as Skrymir followed alongside Aric, together pulling their supply-laden sled. Though his ribs still pained from Hrym's parting attack, Skrymir worked without complaint. Behind him walked Skuld, keeping a watchful eye for any signs of ambush. Skuld and Brunhilda kept a hand at their hilts while Aric kept his bow strung and within easy reach on the sled. Hrym and Geir were still out there after all. They had taken Skrymir's weapons and those of the slain Jotnar and buried them under the supplies on the sled, away from easy access.

Skrymir chuckled quietly to himself as he remembered the

discussion that had led to this arrangement. They had left one of the
bows and one of the swords with the people of Hoddmimis Holt. At
first they had not wanted to bring any extra weapons that Skrymir
might get his hands on, but he had reminded them that they would
need goods to trade for more supplies in Jotunheim. Brunhilda had
been vocal about ensuring that they would not be easily accessible to
him and yet not wanting him walking in front of her. Clearly she
worried that he might have some kind of trap planned with Hrym
that he would trip if he led. So Skuld had suggested keeping him in
the middle and leashed to the sled. That ended up being the most
suitable arrangement to her.

He noted that while they did share a bond of trust, Brunhilda
still kept Skuld at a distance. Perhaps that would be a vulnerability in
their group to exploit, he thought at he looked back. Immediately
Skuld locked eyes with him, almost as if she knew what he had been
thinking. She had an uncanny vigilance that could prove troublesome
for him.

Too bad she had not remained at the village, he thought even
as he gave her a toothy grin. The villagers had been so distraught at
Skuld's departure that Brunhilda, eager as she was to complete her
mission, had given her one final opportunity to stay.

—

The first few days in Jotunheim were quiet and uneventful. Brunhilda
was insufferable, demanding strict sound discipline and snapping at
them whenever anyone started to speak. Skrymir was getting
frustrated with the uncomfortable silence and he could tell that Skuld
did not like it either.

"Hrym might seem brutish and crude, but he's not stupid,"
he offered. Brunhilda turned her head and gave him a glare that he
chose to ignore. "He knows that even with Geir they wouldn't be
able to handle all of us—"

"There is no 'us,'" Brunhilda interrupted. She stopped and
turned to face Skrymir. "You're only alive because you saved that
little girl. And you're only with us because I didn't want to burden the
people of Hoddmimis Holt with holding you prisoner."

"Fair enough," Skrymir bowed. "Still, he wouldn't try
anything against the three of you without backup, and the closest

Jotnar settlement is at least five days northeast of here. Longer if they went all the way back through Isabrot instead of tracking us up through the gap."

"Do you think he'd go after the people of Hoddmimis Holt?" Skuld asked, biting her lower lip. "Maybe I should have stayed with them."

"I don't think you have to worry about them," Skrymir thought aloud. "There are few enough soldiers in this region. Suttungr took most of them south. Those who are still here patrol for deserters from the army and also recruit new soldiers as young Jotnar come of age."

"How many are we talking about?" Brunhilda asked.

"I don't know the exact number," he replied as he mimed counting on his fingers. "Hrym was Suttungr's second-in-command. You should probably ask him." As Brunhilda's hand reached for her sword, he continued with a smirk, "But if I had to guess, I'd say that there are four squads of six that patrol this region." Everyone relaxed a bit and Brunhilda began walking again. "He wouldn't waste the time and manpower to send anyone after Hoddmimis Holt with you as his priority."

"We're your priority?" Brunhilda asked, a self-satisfied smirk on her lips.

"I don't suppose you'll just tell me what your mission is?" Skrymir said in return. After a brief pause he continued, "Well, it was clearly important enough for the Aesir to stage a futile attack and give up Halvard to sneak you through. So your mission would seem to be an Aesir priority as well. That is why we have been pursuing you."

"Why should I believe anything that you say? How do I know that everything you've said thus far isn't a lie?"

He paused again while he considered her question. "I suppose you don't." Brunhilda gave a quick, menacing glance but otherwise didn't acknowledge Skrymir's sneer.

"This is going to be a long trek," Skuld whispered to Aric with a comically exaggerated eye roll. Aric responded with a humorless shrug and grunt.

—

Two days further along, Skuld reported that there were others nearby. "Looks like we've found one of those patrols you mentioned," she said. She had returned from a short scouting expedition while the others ate a light meal of cured meats and unleavened barley bread brought from Hoddmimis Holt. Under Skrymir's guidance they had avoided any run-ins with Jotnar so far.

Brunhilda wiped her mouth. "Six in total?"

"Yeah, it looks as if they're heading north along a trail from somewhere to the southeast, probably Isabrot."

"They're likely heading toward Gastropnir," offered Skrymir. "We should be able to avoid them with ease if we stay within the trees on this side of the road."

"I'd prefer to just deal with them now so we don't have to worry about them flanking us later," Brunhilda said, her hand already on the sword at her hip.

"No killing," Skrymir said with a sharp and definitive tone. "My help is predicated on that one condition."

Brunhilda had started to pull her sword from its scabbard. Aric placed his hand over hers and gently guided the sword back into its scabbard. "There is more than enough dying happening out there," he said, gesturing his arm in a wide arc. "We don't need to kill everyone else from here to... to wherever we're going." Although Aric had not divulged their objective, Skrymir noted Brunhilda's withering stare.

"It's not a bad idea," Skuld joined in. "Even if we killed this patrol and hid their bodies, someone would eventually notice their absence and then step up security in this region. I'm sure speed and secrecy are in the best interest to your mission as well, whatever that might be."

"Fine," Brunhilda pulled her hand away from her sword and from Aric's hand. "No killing." They cleared their campsite and she led them away from the patrol's route.

CHAPTER 34: TO MARKET WE GO

Keeping off of the roads in Niflheim proved to be easy enough. But trudging through the backcountry made their progress slow and difficult. Since the end of the Aesir-Vanir War and under the rule of the Aesir, travel between the isolated Jotnar villages was severely restricted and regulated. In general, supplies flowed in one direction, south to Asgard. Access to raw materials had been limited precisely to prevent the Jotnar nation from rising up again. Even in the face of all of these obstacles, Suttungr had been able to unite the disconnected Jotnar populations and equip them for war.

"We have to find a way to move faster," Brunhilda complained in the evening of the sixth day. "Where are your horses or stags or whatever animals that you ride?"

This was the first time that she addressed Skrymir directly other than to shut him up, and so it took him a moment before he responded. "Are you asking me for information?"

"If I wanted a conversation with you, I'd tell you," she snapped. "Just answer the question. Every moment that we delay, more people die in this war... Aesir and Jotnar."

"And I suppose when you end the war, the Jotnar will just return to serving the great and noble Aesir," he responded, his voice bitter and brow furrowed.

"What are you doing? If you're not here to help me, then why did you come at all? Would you prefer that I find a Jotnar village and take what I need by force?" she said, standing over the seated Jotnar.

Unflinching, Skrymir met her eyes. He let the tension grow thick in the air before answering. "We have aurochs for bearing loads on the few occasions we are allowed to travel," he said with a long exhale. "Most were taken by the army when they mobilized, but

Suttungr would have left some of the smaller or younger ones. These will be the only things that we'll find up here that would suit your purposes. There are no other large beasts out here. They were culled by the vargr, and the vargr in turn were wiped out by the Aesir..." A haunted look crossed his face. "...at least after the incident with Fenrir." Brunhilda nodded knowingly.

"Are we going to see some baby aurochs?" Skuld interjected.

"How are you going to get us some aurochs?" Brunhilda said, ignoring Skuld. She pulled her sword from her scabbard and began running her whet stone along its edge.

"There is a village where they breed them; we should be able to trade some of our supplies to barter for them," Skrymir said as he stood and looked around for landmarks, taking the hint. Night was falling and the waning moon gave little illumination through the thick clouds overhead. After getting his bearings, he said, "We should be able to reach it by next evening. But do we really need aurochs? How much farther are we going? We're already getting close to the last villages in Niflheim..." In an instant his eyes widened and jaw dropped. "Are we going to Yggdrasil?!"

"We can't sacrifice any of our supplies," Brunhilda said and sheathed her sword. "Figure out another way."

"You can't seriously think that we're equipped to make that crossing! There will be no shelter or villages for leagues," Skrymir said incredulously, shaking his head. He turned to Skuld and Aric. "Are you just going to follow her on this fool's errand?"

"She's my responsibility," Aric said, his face betraying no emotion. "If I don't watch out for her, who knows what kind of trouble she'll get into?"

"Are you kidding?" Skuld added, bounding around in excitement. "This is the opportunity of a lifetime. I've been all over the nine realms, but I've never been to Yggdrasil."

"So you see, with four mouths to feed we certainly can't trade our supplies away now. In fact, we'll need to get aurochs and as much food as we can just to make the approach, not even accounting for the return journey." Brunhilda stared at the Jotnar with unwavering eyes, Aric and Skuld on either side of her.

"You're all insane. There's nothing up there," said a beleaguered Skrymir. "How is any of this going to end the war?"

"That's not your concern," Brunhilda said as she waved away

his question. "Your job is to get us there."

After an extended moment of silence staring back at Brunhilda, Skrymir lowered his eyes and sighed.

"I might be able to talk my way into getting us a deal," he said. "But you three will need to stay out of sight when we arrive. I'll go in alone."

"I can just hide in the sled under the supplies," Skuld offered as she mimed burying herself under something and peeking out. "No one will even know that I'm there."

"You'll do no such thing," Brunhilda said to Skuld. "And you," she said to Skrymir, her finger jabbing him in the chest, "you're not to leave my sight. We still have the Jotnar armor. That and these animal skull helmets will be a suitable disguise."

"Fine," he acquiesced. "But you definitely cannot bring that." He nodded at her sword. "That is obviously not a Jotnar-made weapon. It was how I spotted you when you tried to sneak past us at Halvard."

"That won't be a problem," she replied with a smirk. "I'll just wear your weapons." She unbundled the sled and grabbed a satchel that had been buried deep. Untying the knots binding the package she revealed all of the weapons they had taken from the Jotnar killed in Hoddmimis Holt—including Skrymir's frost knife.

—

The next morning, two figures trekked across the half-mile distance from the forest toward the unassuming auroch grazing pastures. Dark shapes shifted back among the trees, watching as the pair pulled a modestly laden sled behind them. This area was still wild, a league or so to the west of a small village. While the ground was covered in deep snow, the aurochs rooted around and seemed to find enough to keep them content and quite fat.

"After our defeat in the Aesir-Vanir War, the old Jotnar fortress of Gastropnir was torn down," Skrymir said in the long, awkward silence. "In the days of the Great Awakening, Gastropnir stood as the gateway to Yggdrasil. It was the staging point for the united armies' final push against the most terrible of the monsters. The locals named this village in Gastropnir's honor."

"What are you blathering on about?" Brunhilda had to push back the horned skull helmet on her head to shoot him a menacing look.

"You should know something about the people who live here," he said, ignoring her. "They take pride in their ancestry and never forgot, even during the generations of Aesir occupation. Now that they're free from your yoke, they would see you as a threat and attack with little hesitation."

"Yes, I know," she replied, pulling the helmet back down over her face. "I won't react or say a word when we're there."

"In the time before the Great Awakening, plant and animal life flourished unchecked all around the World Tree," Skrymir continued as he tucked away a few stray locks of her flaming red hair. Although he could not see them, he could feel her eyes roll. "The ensuing fierce and terrible battles between the monsters and the united peoples left the land scorched and barren. The realms were scoured of predators and the land tamed. Though the greatest of them could not be killed, they fled from the combined might of Mjolnir and Gungnir. Njord, leader of the Vanir, merged his life force with the roots of Yggdrasil to trap those terrible beasts in that deep well beneath the world."

"I know all of that—"

"With these most dangerous creatures trapped underneath Yggdrasil," he continued, "it was decided to turn the surrounding environment into a frozen, desolate barrier between those threats and the civilized realms. And so it was that Gastropnir came to dominate the region and stand watch over the frozen tundra of the north.

"Then during the war, after the Jotnar were betrayed by the Vanir they fled and made their last stand at Gastropnir. As the final stronghold they held out for a time. Yet the Jotnar defeat was inevitable against the combined might of the Aesir and Vanir wielding both Mjolnir and Gungnir. And so the once indomitable fortress was torn asunder. Now, the new Gastropnir stands at the northern edge of the boreal forest of Niflheim, the last populated village of the lands of the exiled Jotnar."

Skrymir eyed Brunhilda, who was clenching her fists. "It's a small village, a shadow of its namesake. The land is harsh and inhospitable to crops of any kind. To our great fortune the wooly aurochs, native to the region, are well suited to living off of the tundra's tough vegetation, and the Jotnar in turn became adept at surviving off of the aurochs. When Suttungr mobilized his army he took the majority of the mature aurochs from around this realm, leaving the people to scrape by with the bare minimum of resources."

"So they don't support Suttungr here?"

"They support his agenda," he said, choosing his words carefully, "and many gave their aurochs willingly. But three years of fighting have tested their resolve. We must tread lightly with how we frame our support of the war. Not all Jotnar follow blindly."

———

Jorunn had been too young to join the army when Suttungr first began recruiting years ago. She had grown up alongside the juvenile aurochs in Gastropnir and would be conscripted when the army recruiters next came through. Although the idea of fighting and killing gave her pause, she would welcome the chance to join her sister and to see the rest of the world. To actually see Jotunheim, the true Jotunheim, would be beyond her wildest dreams.

She was driving a small herd of seventeen aurochs out to pasture when she noticed two people approaching. This part of Jotunheim was so remote that strangers were less of a threat and more of a curiosity. To her keen eyes she could see that they wore the makeshift armor of the Jotnar Army although only one had a helmet, the spiral-horned skull of a Svelbjarg ram. They were soldiers, and soldiers this far north meant they were either recruiters or deserters. Deserters usually did not cause much trouble, only coming into town to purchase supplies, never staying in one place too long for fear of being discovered and forced back into the army. Recruiters, however, were a different matter. Most in Gastropnir saw the draft as a celebratory time. After driving the Aesir out, they looked forward to the chance to continue the fight. It was all for the greater good.

"Greetings!" The male without the helmet shouted in Jotunmal above the low howl of the cold wind coming from the north. *"My*

friend and I are looking to barter."

"Have you come from the front?" Jorunn asked them. She looked at the female with the helmet expectantly. Something about her bearing led Jorunn to see her as the one in charge.

"Please excuse my companion. She lost her tongue and was horribly scarred by the Aesir." The soldiers exchanged a brief glance before he continued. *"We're looking for—"*

"Tell me, have you any word of a warrior named Hertha? From Gastropnir?"

"I, uh… no," he replied. *"That is to say, we don't know anyone by that name, but we have come from the front."*

"She's my sister and a great warrior," Jorunn pressed. *"You must've heard of her exploits on the battlefield. I bet she's defeated scores of Aesir and even killed some valkyries."*

A cough came from the helmeted one. Her companion nudged her with his elbow.

"The battles have been raging all through Asgard," he replied to Jorunn with a weak shrug. *"Much happens that we are not aware of."*

"Oh, well, the village is about a league to the east," Jorunn said, having lost interest in the newcomers. Her shoulders drooped and the smile faded from her face as she pointed over her shoulder. *"Just keep heading toward the ruins and you'll reach it soon enough. The marketplace should be set up by the time you get there."*

"Actually, while we're certainly looking for more supplies," he said and stepped in front of her with a winning smile. *"We are interested in trading with you."*

—

"That went better than I expected," Brunhilda said as they walked toward Gastropnir with two aurochs trailing behind. They had lashed the sled to one of the aurochs, which bore the burden with ease. "How did you get her to accept that deal? There's no chance that that was a fair trade." The youth and Skrymir had spoken in the Jotnar language the whole time, and despite having heard many curses shouted at her, she was not fluent in their tongue.

"These are my people," Skrymir said with casual confidence. "I know how to work with them. I convinced her that this was the best option." Brunhilda gave him a look that suggested she did not believe one word he said. With a sigh he said, "And I may have suggested that this was Suttungr's official business. That instead of recruiting people we needed more aurochs." He waved her off dismissively. "The details don't really matter. Just be glad I was successful. If you had done this on your own, you probably would have wounded or killed her."

"Look, I know that you think the Aesir are all blood-thirsty warmongers," she said, patting and gently stroking the auroch bearing the sled. "But I don't take pleasure in killing anyone, let alone children. When we execute the law of Asgard, it is for the good of the nine realms. Things were much worse before the Great Awakening. Would you rather we return to life in those days? Yes, Aesir celebrate death on the field of battle. All must die at some time, so it is best to die a glorious death of purpose. It is that purpose, not the act of violence, that we celebrate."

"That's all well and good for the Aesir," Skrymir replied in an even tone. "It is your law that you enforce and dispense upon the rest of us. Is it better than the days prior to the Great Awakening? Yes. And it is also preferable to cut off a finger than to lose an entire hand. Best of all would be to give us a voice in what we might choose to sacrifice for our own greater good."

"We follow Odin," Brunhilda snapped, "from Buri to Borr and now Odin. They created the nine realms and drove the monsters away. They know what is best for us. All of us. My faith and loyalty are with Odin unconditionally."

"I'm certain that you've never doubted any of his orders," Skrymir said with a look of skepticism, "but I digress. I doubt we two will find true peace for all the realms. At least it is heartening to know that we can discuss this together and agree that the world may yet improve for the benefit of us all." He turned away as they approached the village.

Brunhilda glared at him. She still felt the sting of Odin's reprimand after Halvard. While she did question some of Odin's decisions, she remained dedicated to her lord and her people. She and Skrymir walked on for a while in an uncomfortable silence as these thoughts swirled in her mind.

"What does that shepherdess think she's going to do with Skuld's coins and those Jotnar swords?" Brunhilda said idly, changing the topic to something less contentious. "I can't imagine that you'll be able to trade with Asgard after this. And all of the fighters went south with Suttungr."

"We've only recently learned metalworking. We have limited access to ore, and most of what we had was used to arm Suttungr's army. And all of the smiths went with the army to repair and maintain the equipment on the frontlines, so refined metal is scarce here. Most likely she'll trade them with someone who will melt them down and reforge them into tools and other useful things. They might even use some of the metal to craft jewelry or some other pieces of art."

Brunhilda raised an eyebrow. "Art? Out here in this barren wasteland?"

"I know that you think that Asgard and the Aesir are the only sources of beauty in the world. We may appear to live simply, but we are not simple people," he said with a hint of scorn in his voice. "In fact, it is precisely these desolate lands that inspire us to create art."

He stopped and crouched near an unremarkable patch of snow. Digging into some of the frost on the ground he uncovered a small patch of purple, low-growing flowers. These plants ordinarily bloom in the summer, but the unnaturally long winter had caught them at the height of the summer season and preserved them in the cold over the past few years. Skrymir plucked one bud, a brilliant shade of purple, and popped it into his mouth.

"There is more to this land than meets the eye," he said with a wink.

CHAPTER 35: VARGR

It had been about an hour since Brunhilda and Skrymir traded for two of the larger juvenile aurochs. Aric stared out from the treeline toward the remaining herd as they grazed, hoping that Brunhilda would be able to restrain herself among her enemies. He and Skuld were well hidden near the treeline to the southwest where the tundra met the forest edge. They had set up a camouflaged blind to keep an eye on the paths to and from Gastropnir. The pastoral scene with the young Jotnar shepherdess tending her flock distracted him for a moment. And the chill morning air and the snow that blanketed everything added to the serenity. In fact, the only sounds were the grunts of the aurochs as they rooted around for food beneath the snow. This far to the north one could almost forget the tragedies they had left in the south.

"What were they like?" Skuld jarred Aric from his tranquility. "Your wife and daughter, I mean."

From the prone position he slowly turned his head to regard her. He was surprised that she had been quiet long enough for him to become distracted. They were both lying on one of the animal skins, staying dry above the snow. And even though he looked at her his gaze was still distant and almost blissful, as if he were a hundred leagues away.

"I know you'd probably prefer to sit here in silence until Brunhilda and Skrymir return, but I cannot be expected to sit quietly for that long," she said in response to Aric's mute stare. "It must have been nice to have a home and family. My parents died long ago, when I was young, so I can understand the feeling of loss." Aric could see a change in her expression as she spoke of the past. There was a distance and sincerity to her face as she continued, "I've lived and traveled with various groups over the years, but I've never really had that feeling of belonging—of family—since. Be thankful that you had as much time with them as you did." Skuld sat up and turned her full attention to Aric with a genuine smile and spoke to him as if they had been lifelong friends. "So tell me about them. Share those memories and celebrate their lives."

Aric dropped his face over the edge of the fur into the snow, then gave a heavy sigh; the barest hint of a smile turned up the corners of his mouth. "You're full of surprises, aren't you?" he said, raising his head. Snow clung to his hair and lingered on his face and beard. "The songs that you sang at Hoddmimis Holt reminded me of the songs my daughter, Una, sang. Especially that first one, about Wodensdaeg. She was so talkative and full of joy. I think you remind me of her too much," he said as he finally sat upright and turned to Skuld. She gave him such a sincere smile that he had to look away.

"She would have been about nine by now"—Aric counted on his fingers—"maybe ten? And though we did much together, she was her mother's daughter. I taught her to fish and hunt, but when Dagmaer taught her to fight..." He paused and looked off as if could actually see her. "Well, that's when Una really truly lit up."

"She sounds like a marvelous child. And she probably would have done better than you have against the Jotnar," Skuld said and gave a little laugh. "Really though, you're doing well and I'm sure that they'd be proud of you."

With a sharp exhale that might have been a laugh, Aric replied, "Dagmaer wasn't exactly a fan of the Aesir. If you think I've been critical or angry with the them, you should have heard her. That's one of the things that I loved about her. She was so strong and independent, though we only really argued about it during the Wodensdaeg Festivals with her asking why we needed to give up so much of our food and bounty to the Aesir. In reply, I would quote our gythja: 'The Aesir provide the bounty for us in the first place, and ask so little in return...'" At that memory Aric's expression turned melancholy and he grew quiet.

"You clearly loved them a great deal," Skuld said in a soothing tone. "No one will ever replace them. However, you know they wouldn't want you to give up on your life any more than you would want them to give up on theirs if your places were reversed. Bottling all of your feelings inside will just make you more miserable.

The Aesir don't mourn death; instead, they celebrate the lives of the fallen."

Aric's eyes snapped into focus and glared at her. "The Aesir do many things, don't they?" he quipped. "You've seen how we live in Midgard. And as we've traveled through Jotnar villages in Niflheim, in every village that we've passed, their poverty has been stark and obvious. You say that you've traveled across the nine realms and visited the other races, yet you speak of the splendor and grandeur of Asgard as if it were something that everyone should celebrate." He took a deep breath. "Tell me, does anyone else live like the Aesir?"

"It's not that simple," Skuld answered, turning her eyes downward. "We owe the Aesir so much for what they did in the Great Awakening. The world was fraught with danger, chaos, and terrible creatures. Even after that, peace did not last. The power struggle between the Jotnar, Aesir, and Vanir during the Aesir-Vanir War spread violence and misery across the nine realms. We live in the greatest period of peace the world has ever known."

"So you're saying that the only way we can live in peace is if the rest of us agree to live life the way the Aesir dictate?" Aric said, raising his voice.

"Shh!" Skuld hissed sharply. "Something's not right." Aric looked as if he might continue but she silenced him with a quick look and a raised hand as she drew her sword from its scabbard.

Aric crept with care to reach his bow and strained to keep quiet as he strung it and nocked an arrow. He sidled up next to Skuld and whispered, "I don't hear anything."

"I know," replied Skuld, barely audible as she looked all around from within their blind. Even the sounds of the rutting aurochs had stopped. She could see that the herd was agitated and the shepherdess had taken up an alert posture. "I haven't heard anything the whole morning, not even a single bird chirp."

Suddenly a blur of white exploded from the snow near the treeline about a hundred yards to the east, on their right, making a beeline for the grazing herd of aurochs. Once out in the open the shape of a wolf was clearly visible. But this was no ordinary wolf; it was larger and more monstrous than any Aric had ever seen near Murtrborg.

"Vargr!" Skuld said in a surprised whisper.

Though it was a formidable beast, the shepherdess took up a position to meet it head on and cut it off before it could reach the herd. She drew a sword from the bundle she had received from Brunhilda and Skrymir. Aric could see that the weight and feel were unfamiliar in her hands as she swung it clumsily. Tossing it aside, she instead firmly gripping her crooked staff in both hands. Though only armed with a piece of sturdy wood capped with a rough, iron ball instead of sharp steel, she appeared confident and unafraid.

"We have to do something," he said, the anxiety in Aric's voice clear.

"The vargr's going for the aurochs and the shepherdess. It looks like she knows what she's doing. Leave this to her," Skuld said, sheathing her sword and placing a hand on Aric's bow. "Brunhilda and Skrymir took all of the Jotnar armor. We can't risk going out there and being spotted." As soon as Aric replaced the arrow into his quiver, another furry blur bolted past their blind on the left, followed by two others. It was not just a lone vargr but a hunting pack. And it did not look like the aurochs were their only prey.

"She's going to be surrounded," said Aric as he once again nocked his arrow and drew his bow.

"This isn't our fight." Skuld had her hand still holding onto Aric's arm. "We can't give ourselves away, it's not safe here."

"We can't just let her die." He pulled his arm free of Skuld's hand and took careful aim. Aric released and let the arrow fly with a whispered prayer. It flew in a long, smooth arc, hitting one of the vargr in the shoulder causing it to stumble just as the shepherdess engaged the first one. The other three vargr stopped and looked around for what had attacked them.

"Damn," Skuld said as the three vargr charged back in their direction. Even the one that Aric had hit was injured but far from dead. She drew her sword and burst forth from their blind.

As Skuld ran headlong to meet them, Aric continued to loose more arrows until he finally struck one in the neck and brought it down just before it reached Skuld. She then clashed with one while the other circled around. It was difficult for Aric to get a clear shot with her so close to them. In desperation he grabbed the sword he had been given back at Hoddmimis Holt and ran to help.

Before he could close the distance, one of the vargr leapt directly at Skuld. Although not quick enough to dodge it, she brought up the point of her sword and caught the vargr under its lower jaw. The blade cut clean through its head, the point and vargr brain matter exiting through the back of its skull. Its momentum carried it forward and, though dead, its body crashed into Skuld, pinning her beneath with her sword immobilized, lodged in the beast.

—

Jorunn blew out a long breath that turned to mist in the chilled air. Her shoulders slumped with the weight of her staff having beaten the first vargr soundly and sent it running with its tail between its legs. Her ears twitched and muscled tensed at the sounds of more fighting. Eyes scanning she saw the second vargr barrel into the stranger in a burst of snow and bright red blood. Rushing over she arrived just in time to fend off the final vargr with her staff. After several sound raps with the iron capped end it fled as well. Jorunn swung her staff with a start when the vargr corpse behind her shifted. Seeing the sword blade sticking out through the beast's skull she realized that the stranger underneath was still alive.

"Thanks for the help," Jorunn said in Jotunmal as she strained to roll the vargr corpse off of Skuld. *"I didn't even see these—"* her words caught in her throat as she got a clear look at the woman and saw the pale skin of her furless face. As another smooth-skinned stranger brandishing a sword ran up to them, Jorunn stumbled back and fumbled for her staff. Although there was fur lining his jaw and upper lip, it did not cover his face and was a pale shade of yellow. They looked more like the Aesir who patrolled Jotunheim though decidedly different. Holding her weapon up in a threatening grip, Jorunn swept it back and forth from the standing stranger to the trapped and unarmed one. *"Who... what are you?!"*

"Wait, wait," the sword-wielding one said as he came to a stop a few feet from them. "We're not here to hurt you. Do you speak the common tongue?"

Jorunn's eyes flicked from his face to the sword in his hand. As if just now realizing he still held it, he slowly crouched and set it down in the snow.

"You're not Jotnar," she said. It was a statement, not a question.

"No," he acknowledged. "I'm Aric and this is Skuld. We're just simple human travelers. We saw that you were in trouble and were just trying to help."

"I am Jorunn. What are you doing with a Jotnar blade?" she asked, eyeing the sword that lay in the snow at his feet.

Aric's eyes followed her gaze to the sword at his feet. As he opened his mouth to reply, Skuld spoke first. "We came across a patrol that had fallen to these vargr. We were too late to save them. And since we didn't want to share their fate, we decided to track the vargr to kill them if we had the opportunity."

"I don't know…" Jorunn said hesitantly as she slackened her grip on the staff.

"We stopped these other vargr from taking you by surprise," Skuld continued with a sharp groan as she pushed at the vargr corpse on top of her. "That's got to count for something."

"You're right. I'm sorry." Her eyes shifted from one to the other with an arched brow. After a moment's hesitation she set her staff back down and bent to pull the vargr off of Skuld. It must have weighed close to two hundred pounds, she thought as Aric joined the effort. With all three working, they rolled the corpse off of her in no time.

Aric helped Skuld to her feet and went to the other vargr to recover any unbroken arrows. Skuld pulled her own sword free from the mass of fur that had been sitting on top of her.

"You might be able to get some use out of these things," Skuld said as she wiped her blade clean. "The meat might not be very pleasant but the skins should prove warm and durable, if not for your own use then at least for trade."

There was a pause before Jorunn responded. Her eyes lingered on Skuld and her mouth was agape. "Thank you. But you killed them, so they are yours by right." After a moment of staring she added, "I'm sorry, did you say that you were humans? I've never seen a human before. I thought you'd be… I don't know, smaller? Different?"

"I understand your confusion," Aric said with a sympathetic smile. "My village in Midgard was isolated and remote. The only time we saw anyone else was during the Wodensdaeg Festivals…" Aric trailed off and gave Skuld a sour look.

"Is he okay?" Jorunn asked after the silence stretched for a little too long.

Skuld gave a little cough to snap Aric from his stupor.

"Right," he continued, shaking his head. "I've heard stories of Jotnar, Dokkalfar, and Ljosalfar and they've always sounded so fanciful, so alien, more akin to imaginary creatures than real people. As a child I imagined the Jotnar to be these giant, monstrous creatures who built the nine realms with their bare hands and carved Asgard from a single massive rock that floated in the sky at the end of rainbows." With his eyes turned to Skuld, Jorunn could not tell if Aric's expression was one of shame or disappointment. With a heavy sigh he said, "Recently I've found that there's a marked difference between those stories and the real world."

"I don't have much with me, but I would like to share some of my food with you. And if you need lodging for the night, you are more than welcome to stay in my home," Jorunn said as she removed her satchel and took out an assortment of root vegetables and a wedge of hard auroch cheese. "It's the least I can do to repay you for your help."

"Thanks for the offer," said Skuld as she grabbed Aric, half leading and half pulling him. "Regrettably we're not staying long here. We're pressed for time."

"Well, if you reconsider, my home will be the first one you encounter traveling east from here. It's the one that smells thoroughly of auroch dung. You'll smell it long before you see it," Jorunn said with a wink and a nod.

And with that they parted ways, Aric and Skuld heading south and Jorunn northwest.

CHAPTER 36: GASTROPNIR

The small village of Gastropnir was a quaint and modest town. Even before Suttungr had recruited all of the able-bodied Jotnar for his army, its presence this deep into Niflheim made it a difficult place in which to flourish. The Aesir-enforced restrictions on travel between Jotnar cities was the only thing that had maintained the small population.

Because of these conditions the Jotnar here were some of the hardiest of them all. And so Suttungr had taken all of the men and women of age when he ousted the local Aesir Army from this region. Those who remained were either too young or too old to fight. Instead of fighting, they aided the war effort by raising the aurochs that were employed by the Jotnar Army.

There were only a dozen or so occupied buildings. They were low structures, distinguishable from the natural surroundings by illuminated spikes of ice and smoke rising from chimneys in thin, curling wisps. They had walls of packed snow and ice reinforced sparingly with wood and insulated with animal hides and auroch wool.

"What is that smell?" Brunhilda whispered to Skrymir as she wrinkled her nose and choked down a gag under her helmet.

Skrymir didn't seem to notice the pungent musk of aurochs and excrement. "The forests provide food and shelter for the animals we used to hunt in this region. Using their wood for fires would be extremely wasteful, so out here we use dried and hardened auroch dung as fuel for our fires."

"I've never understood why your people build fires at all. After so many centuries in Niflheim, aren't you all beings of cold and ice now?" she asked. "Your blood freezes anything it touches, and when you march the very air turns into chilly mists."

"Before the War, Jotunheim was a flourishing place of vast natural beauty, and we were one with the land and thrived with the lush greenery. After the Vanir betrayed us to the Aesir, we were forced to these barren lands. Now in this desolation, we have adapted. The Ethlivald energies that course through our veins have taken on the essence of this land. However, we still enjoy the comforts of a warm hearth and a hot meal. And the fires illuminate the dark nights that grow ever longer in the winter months."

Brunhilda continued walking as she lapsed into a contemplative silence. She had never given any thought to the day-to-day life of Jotnar. In her years stationed with the northern Aesir Army she had put down enough conflicts against and among the Jotnar but she had never taken much time to understand them beyond how to protect against their magics and how to kill them. She never went into the Jotnar towns themselves and only ever engaged them on the field of battle. The role of the valkyrie was not to police the subjects of Asgard; that was the job of the local administrators and the infantry. No, her job was to put them back in their place if they strayed too far out of line.

She snapped back to the present as they entered the main thoroughfare with their aurochs and sled in tow. The small populace had a vibrant energy evident as it awoke to the day and the people set up their shops in the covered marketplace. Market was a bit of an exaggeration, thought Brunhilda, as most of the merchants merely set up their wares in front of their homes. This was a long way from the rich shops along the boulevards in Asgard. Still, these covered interconnected lanes were an effective way of displaying merchandise for browsing in such an inhospitable environment with cold winds blowing.

"Try not to say anything stupid," Skrymir said to her under his breath. Then after a pause and side glance at her, he added, "Actually, just don't say anything. I'll handle the haggling."

She was about to retort when another Jotnar neared them on the path to market. Instead Brunhilda held her tongue and adjusted her skull helmet lower and pulled the animal fur cloak tighter about her neck to make sure her distinctive red hair was fully concealed.

Skrymir looked at ease among his people. He spoke with most of them in the Jotnar tongue, though they sometimes spoke in the Aesir common language. Brunhilda remained wary of him when she could not understand what he said, but she kept to herself and stayed as inconspicuous as possible leading the aurochs.

At the first stand Skrymir gave a hearty greeting to a gnarled Jotnar with silver fur peppered with streaks of blue. The old one had been working on carving various animal bones into ornate jewelry and utilitarian tools. After a lively verbal exchange Skrymir came away with a set of bone needles, an intricate necklace, some knives and other tools, and three bolts of wool for what appeared to be just a handshake. Next they moved to a matronly Jotnar peddling blankets and clothing woven from auroch wool. Skrymir spoke with the old woman and pointed to the carver several times during their conversation. He gave the bolts of wool, needles, and jewelry to her and she pulled out two fluffy woolen blankets and two finely crafted tunics. With a wink and a polite laugh Skrymir accepted the items. They stopped at other stalls before returning to the bone carver. Of everything that they had collected along the way they kept about half: the blankets, some root vegetables, a wheel of auroch cheese, and the bone knives.

As they moved through more of these transactions with other merchants she really began to take notice of the genuine kindness and affection that the people showed to each other. Skrymir's smile and easy manner elicited smiles and laughter from the older Jotnar. And with each transaction he negotiated an extra little treat that he would give to a nearby child. In fact, he was so affable that none gave her much notice.

It was clear that these people were struggling to get by, and yet, despite their hardships, there was a warmth to their demeanor and interaction that was often lost in the bustle of Asgard. Certainly there was camaraderie amongst the soldiers and between the Aesir in general, though it was often brief and in passing as they conducted business; it lacked the emotional depth of this simple life and close community though. Even thinking back on the people of Hoddmimis Holt Brunhilda started to understand the strong ties that form when people worked together for their collective survival.

She saw this everywhere she looked. Children helped their elders set up their stands and display their wares. The shopkeepers gave treats and toys to the young who visited. During their morning of browsing and bargaining, she saw no signs of unrest or conflict, no drunken brawls, no arguments more heated than simple haggling.

After no time at all they had their supplies purchased and secured to the sled and harnessed to the aurochs. For the first time she began to appreciate Skrymir's presence.

"That went pretty well," Brunhilda said to him once they had left Gastropnir in the distance. "I'm glad I didn't kill you."

Skrymir responded with a wry smile and a slight chuckle, "So am I."

———

Suttungr rode in silence, alone, even as his vast army marched around him. The expansive northern territories, once controlled by the Aesir and annexed from the Jotnar after the Aesir-Vanir War, were now reclaimed. A long road lay ahead of them, and at its end was the shining city of Asgard. Not since the Jotnar and Vanir marched united had the power of the Aesir been challenged.

"*We haven't had any updates from Hrym since they left Isabrot pass,*" Hertha said, riding up to him. "*Reports from Niflheim have been sparse and there has been no news of the valkyries.*"

"*Hrym will not fail me,*" Suttungr said with certainty. "*Skrymir, however, may be more of a liability. Perhaps I should not have sent him along.*"

"*He has shown some skill on the battlefield,*" mused Hertha. "*I should think he would be an asset in a fight. And I think that you underestimate Hrym. He'll keep Skrymir on a short leash. Hrym won't let Skrymir impede his duty to you.*"

"*He has openly questioned my tactics and my motives,*" he replied in a tone so even and icy that it carried more malice than if he had shouted in rage. It was enough to wither the confident and headstrong Hertha to silence. "*I question Skrymir's intention, not his ability. Before we are done with this war, we will see his true purpose.*"

"*The war is nearly over. You've done what no one thought possible,*" said Hertha after a brief pause. "*You've brought the Aesir to their knees.*" With Hrym away on his mission, she was the senior commander for the Jotnar Army and reported directly to Suttungr. She attended to her duties with diligence and enthusiasm, always trying to prove herself and her abilities. In stature she was the last person who would inspire the moniker, frost giant, yet she carried herself with the confidence and bearing of the name. *"Victory will soon be ours."*

"Now is not the time to become overconfident," admonished Suttungr. *"The Aesir had grown lax with the security of their outer territories. They were ill prepared to meet a force as well organized as ours. But even during the Aesir-Vanir War the stronghold of Asgard was never breached. By now Odin will have recalled their troops from the south to reinforce their position. That will be the true test of our might."*

Turning to look at her directly, he continued with a serious and measured voice, *"And that is where both Thor and Odin await us."*

"Yes sir," Hertha replied in a more humble and subdued tone. *"We understand the stakes of losing our capital. And though they have underestimated us in the past, we will not do the same to them."*

CHAPTER 37: BEWARE SLEEPING DRAGONS

Traveling in the lee of the two aurochs afforded protection from the biting wind but put the group downwind of the pungent beasts. Skrymir had been the only one not to complain about the smell, though they all adjusted to it in time. However, the odor was a small price to pay for the aurochs' benefits. The daily march was now less of a slow, morale-draining slog and simply a bland, mind-numbing stroll through a vast, featureless wasteland. Even loaded with all of the supplies they had procured at Gastropnir, they now covered the same distance in half the time.

Brunhilda kept herself occupied during the monotonous trek by checking and rechecking their rapidly dwindling stores. After departing Gastropnir she had taken sole responsibility for maintaining and distributing the food. Even rationing their meals she could already see that they would not have enough for the return trip. She was glad for the furs and the helmet as they concealed her face. As an Aesir and a valkyrie Brunhilda knew that she could survive on much less, but to battle a dragon she would need to keep up her strength. Looking at the others she knew that not all of them would survive. Her eyes lingered on Skrymir for a long moment before she shook her head, remembering his affable nature in Gastropnir.

At the very least they would not need both aurochs to pull an empty sled, she thought as she patted the wooly haunches of the larger one. The young aurochs proved to be strong and resilient, their pace never flagging even on the limited feed they had. Whenever they paused to rest they gorged on all of the purple buds and other vegetation they could find beneath the snow.

"Is that it or have I finally gone crazy from the midnight sun?" Skuld asked as she pulled down the furs covering her nose and mouth, her voice had a mixture of hope and exhaustion. A flash of green appeared on the horizon, far to the north. The sun remained obscured behind the clouds overhead, and yet the light of day lasted longer and longer the farther north they traveled. For the last few days the sun refused to set, making their slumber fitful and restless. Even Skuld's usual attempts at levity and conversation had waned in the face of these conditions. Not that it would have mattered as the bitter cold had forced them to cover their heads and faces with insulation, muffling anything they might have said.

"That is it," Brunhilda said with a relieved exhale, her breath clouding and freezing in the frigid air.

"So now that we're here," Skrymir said, "will you please tell me what we're doing at Yggdrasil? Last I heard, Njord, the Vanir king of old, had sacrificed his life to bind the worst of the old monsters beneath the tree—" He stopped mid-thought and his eyes grew wide. "Wait, we're not unleashing the monsters on the Jotnar, are we?"

"No," Brunhilda said quickly. "There's a dragon—"

"A dragon!" Skuld interrupted with excitement in her voice. "Are we taming a dragon and riding it into battle?"

"Nidhogg was the last great monster that survived the Great Awakening. Supposedly Odin slayed it—but that was a lie and even he could not kill the thing and merely trapped it." Skrymir said with rising anger, "Unleashing a beast like that will destroy the world, not save it."

"I won't be a party to that," Aric said.

"Calm down," Brunhilda interjected, raising her hands for silence. "Yes, Nidhogg survives. However, we are not turning it loose on the Jotnar or anyone else."

Aric and Skrymir looked relieved but Skuld had a disappointed look on her face. "Will we still get to see the dragon?" she asked with a pout on her face.

"Then what are we doing here?" added Skrymir.

"We're here to retrieve the spear, Gungnir, which should still be lodged in the dragon's flank. Odin believes that is the only weapon powerful enough to pierce Suttungr's magical defenses and allow us to kill him. Just him," Brunhilda said with emphasis to Skrymir. "This rebellion will collapse with his death and we'll return the nine realms to peace." Turning to Aric she added, "Perhaps with some changes. I promise to advocate to Odin personally."

To Skuld she said, "And yes, we will get to see a dragon up close."

"So we're going to sneak up to a dragon, remove a spear from its side, and get away? How are we supposed to do that?" asked Aric, his mouth agape and his hand pulling at the hair atop his head. For someone who had never traveled beyond the borders of his small village before, Brunhilda thought he was taking all of this rather well. She could not help but admire him, facing down monstrous wolves that terrified him and standing up to people he had once revered as gods. And now he would encounter an ancient terror from the old world. Humans were proving to be tougher and more resilient than she had ever expected.

Brunhilda looked at her motley crew of two humans and a Jotnar, and her words caught in her throat. She was supposed to be here with two other skilled valkyries, with her friends. Yet these strangers had followed her, had put their faith in her, and she had, in turn, come to trust them. So she spoke honestly and said, "I have no idea."

She made eye contact with each of them in turn. As she remembered what they had all gone through to get here, thought about how they were prepared to work together and overcome whatever they might encounter, she smiled and said, "But I have faith that together we'll figure something out."

"Faith?" Skrymir said with a hint of teasing in his voice. "I'd much rather have a plan."

—

Brunhilda, Aric, Skuld, and Skrymir crept on their bellies and peered over the cliff edge into the bowl-like expanse where they expected to find Yggdrasil and Nidhogg. The broad green canopy of the World Tree reached high overhead, here where the sun still shone unobscured. This valley was the polar opposite of the caldera of Hoddmimis Holt. It was desolate save for the giant tree at its center. Brunhilda's spirits fell when she saw no signs of edible plant or animal life. The lush vegetation that had once flourished here had been scorched by dragonfire. A light mist circled the tree's base as water continued to flow from the nearby spring. There, along its edges, life was slowly returning.

Not far from there they saw the source of all of the devastation. The long, lithe body of a dragon was coiled into a dark, spiraling, black mass. Obsidian scales covered in hardened spikes jutted out all along the creature's back. The hard, sharp features were enhanced by dew from the mist, glinting in the light filtered through the leaves. Its features were difficult to discern, yet even at this distance it sent a shiver along the spines of all who beheld it.

The arctic winds that had dogged them across the barren tundra of Niflheim stopped abruptly here at Yggdrasil; the air was still and preternaturally quiet in the valley. The sides were formed of granite and covered by ice as smooth as glass and harder than steel. The remnants of an ancient landslide littered one side. Brunhilda pointed out the only access, a hidden, narrow crevasse carved into the southwest wall. Claw marks marred these faces. The dragon had been unsuccessful in widening this passage and using it to climb out. With its size and bulk, its only avenue of escape was by air.

Nidhogg itself was a hundred yards away from the roots of Yggdrasil. The haft of Gungnir could be seen jutting forth from its right flank, sparkling in the daylight and pinning the dragon's right wing. By Brunhilda's accounting it had been embedded in the beast for over a century.

"After all of the stories of the Aesir and Jotnar that had proven to be gross exaggerations of reality," Aric said, his voice cracked with fear and awe, "those of Nidhogg fall woefully short."

"Is it dead?" whispered Skuld. She sounded disappointed. Her glib remark undercut the gravity of the awesome creature before them.

Minutes passed before they saw the slightest rise and fall of the dragon's chest.

"The beast looks to be in a heavy slumber," observed Skrymir. "Possibly hibernating."

"Hibernation makes sense," Skuld said in agreement. "With Niflheim surrounding this pit, no prey would have stumbled in to feed the dragon in years or even decades. It's a wonder that it's still alive at all."

"Maybe this will be easier than I thought," Brunhilda said

under her breath.

—

The plan had sounded simple enough. The humans would circle around to Yggdrasil and hide among the roots, bows at the ready should the dragon awake. Brunhilda would have the dangerous task of approaching Nidhogg and retrieving the spear. And, if the opportunity were there, she would thrust the spear in deeper to slay the beast once and for all. The primary objective remained to retrieve the spear, and Nidhogg's demise was secondary.

Any movement of Gungnir from Nidhogg's side would surely wake the beast no matter how deeply it slept, and Aric and Skuld would be ready with bows and arrows to draw the creature's attention. With the spear in hand, Brunhilda and Skrymir would rush back to the crevasse and then up to their waiting aurochs. Then they would distract the dragon while Aric and Skuld made their own escape.

Getting down through the crevasse was simple enough. Skrymir anchored a rope from the opening into the valley below. He and Brunhilda took up their positions behind some debris from the landslide about fifty yards from the still form of the dragon. The boulders that had crashed and scattered long ago remained rough and jagged with a broad expanse of scree between them and Nidhogg.

Skuld had to pull Aric along the perimeter of the bowl to the far side of Yggdrasil. The scree and other debris from the landslide made moving quietly nearly impossible, yet despite the noise the slumbering dragon did not stir.

From their hiding place, Brunhilda and Skrymir winced at every miniature landslide created as Aric and Skuld moved across the loose gravel. "Could they possibly make any more noise?" Skrymir hissed through his teeth.

He seemed even more nervous and anxious than Brunhilda felt; sweat beaded all across his forehead, and she thought she detected a slight tremor in his hand. Now that they were closer they could see Nidhogg's head covered in ridges of spikes, the sword-like teeth that lined its jaws, its silvery talons as long as spears contrasted against the shimmering, black scales. The familiar scent of sulfur burned her nostrils. Unlike the pervasive, ambient odor of Hoddmimis Holt, the source here was the dragon. She did not think any less of Skrymir for his fear as she recalled the first time that she bore witness to this terrible creature.

Brunhilda looked at him with sincere concern. "Are you okay?"

"We're about to tear out a scab from a monstrous dragon, with teeth and claws larger than we are, that even the alliance of the Great Awakening couldn't kill," Skrymir said with biting condescension. "Of course I'm not okay."

"It breathes fire too," Brunhilda said with a wink. Her own fears were buried deep down, and all she could feel was the blood pumping adrenaline in her as the memories of her fallen sisters-in-arms, Hilder and Skogul, bolstered her strength. Their deaths would not be in vain. Brunhilda steeled herself and ran through the details in her mind. With Gungnir embedded in the dragon for so long, she would need to pour her own life energy into the spear to empower it and cut it free. Freya had instructed her, all three of them, in the principles of performing such a feat. Brunhilda was confident that she would not fail and told herself as much; still, she could not dispel a small kernel of doubt.

So it was with little surprise when there was a commotion around the roots of Yggdrasil and the massive bulk of Nidhogg began to stir.

—

"How are you tripping over every single stone?" hissed an exasperated Skuld.

"How are you not?" Aric responded in a harsh and defensive whisper. "This area is made entirely of loose stone and ice and gravel." Despite his tone he was impressed at Skuld's deft footwork across the debris. If Aric had not been distracted and watching his own feet, he would have been amazed by her ability to dance over the ground.

After what seemed like an eternity they at last arrived at Yggdrasil. The expansive root system stretched out in a hundred yard radius from the trunk and rose to thirty feet above ground level. Crouching low, they looked over the low roots at the edge to check on Nidhogg. To his surprise their noisy trek had not elicited any reaction from the beast, and both Aric and Skuld breathed a sigh of relief.

Yggdrasil was a tree of near incomprehensible size. The trunk was wider around than four of Murtrborg's town square. Its canopy stretched above where clouds would normally be. And it was at this point that Aric realized that he could once again see the clear blue sky. The upper boughs of the tree were covered in broad, verdant leaves that drank in the light of the sun and cast this valley in an ethereal, dappled light. He had been so awestruck at the fantastic nature of the dragon that he had been blind to the grand majesty of this tree from which all life had sprung.

Even the perimeter roots were thicker around than three people standing abreast. The tree itself moved and swayed though he felt no wind, and Aric could swear the roots themselves shifted to give them a path to walk along. As they worked their way closer, Aric and Skuld barely had to duck their heads. The roots indeed appeared to have a life of their own, moving and flowing around them, opening up a corridor as Skuld led the way. Looking toward the heart of the tree, the branching root systems became more labyrinthine as they disappeared into the darkness. Aric thought he could see a strange light emanating from somewhere beyond the murky depths.

"Hey," Skuld said as she grasped Aric by the shoulder. "Are you okay?"

"What? Yeah," Aric said, shaking his head to clear the fog from his mind. "Did you see… Something's in there."

"All of the worst monsters from before the Great Awakening are trapped deep within there, from the ancient days when the Aesir, Vanir, and Jotnar worked together for the collective good," Skuld said, her voice dreamy and nostalgic. "At least that's what the stories say. Whatever might actually be there hasn't come out to disturb the slumbering dragon in all of this time so I think we'll be okay. Come on, we need to get up higher to cover Brunhilda and Skrymir when they approach."

217

She was about to turn back and continue on their path, but then she leapt toward Aric and tackled him down to the twining roots that made up the ground beneath their feet, knocking the wind out of him. At the same instant a dark, monstrous claw swiped above their heads. Skuld had her sword drawn before she stood, coming up into a low guard position. Another claw came at them from their right flank, and this time Skuld's sword came up to intercept it. Bright sparks erupted from the point of contact as the sword itself glowed against the shadowy limb. The claw recoiled as an inhuman scream echoed in the inky blackness beneath the tree. In quick succession more claws and dark shapes began emerging from the deep shadows of Yggdrasil's roots.

Aric had drawn his own sword now. But while Skuld's strikes seemed to have a significant effect on the claws, his cuts elicited no reaction at all. And as more grasping limbs began emerging from the darkness, he struck to no avail and silently rued not taking advantage of Brunhilda's offers of combat training.

"How are you doing that?" he shouted as Skuld's sword struck back another claw in a brilliant flash of light, forcing it to retreat.

She hacked at two more attacks from wicked claws both scaled and furred. "Run!" she shouted. More roars and screams threatened from below as Skuld hauled Aric behind her and they ran back out away from Yggdrasil's depths. Aric could swear that the roots were closing in behind them to contain the shadowy monsters.

When they emerged back into the sunlit realm of the World Tree's canopy, they were greeted by a terrifying sight. Nidhogg had awoken and was looking right at them. Surprised, it snapped its jaws at them from the front while the dark claws reached from behind. Skuld had just enough time to push Aric to the right as she leapt to the left, and they both fell and tumbled over the tangle of roots, coming to a stop where the ground and the roots met. Somehow they had held onto their respective weapons, though most of Aric's arrows had spilled free from his quiver. Nidhogg moved in slow, swaying arcs, as if it were still half asleep, its eyes blinking drowsily. From Yggdrasil the claws reached for and attacked everything, including the dragon.

Aric scrambled to retrieve his arrows, and Nidhogg turned its attention to him. As its neck cocked in preparation to strike, an arrow struck it from behind. The arrow itself was deflected by the creature's hardened scales, yet its impact was enough to get the dragon's attention. Aric could just see Skrymir ducking back behind a boulder. Nidhogg whirled around with more annoyance than anger.

Yggdrasil's roots were now a seething mass of clawed limbs and fanged mouths trying to break through. Skuld stayed busy with a sword in hand. Each strike of her blade upon the dark limbs brought about bright flashes and sparks, giving her a brief respite from them as they recoiled. But that commotion drew Nidhogg to her, its eyes focused on the flashes. With its tail, Nidhogg alternated between flailing at the boulders behind which Skrymir and Brunhilda hid and crashing against the roots holding back the grasping claws.

Aric found himself stuck among the roots. He could not seek refuge there for the claws were ever present and grasping. And there was no other cover between him and the others. Skrymir was doing his best to distract Nidhogg, firing arrow after arrow at its head, though these just bounced off as the beast became fixated on Aric, Skuld, and the grasping creatures.

As the dragon continued to snap and thrash, smoke and embers began to spew from its nostrils. When Skrymir's next arrow found its mark and glanced off of Nidhogg's eye, it spun in his direction and belched out a short gout of flame. Skrymir escaped just barely singed, though his bow was not so lucky and it burned to ash.

He was yelling to Brunhilda as a larger blaze burst forth and enveloped the rock he was hiding behind. Aric feared the worst until he saw the Jotnar pop his head out from behind Brunhilda's boulder. As soon as the flames died down, Nidhogg's head emerged above the rock and its claw crashed down where Skrymir had been. The beast turned its paw and looked beneath before unleashing a deafening roar. It raised its head and was about to continue around the other rocks when Aric's arrow struck the side of its head, drawing it back toward Yggdrasil.

Nidhogg darted straight for Yggdrasil, bellowing flame from its gaping maw. Once again Skuld reacted with uncanny reflexes and pulled Aric to safety behind a thick clump of roots that closed against the blaze. They narrowly avoided the fire yet they were near enough to feel the intense, searing heat. When his eyes adjusted to the darkness he saw a path in Yggdrasil's roots leading away from the inferno. Despite the intensity of the flames, the tree itself did not catch fire.

Roaring, Nidhogg battered the roots with its tail, knocking them to the ground. Aric stumbled and fell out into the open area away from the tree while Skuld fell farther into the winding root system. The dragon pounced and was on Aric in a flash, gripping him in its claw with crushing force, its head drawn back, mouth open, smoke and saliva coming out.

Brunhilda and Skrymir burst out of cover and raced across the open terrain. Even though she moved inhumanly fast, Aric could see that she would not to reach him in time.

He stared into the gaping, tooth-lined jaws, ready and resigned—until a shadowy claw shot out from the roots and grabbed the dragon's foreleg that was holding him. The startled Nidhogg dropped its prey. As Aric fell, he could see more and more snaking limbs reach out, grasping and pulling Nidhogg toward the roots. The dragon strained and snapped at the claws, yet for each one that it pulled off, two more took its place. As the creature was dragged closer to Yggdrasil, more and more claws took hold and the roots themselves seemed to come alive and entangle Nidhogg. Skuld emerged from the roots and helped Aric to his feet.

"You lured the claws back?" rasped Aric, injured but still alive. His breathing was labored as he rose, his arm clasped around his left ribs in pain. He probably had a few cracked ribs from Nidhogg's crushing grip and the fall.

"Come on," Skuld replied, pulling Aric with urgency, "we're not safe yet."

—

As Nidhogg struggled and pulled against the claws, limbs crashing and fire spewing forth, Brunhilda and Skrymir caught up to Aric and Skuld, who were standing just beyond the reach of the dragon. Skrymir helped to support Aric, who was holding his side and grimacing. Meanwhile, Brunhilda assessed the scene before them. Nidhogg's attention was fully focused on the shadowy monster claws and snaking tendrils. Though it fought with all of its strength, the claws and roots held it more or less in place. This was her chance, the opportunity that she needed to get to Gungnir. And so she took it.

Brunhilda threw down her sword, its golden pommel glinting in the light as it hit the ground. She ran as fast as her feet could carry her toward Nidhogg, her eyes fixed on the spear jutting from its pinned right wing. She did not hear the shouts from Skrymir or Skuld; her focus, all of her concentration was on Gungnir. The dragon's tail lashed out at her, and she vaulted over that with ease. The return swing almost caught her in the head, but she tucked and rolled beneath it, never losing her momentum. Surging forth, she leapt onto the beast's haunch and raced up along its flank, her goal in sight. When she was within a yard, Brunhilda threw herself forward, anticipating some last minute turn of fortune that would strip away this victory.

It did not come. Instead she felt the haft of Gungnir in her hands. She held on with every fiber of her being as Nidhogg continued to buck and struggle against the shadowy claws surging from the roots of Yggdrasil, flames bloomed all around her as the monstrous dragon bucked and thrashed. Securing her grip on the spear, she set her feet on either side and pulled with all of her strength. But the spear would not budge. The flesh had cauterized around the wound ages ago and the scar tissue had healed around it. The blade was locked, wedged into the iron-hard scales.

Freya's image came unbidden into her mind. She felt Hilder and Skogul's presence as well. Thinking of her fallen friends and her mentor, she took a calming breath and steeled herself. Reaching deep within, Brunhilda opened her life's energy up to Gungnir. Even astride the thrashing Nidhogg while trying to tap into the primordial energy inside, she held on. At first there was nothing, just the starbursts against blackness of her tightly shut eyes. The physical and mental strain taxed her mind and body. Still, she could not give up. She thought of the reasons for which she fought: for the nine realms, for Asgard, for Freya, for Skogul and Hilder, and for her new companions, friends, two humans… and even a Jotnar. And as she thought of them all, a surge of energy and light joined her with Gungnir and completed the link with the power of Yggdrasil.

In that instant the spear flashed with a brilliant intensity. Everyone was momentarily blinded; ghost images flickered in their vision as they squinted, rubbed their eyes, and blinked furiously.

Nidhogg spasmed and bucked as Gungnir came to life. The beast screamed in pain. With Brunhilda's outpouring of energy, Gungnir easily cut through the scar tissue and the dragon's scaly hide. But the intense burst of power had overwhelmed her, and both she and the spear were thrown free as Nidhogg twisted and writhed. In mid-air Brunhilda, utterly exhausted by the power expended, faded in and out of consciousness and lost her grip on the spear. Immediately Gungnir's power dissipated and fell to the ground, drained and powerless.

—

"What happened?" asked a groggy Brunhilda as Skuld cradled her in her lap. "Did we win?"

Skuld had been the first to regain her sight and rushed to Brunhilda's aid. Looking around she saw Aric, who was injured, slowly rising. He was still shaking off the blinding effects, the heels of his palms pressing against his eyes.

"You were amazing," reassured Skuld. "You tapped into Gungnir and pulled it free. The power was incredible."

"Where is it?" Brunhilda said as she blinked, her eyes searching. She struggled to sit up as Skuld held her and spoke to her with a soothing voice and gentle strokes.

"No need to worry, child," Skuld said, keeping eye contact with Brunhilda as she pointed in the direction it had fallen. "It's just over there—"

Skuld's breath caught as she looked down and saw Gungnir's blade jutting out through her abdomen. The bright, golden glow of Reginvald shone from the wound, radiating around the blade of the spear. She clutched at her wound as the blade was withdrawn and she fell forward, a look of pain and confusion on her face.

Brunhilda rolled and scrambled back a foot, staring aghast as Skuld slumped over. The unflappable valkyrie was stunned and shell shocked, for holding Gungnir was Hrym, flanked on either side by Skrymir and Geir.

CHAPTER 38: INTERLUDE

Sif stood atop the towering wall of the fortifications that encircled the entrance to the Rainbow Bridge, the Bifrost Skjaldborg. The hundred-foot-high shield wall surrounded an entire district of residents. It stretched in an arc terminating on each side at the sheer western cliffs. The only way to access Asgard was to cross the bridge. On the western side, secure within the wall, lived the non-Aesir citizens who worked in Asgard. Since the uprising began, refugees from all over were brought to shelter here. There was a flurry of activity as troops and engineers worked at a fevered pace to secure the defenses. The last of the reserve troops from the south had returned the day before and were resting after their forced march to Asgard.

"Has there been any sighting of Hilder and her team?"

Sif turned to see Thor's approach. "Nothing, sir. The scouts report that the Jotnar Army is a day's march away," she replied. "If they are still out there, the entire enemy host now stands between them and us. As for our defenses, we haven't had to use them in an age but they were in good condition and did not require much service to be made fully operational. The troops from the southern territories have all returned and are resting or performing their drills to prepare for a siege."

"Good. After we break the Jotnar's first attack, we should be in a position to counterattack and crush their army."

"They've kept us on the defensive throughout their campaign. Do you think that they'll be that predictable?"

"I fully anticipate some scheme or stratagem," Thor said as he shifted Mjolnir in an unusual display of nervous energy. "And with Hilder's team not yet returned we are in a weak position against

Suttungr, but this is our home and we are prepared. I am fully recovered and have learned much since our last encounter; he will not catch me unaware again. Should Suttungr show himself, I shall have the upper hand this time." His grip tightened around Mjolnir, a slight crackle of power flashing across its head.

"Certainly, sir," Sif said and bowed with stiff formality. "I am confident in our defenses and in your leadership." She added with a gentle hand on his arm and a sincere whisper, "Still, I would prefer to have both Gungnir and Mjolnir on our side when Suttungr arrives."

Thor made no reply as he stared across the boundless plain before them.

———

Odin sat in the darkened war room, accompanied only by his animal menagerie. Huginn perched on his shoulder and Muninn kept a watchful eye from atop the throne while the wolves slumbered, their legs twitching as they dreamt. The torches were extinguished and only the glowing embers in the braziers illuminated the room.

Odin's one good eye stared intently at the relief map carved into the table. The pieces told a story of stunning defeats and brilliant tactical maneuvering. Three divisions of Aesir troops were on the move from the borders of Alfheim and Svartalfheim. They would not arrive in time. Jotnar Army tokens had cut a swath of destruction through Midgard and reclaimed the former realm of Jotunheim; they raced through the mostly abandoned realm of Asgard, its citizens safe behind the defenses of the Bifrost Skjaldborg.

Muninn let out a sharp caw.

"Yes," Odin said as if in reply. "We have underestimated him." Reaching out with his right hand, he grasped the token representing the Jotnar Army and slid it toward the capital city of Asgard.

He picked up the piece representing Suttungr and looked at it carefully. "You have cost me much, Loki," he murmured to it. "The blood of Baldur and Freya, Gunnar, and many more are on your head. You are responsible for the suffering of hundreds of thousands of my people. I will exact revenge... justice, with my own hands." The wooden piece snapped in Odin's grip.

Standing, he drew his sword and set it upon the table with a heavy thud. It caught some of the dim light from the brazier yet it glowed brighter; its own light, emanating from the runes, emblazoned down the length of the blade. He stared at it with a bright, burning look in his eye. "You're not the only one with a trick or two."

CHAPTER 39: TRIUMPHANT

Aric's vision cleared at last as the world came back into focus. He saw Hrym standing over the prone form of Skuld with Gungnir in his hand, the blade illuminated with a golden glow and stained with blood. Skrymir and Geir stood with him.

He watched as Brunhilda rose unsteadily on trembling legs. She reached a shaky hand to her empty scabbard. A quick look showed no weapons nearby, but still she charged. Her punches were weak and Hrym allowed them to land, a look of disdain on his face. She dodged a lazy swing by him but was caught by a fist across the face in a following strike. Her body went limp and she was unconscious before she hit the ground.

"I'm going to enjoy breaking your spirit," said Hrym with a smirk as he kicked her unmoving form.

As Aric stood, a sharp pain lanced through his chest. His ribs were definitely cracked. Unsheathing his sword, he ran straight at the Jotnar. Not for the first time but perhaps for the last he regretted not taking combat training more seriously and whispered an apology to Brunhilda.

As those last word crossed his lips, Geir stepped forward with a lazy thrust of his spear; neither Hrym nor Skrymir had bothered to raise their weapons. Aric brought up his sword, but his blade slid along the length of the shaft, only deflecting slightly as he tried to push it away, and all that he accomplished was that the spear sliced him across the gut instead of piercing his heart. Aric dropped the sword and clutched the wound, slowly bleeding out. He had avoided an instantaneous death and was instead rewarded with a slow, agonizing one. Kicking the sword away, Geir sneered at Aric and spat on him, as if he were not worthy of a swift warrior's death.

"I must say that I was skeptical when you first proposed this plan, Skrymir," Hrym said as he examined Gungnir and ran his fingers along the runes, "but this worked out better than I could have hoped for."

"Why?" Skuld gasped as she lay at his feet, her life's blood spilling out. "We trusted you."

"I told you," Skrymir replied, avoiding looking her in the eyes, "the wellbeing of the Jotnar people is my priority. That has always been my goal. It is a promise I made long ago to someone I cherished. I failed her once; I will not fail her again."

—

A powerful roar came from the direction of Yggdrasil. Nidhogg was still struggling against the claws and roots. A smile curled at Hrym's mouth as he caught sight of the trapped beast.

"Finish them and let's be done with this," Hrym said to Skrymir and Geir.

"Why don't you do it?" Skrymir asked, not looking at Skuld, Aric, or Brunhilda.

"I have larger prey to attend to."

Hrym turned and hefted Gungnir in both hands, and he strutted toward the pinned dragon. Geir quickly grasped his intent and was only too happy to follow his leader.

"You should be careful," Skrymir called out after them. With Aric and Skuld fatally wounded his eyes lingered on Brunhilda. He hung his head and sheathed his sword.

"I have the opportunity to do what Odin and the entire host of the Great Awakening could not," Hrym said and raised his arms with arrogance. He and Geir stood before the restrained dragon, just beyond the reach of the sinister claws. "I will be Hrym, slayer of Nidhogg!"

"Hrym, dragonslayer!" Geir chanted.

Hrym stared at Gungnir. Turning it over a few times he gave the spear a shake, looking for the telltale glow of power and energy. He gripped it tighter and raised it toward the sky, willing it to come to life. Still nothing happened. Looking around he could see Geir chanting behind him, unaware of his hesitation. In a flourish Hrym swiped at a rock on the ground. The blade cut through with almost no resistance, splitting it in half.

A smirk rose to his lips as he covered the last six yards to Nidhogg. He raised Gungnir and struck with all of his might. The blade pierced the thick scales of the dragon's eyelid and then came to an abrupt stop. There was no energy, no glow of magic, no hidden power unlocked in this moment.

The beast unleashed a terrifying roar and, with a surge of strength, pulled and tore its head free from the shadowy claws. In a flash, the spiked obsidian head lashed out and snapped in a flurry of teeth and fire. Geir pushed Hrym out of the way, and the gaping maw devoured him instead. Geir was dead in an instant, incinerated in a maelstrom of flames before the dragon's jaws closed upon him. On the ground a few feet away, Hrym desperately patted at the flames that caught on his clothes. The right side of his body was black and burned, though he was able to scramble away out of Nidhogg's reach, still clutching Gungnir.

Skrymir picked up Brunhilda and raced back toward the crevasse out of the valley. Hrym followed right behind after clawing himself out of the still smoldering armor. Even as it dropped to the ground the metal was all that remained, the dragon's fire having incinerated the hide and leather parts in seconds.

It would be a long journey to catch up with Suttungr at Asgard, but they had survived. With the aurochs and with Gungnir in their possession, the way back would speed by. The loss of Geir was unfortunate, but Hrym was not weighed down by his sacrifice. Their task had been a resounding success. And though he had not succeeded in killing Nidhogg, he would still return triumphant. He would be the one who brought Gungnir back to the Jotnar people.

CHAPTER 40: THE SIEGE BEGINS

Thor and Sif observed from overhead as another volley of arrows rained down on the Jotnar. "Fall back!" shouted Suttungr from below. While his spelled armor deflected most of the arrows for him, the other Jotnar were not so fortunate. A number of those struck were revealed to be mirages that vanished upon impact. Still, many more of the casualties were very real. The bodies strewn about him were his soldiers, his followers, his people. Frost covered the ground and spread as the life drained from the fallen. Yet as the Jotnar retreated, Suttungr waved tauntingly to Thor, baiting him even while standing amid the corpses of his fallen troops.

The great shield wall cast a long shadow, even with the sun shrouded by the clouds that accompanied the Jotnar Army. As Suttungr withdrew, cheers rose from the parapet high above. This was the first reported loss of the Jotnar Army under the direct leadership of Suttungr. They fell back to a position just beyond the range of the Aesir archers, and as the sun climbed to its zenith, the Jotnar set about laying their defenses, pitching camp, and digging in for the siege to come.

"Suttungr was right there," Thor exclaimed in frustration. "We should go after them and crush them as they lick their wounds, not let them fortify and tend to their wounded."

"You know that would be a foolish mistake," Sif replied. "The roads from Jotunheim to Bifrost are littered with the frozen and shattered bodies of those who have stood against Suttungr in battle. You and Brunhilda are the only exceptions, and even still, you were brought low and nearly died."

"Yes, yes, I know the plan," he said with anger rising in his voice. "But here we have the advantage. We are Aesir; we do not cower behind walls."

"And that is exactly what they want," Sif said, sighing with strained patience. "They've been beating us, taking advantage of our strategies. It's clear that they have knowledge of our tactics, and if Freya were still with us she would give you the same counsel. All of his magic defenses won't help him to breach our walls. We can hold them back here, whittling away at their forces on every attack. It will also allow us to bide our time for the southern division to smash them from behind or for Hilder, Skogul, and Brunhilda to get Gungnir and bring it home. That was Freya's plan, and it's a good one. We owe it to her to see it through."

Thor looked out as the Jotnar Army continued building their encampment for the long siege ahead. "They'd better hurry because the Jotnar aren't done yet. Suttungr will have something planned for this."

———

"They're cowering behind their precious wall," reported Hertha as she strode toward Suttungr. *"They don't appear to have taken the bait."*

"I suppose they are capable of learning. We knew it would come to this eventually," he replied. *"You have the designs for the siege engines?"*

"Yes, m'lord," she said with a slight nod. *"Our forces are establishing the forward defenses, and our reserves are gathering the resources to build your... contraptions."*

"Good. They're trapped in their little paradise," Suttungr said as they entered his command tent. *"We've managed to keep this war on our terms. This will be no different, just as I had planned. That shining city that they lord over all of the other realms will be their tomb."*

In the first, brief moment when they entered the darkness of the tent, Hertha thought that she saw a dull glow emanate from his skin. As her eyes adjusted to the different lighting inside, the effect vanished. She helped him remove his armor with precise and practiced movements. It was then that Hertha noticed a broken arrow shaft jutting out from above his shoulder; it had found a gap between the metal plates of his armor.

"Sir, you're injured," she said with a start. *"Shall I get the healers?"*

"No, let them tend to our wounded soldiers," he said as he grabbed it with his left hand. A golden light bloomed at the point of contact

and grew in intensity. The barbed arrowhead tore flesh as he ripped it out. Despite the broad blades of the arrow, no blood spilled forth and not even the slightest grimace showed on Suttungr's stoic face. Hertha stood in awe of the sight.

"Every defense has its weakness," he continued as if nothing had happened, throwing the arrow onto the floor. *"We need to attack theirs before they find ours."*

CHAPTER 41: GUNGNIR RETURNED

"It's Gungnir, Skrymir," Hrym shouted from atop an auroch. He raised the spear high until a powerful gust of wind nearly tore it from his grip. He bent down low and held the weapon in his lap as he looked back at Skrymir. *"Did you ever think that you'd see it in person?"*

A line of four aurochs were the only sign of life in the boundless white tundra. Hrym and Skrymir each rode atop one, leashed to another. Aric's sled was still bound to one of the animals though there were almost no food supplies remaining. Brunhilda was bound and draped across an auroch with Hrym's massive torso leaning over her, holding her in place as the group raced southward.

"You didn't have to kill them," Skrymir shouted back from the other auroch. *"The humans posed no threat to us."*

"They were dead anyway. Without these" —Hrym patted the auroch beneath him— *"they would have been stranded there, left to die of starvation or devoured by Nidhogg should it break free from those demon claws. What in Hel's name were those things?"* Despite the cold, the two Jotnar seemed rather comfortable; recalling the shadowy appendages, however, sent shivers down Hrym's spine.

"Monsters of the past," Skrymir said in a hollow tone. *"Though they say the Great Awakening culled them from the world, most were simply driven into hiding or trapped beneath Yggdrasil."* The haunted look in his eyes were lost to the driving snow as they continued on their way through the Niflheim wastes. The fierce arctic gales and the thought of such an immense concentration of terrible monsters was enough to leave them in an uncomfortable silence.

—

They rode for two days straight without rest. At last the aurochs reached their point of exhaustion and Skrymir convinced Hrym to a rest stop. *"We don't want them to die,"* he said practically. *"We'd be stranded leagues away from Gastropnir.*" Hrym only grunted consent.

The windswept barrens of Niflheim stretched out around them in every direction. When they finally came to a stop, the aurochs collapsed in exhaustion, their breathing heavy and labored though they were otherwise unaffected by the cold and biting winds. Skrymir arranged them into a berm and set up their gear against their leeward side. Though the Jotnar were fairly inured to the cold, spending this long in the severe conditions of Niflheim was beginning to chill even their bones. This was meager shelter, but it would have to do. Brunhilda was in terrible shape. Her injuries left her more vulnerable to the harsh weather.

"*I will guard the prisoner,*" Hrym announced with a leering smile as he lifted Brunhilda and held her against him. Though weak and exhausted, she still mustered enough strength to struggle against him.

"*That won't be necessary.*" Skrymir placed a hand upon the hilt of his sword as he addressed Hrym. "*We are not savages. We are Jotnar and will conduct ourselves with the dignity of Yggdrasil's first children.*"

"*You should be careful, Skrymir,*" Hrym said, baring his teeth, his grip tightening around Gungnir in his free hand. But unlike the moment when Brunhilda wielded it, it had yet to react to his will. "*You don't stand a chance against me. We staged the fight in that pissant human village.*"

Skrymir did not reply and just steeled his glare at Hrym. The conviction in his unwavering eyes burned with frightening intensity. Even Brunhilda, who did not understand what they said and was still in Hrym's grasp ceased her struggling.

"*As you say,*" Hrym said after a long moment. "*Let her be your responsibility.*" With that, he pushed her toward Skrymir, who caught her with both hands as she stumbled. He had never actually drawn his sword.

"I'm still going to kill you for betraying us," Brunhilda hissed at him through clenched teeth. An unimpressed Skrymir did not even bother addressing her hollow threat. He just shoved her off of her feet and down into the sheltering nook of the resting—and especially pungent—aurochs.

—

It was a dark, moonless night weeks later when two aurochs arrived at the Jotnar camp besieging Bifrost. The clouds that had spread from Niflheim and covered Midgard blocked out the twinkling stars above Asgard as well.

During the day the sun itself only cast the world in a cold, gray twilight. So it was that night found the dim bonfires of both fronts barely illuminating the edges of the battlefield. The newcomers arrived unseen by the Aesir scouts, who were straining their vision against the darkness.

Even in the Jotnar camp their arrival was received with little fanfare, though Hertha hurried to Hrym's side to greet him. Hrym and Skrymir were exhausted and the aurochs they rode were not the same as the ones they had left Yggdrasil with. Having picked up fresh mounts at Gastropnir and every possible point along the way, they had made it to Asgard in remarkable time.

Hertha brought them straight away to Suttungr's tent at the center of camp. They scarcely noticed the construction going on as they walked; and despite their grueling journey, Hrym insisted on carrying Gungnir. Skrymir had no objection to Hertha's help and gladly handed off Brunhilda after cutting her legs free of their bonds. She had been trussed up like a wayward auroch calf after so many escape attempts. Her legs were shaky after being bound for so long. Still, as they walked through the Jotnar camp she managed to stand tall and defiant.

Skrymir and Hrym collapsed into a kneeling position before Suttungr when they entered his tent. Hertha knelt as well after knocking Brunhilda to her knees. A brazier burned with intensity in the center of Suttungr's personal tent. His armor hung in the corner, the faint glow emanating from it that was more than just the reflected light of the fire. The bed was covered in furs and there was a workbench along the far side as well as a table heaped with maps and messages.

"Your mission was a success," Suttungr stated as his eyes moved from the blazing red hair of the kneeling valkyrie to the runes shimmering across the surface of the spear.

"Yes, my lord," Hrym said with a humility and deference Skrymir had not seen in him before. Hrym presented Gungnir to

234

Suttungr, holding the spear in open palms above his bowed head.

"Ah, Gungnir," Suttungr's voice cracked, betraying a hint of emotion as he beheld the legendary weapon. He took hold of the spear and at the moment of contact it gave off a subdued glow of blue light. Hrym's look of disappointment and envy did not escape Skrymir's eye.

"So this was Odin's brilliant plan. In attempting to save himself, he has delivered to me the very instrument of his downfall," Suttungr said as he looked at Brunhilda, his voice rife with malice and contempt.

"Even with Gungnir you won't get anywhere near Odin," Brunhilda spat at him. "Thor still wields Mjolnir and he will crush that smug grin off of your face!"

"The whole host of Aesir, least of all Thor and his hammer, have not stopped us from tearing a path of death and destruction across the realms to Asgard's door," said Suttungr. "And now with Gungnir in my possession, the indomitable wall of the Bifrost Skjaldborg will crumble before me. I will kill Odin last so that he may watch everything he loves burn and know that this was all his fault!" It was the first time Skrymir had ever seen Suttungr show so much naked emotion. In that display, the beauty of his face betrayed a frightening countenance that shocked them all.

Suttungr went to the kneeling yet somehow still insolent Brunhilda. He placed his hand upon her chin, and small sparks of frost crackled against her skin. "I understand that we have you to thank for pulling the spear free from that infernal beast. And so I grant you your life. After we raze Asgard to the ground and slaughter everyone within, you will be the last Aesir, cursed to live alone with your failure."

CHAPTER 42: FAILED ONCE MORE

A golden sun blazed in the brilliant sapphire sky above. The emerald greens of the lush forest were achingly vibrant to Aric's weary eyes. He found himself chasing after Una into the woods near their home, just up the shore from the fjord where they fished. She was quick and small and always seemed to be just beyond his reach and out of sight. She flitted and danced between the golden rays of sunlight, always disappearing behind a tree before he could glimpse her, but the lilting chime of her laughter reassured Aric that she was there.

The dappled rays shone hazily through the leaves. Light and shadow played throughout the woods and made it difficult for Aric to see how far everything was, where he was, even when he was. Yet he still laughed every time he heard the trill of Una's giggles.

Somewhere behind him, beyond the trees, Dagmaer called out to Aric, asking him to return. "Come on, Una, it's time to go home," Aric said as he stopped running. Turning to locate the source of her giggles, he said again, "Playtime is over. We'd better get back before your mother becomes cross."

Turning again as he heard giggling behind him, he tripped as a root rose up out of the ground. It had not been there before. It was almost as if it had tangled his feet on purpose. Aric fell flat on his face, or maybe the ground had fallen up into him. He rolled over onto his back and rubbed the dirt from his eyes; his nose felt like it might be broken, but there was no blood. When he opened his eyes, he saw Una standing over him.

"It's not your fault, pabbi," she said with her measured and too-mature-for-her-age tone. "You did the best that you could."

She turned and walked out of his field of vision and her disembodied voice added, "But you still failed."

—

The canopy of leaves overhead was still and silent. Aric's eyes blinked then squeezed shut. Tears streamed down his cheek, and he let out a long exhale. The green of the leaves and the golden orb of the sun were a welcome sight, though everything appeared as if he were looking at it through a long, dark tunnel. With a sudden jolt the leaves shook violently overhead. Aric turned his head and saw that the dragon was still trapped in a tangle of dark, grasping claws and twining roots. Each surge of its body rocked Yggdrasil from base to bough.

Aric was on his back, his left hand held tight across his body. He tried to stanch the flow of blood from the wound in his gut. Though he had no experience with battlefield injuries, he knew, deep down, that the cold touch of death was crawling through his veins, outward from the gaping cut. He could not even draw enough breath to call for help.

Closing his eyes, that all-encompassing darkness brought back the faces of all he had failed. Quick, agonizing flashes tormented him; Dagmaer and Una he had become accustomed to, yet seeing them so vividly stabbed at his heart. Now that bitter agony was joined by the faces of Skuld and Brunhilda. His eyes snapped open and he coughed up a bit of blood.

"I'm sorry." His lips formed the words, though no sound escaped his throat. He begged forgiveness of the leaves, of everyone, and of no one in particular. "I'm so sorry. I let you all down."

CHAPTER 43: STRATAGEM

A thick morning fog flowed in from the west, enveloping the landscape in a blanket of eerie silence. What had once been the Jotnar bonfires to the Aesir on watch now emerged as ghostly sprites, floating forward in the rolling mist. As they drew closer to the Bifrost Skjaldborg, it became clear to the Aesir defenders that these lights sat atop six massive siege engines, pushed by teams of aurochs they could hear braying from within. The towers moved at a slow, deliberate pace, bristling with spears and followed by the bulk of the Jotnar Army, led by Hertha. Suttungr marched in their midst. He wielded Gungnir with casual grace, unhurried as if in a ceremonial parade. Hrym and Skrymir flanked him on either side in places of honor.

Brunhilda walked forward, led by a chain that Skrymir held. Her wrists were shackled together with heavy metal manacles taken from defeated Aesir armies, used to bind their prisoners. She had been stripped of her Jotnar armor disguise and wore simple clothes. Suttungr stopped and held Gungnir aloft. Hertha halted the advance and the army roared as they clamored, awaiting the signal to attack. From their current position, four hundred yards away, they had an expansive view of the plains that lay before the towering Bifrost Skjaldborg.

Brunhilda spat at Suttungr. "Asgard will bury you. The border territories were ill fortified. Here, against the Bifrost Skjaldborg, is where we break you!"

"You and your vaunted valkyries fell before our might," Hrym said, and with a heavy shove he knocked Brunhilda to the ground. He drew his blade and stabbed it into the dirt beside her head.

"Enough," Suttungr interrupted. He pulled Brunhilda up by the hair into a kneeling position. Curling his right hand into a fist around Brunhilda's chains, he struck it against the ground and created a spike of swirling ice that anchored her in place. "You may watch the destruction of your home and your people from here."

He turned away and gestured to Hertha. From the head of the column she nodded and brought a grand twisting horn to her lips. A trumpet blast broke through the still morning air, and the attack began.

The first volley of Aesir arrows began as soon as the towers were in range. The pitch-covered, flaming arrows stuck but did little to the towers. The leather-covered walls were coated in a layer of frost that quenched each flame as soon as they hit. The main body of the army held back just out of range of the Aesir archers as the towers continued their slow, steady march forward.

But the towers had been constructed in haste and in the dark, and after several volleys the first tower ground to a halt, its drivers and aurochs slain beneath a hailstorm of precision shots. Two other towers slowed as well, each one stopping closer and closer to the Skjaldborg.

When the three remaining towers got to within a hundred yards of the wall, Suttungr signaled and Hertha blew the horn again. The Jotnar Army charged with weapons raised high.

A bolt of lightning struck the closest tower. Although a thick layer of clouds covered the sky overhead, it had originated from atop the wall, from Mjolnir. However, when it hit the metal in the tower's frame the power was redirected and the magic energy ignited the sapper charges within. The mixture of Ethlivald and Reginvald forces resulted in a blast of Jotnar frost magic a thousand times more devastating than when Thor struck Suttungr back in Halvard so long ago.

The ice wave hit the Bifrost Skjaldborg with terrible force and knocked back many of the defenders standing upon the ramparts. Dozens of soldiers fell from the top, plummeting a hundred feet to the ground below. Ice fragments erupted through the stone of the wall made brittle by the cold. The two other towers were caught in the radius of the blast and erupted in secondary explosions. When the dust and smoke cleared, all that was left of the towers were aurochs and their drivers, encased in spires of ice.

Suttungr ran ahead of the frontline of Jotnar soldiers. With Gungnir's blade he met the shockwave head on and dispelled it as Odin had done to Nidhogg's flame so long ago. Reaching deep into the energies connected through the ancient weapon, Suttungr tapped into a small fraction of its power. With a slashing arc of the spear, the once indomitable wall of the Bifrost Skjaldborg was rent asunder and collapsed before him in a shower of ice and stone, the rest of the Aesir defenders falling with it.

CHAPTER 44: CONFESSIONS

"Aric."

The whisper broke through the darkness. He felt as though he had been hearing it for a while, but only just now did he comprehend it and recognize his name.

"Aric, are you awake?" The disembodied voice came to him again; it sounded sweet and familiar. Slowly the darkness gave way to a brightening green haze his eyes fluttered open. "Wake up." Once again he saw the expansive canopy of leaves above him and then recalled where he was.

"Dagmaer?" he said. His memories of recent events returned. "How long have we been here?" Aric turned his head toward the source of the voice. There was a hand on his shoulder and for a brief moment, as he looked, he thought that he saw her.

He blinked and realized that it was only Skuld. She was lying face down in the dirt, hair splayed all about and with her arm outstretched, clutching him tightly. Looking beyond her he could see a trail of blood marking her path; it was shimmering and golden.

With great effort he extricated himself from her grasp and sat up. He crawled over to her still form and shook her shoulder. Aric panicked. She couldn't be dead. She had just spoken, hadn't she? Relief swept over him as she groaned. Although slow in reacting she at last rolled onto her side.

"It's been almost three days. I was beginning to worry," she said, propping herself on one arm and coughing into her hand. "I'm glad that you're finally awake." As she sat upright her hair fell away from her face, and what Aric saw startled him. He fell backwards and scrambled an extra yard back.

"You—You're not Skuld." Aric said with little conviction. He was not so much frightened by what he saw but rather startled by the striking visage before him.

"I am her. Or rather, she was me." She rose to her full height, though she was still weak and unsteady.

"And who are you?"

"I am Freya of the Aesir," she stated, power resonating even in the utterance of the name, "daughter of Njord, first king of the Vanir." The authority of her voice lost some of its power with the frailty of her current condition. Shimmering golden blood still flowed from the wound in her chest though she clutched at it with her hand.

Aric looked to his own stabbed gut. To his amazement it no longer bled, though neither was it fully healed. Looking through the tear in his clothes, he thought it resembled a poorly mended scar.

"You're Freya! You're Skuld?" he asked his voice fraught with confusion. "How... When... I don't understand."

"I came to help Brunhilda. We sent her team of valkyries on this mission to retrieve Gungnir. Sadly, some time after they broke through the Jotnar lines at Halvard, the other two died. I had been keeping track of them with a small bit of magic. Soon after that my own army was attacked. I knew then that the situation was more dire than we had first assumed. We needed Gungnir. But now—"

Finally her strength gave out and she started to falter. Aric rushed to her side on instinct and caught her before she fell.

"Now the Jotnar have the spear, and you're bleeding to death," Aric continued for her as they both sat on the ground. "You healed me, didn't you? With your powers? Can't you use your divine Aesir magic to heal yourself?"

"You are a simpler matter than I." She doubled over as she coughed up blood. "Your injury by an ordinary spear required only a small fraction of my power. Were I injured similarly, it would require even less. However, Gungnir's power is great and wounds inflicted by it cannot be so easily mended." Aric helped her lie back and held her in his lap as she spoke.

"You have demonstrated exceptional bravery and a caring heart. You still have a role to play in all of this, Aric," she said, grasping at his tunic with a sense of urgency. "The Aesir still need your help,"

"I've already lost everything... lost everything twice. I have nothing more to give, nothing left to lose."

"The very existence of the nine realms is at stake, and Brunhilda needs you. I can still sense her through my magic. Suttungr has promised to cleanse the realms of every Aesir. And if he wields Gungnir in battle against Thor and Odin, he will destroy Asgard; even then his rage will not be sated. He will bring destruction on all of the other realms, just as he has already done to Jotunheim and Midgard."

"But what can I do against gods and monsters?" pleaded Aric.

"You have more power than you think," Freya said with gentle reassurance as her muscles relaxed. "You've faced down Jotnar warriors, terrifying vargr, and even the most powerful dragon the nine realms have ever known. Though my power will not save me, I will imbue you with all that I have left." She raised her hand to his forehead. A soft, warm glow bloomed from the point of contact and spread throughout his body. "Use it to save Brunhilda. You've proven to be clever and brave. I'm sure you'll think of something."

The power hit Aric hard. This infusion of power into his frail human body was too much for him. Despite his best efforts to stay awake, after several painful moments he succumbed and fell unconscious.

Freya's hand went limp and her body eased into his lap. Somewhere in the back of his mind, Aric could feel her pass and once again he was left alone, cradling a lifeless body.

As the power flowed and shifted to find room within his meager frame, he experienced the dreamlike sensation of seeing himself from the outside. It reminded him of a similar scene not so long ago, when he cradled his own daughter in his arms as her life faded. She had looked up at him from his lap until the spark of light was extinguished from her eyes.

CHAPTER 45: BIFROST SKJALDBORG

The battle raged and the fighting was brutal. Chaos and the din of battle resounded throughout the plains as the Aesir forces pushed back against the bulk of the Jotnar Army. Suttungr was unstoppable with Gungnir, though the rest of the Jotnar Army was far outmatched by the Aesir forces.

After Suttungr toppled the Biforst Skjaldborg, the Aesir rallied to meet the Jotnar onslaught head on with Sif in the lead. She had seen Thor hold on against the ice blast, but when the Skjaldborg collapsed he had fallen too, lost among the cascade of rubble. With the Jotnar surging through the gap behind their leaders, there was no time for her to search the debris for Thor or the others. Without missing a beat Sif took up command of the army. If Suttungr made it to the bridge, there would be no stopping the Jotnar Army from slaughtering everyone within the capital. This was their last and only chance to break the Jotnar blitz.

"Form up on me," shouted Sif. "Engage their flanks, press in on them. Limit Suttungr's movements! If he breaks through, fall back and leave him to me!"

The Jotnar Army was far less skilled than the Aesir, yet they made up for that deficiency in sheer numbers, pushing through the destruction of the wall. With help from valkyries, the remaining Aesir soldiers moved their line forward, even over the rough terrain of the debris field, over the bodies of their fallen comrades. Hundreds of Aesir threw their bodies against the Jotnar onslaught. They pushed the less disciplined lines of the Jotnar into Suttungr, surrounding him with his own troops, keeping him from using Gungnir to its full effect.

"Jotnar, push out the flanks!" Suttungr's voice carried above the din, and his troops adapted and moved according to his order. The mountainous Hrym forced his way out against the shields of the Aesir. With powerful swings of his cleaver he hammered out space along the right flank. Hertha bolstered the left flank, rallying Jotnar to her and leading by example. Her stout frame held fast against the Aesir attacks. Skrymir found a mound of rocks near what was left of the wall and fired arrow after arrow into the Aesir line.

After extricating himself from his own troops, Suttungr laid into the defenders of Asgard. In a matter of minutes he cut down a dozen foes. Then the Aesir line opened up as Sif stepped forward. She wore a tabard emblazoned with the crest of Asgard. Her rank as commander of the city guard was signified by the gold trim of her armor. Many of the Jotnar withered away as she approached, wielding her sturdy round shield and bloodstained sword. Braids of honey-colored hair billowed out from the back of her helmet. Suttungr gave a nod of recognition—whether to her or her rank, she did not care—and they engaged each other with no other pomp or delay.

Several Aesir and even some Jotnar fell to Suttungr's wild swings with Gungnir. Sif was skilled enough to avoid his first swings. Likewise he blocked her counters, the wooden shaft of the spear proving more than capable of withstanding Sif's spelled blade. Suttungr's next attacks were not directed at her but at her weapons. The spear split her shield and then broke her sword in his following attack. As she reeled, Sif had a brief moment to take in the battlefield; the sheer number of slain Aesir was staggering. This was not the time to mourn them for they had achieved greatness and died in glorious battle; but in death they no longer had need of their weapons. Sif rolled to the side, and in one smooth motion she picked up two swords, one in each hand. She blocked Gungnir by the shaft, avoiding contact with the blade. With each parry she tried to turn the blade against nearby Jotnar. And although she often created openings to attack, she knew enough not to strike Suttungr with her spelled Aesir weapons. Instead she used the rubble of the Skjaldborg to her advantage, leading him onto loose rocks and uneven terrain. She batted stones at him, looking for any opportunity to disarm him. Yet for every technique and stratagem that she employed, he was never as vulnerable as she hoped. Each time that she thought she had him at a disadvantage, he broke the momentum of the fight, avoiding her trap.

It was after a long exchange, when they clashed with their

weapons locked together—her blades and guards trapping Gungnir's haft—that she truly began to worry. When the Bifrost Skjaldborg fell, she knew that they had dangerously miscalculated. And now, for the first time, she realized that they were facing annihilation. Loki had never been this skilled in combat.

Her opponent absorbed everything she threw at him. He continued to surprise her with the depth of his knowledge of Aesir methods and skills. The flow of the fight never left his control. Now she could see his machinations. After opening with a few wild attacks to give her a false sense of security, he took up a different stance and went on the offensive.

All the while, the tide of battle moved in sync with their fight; when she had pushed him back, so too did the Aesir Army surge against the Jotnar. Now, as if connected to him, the entire Jotnar Army swelled forward with his attacks. Sif was barely able to raise her guard. Blow after blow she was pushed back along with the Aesir lines, the Jotnar Army cheering at each step.

From somewhere deep inside, she drew upon her reserves and rallied. Suttungr was more skilled than she had given him credit for; they had all underestimated him. That hubris had cost them. It had cost them Halvard, Freya, Gunnar, and all of Midgard. This was their last stand, their last chance to defeat Suttungr. If they could not hold him here, they would lose Asgard. They would lose everything. So with a battlecry rising from the depths of her very soul, she fought back. Her swords locked with Gungnir again. She would hold the line this day or die in the effort.

CHAPTER 46: THE LESSER EVIL

Nidhogg lay quiet at the base of Yggdrasil yet seethed with impotent fury, smoke and fire spewing from its nostrils. Entangled by grasping claws and roots, it had stopped struggling against its restraints for now. The meal provided by Geir's sacrifice had given it a bit of nourishment, though it whetted the dragon's appetite more than sated it.

Aric snapped awake then, gasping for breath. He sat up and looked around. Rocks scorched by dragonfire spoke of recent events. The land between him and Yggdrasil was gouged by the beast's wicked talons, the rocks churned by its thrashing tail. And yet the valley was now calm. Not even smoke lingered from the charred ground. Blazing overhead, the sun indicated that it was near midday, though Aric had to wonder how many days had passed. His wounds were healed without a trace and he flexed and stretched to confirm this. The eerie silence was broken by a sound of scraping coming from the direction of Yggdrasil.

Nidhogg glared as Aric stood. A deep growl reverberated through the valley, the low timbre penetrating through to the human's very core. Aric turned to face it and locked eyes with the fearsome creature's good eye. Its lids narrowed as they stared. The dragon's eye flicked toward a pile of debris nearby and then back to Aric.

Breaking eye contact, Aric took a quick glance around him. Skuld's body was nowhere to be seen, yet her shimmering blood still stained the ground and his clothes. A distinctive gold hilt caught his attention. He walked over to it and stared at length, remembering Skuld's last words. Brunhilda was still alive. Picking up the sword, he hoped to someday return it to its rightful owner—if they both lived that long. Nearby he noticed Hrym's armor had been burned and partially melted. Despite that, enough of the skull shoulder armor and metal remained intact to be recognizable. Aric looked from the pile back toward the dragon, and an idea began to take shape.

The dragon tensed, muscles straining against the roots and dark claws as Aric approached. Quick shifts threatened to break the dragon free from its restraints at any moment. It even managed to snap at him although the shadowy appendages and tendrils held fast. These threats of hostility were hollow, though to Aric they were no less terrifying.

He carried the remnants of Hrym's armor. Arms outstretched, Aric presented it to the captive creature. He laid it down within its field of view and unsheathed Brunhilda's sword. "Easy now," Aric said in a soothing tone. Nidhogg snapped at him again and caught only air, coils of smoke and flame billowed from its nostrils. "Okay, I know that you probably don't understand me, but you probably recognize this," Aric said, shifting his gaze toward the armor. The dragon's good eye followed Aric's line of sight and again emitted a menacing growl. Aric raised his sword and brought it down on the armor.

"Same enemies," he said aloud, as if speaking slower and louder to a dragon would help it understand him. To emphasize the point, he gave it a good, swift kick. Perhaps Nidhogg understood or perhaps it was simply tired, but its growl quieted slightly as it turned its attention away from the pile of armor back to Aric. They regarded each other for a long time.

With one tentative step after another, Aric approached the beast. His first step was met with a renewed growl, though much less threatening. He slowed and held out his left hand, palm facing it and tried to speak in slow, soothing tones. The dragon did not relax so much as become a little less tense.

The walk seemed to take an eternity until Aric found himself just beyond the reach of the grasping shadowy claws. They took a futile swipe at him. As he raised his sword, Aric really hoped that he knew what he was doing. Nidhogg tensed but did not react otherwise as the sword came down. When the blade hit one of the claws, a bright light flashed, and Aric felt Freya's power flowing down his arms through the blade. However, it was not an instant victory. He worked hard to hack away and fight off each and every claw.

It was slow and laborious work. The sun sat just above the rim of the crater, its waning light still illuminating Yggdrasil's leafy canopy. The dragon had remained still and calm and was now flexing and stretching against the roots that still entangled it, the final restraints holding it in place. While chopping away at the claws, Aric had avoided damaging the roots themselves. He didn't know what exactly made the World Tree so important, but he felt its power instinctually and treated it with reverence.

Aric sheathed the sword and approached, the golden hilt the only hint of color in the gathering twilight. He was almost in a trance when he laid his hands upon one of the roots, and to his surprise a long piece came off in his grasp. A flash, like something remembered from his childhood, raced through his mind.

Suddenly he understood. At the conclusion of the Great Awakening, when the Jotnar, Vanir, and Aesir had worked together to tame the land and cleanse it of monsters, the Vanir leader, Njord, had sacrificed his life's energy to merge with Yggdrasil and imprison the remaining beasts beneath its roots. In doing so, he left the physical plane of existence and his spirit and essence joined with the World Tree. Now, the part that remembered his daughter Freya responded to her essence, coming from within Aric. After the first root was removed, Aric waved the gnarled staff and the other roots responded. All at once they retracted, freeing the captive dragon before returning to their original configuration.

Nidhogg stood to its full height and shook itself with vigor and revelry. Its right wing appeared atrophied though otherwise functional as it spread out and took a few tentative flaps. Aric retreated to a safe distance. They circled each other warily, and when Nidhogg was at the pile of Hrym's armor, it spat a fiery blast at it and leapt into the sky.

The armor ignited into an intense pyre. Metal turned molten and the animal bone cracked and splintered in the extreme heat. The dragon's takeoff was less than graceful. Its first leap got it just to the top of the cliff. That was enough for the beast to gain purchase with its forelegs. With a few additional wing beats it crested the edge and leapt again, rising into the gray sky beyond the canopy of Yggdrasil, heading south.

Aric stood alone, watching the shrinking silhouette in the sky. His body felt rejuvenated, better than he ever had before. His heart and mind were still heavy though. "I hope I did the right thing," he said aloud as he leaned on the root staff. Deep down, buried somewhere in the back of his mind, a little voice said, *I hope so too.*

A part of him wished that the dragon would have allowed him to ride it into battle, like some mythic hero. But he knew that his was not that kind of story and he was no hero. He had failed those closest to him and now had unleashed a force of unrivaled danger upon the world. His only source of comfort was to hope that it was better than the alternative.

CHAPTER 47: THE DUEL

Once again Sif and Suttungr were at an impasse, weapons locked. Their faces were inches apart, separated by their helmet. She could see the fire in his eyes as she gritted her teeth and tried to hold her ground. Her arms trembled as he continued to push forward, gaining the upper hand little by little. Suttungr and the Jotnar line were now fifty yards beyond the wall and steadily advancing. Suddenly, a spear nicked her side as it passed by and struck Suttungr full in the torso. The force of the impact and the resulting burst of magic threw them apart in a swirl of ice and light.

Sif leapt to her feet and looked over her shoulder to find a familiar figure step forward from the sea of Aesir soldiers. His eye had a wicked gleam not seen in years. He wore no helmet, his full beard and long locks billowed amid the chaos of battle. Once, long ago, his armor blazed with polished steel and gold trim. Now its light came from the power of the runes etched across its surface. Fine auroch wool lined his collar and caught that glow surrounding his head with a golden aura. In his right hand he wielded a brilliant and ornate blade. In his left was a sturdy oak shield, three feet across with a golden boss in the center and the crest of Asgard painted around it. Odin, king of Asgard and ruler of the nine realms, had arrived.

Fighting up and down the frontline paused at the sight of Odin and Sif standing side by side. Hrym rushed over to Suttungr while Skrymir approached at a more leisurely pace. Soldiers on both sides hesitated in anticipation of the clash to come.

Breaking the tension, Hertha shouted an order in Jotunmal and the Jotnar line surged once more. Their soldiers continued to pour through the gap in the wall next to her. She was standing atop a six-foot high rubble pile of the Skjaldborg and still could barely be seen above the fray. As she took a step toward Suttungr, the mound erupted in a deafening explosion. Hertha was sent flying, her body crashing into her own soldiers. Dozens of other Jotnar in proximity were also injured by the blast and flying shrapnel.

Emerging from the crater left in the wake of the explosion was Thor. Mjolnir glowed with residual power cutting through the haze of smoke and dust. He was covered in cuts and bruises even as the telltale glow of Aesir magic flared to heal the more severe injuries. Crushed and dented he stripped off his helmet and cuirass and roared. The Jotnar yet to enter the breach faltered at such a miraculous recovery.

"Odin is mine," Suttungr said, his voice full of malice. He waved toward Thor and said to Hrym and Skrymir, "Kill Thor and bring Mjolnir to me."

Skrymir loosed a volley of arrows at Sif. Odin stepped in between and blocked the shots with his shield. They were pinned in place by the barrage as Hrym ran toward Thor.

Sif grasped the tactic in an instant and left Odin's protection in pursuit of Hrym. She was faster than the lumbering giant but was slowed down having to dodge and deflect Skrymir's near constant onslaught of arrows. With a quick glance back she saw Odin pick up a discarded spear and hurl it at the archer. Skrymir shifted to the side, avoiding the throw. He reacted to the attack with an arrow at the ready, aimed at Odin. But Suttungr raised his hand in front of him, and Skrymir lowered his bow. Their fight had come at last.

CHAPTER 48: REVEALED

The two titans faced each other while the maelstrom of battle raged all around them. They were at the eye of the storm. The disciplined Aesir Army found themselves pushed to the limits as berserking waves of Jotnar smashed into their lines. Yet even then they fought with indefatigable strength, holding back the tide. They had to, for they were the only thing between this horde and their home, the shining city of Asgard. With the Bifrost Bridge at their back, there was no retreat, no quarter. They would hold the Jotnar Army here or they would lose everything. The roar of the falls were drowned out by the bedlam of war.

Odin was not the greatest Aesir warrior. His loss to Nidhogg had been humbling and yet enlightening. Since that day he had led his people using his immense power and wisdom. He had recognized the power of Gungnir when the Skjaldborg was sundered. Seeing it again was unsettling as he recalled the last time he had wielded it. It was his most agonizing failure come back to haunt him.

After that defeat Odin left combat to others. Freya planned, and Thor fought. There had been one incident that brought the Aesir king back to the field, and for that endeavor he had needed a suitable weapon to replace Gungnir, as he had already bestowed Mjolnir to his first son, Thor. In that battle he wielded perhaps the greatest sword ever crafted. Gathering the most skilled smiths, they forged a weapon worthy of the greatest king in the nine realms. Without access to wood from Yggdrasil it would never be as powerful as either Gungnir or Mjolnir. Still, it was imbued with the strength and magic of the Aesir. It cut through armor like it was cloth, but it would never shatter a wall or raze mountains. It was a weapon that would put any other to shame if not for the fact that it existed in the same world as Gungnir.

"You've finally come out of hiding to the field of battle," Suttungr said imperiously. "I was wondering how much more of your precious kingdom I would have to destroy before you faced me yourself."

"You always did talk too much, Loki," Odin said, and he attacked.

Suttungr parried the blow with ease. "Loki?" he replied with a sneer as he launched his own counterattack. "You still don't know who I am. I suppose it's not so much surprising as it is disappointing."

"It matters little to me, since you'll be dead soon," Odin retorted as he pressed the offensive. "For all of this you will die in obscurity, your corpse to rot here. No burial or funeral pyre for you, no bard to sing your tale." Where Sif had failed in using the environment to her advantage, Odin kept Suttungr off balance, delivering pointed hits at the Jotnar's less armored extremities. It would be a death of a thousand cuts, yet each wound healed in a flare of golden energy. Their movements showed similarities. Suttungr's fighting style had some elements of Jotnar ferocity with the balance and discipline of the Aesir. They both fought with blinding speed and lethal force. The soldiers engaging around them moved to give them a wide berth.

Suttungr surged with each attack, his entire focus was on Odin. All around him, his army faltered without leadership as the Aesir began to turn the tide. Hertha was missing, Hrym and Skrymir were occupied and still Suttungr did not take up command of his army. Their war, their struggle against the Aesir, fighting for the Jotnar people, all of that was ignored. Now, Suttungr had his own agenda.

For Odin, there was an exuberance in his demeanor. It had been a long time since he had engaged in combat with his life at stake. The old fire of the one who had sought to slay Nidhogg resurfaced. In spite of the bloody carnage of war, or perhaps because of it, a broad grin spread across Odin's lips.

As the battle raged on, the combatants proved evenly matched. Odin avoided Gungnir's blade and parried the haft only. The front of the surrounding battle had ground to a halt as the Aesir at last stopped losing ground and started retaking it.

After a furious exchange they separated and paused in a brief respite. Both were covered in the blood of the soldiers that they had carved through on their path toward each other. In that moment there was the spark of recognition in Odin at the terrible cost in life of this conflict. His smile faded as he regained some measure of awareness of the toll this was taking from those he ruled over, those who followed his orders and trusted in his judgement and wisdom. His face hardened with a steely resolve; their fight would determine the outcome of this battle. This understanding registered to them both as they raised their weapons in preparation for a final exchange that they knew would leave one of them dead and the other triumphant.

Odin came in with blazing speed, faster and with more conviction than he had shown thus far. It was a daring gambit that could end the fight in one fell stroke. He feinted with a high one-handed slash aimed at Suttungr's exposed throat. Then, at the last moment, he disengaged and struck with a riposte, stabbing through a weak point where the armor segmented. Suttungr had charged as well but he had not brought up his weapon to guard, instead allowing the blow to land. The freezing explosion that almost fell Brunhilda and was the downfall of Gunnar was markedly absent. In its place there was only the sickening squelch of stabbed flesh and a dim flash of defensive wards as the blade found its mark.

Suttungr looked down at the sword, his head cocked to one side. Odin saw his eyes widen in surprise with the realization that it was an ordinary weapon, a sharpened piece of steel not imbued with Reginvald. Odin had gambled that Suttungr's defenses were predicated on his enemies using weapons imbued with Aesir magic. Now the Aesir king took a step back, smiling as his foe clutched at the sword protruding from his chest.

"You always were a deluded, ignorant old fool," Suttungr said with a wet cough. The simple sword had done its job. There had been no explosive reaction, no block of ice encasing him. Odin's attack had pierced deep, the blade slipping between his ribs. But then the self-satisfied smirk on Odin's face faded as Suttungr pulled out the sword with a squelch and tossed it aside. A bright, golden glow of

Mithlivald erupted from his wound instead of blood as the cut healed in seconds.

—

Thor climbed out of the crater just in time to meet the charging, hulking form of Hrym. The massive Jotnar swung at him with his cleaver-like blade with such force it would have downed a tree in a single stroke. Thor easily dodged and fought back. He was surprised by Hrym's speed and dexterity as the Jotnar avoided the brunt of the strike and turned his sword back into a downward cutting stroke.

Bringing up Mjolnir, Thor blocked the swing with the shaft of the hammer. The powerful blow dropped the mighty Aesir to one knee. Thor pushed back, throwing the Jotnar back a couple of steps as he rose back up to both feet. He was weakened but still defiant; he would not be felled by a simple brute like Hrym.

Hrym's next attacks were more measured and calculating. He displayed more control and skill than Thor was expecting. His poise and composure with the blade was excellent and the ground that Thor had gained in pushing him back was lost. In an instant Thor found himself forced to the edge of the crater.

Just as Hrym attempted to make him fall back over the edge, Sif leapt in and attacked. Between the two of them, Sif and Thor kept Hrym on the defensive. Thor would never openly admit it but he was glad that Sif had arrived at that moment. If he had fallen into the crater the fight would have ended. Together, the duo disarmed the Jotnar in three moves.

"You may have beaten me, but I gladly sacrifice my life for his," Hrym said and pointed to Odin and Suttungr's fight. They turned just in time to see Suttungr pull Odin's sword from his chest and throw it away. He turned back to Odin and, with a swing of Gungnir, cut the Lord of the Aesir across the chest. The blade sliced through his armor and a spray of blood arced out from the wound.

—

"Ungrateful whelp," Odin spat. His armor was split and he held his arm across the superficial gash across his chest. It was bleeding but only skin deep. "I never should have allowed you and Jarnsaxa into

Asgard."

"No!" Suttungr shouted in an outburst of rage, kicking Odin in the ribs. "You don't get to say her name!"

He took a breath and addressed Odin more calmly, a knowing sneer on his lips. "You all think that I'm Loki, don't you?" Suttungr taunted as he stood above the fallen Odin. Blood continued to flow from the cut. Golden light poured from it as Odin's Mithlivald power worked to heal it to no avail. Pieces of his armor slid off, sliced through by Gungnir's blade.

"Of course next to Thor I was always practically invisible to you," Suttungr said. He tossed aside his helmet and released the glamour that he had been holding. The golden mirage of Suttungr's face shattered to reveal a terribly burned visage. And yet, despite the disfiguring scars, a father would always recognize his son.

"Baldur?" The name escaped Odin's lips in a whisper. It was the last word he would ever speak to his prodigal son.

Baldur raised the spear, its blade glowing bright with all of the power he could pour into it. Then, before he could bring it down, a powerful roar thundered from the north and echoed through the plains, shaking every living creature who heard it to the core.

CHAPTER 49: NIDHOGG'S FURY

Time ground to a stop as the sounds of battle came to an abrupt halt. Only the reverberation of the roar could be heard as all of the combatants turned to face a horror that had not been seen in the nine realms for centuries. Only the eldest of the Aesir and Jotnar had lived through the terror of its reign. Nevertheless, the primal ferocity of the roar hit everyone immediately.

The great beast announced itself from beyond the horizon and arrived soon after with blinding speed. Its time spent trapped at Yggdrasil seemed to have had no impact on its strength and agility. Only its rage and hunger seemed to have been affected by its imprisonment; stoked to a white-hot ball of wrath and devastation, it was a force of nature to cower before, not a creature to be fought.

Nidhogg crashed to the ground just inside the Bifrost Skjaldborg with no regard for either army beneath its feet. Dozens of nearby Jotnar and Aesir soldiers were incinerated in the searing fire. Sif, Thor, and Hrym all dove into the crater, avoiding the conflagration. Even within that shelter they could feel the scorching heat of the flames that flowed above them buffeted by the lip of the crater.

Before Thor and Sif could react to the presence of the foe in their midst, the dragon's head came up over the rim of the crater and in one fluid motion snapped closed around Hrym. The crunch of the armor and bones was lost amidst Hrym's screams of agony. Even half-eaten he fought, holding the jaws open. His struggles and cries ended abruptly as Nidhogg tossed its head back and swallowed the Jotnar in a fiery gulp.

With its vengeance complete, its ravenous hunger took over. As it turned its attention to the two left in the crater, a spear struck the back of its head as Hertha shouted in rage at the loss of Hrym.

—

The battlefield became a chaotic morass as many of the Jotnar fled. Pockets of fighting resumed, but this was a creature whose like no one had seen for centuries. Those closest to the raging dragon froze in terror. Even some of the disciplined and unflappable Aesir soldiers fell back, though they did not retreat even faced with this eldritch horror.

Baldur, however, would not be distracted from his goal. He turned back to Odin, knowing time was limited; Nidhogg would tear through everyone here in moments. Without looking he knew that his troops were fleeing from the monster. This battle, perhaps even this war, was lost in the face of the threat posed by the fearsome dragon. Yet his thoughts did not linger on those things; instead all of his hatred and will focused in on Odin. At last he would have his satisfaction.

As he again raised Gungnir for the killing blow, a blade erupted through his chest. It was the simple blade that Odin had wielded, but it came from behind him. Baldur turned and found himself standing face to face with Skrymir.

—

"I knew it was you, Baldur," he said. Tossing aside his helmet and releasing his own glamour, Skrymir revealed his true identity. Just like Baldur, his own face was a mass of burned skin and scar tissue. In addition, scattered all across his skin were patches of pale blue fur.

"Loki," Baldur wheezed.

And in one fell stroke Loki drew his frost blade, grabbed Gungnir, and cut off Baldur's hand. The magic barrier of his armor did little against the Ethlivald weapon. As the golden healing Mithlivald energies began to bloom at the severed wrist and around the sword in Baldur's chest, Loki swung Gungnir in an arc and beheaded the leader of the Jotnar uprising. As the body crumpled to the ground, all hints of magic evaporated in an ethereal mist. Even his armor lost its luster and faded in splendor.

"That is the fate of any Aesir who would seek to control or

oppress the Jotnar people," Loki stated emphatically, now holding Gungnir pointed at the fallen Odin. "We have retaken Jotunheim and now—"

He was cut off as a full-throated roar hit him. This was not the bestial roar of a half-starved, feral animal searching for prey. It was the sorrowful cry of one who had lost a brother not once, but twice.

Thor swung Mjolnir with both hands his face contorted with grief and anger. Loki reacted fast enough to only take a glancing blow from the legendary weapon. However, even that light impact threw him clear of Odin and off of his feet. Sif rushed over and helped her king. While they fled to safety, Thor pressed the attack in blind rage. This time Loki was prepared and dodged a flurry of his wild swings. He weaved and dodged, keeping his distance, waiting for an opening that he could exploit. The spear was an unfamiliar weapon for him and it took him a few moments to find his range while sidestepping the charging Thor.

After getting some distance and regaining his footing, Loki saw an opening and swung Gungnir. Even in his muddled state of mind Thor was far and away a better fighter than Loki and intercepted his strike. Their primal emotions poured through them into these two powerful weapons, flares of energy arcing from them, one blue the other golden. The energy coursing from Yggdrasil flowed through their bodies, the sharp smell of ozone heavy in the air. When the weapons collided, a concussive shock wave erupted and knocked down everyone within a hundred yards. The explosion brought all fighting to a stop as even those still standing felt the blast wave roll over them. Everyone's attention was drawn to the clarion call of such immense power—including Nidhogg's.

—

Although the dragon was on the other side of the battlefield devouring prey both Jotnar and Aesir, that detonation seized its attention. Now the dragon spied a familiar figure. Despite the ages since their fateful encounter, the dragon recognized the one responsible for its long imprisonment at the base of Yggdrasil. Odin may have grown older, but the smell of his blood was unmistakable and, after all of this time, irresistible.

260

Still alive Hertha shouted after the dragon and hurled a spear at it. But now it was focused and its hunger for vengeance would not be denied. The terrifying beast's excitement was palpable as it leapt into the air, wings spread, in a swift, low arc on its way to this prized prey.

CHAPTER 50: THUNDER AND LIGHTNING

A terrible danger threatened Asgard. Massed forces have tried to destroy it before. All were defeated or turned back in the past. Now its downfall seemed inevitable. First, Suttungr breached the Bifrost Skjaldborg, and now the invincible dragon, Nidhogg, darkened the sky, poised to lay waste to the eternal city.

The Jotnar Army scattered and was in full retreat to the north; their leaders were dead and an ancient horror raged in their midst. The Aesir Army could not pursue and was instead falling back itself, to protect their capital and do what little it could against the indomitable cataclysm that was Nidhogg. The explosion from Gungnir and Mjolnir clashing had tossed Loki back into the fleeing Jotnar host, lost in the sea of animal hides and armor covering the bodies strewn about the battlefield. Thor was unconscious among the other Aesir, laid low by the same blast.

All the world appeared to hold its breath as the immense beast flew through the sky. As it passed overhead a solitary figure pushed through the crowd, against the stream of fleeing Jotnar. Alone at the cratered epicenter of the explosion, the figure knelt and grasped both Mjolnir and Gungnir, the hammer in her left and the spear in her right. Power surged through her.

—

The moment Loki took off Baldur's head, all of his magic had dissipated. The most visible effect was on his armor and its radiant glow. Farther away the ice that he had conjured to bind Brunhilda also faded. Without that additional encumbrance it took little effort to extricate herself from the shackles. Too often in the past she had found herself bound by Aesir irons.

Now unleashed, she could do something after having watched as her fellow Aesir were cut down by Suttungr. The guilt was overpowering seeing others suffer for her own failures.

She had rushed headlong into the battle. At first her plan was to go to Odin's aid. She had grabbed the first sword that she could find and ran into the battle. She encountered some resistance from the crowd of Jotnar soldiers fleeing the great dragon. But they did not attack her, did not even see her as they were blinded by fear, running away in terror. Even in the face of Skrymir's betrayal she held to her promise and did not harm any Jotnar that posed no direct threat to her or other Aesir.

Between the dragon and their leader being beheaded, their motivation to fight was lost. The explosion from the clash of Mjolnir and Gungnir had sent all of the remaining Jotnar into full retreat. She could still feel the lingering power of the detonation even though she had been outside its range. Her skin tingled with the energy in the air and her nose recognized that distinct smell left after a lightning strike.

Seeing the two legendary weapons on the ground, she knew that they held the key to this battle. When she knelt and picked them both up, she not only felt their power but she felt their wisdom as well.

———

It was like touching the surface of a glacier and getting only the barest hint of the enormity of all of the water trapped within. If all of that water was unleashed, the power and destruction that would spill forth was almost incomprehensible.

So now she grasped a fraction of the whole. And although she only understood a little, it was enough. The situation was desperate, so without the full knowledge of what would happen, she threw Gungnir sure and true at the dragon as it passed overhead.

It found its mark and pierced Nidhogg's flank. So focused was the beast on its ancient foe that it did not appear to register the impact, continuing on its path toward Odin.

Brunhilda then raised Mjolnir in both hands and unleashed the floodgates, opened her entire being and all that Mjolnir would accept. That energy erupted in a brilliant explosion of light and magic. And when the bolt of Reginvald struck, true power was witnessed by all.

The bolt did not hit Nidhogg, nor was it intended to. It struck Gungnir, and the clash of energies detonated the spear in a spectacular and brilliant burst of light. The explosion radiated out in a sphere that ripped through the air as it expanded, flattening the Jotnar and Aesir Army, all who stood directly below.

The last image that Brunhilda saw was the intense, bright energy bolt unleashed by Mjolnir. Using Gungnir before had left her weakened; this effort, however, drained her to the core. Even before the explosion her eyes had fluttered closed and rolled back into her head. Mjolnir dropped from her limp hand with a dull thud shortly before her own body followed.

—

The battlefield was littered with the bodies of the dead. Both the Jotnar and Aesir armies had been laid low by the fighting and then further decimated when Nidhogg had arrived. The Jotnar Army was in full retreat. Among them was Loki; his ears were bleeding and the capillaries in his eyes had burst as a result of the explosion. The Aesir forces were in no better shape and were unable to pursue. An unarmed Thor staggered on unsteady feet, Brunhilda lay unconscious, and Sif raced back to Asgard carrying the wounded Odin.

EPILOGUE

Bright light flooded the room as Brunhilda's eyes opened. The afterimage from Mjolnir was still seared into her retinas. As her vision cleared, the room around her came into focus. She had a vague awareness of a flurry of activity, with many people nearby, and fleeting recollections of having awakened before. Now, however, her room was silent.

It was an airy space with tall windows. Outside she could see the steel-gray sky. She used her arm to prop herself up trying to get a better view of her surroundings, and almost immediately the room spun and her head swam, and she fell back into the soft, downy pillow and mattress. The feel and comfort of the rich linens let her know that she was once again in the warmth and security of Asgard. There was a sense of relief that faded as she recalled all of her fallen comrades... friends. Once again she was reminded of the vast gulf between the Aesir and everyone else. Here she recuperated in comfort whereas her friends had died in harsh wastelands, far from their homes. Everything hurt, though it was more of a dull ache and soreness than actual pain. Her physical injuries would heal, but she would forever carry the memories of all she had done and witnessed. And despite the feeling of immense fatigue, she could still feel the phantom tingle of power lingering in her body, a reminder of when the energy of the World Tree had flowed through her.

"Take it easy now," a familiar voice came from the far side of the room. "You've been unconscious for almost a week."

"Thor, Odin... Bifrost, Nidhogg... what happened?" she said shifting and pulling the blankets off as she turned her head to focus on the figure opposite the windows.

"We won. Or rather more accurately, you saved us," said

Odin as he approached closer to the bed. Brunhilda's eyes drifted to his bandaged torso, visible through a loose robe cinched at the waist. "Fostra Eira is quite skilled, but Gungnir's power is far beyond her healing arts," he said, following her gaze.

"Sire," she said, trying to get out of bed to kneel before him. He laid a gentle hand upon her shoulder to slow her down and help her to sit upright at the edge of the bed.

"You did what none before you was able to do. Not the alliance of the Great Awakening, not Borr, not even I." His tone was as stern and measured as ever, yet she thought that there was a hint of warmth in his voice. Nevertheless she was quite groggy and could not be certain that she was not dreaming or hallucinating this entire exchange. She leaned on his arm as she stood.

At the open window the brisk air helped to clear her head. The buzz of activity around the Bifrost Skjaldborg, visible from this lofty vantage point, caught her attention. Even at this distance she could recognize the unarmored soldiers working alongside other laborers to rebuild the fallen battlement. By design there was much care taken in the planning of all the structures of Asgard, yet here there was a sense of urgency to the construction that trumped their traditional, exacting standards.

"Why are they working so hastily? Did we not win?" she asked.

"Look around." Odin pointed along the horizon stretching out beyond the construction. The ground was still littered with the bodies of the fallen, tinted a shade of blue. Jotnar blood covered the ground with a layer of ice that left the slain soldiers in horrifying and painful visages of death. The rubble was cemented in place in a similar fashion. And as she followed his gaze above, she saw that the clouds continued to cover the land in a gray, directionless light.

"The clouds are still here. When Baldur died, his magic died with him," she said as she rubbed her wrists where they had been shackled. After a moment she turned her face to Odin. "Didn't it?"

"We won the battle and defeated Sutt—Baldur," he said with melancholy in his voice.

Brunhilda stood in silence, no words of comfort seemed appropriate for a moment like this.

"What Baldur began has become larger than him. The spreading darkness has taken on a life of its own. He was the spark that ignited a blaze. We will need to extinguish this before it grows out of control and covers the world in darkness. No, this is far from over. The Jotnar were beaten but they were not defeated. Loki will assume leadership of them and pick up where Baldur left off. We will not make the same mistakes as before. First we will secure our home and honor our glorious fallen. Then we will destroy them."

—

Even above Yggdrasil the blue sky and bright sun had been replaced with a soft veil of gray. In the canopy above a single leaf fell. It was the first leaf to ever be shed by the mighty tree since the world began. Soon it was followed by another and another, one after the other.

A cold, melted lump of metal, long since extinguished was the only thing to bear witness to this inauspicious event.

The tree's roots shuddered and cracked along a faultline, up through the trunk. The roots nearest the opening turned dark and lifeless, no longer alive and shifting. The valley surrounding the World Tree grew deathly calm and quiet. In the shadowed recesses beneath the towering tree, a pair of eyes glowed with reflected light. Just beyond the edge of the darkness a wicked claw reached out to test its newfound and long-denied freedom.

END

GLOSSARY

A

Aesir - The second race of sentient beings birthed from Yggdrasil, the World Tree. They are a people characterized by a proclivity to order and structure. Their home is the realm of Asgard and their capital city is also called Asgard. Their physical traits consist of various shades of blonde and red hair with fair skin complexion.

Alfheim - Realm of the Ljosalfar, represented by emerald. Dense forests form the basis for all of the lumber used throughout the realms. Their base resources are exchanged for the resources of the other realms.

Aric - Male human. Husband of Dagmaer, father of Una. Descended from a long line of fishermen in the village of Murtrborg in the northwest region of Midgard.

Asgard - Name of the realm and also the capital city for the Aesir, represented by quartz. Originally in the southeast, after the Aesir-Vanir War Asgard annexed the territories of Vanaheim and Jotunheim. On an island off of the east coast, the capital city is connected to the continent via Bifrost, the Rainbow Bridge. Capital of the nine realms, its temperate climate and rich, arable lands are labored and harvested by other races for raw materials while the Aesir consume and produce art and wealth.

Auroch - A wooly herding bovine that provides resources and sustenance for many of the northern peoples. Their milk, wool, and meat supply food and clothes in the otherwise barren regions in Niflheim. They may also serve as pack animals, capable of hauling heavy loads over long distances.

B

Baldur - Male Aesir. Second son of Odin and Frigg.

Bestla - Female Jotnar. Leader during Great Awakening, wife of Borr, mother of Odin.

Bifrost - The Rainbow Bridge. Several theories exist as to the name. The single-span bridge has only one immense arch underneath recalling the shape of a rainbow. Also, the waterfalls that flow on each side of the bridge generate dense mists that refract brilliant rainbows throughout the day.

Bifrost Skjaldborg – The shield wall erected to defend access to the western entrance to Bifrost, the Rainbow Bridge.

Birgjavale - Medium-sized city in the realm of Asgard.

Boelthor - Male Jotnar. First leader of Jotnar, he bound his spirit to the spear, Gungnir, during the Great Awakening.

Borghild - Female Jotnar. Senior soldier in Jotnar Army.

Borr - Male Aesir. Leader during Great awakening. Husband to Bestla, father of Odin.

Bragi - Male Vanir. Husband of Ydun.

Bruborg - Large human city bordering the former Vanaheim.

Brunhilda - Female Aesir. Hot-headed valkyrie with red hair.

Buri - Male Aesir. First king of the Aesir, he bound his spirit to Mjolnir during the Great Awakening. Father of Borr, grandfather to Odin.

C

Calder Lake - Large lake in central Midgard near Jotunheim. It is fed by a tributary of the Calder River. Halvard was built on the cliffs on its eastern edge.

Calder River - Originating from snowmelt in the Svelbjarg mountains, it flows west toward the sea emptying out in a fjord near Murtrborg.

D

Dagmaer - Female human. Wife of Aric, mother of Una.

Dokkalfar - The race of stout and stocky people who live underground and mine the mountainous realm of Svartalfheim. Primarily subterranean dwellers, they have pale complexions often hidden under layers of dirt and grime.

Dragons - In the days before the Great Awakening they were the apex predators. With broad wings and powerful claws, they dominated the land and the skies. Dragons are solitary by nature, so the alliance of the Great Awakening undertook the arduous task of tracking them down and eliminating them one by one, until Nidhogg was the only one that remained. A dragon's arsenal includes a fiery breath, razor-sharp claws and teeth, and iron-hard scales that cover its entire body.

E

Eira - Female Vanir. Chief healer of Asgard. Her title is Fostra, Fostra Eira.

Eldjotnar - The faction of the Jotnar population exiled to live in Muspelheim. Among the volcanic activity in the realm they developed into auburn- and brown-coated versions of the Jotnar of the north. Their Ethlivald power is more expressive of fire than the cold of the Jotnar.

Ethlivald - The spectrum of energy associated with Jotnar, manifesting green in color originally. Its effects enhance natural phenomena such as increasing plant growth or ambient weather conditions.

F

Fafnir - Female lindworm. This powerful lindworm was trapped beneath Yggdrasil during the Great Awakening.

Fenrir - Male vargr. Fenrir is an extraordinary vargr that terrorized Jotunheim years earlier.

Fostra – Title given to those who practice the healing arts of Mithlivald as a profession.

Freya - Female Vanir. Daughter of Njord. Leader during Aesir-Vanir War. Chief military leader of the Aesir council.

Freyr - Male Vanir. Son of Njord, brother of Freya.

Frigg - Female Aesir. Official counsel and wife to Odin. Chief advisor to Odin on all matters.

Frode - Male human. Leader of Hoddmimis Holt. Though using the title of gothi, he has no direct connection with Asgard or the Aesir.

G

Garmr - Male hound. A massive feral dog of the Great Awakening era trapped beneath Yggdrasil by Njord.

Gastropnir - *archaic,* northern stronghold deep within Niflheim. Staging point for final push of Great Awakening.
modern, a small village nestled in the shadow of the ruins of the former stronghold.

Geir - Male Jotnar. Spear-wielding soldier, loyal to Hrym.

Geri and Freki - Male and female respectively. Wolfhounds that prowl Asgard as Odin's companions.

Gjallarhorn - A massive trumpet fashioned from a giant dragon's horn. Wielded by Heimdall and only blown if enemies approach Asgard.

Gothi - Masculine. Title for the local human civic and spiritual leader.

Gungnir - Ancient spear used during the Great Awakening. The shaft is six feet long and the blade is an additional two feet beyond that. The spear is covered with intricate knot patterns and runes, Boelthor's spirit ties this weapon to the Ethlivald/chaotic end of the magic spectrum.

Gunnar - Female Vanir. Leader of the valkyries.

Gythja - Feminine. Title for the local human civic and spiritual leader.

H

Halvard - Central commercial and military hub in the former Jotunheim. Situated on the eastern cliffs above Calder Lake.

Hege - Female human. Gythja of Murtrborg.

Heimdall - Male Aesir. Herald of Asgard. Watchman and in charge of blowing the great trumpet Gjallarhorn to warn of approaching enemies.

Hel - Land of the dead, represented by onyx. An untouched stretch of mist shrouded land in the south considered sacrosanct by all.

Hertha - Female Jotnar. Sister to Jorunn. Second-in-command to Suttungr in Hrym's absence.

Hilder - Female Vanir. A fun-loving Valkyrie.

Hoddmimis Holt - Small hamlet hidden in a caldera nestled in the Svelbjarg Range. Its hot springs are a result of the volcanic activity of the caldera. They are mineral rich and rejuvenating.

Hofborg - Medium-sized city in Vanaheim before unification with Asgard.

Hrodi - An expletive or insult literally meaning "snot."

Hrym - Male Jotnar. Second-in-command to Suttungr, physically powerful and fiercely loyal.

Huginn and Muninn - Female ravens. Many believe that they speak to Odin and report on events in the nine realms.

Human - The last of the races to emerge from Yggdrasil. They excel in the cultivation of the land for the production of food. As such, they are the second most populous of the races, just behind the Jotnar. They wield no magic, though they have a penchant for construction and engineering.

I

Isabrot - The town near Isabrot Pass that is the primary staging area for all Aesir Army action in Niflheim.

Isabrot Pass - Outpost guarding the only widely known overland path between Jotunheim and Niflheim in the Svelbjarg Mountain Range.

Iss Ethlivald - Variant of Ethlivald that is an expression of the ice and cold of Nyr Jotunheim in Niflheim. Manifests as blue in color.

J

Jormungandr - Female serpent. The first beast driven down beneath Yggdrasil. At the time of its imprisonment, it was a creature of average size and power. Having spent the most time nestled among Yggdrasil's roots, it has grown the most embittered and the most powerful.

Jorunn - Female Jotnar. Hertha's younger sister and auroch herder.

Jotnar - The first race of sentient beings birthed from Yggdrasil. They are covered in fur and their current coloration generally falls in the blue range of hues. They have a strong bond with their natural environment. Their magic is known as Ethlivald, though over generations in Niflheim it has become known as Iss Ethlivald.

Jotunheim - Jotnar, represented by amethyst in heraldry. Jotnar are used as a permanent pool of slave labor. Stone for building and aurochs are the primary resources of the modern Jotunheim. The original lands flourished with all manner of resources, primarily food and lumber.

K

Kaupstefna - Covered marketplace most commonly used in the harsh environment of Jotunheim by the Jotnar.

Knute - Male Jotnar. A bonecarver and an older generation Jotnar who lived through the Aesir-Vanir War. Remembers the verdant Jotunheim and is an elder and leader of Gastropnir, both in the past and the present.

L

Lif - Female human. Resident of Hoddmimis Holt.

Lindworms – Lizard-like creatures that are wingless and have only two appendages. They slither and crawl on their bellies and are heavily armored on their dorsal side. Their scales and coloration resemble rocks, giving them natural camouflage. Their broad, triangular heads make them ideal burrowers. Unlike dragons, lindworms do not breathe fire, but they can emit noxious gas and their saliva is toxic.

Ljosalfar - The lithe and graceful people of Alfheim. Generally dark of complexion. Their lives are spent outdoors among the trees and plains of Alfheim.

Loki - Male Jotnar. Has a complicated relationship with the Aesir, with specific ties to Baldur and his death.

M

Midgard - Human realm, represented by pearl in heraldry. Vast, open plains of farmlands and grazing pastures for animals. Humans work the land and produce the majority of food that is sent to the other realms.

Mithlivald - The spectrum of magical energy associated with the Vanir. It is a bridging energy that may be used to heal organic and repair inorganic material. It may also be utilized to amplify Reginvald or Ethlivald. Manifests as white in color on its own, though takes on the color of any energy used alongside it.

Mjolnir - A massive warhammer with a shaft four feet in length and a head with a blunt surface on one face and a spike on the other. The metal is iron and is embossed with a delicate filigree of Celtic knots and runes. Imbued with Buri's life essence, the hammer leans to the ordered Aesir-Reginvald spectrum.

Mjodrmork - Farming community in southwestern Midgard near Alfheim, known for their honey.

Murtrborg - Small village along the coast in northwest Midgard, not far from the Svelbjarg Range.

Muspelheim - Eldjotnar realm, represented by garnet in heraldry. Ingots of metal from Svartalfheim are brought to the forges here to be shaped into tools and weapons for the other realms.

N

Nidhogg - Dragon. A powerful monster from before the Great Awakening and the only one to survive and escape imprisonment beneath Yggdrasil by Njord.

Niflheim - Realm of ice and cold, represented by sapphire in heraldry. It is a barren wasteland that serves as a buffer zone that surrounds and shelters Yggdrasil.

Njord - Male Vanir. First leader, father of Freya and Freyr. His spirit was bound to Yggdrasil to entrap those monsters that could not be killed.

Nyr Jotunheim (New Jotunheim) - The new lands set aside for the Jotnar within Niflheim. Accessible only via Issabrot Pass. Though initially a desolate tundra, it has since become a thriving boreal forest region under the nurturing care of the Jotnar. It is officially designated as Jotunheim.

O

Odin - Male Aesir. Although Odin is recognized as full Aesir, his true lineage is half Aesir, half Jotnar. Leader during Aesir-Vanir War. Husband to Frigg, father of Thor and Baldur.

Odr - Male Vanir. Leader of the Vanir during the Aesir-Vanir War alongside Freya, and husband to her. Freya's bargaining with Thor not only betrayed the Jotnar people, it undermined Odr's authority and standing. Though he was afforded a position within the unified Aesir-Vanir nation, he soon left, never to be heard from again. Freya often takes lengthy journeys under the pretense of searching for him.

R

Reginvald - The spectrum of energy associated with the Aesir. Primarily a magic used to shape and bend the natural world into more ordered structures. Manifests with a golden color.

S

Sif - Female Aesir. Commander of the Asgard City Guards and all domestic forces.

Skogul - Female valkyrie. Half Aesir (father) half Vanir (mother).

Skuld - Female human. Minstrel and actress with a theater troupe.

Sleipnir - Male horse. One of the few friendly creatures of power that existed before the Great Awakening. Though forever wild, it created a bond with Borr that transferred to Odin after the ancient Aesir leader passed.

Svelbjarg Rams - These elusive creatures climb the Svelbjarg range to heights that no other terrestrial creature could aspire. Their hides are prized. They often defend territories by butting heads with rival males. The force of these impacts is so impressive that the air reverberates with each impact. As such, many Jotnar see their skulls as ideal for use as helmets, and their rarity makes such helmets rare pieces of prestige among the Jotnar.

Suttungr - Male Jotnar. Leader of the Jotnar during the uprising.

Svartalfheim - Realm of the Dokkalfar, represented by ruby in heraldry. The mines provide ore, precious gems, and minerals for artisans in Asgard, and the base materials for the military-industrial complex in Muspelheim.

Svelbjarg Mountains - Mountain range that forms the border between Niflheim and the other realms.

T

Thor - Male Aesir. First son of Odin and Frigg. Heir to Asgard.

Thrym - Male Jotnar. Leader of the Jotnar during Aesir-Vanir war.

Tyr - Male Aesir. Decorated military officer, still insists on leading field missions.

U

Una - Female human. Daughter of Aric and Dagmaer.

Utgard - Former capital city of Jotunheim. Razed to the ground during the Aesir-Vanir War. Its ruins should exist somewhere south of the Svelbjarg Mountains, but the true location is lost to the ages, reclaimed by the forests.

V

Vanaheim - Realm of the Vanir, represented by amber in heraldry. As with Old Jotunheim and Asgard, Vanaheim was a land well suited for the growth and production of all resources. Currently merged with Asgard into one realm, though some lands are used as farms and worked by human serfs.

Vali - Male Vanir. Captain of the northern Aesir Army based in Halvard.

Vanir - One of the three magical races of the world. They have skin of various shades of gold and tan with dark hair. They wield the magics of restoration and balance known as Mithlivald.

Vargr - Though somewhat similar in appearance to wolves, vargr are a separate species. Their fur is much more coarse, coalescing in a mane of thick, sharp spikes. They are larger and more vicious than any other predator after the Great Awakening. Primarily solitary creatures, it takes extraordinary circumstances for them to work together as a pack.

Veizlakr - Eastern farming community that produces much of the grain distributed throughout the realms.

Y

Ydun - Female Vanir. Wife of Bragi.

Ylva - Female Jotnar. Hailing from the Niflheim border region, she is not much of a soldier but is an excellent hunter and tracker.

Ymir - The continent that contains all of the nine realms. The term is only used by the Jotnar who resent the concept of the land parceled out as the nine realms.

ACKNOWLEDGEMENTS

A special thanks to James Zhang for being a great friend and sounding board and for getting me off of my butt to actually write this book.

Thanks to Joel Abraham, Gail Yui, Dilek Sanver-Wang, Silke Fußbroich, and Hadley Langosy for your insightful feedback and encouragement. Thanks to my editor, Olivia Ngai, for keeping my narrative focused and coherent. My deepest gratitude to Kathleen Weng and the Absolute Dragons family for all of the friendships, crazy adventures, and life experiences. A special thanks to Marty McCall and Gloria Leung for your generosity and hospitality week in and week out. And thanks to the rest of the Wednesday Night Crew for all of the input and great conversions over the years.

Finally, a big, heartfelt thanks to my parents and brother for a lifetime of support and care.

AUTHOR BIO

Andy Wang lives in the San Francisco Bay Area where he works as a concept artist in the video game industry. Over the past twelve years he has worked on creating and adapting visually diverse and interesting game worlds.

As an undergraduate he studied Integrative Biology at UC Berkeley and then earned his Master of Fine Arts degree in illustration from the Academy of Art University in San Francisco. Andy's MFA coursework and thesis centered on sequential art and storytelling. His degree project was the first chapter for a proposed graphic novel exploring the characters, world, and themes of Norse mythology. That material laid the foundation for this novel.

Made in the USA
San Bernardino, CA
21 November 2018